'118

FEB 2018

The King's Charter

Yet another James Goodfellow Investigation

Clive F Sorrell

authorHOUSE®

AuthorHouse™ UK
1663 Liberty Drive
Bloomington, IN 47403 USA
www.authorhouse.co.uk
Phone: 0800.197.4150

© 2017 Clive F Sorrell. All rights reserved.

No part of this book may be reproduced, stored in a retrieval system, or transmitted by any means without the written permission of the author.

Clive Frederick Sorrell has asserted his right under the Copyright, Design and Patents Act, 1988 to be identified as the author of this work.

This novel is a work of fiction. Names and characters are the product of the author's imagination and any resemblance to actual persons, living or dead, is entirely coincidental.

Published by AuthorHouse 04/12/2017

ISBN: 978-1-5246-7987-3 (sc)
ISBN: 978-1-5246-7988-0 (hc)
ISBN: 978-1-5246-7989-7 (e)

Print information available on the last page.

Any people depicted in stock imagery provided by Thinkstock are models, and such images are being used for illustrative purposes only. Certain stock imagery © Thinkstock.

This book is printed on acid-free paper.

Because of the dynamic nature of the Internet, any web addresses or links contained in this book may have changed since publication and may no longer be valid. The views expressed in this work are solely those of the author and do not necessarily reflect the views of the publisher, and the publisher hereby disclaims any responsibility for them.

In
Memory
of
Sophia

BOOKS BY THIS AUTHOR – PUBLISHED BY AUTHORHOUSE

Stories For Dark and Stormy Nights
Siddiqui
Kawthar
Jumana
Duress - the Life and Death of a Ton-Up
Ingrid's Children
The Distant Cousin

PROLOGUE

THE EXCOMMUNICATED KING JOHN had taken ill shortly after leaving Spalding and unable to stay with his amassed treasure he was forced to take the longer route by way of Wisbech Castle. He stopped at the Cistercian abbey on the following day and relied on the monks and their prayers to restore him to good health. The king had planned to rejoin the heavily guarded treasure at Bishop's Lynn but as fate would have it he could only travel as far as Newark Castle.

A total of 2,650 soldiers and servants had been left to protect the royal procession of forty-five heavy carts. The commanders had been instructed to take the shorter and more direct route across the wide Wellstream estuary, forcing the drawn-out convoy to use the treacherous tidal causeway that had been marked infrequently with willow withies.

Soldiers watched with growing concern as a dense sea mist roiled over the mud flats, enveloping the carts in a clammy cloak of invisibility. The oxen handlers were finding it impossible to see the carts in front of them and the straining beasts were urged on with the frequent sting of whips. A combination of sedimentary mud and sand sucked at the cartwheels, slowing them down. This further frustrated the men who shouted and whipped the suffering beasts even harder.

The elderly guide hired for the crossing was a local man and was walking beside the second cart with his hand resting on the whippletree when it jerked violently. He fell and was instantly crushed beneath the iron-rimmed wheels. The dying man was half buried beneath the cart, his blood staining the fine silt, but the soldiers turned their heads away and kept plodding on. They didn't dare pause to help the screaming man for the encroaching mist was now beginning to conceal the line of withies. The gasping man was soon silenced as he was driven deeper into the seabed by the following oxen and carts.

The procession had reached the midway point on the causeway when, without warning, the wheels of the lead cart plunged deep into the mud. The yoked oxen struggled to pull it free but were unable to shift it an inch. The convoy closed up and came to a steaming standstill as a dozen men-at-arms hurried to put their shoulders to the stricken cart. Swords, shields and chests of chain mail were discarded to lighten the load but the wheels refused to turn. Within minutes the oxen were up to their knees in the morass with clouds of vapour rising from distended nostrils.

Wagons began to pull out of line in an attempt to pass the obstruction but these encountered a more treacherous surface and were also bogged down. The beasts bellowed their pain as they were lashed mercilessly. Some carts set off at a sharp angle in the foolish hope of reaching the mainland sooner but they suffered a similar fate in the turning tide.

Voices called out in terror as the scudding clouds closed and blackened the sky. Many left their carts and struggled in the direction they thought the next guide pole would be. Unable to see the horizon in the dark even veterans who had fought in Brittany, Bouvines and against the barons of England discarded their armour, their heavy leather tunics and gambesons before mistakenly making their way into the incoming tide and the open sea to perish most horribly.

Pandemonium arose as hundreds of soldiers, servants and women shouted, screamed and prayed until one plaintive cry of anguish, not unlike that of a seagull, signalled the end.

Two and a half thousand people perished that night as well as King John's plan to overcome the barons and reunite the kingdom.

As the king made his way to the Cistercian abbey at Swineshead two common men-at-arms were urging their oxen towards the small county town of March. Their good fortune had placed them at the rear of the convoy and as the cart in front of them descended onto the sands to make the estuary crossing they had lingered until it was a vague shadow before turning their span and taking the road inland.

Geoffrey and Hugh were two disreputable brothers who had fought and lost in Angevin Normandy and had survived battling both the French knights and the English barons in Exeter. They were tired and wanted to go home with more than just a few pence. The cart given into their care was loaded with bedding, spare clothing and cooking utensils. Stealing such worthless items would never have crossed their minds but the discovery of a small, iron-banded oak chest hidden in the cart changed everything.

The mystery chest was uncovered in Spalding when a deep hole in the road jolted the cart. Both men knew that all items of value, including the royal regalia and many barrels of silver coins had been secured in the first fifteen carts but their curiosity was stirred and a few hefty blows sprung the lock. Being the most courageous Geoffrey raised the lid and uncovered a large package wrapped in soft doeskin. Silk pouches filled with coins were packed around it and Hugh nervously lifted it out for his brother to see.

With large callused hands that were more used to wielding a battle-axe than handling delicate items Geoffrey slowly unwrapped the package and they gasped when they saw the gleam and glitter of silver and precious jewels. Geoffrey was holding the crown of England. It would mean death if they were caught and Hugh snatched up the skin and re-covered the priceless symbol of power before putting back in the chest with all the pouches and closing the lid firmly.

The two brothers whispered throughout the night, discussing what to do with their unexpected find. The coronation regalia had evidently been hidden in separate carts, well away from the main bulk of the treasure to provide extra security. They knew that the broken lock would immediately be noticed when the chest was unloaded at Bishop's Lynn and being hung, drawn and quartered was not an end either man had envisaged for himself.

Mid-afternoon, when the cooking fires were being doused, Geoffrey decided that their only option was to steal the chest and the treasure it contained.

Hugh was horrified but Geoffrey assured him they could hide everything in a safe place before taking a ship to the continent. There they would work as mercenary soldiers before returning a few years later when the *hu et cri* had ceased. The gold crown could be broken into very small insignificant pieces which they would sell in different market towns while keeping the pearls and the jewels separate. The gems would be sold in France where they would live out the rest of their lives in luxury.

All of Hugh's misgivings evaporated while his brother outlined the plan and he readily agreed. They were unaware of the fateful causeway crossing which resulted in the loss of the entire precious cargo in the estuary mud. Concealing their theft and hiding in France was completely unnecessary.

The night was pitch black and the same fateful sea mist was now creeping in behind them making visibility impossible by the time they drew close to Ravens' Wood, a forested area little known to the brothers. As they were still ten miles from March Hugh suggested that they enter the wood and hide the chest before daring to continue on to the marshland town.

They found a small cart track and as Hugh walked before the oxen holding a flaring torch aloft they penetrated deep into the wood. The pitch-soaked bundle of twigs was beginning to splutter in the damp air when they spotted the perfect hiding place.

A solitary oak, young yet majestic in size, provided an ideal landmark that would last for centuries. Lightning had blasted away one of its larger branches leaving a deep cleft in the distorted trunk. It was at head height and with a little coaxing the chest went in and dropped out of sight in the large cavity. Hugh then took the doeskin pouch and buried it in a deep pit at the foot of the tree between two visible roots.

'It'll be safe here while we spend the night in the village inn and then we can retrieve it in the morning and head for the nearest port.'

'Why so deep?' Geoffrey asked.

'To prevent any casual traveller finding it.'

They filled in the hole and scattered moss and leaves on top before Hugh used his sword to cut a deep line in the tree at ground level. He rubbed mud into the wound to hide its freshness.

'That'll save us digging all round the tree should we forget where we buried the damned thing in the dark,' he explained.

The brothers swore an oath that neither would touch the chest or the crown without the other being present. They spat on their palms and slapped their hands together before continuing on towards March and the promise of a warm hearth and a hotpot meal.

As the cart slowly trundled into the thickening mist Hugh walked ahead with one of the few remaining flares held high to guide his brother. They had hardly travelled more than three miles from the wood when a large group of heavily armed men materialized from the mist and challenged them.

The brothers immediately sensed that the group was one of the many itinerant bands of thieves who preyed on those who dared to venture out at night. They both began unsheathing their swords but their blades had hardly cleared leather before the rogues swiftly overwhelmed them.

Geoffrey had been sitting high on the wagon and he suffered upward sword thrusts from two burly men who smelt of stale beer and urine. One sliced beneath the hardened tunic, penetrating his stomach and severing his spinal cord. As Geoffrey toppled from the cart Hugh was gripped by three more ruffians while a fourth clubbed the sword from his hand, rendering him defenceless. As he fell beneath their combined weight one knelt upon his back, pinning him to the ground. A thin *poignard* was thrust into his back, puncturing a lung, and after three more violent thrusts Hugh was left to drown slowly in his own blood.

Satisfied that their victims were mortally wounded the band of men ransacked the wagon. They stripped the dying men and argued over the meagre purses before unharnessing the oxen. These would fetch a princely sum at the weekend market where ownership was never questioned. As the ruffians evaporated into the cloying mist one lingered to make sure nothing of value had been overlooked. Ransacking the heaps of casually tossed clothing and bedding he found a roll of vellum wrapped in one of the blankets. The large piece of soft skin was covered in Latin script that he was unable to decipher. He rolled it up and tucked it beneath his filthy shirt, planning to have it valued later by someone who could read. Pitiful sounds from the dying Hugh drew his attention and he administered a merciful *coup de grâce*. He dragged the naked corpses into the undergrowth and covered them with bracken.

The brothers' dream of a life of leisure ended as a banquet for ravens, wolves and wild boars.

1

JAMES GOODFELLOW STRETCHED, opened his eyes and was instantly blinded by a dazzling shaft of sunlight. With a muffled curse he rolled away from the window and pulled the duvet over his head. Jennifer had placed a cup of tea on the bedside table, hidden the TV remote and opened the curtains before going back downstairs. It was her way of getting him out of bed on a Sunday morning in time for the cooked breakfast she always prepared.

Stretching lazily and listening to his wife clattering in the kitchen he thought about the sequence of events that had brought him to this happy place.

Despite his Oxford degree in microbiology James had always wanted to be a detective and after a number of career changes, each ending in disaster because of his undiagnosed narcolepsy, he had joined the police force where he was soon promoted to Detective Constable. His posting to East Steading changed his life in ways he could never have anticipated. First, he fell for a very attractive constable called Jennifer Kent who later became his wife and second, an inopportune attack revealed his awkward medical condition and following a gentle but firm nudge from senior officers he was compelled to resign.

James was determined to pursue a crime-fighting career and he opened his own detective agency, Goodfellow Investigations, next-door to the Forbidden City, a Chinese restaurant in the small town of East Steading. He still lives in the same flat above the agency. His first big case took him to Germany where he was able to save a number of orphans from ruthless scientists who were conducting abhorrent pharmaceutical experiments. Despite his traumatic experience one child grew to love James and Jennifer more than any parents could ever wish and, after unravelling miles of red tape, they adopted him.

Suddenly, that same happy bundle of eight-year-old energy burst into the room and leapt upon the bed. The weekend was always their special time and they spent hours making model aircraft and flying them in the park. Jennifer kept their energy levels stoked high with a big breakfast and a well-stocked picnic basket.

They wrestled for a few minutes until Claudiu was out of breath. James quickly jumped out of bed and put on his dressing gown before both hurried down the stairs and into the kitchen.

'What's on the agenda today?' Jennifer asked as she topped baked beans and sausages with fried eggs while James poured freshly squeezed orange juice for Claudiu.

'Fly the Tiger Moth,' exclaimed Claudiu as he waved his hands in the air to simulate aerobatic manoeuvres. 'Pl-e-e-ase can we go and fly the Tiger?' he implored as he grabbed the sleeve of James' dressing gown and used his big brown eyes to put on the pressure.

James was a soft touch when it came to Claudiu's happiness and was about to agree to the plan when the phone on the hallstand table rang. He looked at Jennifer and shrugged as if to ask who could be calling on Sunday at nine o'clock in the morning.

'How would I know?' she asked, reading his mind and leaving the room to answer the insistent ringing. James put a finger to his lips to keep Claudiu quiet as he strained to hear who she was speaking to. After a few seconds she returned, her face as white as a sheet.

'It's Agnes, she wants to talk to you.' Jennifer sat down and took a gulp from the scalding cup of tea. 'Bad news, James,' she whispered. James went to the phone while Claudiu looked at Jennifer's distressed expression with childish concern.

James picked up the handset. 'It's James, Miss Lightbody, what's wrong?"

'It's my cousin Daniel, Mr Goodfellow.' There was a long pause and James could hear his secretary suppressing some sobbing. 'He's been killed. I've just received a call from the local police in Wisbech and they told me that he had an accident whilst felling a tree. They wouldn't give me any details over the phone and I'm at a loss as to what I should do.'

'My God, I'm so sorry, Miss Lightbody. Where are you now?'

'I'm at home. I received the call on my way back from the office where I went to get some papers.'

'Then I want you to phone for a taxi and come straight back here while I try to find out what happened. Jennifer and I will be waiting with a fresh pot of tea.' James waited until he heard the connection being broken before returning to the kitchen.

'I guess you overheard. I'll phone Wisbech and see what it is that they can't tell her over the phone.'

Jennifer nodded. 'She sounded very distraught so I'll go and prepare the guest room. Agnes can't possibly stay all by herself in that big old house of hers tonight.'

Claudiu had been looking from one to the other with a big question mark in his eyes and James took his hand. 'I'm sorry son, but we'll have to fly the Tiger on another day. Our friend, Agnes, has had some very sad news and we have to look after her.'

'I'll go and help Mum,' Claudiu announced bravely and hurried to catch up with Jennifer who was climbing the stairs carrying fresh sheets she had taken from the airing cupboard.

James dialled directory enquiries and asked to be connected to Wisbech police station. He waited for an interminable length of time before an authoritative voice said brusquely, 'Wisbech Constabulary. How can I help you?'

James gave his name and said he was enquiring about the man who had been killed in an area called Ravens' Wood. He explained that he was a private investigator working for the aunt who had agreed to identify the body whilst the deceased's wife was away in Bristol.

'If you're a bona fide licensed investigator then you should know that I cannot give any information over the phone, especially to someone who isn't related, *sir*.' The stress on the last word didn't go unnoticed by James. 'Your client will have to come to Wisbech to formally identify the body and then she will be informed of the circumstances that led to the fatality.' This was said with clipped formality that lacked any emotion and James knew he wouldn't get any further. He reluctantly thanked the constable and hung up.

'Miss Lightbody and I will have to visit Norfolk,' James shouted up the stairs as he dialled the number for East Steading railway station. There was a muffled reply from the bedroom but before he could call out again a very efficient booking clerk came on the line and gave him the train times to Wisbech. He put the phone down and as if on cue the front doorbell rang. Agnes was standing outside with red-rimmed eyes and James gave her a long reassuring hug before taking her into the kitchen. He poured a cup of tea and without asking spooned sugar into the cup.

'You know very well that I don't take sugar, James.'

'Hot, sweet tea was made for times like this, Miss Lightbody,' he said softly as he slid the cup across the table. 'Now drink up before you say another word. You'll be staying here with us tonight and I won't take any arguments from you. You need friends close by to look after you.'

His secretary cradled the hot cup in her hands and took a tentative sip. 'I – I – I didn't have time to bring anything. Not even a toothbrush,' she whispered apologetically.

'Jennifer will have everything you need and tomorrow you and I will travel to Wisbech to find out what happened.'

'The officer who phoned wouldn't tell me anything and –'

Jennifer entered the kitchen and immediately put her arms around the slender woman's shoulders. 'Oh, you poor dear,' she exclaimed. 'What you need is a good shot of brandy in that.' She pointed to the half-empty cup and James hurried to the cupboard to search for the bottle that only came out to flame the steamed fruit pudding at Christmas.

Agnes couldn't help smiling: first sickly sweet tea and now brandy which she detested. She felt a surge of love for the two people and she squeezed Jennifer's hand.

'I'll take Claudiu to school tomorrow and Inspector Tilley will understand if I leave early to pick him up which will give you the whole day to get to Norfolk and back,' Jennifer said and James, who normally did the collection at the school gates, nodded appreciatively.

Jennifer had been a police officer for three years and during that time had gained rapid promotion to detective and then, on her own merit, detective sergeant. James had first met her when she was a junior police constable at the same station house. That was shortly before his resignation when the narcolepsy grew stronger. His seniors had noticed how he was apt to fall asleep on the job, sometimes for no reason other than a car backfiring or somebody telling a particularly funny joke.

'Daniel loved the country,' Agnes suddenly said as though she had a need to explain why her cousin didn't live near her in a big town. 'When Tom Rogers gave Daniel the responsibility of looking after Ravens' Wood he was over the moon. He did nothing but talk about his plans for the wood for weeks on end.'

'Tom Rogers?' Jennifer asked.

'He was Daniel's employer and had inherited four hundred acres of prime Norfolk farmland from his father. That was ten years ago and in that time he lost his wife to cancer and resigned himself to a quiet bachelor existence growing oil-seed rape and sugar beet.'

'Why was Daniel so excited about Ravens' Wood?' James asked in a quiet voice.

'It seems that there is a very old oak tree in the middle of the wood that was close to being one thousand years old. Tom had asked a tree surgeon in Spalding to take a look at it and it was found to be rotten to the core. It was dangerous and had to come down but the tree surgeon wanted too much money for the task.'

'Daniel volunteered to do it?' Jennifer asked, guessing that this may have been the cause of the fatal accident.

'The tree surgeon had quoted eighteen hundred pounds and the right to dispose of the felled timber. Daniel said he would do it for five hundred and cut the wood into disposable logs for Tom Rogers to sell. It would be enough to buy Margaret, Daniel's wife, a new stove she had set her heart on.'

Jennifer sat down beside Agnes and laid an arm across her shoulders. 'I remember when Daniel came to East Steading last month to tell you all about it,' Jennifer murmured.

'I was so proud of him.'

There was a catch in Agnes' throat and Jennifer knew she was close to crying. 'Let's go upstairs and I'll show you your room, Agnes. I think you'll be comfortable there. Then you can say hello to Claudiu who's dying to show you his latest model plane.'

The flicker of a smile appeared and then disappeared as fast as it had come. The two women left the kitchen and James sank down into his chair with an inaudible sigh and reached for the Christmas brandy.

Early the next morning Agnes made her appearance and smiled at the busy family as she entered the kitchen.

'I was lured away from that very comfortable bed by the delicious smell of bacon, Jennifer,' she said as Claudiu placed a glass of orange juice by her elbow. Agnes ruffled his hair and bid him good morning and he laughed whilst self-consciously brushing it back into place with his hand. He returned to his chair and the half-finished bowl of frosted flakes.

Agnes knew Claudiu's background well for she had been instrumental in helping her employer track down the kidnappers and bringing them all to justice. Since arriving in East Steading the two had become very close friends and Agnes had occasionally joined the family on their picnics to escape the boredom of her lonely weekends in the house.

'We have an hour before the train leaves which gives us plenty of time for breakfast and to get ready,' James informed his secretary as she began to nibble half-heartedly at the generous plate of food Jennifer had placed before her.

They arrived in Kings Lynn station at 1.30 p.m. and James hired an economy Chevy Aveo to drive the thirteen miles to Wisbech police station – Agnes never permitted unmerited expenditure when it came from the Goodfellow Investigations fund of petty cash.

They drove for twenty minutes in silence, Agnes sifting through memories of her favourite cousin while James focused on the portable sat-nav screen he had brought from the office. He found a convenient space to park that was only one hundred yards from the police station and hadn't been disfigured by yellow lines. It was a long, two-storey building in dull cream brick that stood facing the River Nene. Blue railings and a steel gate across the road marked the private access ramp and concrete steps of the Wisbech yacht harbour.

A uniformed constable was leaving the police station as they approached the main entrance. He paused to hold one of the imposing double doors open for Agnes and James nodded his thanks as he followed her in. After presenting identification and giving their reason for the visit to the desk sergeant they were asked to take a seat. While waiting the sergeant told them that Daniel's death was being treated as suicide and Agnes was rendered speechless.

'Daniel would never do such a thing!' she stuttered and James was inclined to agree for he had met the young man and admired his enthusiasm for life and everything he was involved in.

They were kept waiting for twenty minutes before a constable took them to meet a Sergeant Tanner, the senior officer overseeing the incident.

'Only a sergeant,' James observed quietly. 'Surely a violent death should warrant an inspector?'

'Not for a suicide, sir,' the constable answered as he showed them into an empty office. 'If you would like to take a seat Sergeant Tanner will be with you shortly. Would you like a cup of tea or coffee?' They declined and he shrugged indifferently, closing the door behind him.

Sergeant Tanner was a corpulent figure with a tunic that fought hard to control the mass constrained within. He bustled in followed by a middle-aged woman wearing a navy-blue suit. It was the style of fashion that Agnes admired and wore herself. She was introduced as the medical examiner and they were told she would be taking Agnes to identify the deceased.

'I will be accompanying Miss Lightbody,' James declared firmly as he handed his business card to the sergeant. 'She may need my support.'

Tanner returned the card with the suggestion of a condescending smile on his lips and gave his permission in a grudging tone of voice.

'This way please,' the medical examiner requested and they followed her to the room where Daniel had been laid out in preparation for Agnes' arrival.

One wall was lined with stainless steel doors but it was the figure draped in white cotton sheeting on a solitary table in the small room that immediately gained their attention.

'I'm here, Miss Lightbody,' James whispered as he saw her shoulders draw back as though trying to delay the inevitable.

'It would appear, from my initial inspection at the scene, that the deceased used a chainsaw to sever his own carotid artery, causing copious bleeding and certain death.' The sergeant's words sounded sterile and heartless as they echoed round the tile-walled chamber. The medical examiner had remained silent during his summation.

'He was found at the foot of a giant oak that he had arranged with his employer, Mr Tom Rogers, to bring down for the sum of five hundred pounds. We can only assume that the task depressed him and that he chose to take his own life rather than that of the tree.'

'Rubbish!' Agnes blurted out.

'I beg your pardon, madam?'

'Daniel loved his own life too much to end it.'

The woman drew the sheet back enough to reveal the face only and Agnes gasped, blood draining from her face. 'Yes. I can identify this person as my cousin Daniel Lightbody and damn the person who did this dreadful thing to him.'

Once back in the office Agnes repeated her words.

'Madam, all evidence is to the contrary,' the sergeant stated with a tone of finality that forestalled any further argument. 'Would you please sign the official statement that you have identified the deceased as Mr Daniel Lightbody, residing at Crags Bottom Cottage, Newton.'

While Agnes signed the form James hurried back to the shrouded figure and threw the sheet back completely.

'What are you doing,' the medical examiner exclaimed in a shocked voice.

'I need to see how this man committed suicide,' James replied as he studied the gaping wound in the side of the neck. 'Apart from the obvious damage he also shows signs of bruising and what seems to be a blow to the back of the head.'

'Those were undoubtedly caused by his fall from the tree he was cutting. I presume that the chainsaw he was using on himself caused that fatal cut in the side of the neck. He then fell to the foot of the tree where he was found roughly three hours later.'

'Halfway up a tree is a strange place to kill yourself and surely there would be signs of scratching on the arms and face from falling through the lower branches!' James commented as he leant over the corpse to take a closer look at the damage.

'I was told that the smaller branches had already been cleared and that the deceased was starting to work his way down on the larger ones.' The woman shuffled her feet and then seemed to make up her mind about something. 'You will have to leave now as it is against the rules to allow anyone who isn't a relative to be in here.' She pulled the sheet to re-cover the corpse and James reluctantly walked towards the door.

'There will be a full post mortem?' he inquired and she nodded. James gave her his card and a request to call him if anything untoward was found.

The King's Charter

'I will let you know but only if the coroner permits me to do so.'

James left and went back to the office. The pompous sergeant was behind his desk and Agnes was sitting beside a younger woman on the leather settee. She was a small brunette with tears running down her cheeks and a completely lost expression on her rather attractive face. Agnes explained who James was and then said, 'This is Margaret, Daniel's wife. She has only just arrived from Bristol where she was visiting her sister. She was able to catch the fast train when notified of the accident.'

The sergeant was starting to correct Agnes when James interrupted. 'I'm so glad Agnes could do the identification for you, Mrs Lightbody. It's a very traumatic experience that nobody should ever be subjected to.'

James felt massive sympathy for the new widow and then anger that a junior officer's speculation had been accepted as the truth. 'I have a strong feeling that there is more to this than a tragic accident but I will need Sergeant Tanner's permission to visit the scene of the tragedy before I can say any more.'

Tanner looked at James suspiciously. 'Are you still doubting that it was suicide, Mr Goodfellow?' he questioned and James felt the office temperature plunge.

Margaret leapt to her feet to confront the officer. 'Suicide? You think it was a suicide?' she shouted. 'Daniel could no more take his own life than he could mine.'

Tanner shrunk back into his chair and James led Margaret back to Agnes. 'Nobody is saying Daniel would do such a thing, Margaret,' he said softly while glaring at the sergeant, daring him to contradict.

'Then what did he mean?' She slumped down beside Agnes who once more comforted the desolate woman.

'They have to consider every possibility. It's what the police are paid to do and they will be investigating every possible angle to discover what actually happened in the wood.'

James went to stand before the sergeant. 'That's why Sergeant Tanner will give me the necessary permission to continue working on the case in my own way and do a little investigating of my own.' With his back turned to the women James raised an eyebrow and waited for the officer's response.

'As Ravens' Wood hasn't officially been listed as a crime scene you are perfectly free to enter and waste your time.' The condescension was back and James turned away and ushered the two women from the room.

'I'll let you know whether I've been wasting my time or not, Sergeant,' James said before closing the door.

As they walked to the car Agnes took the widow's arm and said, 'I suggest that I stay with you for a couple of days, Margaret.' She turned to James who was unlocking the car. 'I know the address, it's on the outskirts of Newton so I'll be able to direct you.'

James nodded, checked all seat belts were fastened and pulled away. With excellent navigation from the back seat they were soon outside a charming stone cottage within a stone's throw of the small village that could hardly be home to more than a thousand souls. As soon as they had entered Agnes busied herself with the kettle while James sat Margaret in the small front room and tucked a hand-embroidered throw about her legs. He had seen a compact suitcase standing in the hall and knew that she hadn't even had time to unpack on her arrival home before the taxi took her to Wisbech. Movement in the corner of his eye caught his attention and he was about to take action when a rather elderly cocker spaniel appeared from behind the settee and waddled towards her mistress. Her ears swung lazily as she turned to look at James with eyes that could charm the devil himself and he held his hand out.

'She's very friendly, James,' Margaret murmured having noticed his initial reaction. 'This is Tammy. She's thirteen years old and a trifle too arthritic to tackle burglars or private detectives.'

'She's lovely,' James said as he fondled one of the long silky ears. 'Miss Lightbody, while you and Tammy keep Margaret company I'll go and take a look at Ravens' Wood,' he said and then murmured, 'which way do I go, Margaret?'

'Do you always call Agnes by her surname?'

'It's a habit I haven't been able to change even though, after all the cases we've been involved in, I like to think we have more than an employer–employee relationship.'

'That's nice,' Margaret whispered to herself and then seemed to jolt awake before adding, 'continue along Fen road until you see an old wooden sign for Roger's Farm. Take that and drive for three miles and after passing an old farmhouse and two dilapidated barns you'll see a dirt track on your left that leads straight to the heart of the wood. You'll find Oliver Cromwell there.'

'Oliver Cromwell?'

'Yes. It is one of the oldest oaks in the county, said to date back to medieval times. It's the one that Daniel was supposed to fell for Tom Rogers.'

She bent her head and sobbed into a wad of tissues and James patted her shoulder, stroked Tammy once, and left the cottage.

The instructions had been clear; the drive proved uneventful and he parked the car on the fringe of the woodland and walked along the rutted road that acted as a firebreak until he saw what could only be the biggest oak he had ever encountered.

This must be it, he thought as he gazed upward. The main branches were naked, the result of a chainsaw expert, and as he looked up he could see the last of the rain clouds moving apart to reveal a duck-egg-blue sky. The temperature had risen and he slipped his jacket off while walking around the massive bole wondering how a simple tree could possibly live for hundreds of years when humans struggle to survive for only a few decades. Midway round Oliver Cromwell he stopped and stared at some deep cuts, gaping wounds that disfigured the ancient bark just above head height. It was an ugly assault on a thing of beauty.

To what purpose would Daniel use his chainsaw there, he thought. The first wedge removed is usually cut between knee and waist height when felling the main trunk of a tree the size of Oliver Cromwell.

After leaving university with a degree in microbiology James was offered a position with a leading forestry company and knew every tree disease. He had helped in felling badly stricken trees and knew most of the techniques employed by forest rangers. James shaded his eyes with his hand and with neck muscles straining looked up to the top of the tree. He shook his head for he knew there had to be a lot more trimming done before Daniel could have tried laying Cromwell down without damaging any of the surrounding trees.

James continued round the bole until he identified where Daniel's body had lain. Decomposing leaf litter and fungi had been crushed and there was a large dark stain where blood had flowed and been blotted by the woodland detritus. Abandoned police tape lay on the ground surrounding the depression that was ten paces from the trunk. Looking up again James could see that there wasn't a branch strong enough to support Daniel that would make such a fall acceptable. Stroking the side of his nose with a forefinger he walked back to the tree. There he looked round at the offcut branches and propped one of the shorter logs against the trunk. He stepped up to stand on the end and inspect the deep cut in the side of the tree.

It wasn't just a savage mutilation of the trunk but a neat wedge cut into the side of a deeper, much older cavity. Daniel, or possibly someone else, had used the chainsaw to enlarge a natural opening for a purpose he was not immediately sure about. James took a small Maglite from his pocket and shone it inside the tree. The bottom of the hole was only two feet from the entrance and the pale yellow light revealed the unnatural imprint of an oblong shape in the thick moss and rotten pieces of pulped wood at the bottom of the cavity.

Something had stood hidden there for a very long time, he thought as he reached in and ran his fingers lightly around the inside of the bole. An object had been dragged up and out of the cavity, deeply scoring the inside. The oak had clearly grown in an attempt to repair the original hole that was probably caused by lightning many years ago. This meant that after natural growth whatever had been placed in there at the time could no longer be retrieved without being physically cut from the living tree.

James jumped down and began to go round the tree in ever-widening circles until he was walking through a large patch of tall stinging nettles. He was fifty yards from Oliver Cromwell when, on closer observation, it was clear that someone else had walked into the weeds. He pulled the sleeves of his jacket down to cover his hands and pushed his way into the dense patch until the toe of his shoe struck something hard lying in the undergrowth.

Using his feet James exposed what appeared to be an old iron box. It was a yard long and half a yard high and wide. Considerable corrosion over the years meant that the metal readily shed orange flakes when touched. It was also clear from the distorted hasp that the key lock had been forced many years ago. He bent down and lifted the lid to find that apart from a few fragments of rotting material it was completely empty.

'What did Daniel find inside?' James muttered aloud as he struggled to lift the heavy chest. 'And why did he hide it so far from the tree?' James was now convinced that Daniel didn't take his own life; nor was his death an accident. 'He'd discovered a chest and some bastard took it from him.'

James had exposed a very bloody murder and the motive had to be the contents of the chest.

2

THE SUN HAD BEGUN to set as the hire car stopped outside the cottage in Newton. Agnes opened the door and waved excitedly for James to hurry in, a curious Tammy standing by her with tail erect.

'I have Daphne Sampson on the line,' she said as he drew near.

'Who?'

'The medical examiner we met this afternoon.'

James took the receiver from the hallstand. 'Mrs Sampson?' he asked as Agnes moved in closer to pick up what was being said. He listened attentively as the woman gave him a brief description of the autopsy results. When she had finished James hung up with a gleam in his eye.

'It's something terrible, isn't it?' Agnes asked, for she had learnt how to read her employer's face. James nodded and led the way into the kitchen where Margaret was preparing an early supper. Tammy trotted past them and went straight to her basket.

'I think you should hear this, too,' he said as he sat at the table. 'The medical examiner has found that Daniel wasn't killed by the chainsaw. He was already dead when he received those cuts on his neck.'

Margaret, eyes fixed on James, held a hand to her mouth as she continued stirring the simmering gravy. 'So it couldn't possibly be suicide? Daniel didn't kill himself?'

'No,' James said firmly. 'Nor was it an accident. They found marks on the second cervical vertebra consistent with a thin and exceptionally sharp blade. Daniel had been brutally attacked with a knife before the chainsaw was used to disguise the manner of his death.'

Margaret gasped and Agnes hurried to her side.

'I'm sorry if I shocked you, Margaret, but I thought you should know before the police came.'

'He was murdered,' Agnes said softly, more to herself than anyone present and then she loudly exclaimed, 'But, why? Who would want to do such a thing?'

'I have a feeling that the motive may have been the contents of an old iron chest that I found hidden a short distance from the tree known as Oliver Cromwell.'

Agnes sat beside Margaret and took her hand. 'Have you still got the chest?' she asked.

'Yes. It's in the car and I'll take it to Wisbech police station in the morning. Meanwhile I'll go and look for a hotel that is suitably close to this house.'

Margaret's head lifted. 'You don't have to do that, James,' she sobbed. 'You can both stay here. I've got two spare bedrooms and it won't take long to put fresh linen on the beds.' She stood up and returned to stirring the gravy while Agnes checked the chicken in the oven. James admired the women who were both showing exceptional fortitude and left the cottage to retrieve the mysterious iron chest from the car and photograph it from all possible angles.

The next day began with a storm and a deafening clap of thunder that woke James from a restless sleep. He had always found it difficult to sleep at night and his narcolepsy compelled him to take two or three short naps during the day to prevent any attack at an inopportune moment.

James swung his legs round and sat on the edge of the bed. Taking a small box from his toiletry bag he swallowed a sodium oxybate tablet called Xyrem. This helped in countering the cataplexy, hallucinations and sleeping problems but quite often caused bouts of nausea and dizziness. He took a quick gulp of water and went about getting ready for the day.

The storm had passed and left the sky a washed-out grey that threatened no more than light showers when he went downstairs. Agnes was in the kitchen preparing breakfast and the smell of crispy bacon caused James to salivate. Agnes greeted him with a smile and in answer to his unspoken question she explained, 'Margaret's still upstairs. She's not feeling too good, poor thing, so I'll take her a tray.'

He gave an understanding nod and poured the freshly brewed coffee for them both. As he sat sipping the smooth Nicaraguan coffee his mind ran over the facts from the day before. The road to the farmhouse would have little traffic and the farmer or labourers would be the only people using the rough track leading to Ravens' Wood. James made a mental note to visit Tom Rogers and see what he knew about Oliver Cromwell.

On the way to Wisbech James suddenly realized that he hadn't spoken to Jennifer since his arrival in Newton. He pulled into a lay-by that overlooked the green billiard table of north Norfolk and used his mobile to apologize for not telling her that he was staying at Margaret Lightbody's home. After ten minutes of conciliatory platitudes he had cooled her temper and brought her up to date on the latest news. James then mentally ducked as he told her of his plan to stay a few days more.

'You do realize that Inspector Tilley will go up the wall if I keep leaving mid-afternoon to pick up Claudiu?'

James could hear the frustration in her voice, 'I'll try not to be away for too long and if you want I'll give Tilley a call myself and explain the situation.'

'Don't you dare. I'm in enough trouble as it is.'

They said their goodbyes and James went to Wisbech police station where he found Sergeant Tanner on duty. He greeted James gruffly with a few brief words and after leading James to his office he described what he had seen and found at the old oak.

'So you think it's a crime scene now?' the sergeant mocked as he took a memo from his in-tray. 'What makes you think a rusty box so far from the tree has the power to turn a simple suicide into a murder?' He yawned and started reading the memo in his hand.

'Logic tells me that a young, happily married man doesn't suddenly take his own life for no reason at all; and certainly not up in a tree. Daniel Lightbody found something in that hollow tree that needed a chainsaw to get it out. That means it had been there a long time and –' James got no further as the sergeant suddenly sat bolt upright with a curse on his lips.

'It would seem, Goodfellow, that you may have stumbled on something and I need to see that iron box as soon as possible.' Tanner turned the memo face down on his desk and stood up. 'Where is it?' he demanded.

'I put it in the trunk of my car this morning.'

'Give me your keys now!' Tanner snatched them from the outstretched hand and dashed from the room. James was left alone with a puzzled expression on his face until he reached across the desk, took the memo and read that it was a summary of the medical examiner's findings. James nodded with satisfaction, replaced the memo as he had found it and sat back to await the return of the sergeant.

Tanner soon returned to sit on the corner of his desk and stare down at James with one leg swinging nervously. 'We will need your fingerprints, Goodfellow,' he snapped. 'To eliminate you from our inquiry.'

'You'll find my prints are already on record.'

A satisfied expression crossed the officer's face. 'Been in trouble before, have we?'

'Not exactly, Sergeant, I was a detective constable before my disability brought about retirement.'

The leg stopped swinging and Tanner walked around the desk and sat down with what seemed a sympathetic look on his face. 'I have sent the chest to the laboratory for checking and the latest post mortem results indicate that the wound wasn't self-inflicted. That will be of some relief to the widow.'

'Her husband's dead. I don't think anything will relieve her of that loss, Sergeant.' James stood up and walked to the window before speaking again. 'Who else was interested in Oliver Cromwell apart from Daniel's employer?'

'Nobody, unless of course you mean Mr Bernard Davies.'

'Who is he?'

'Mr Davies is a highly respected member of our community, a Rotarian who gives generously to support the local school.'

'I wasn't asking for a character reference just simply what he does,' James said patiently.

'He runs a landscape garden business and is a professional tree surgeon. Many people use his services including myself. I had a troublesome willow that was undermining my house and he –'

'Did he know about Oliver Cromwell?' James interrupted.

'I heard that he was asked to give his opinion on the state of the tree by Tom Rogers who owns Ravens' Wood. It would appear that the tree had reached a critical stage and that the weight of the branches threatened to crush the rotten section in the lower trunk.'

'That's all?'

'Wait a minute, what are you insinuating?'

James ignored the question, stood up and left the room, leaving the officer with a dumbfounded expression. On his way out he retrieved his car keys from the constable at the front desk and discovered that the forensic people hadn't bothered to relock the car or even to close the trunk. The light rain had soaked the case containing his laptop and he made a mental note to send the bill to Sergeant Tanner. His smartphone soon sourced the garden centre and he flicked the satnav on and started the engine.

The countryside was still flat and the grey sky vast as he drove through the misty rain thinking about his strategy in handling Mr Davies. The empty road seemed to stretch away into infinity and James' eyelids were beginning to droop when a billboard flashed past announcing Green Fingers Garden Centre – 300 Yards.

He slowed the car and pulled into the car park of what, at first glance, seemed to be a supermarket complex. Steel trolleys of the kind used for carrying heavy ceramic plant pots lined the pathway to the entrance. He asked for Bernard Davies and followed a youth wearing thorn-proof gloves and a rubber apron to a door labelled Managing Director.

It was some time before the door opened and a stout man in a grey three-piece suit emerged. His bald pate glistened beneath the fluorescent tubes and he extended a pudgy hand. 'Good morning, sir, how can I help you?' His sideburns ran down to join a bushy moustache that partially disguised protruding top teeth. James took the hand as he gave his name and was repulsed by the moist touch of the man's limp grip.

'I understand you surveyed the giant oak tree in Ravens' Wood that is locally known as –'

'Oliver Cromwell. Yes, you are quite correct, I did take a look at the tree and was asked by Mr Tom Rogers to bring it down after I diagnosed the extent of the internal rot.' As Davies was talking he ushered James into the office and offered him a seat.

'But the contract was given to the farmer's employee, Daniel Lightbody. Do you know why?'

'What business is this of yours?' he asked, his voice hardening.

'I am investigating the death of Mr Lightbody.' There was no reaction from Davies. 'You may have heard that he was murdered with his own chainsaw.' This time there was a change and James watched the blood drain from the man's face.

'Murdered? Nobody said anything about him being killed,' he exclaimed.

'What do you mean by nobody said anything?'

Davies fiddled with an HB pencil that had been lying next to a half-completed crossword. 'Nothing, I didn't mean anybody.'

'It appears that you told some people about a steel chest you had seen hidden in the oak when you were doing your assessment of the rot damage and –'

'No, I know nothing.' The pencil snapped in half and Davies jumped to his feet. 'I want you to get out of my office before I'm forced to call the police.'

'No need, Mr Davies, they're here already.' James pointed out of the window to where a blue-and-white car was pulling up outside the warehouse. A tall stranger in a dark suit got out and was followed by the more familiar figure of Sergeant Tanner. 'I'll wait for them here if you don't mind,' James said with the hint of a smile as he turned in the swivel chair to face the door. Davies returned to his seat with a light sheen covering his forehead and tugged at his striped tie to undo the top shirt button.

There was a polite tap on the door and it opened before Davies could respond. Sergeant Tanner entered the room and stood to one side as though ushering in royalty. His superior entered and introduced himself as Chief Inspector Cheswell.

Tanner eyed James suspiciously. 'What are you doing here?'

'Annoying me and I want you to arrest him for trespass or at least throw him off my property,' Davies demanded.

James ignored the blustering man to answer the sergeant. 'I'm here because Mr Davies was the first to find the iron chest and he informed others but refuses to tell me who they were.'

Cheswell sat in the only other spare chair and fixed James with a cold look. 'This case has nothing to do with you or any other members of the public and I will have to ask that you do as Mr Davies requests and leave immediately. The sergeant has informed me that you were causing trouble in his office earlier today which is to be expected from someone in your line of work.'

James knew he wouldn't gain anything further as it was clear that the inspector was the tree surgeon's friend; his animosity was compounded by his intense dislike of private investigators. He nodded to both officers, ignored Davies, and left the office.

Mulling over what he had learned so far James drove back to Ravens' Wood and after passing the farmhouse he arrived at the rough track that led to the woodland. A constable unwinding lengths of yellow crime scene tape now prevented any further access. As James turned the car the police office held up his hand and went to the driver's window.

'Why did you want to go to the woods, sir,' he asked using the most officious tone of voice he could muster.

James smiled. 'Just for a bit of bird-watching, officer, it's my hobby,' he explained with a broad smile.

The constable wasn't convinced. 'I will need to know your name and address,' he said gruffly as he took a notebook from his top pocket. When James finally left he glanced in the rear-view mirror and saw the officer jot down his number. James decided to do some sleuthing at the farmhouse and pulled into the driveway. A long-wheelbase Land Rover was parked in front of the ivy-covered house and a casual touch of the bonnet showed that it was still warm.

He rang the doorbell and the studded oak door swung open almost immediately and an older man stood facing James. His hair was on the brink of turning silver and his blue intelligent eyes studied the dark suit with a look normally reserved for double-glazing salesmen and Jehovah's Witnesses.

'You're not from around here,' were his first words and James had to smile as he introduced himself and shook the callused hand of a man who had worked the land all his life.

'I am the employer of Miss Agnes Lightbody, and I'm here to investigate the death of Daniel, her cousin,' James explained.

Tom Rogers stepped to one side and waved the investigator in. 'I know who you are,' he exclaimed as he led James down the hall and into the kitchen. 'Margaret used to boast to Daniel about her cousin working for a private detective who solves murders in the city.'

'Well, East Steading isn't quite a metropolis but it's close enough,' James said with a smile and nodded his head as Rogers took a teapot from the warming plate of the Aga and held it up. He poured a rich builder's brew into both cups and slid one across the table.

'How can I help you?'

James used the milk jug to soften the taste. 'I'm trying to piece together as much information about the actual day that Daniel was killed as I –'

'It was an accident!' Rogers exclaimed slopping tea into his saucer. 'Daniel had a frightful accident; I'll never believe he committed suicide. I know that chainsaws are tricky buggers to handle at the best of times and accidents often happen –'

'I'm sorry, Mr Rogers, it was no accident as the latest evidence has shown that his throat was sliced with a knife. Only when he was dead was a chainsaw used to make it look as though he'd had an accident or taken his own life.'

As Rogers slumped heavily into the ancient Windsor chair James watched dust motes rising from the cushion in the shafts of light that were now streaming through the mullioned windows. The sun had broken through the leaden clouds and the flat landscape beyond the glass had been transformed into a green patchwork mottled with shadows that were slowly drifting south.

'Why? Why would anyone want to kill such a fine young man?' His voice broke with emotion. 'He was like a son to me.'

'That's why I'm here, Mr Rogers. I'm determined to find out who the culprit was and I'm hoping you will be able to help me.'

'How?' Rogers took a sip from the cup with a shaking hand.

'I'd like to know something about the people who associated with Bernard Davies on a social level.'

'Good grief, do you suspect Davies!'

'Not at all, but it's my belief that he told people about a mystery chest hidden in the tree centuries ago and they may have spoken to others or even had a hand in Daniel's death personally. It's those people I'd like to have a quiet chat with.'

There was a long pause as the farmer thought deeply. He pinched the top of his nose and then raised his head. 'Davies has a number of people working for him but there are two who he seems to trust more than anyone else. They always seem to appear when he's talking business with clients. I've also seen them put their heads together whenever drinking in the Old Windmill. They usually sit in the far corner whispering and looking as if they're planning something a bit dishonest. I wouldn't be at all surprised if they were involved somehow. They've been caught a few times pilfering in the local shop and poaching.'

'What are their names?'

'One is called Cartwright. I never learned his first name. The other I don't know but you can easily spot him.'

'Why is that?'

'Because he's an albino.' Rogers poured the spilt tea from the saucer into his cup and took another sip. 'White hair, pink eyes and from what I've heard Cartwright and this fellow were originally itinerant farm labourers from Essex. Davies took them on last autumn for a bit of hedge trimming and lawn cutting for a number of private estates in the Newton area. They did a reasonable job for him, stayed on and now Davies employs them full-time for his tree pollarding and felling contracts.'

'Do you know where I can find them apart from at the garden centre?' James inquired as he stood up in preparation to leave.

Rogers pulled a face before muttering; 'You'll find them in the Old Windmill from seven to closing time.'

'Are they heavy drinkers?'

'They put down bitter like men lost in the Sahara. After the eighth pint their mood changes and the albino wants to fight the first person to cross him which is usually the barman when he rings time.'

'And he can handle them both?' James raised an eyebrow.

Roger chuckled, 'Alan may be small but he's smart. He simply holds his mobile up for the two to see and threatens to speed-dial the police unless they leave. He'd learnt that trick from the landlord of the Eagles' Nest in Newton where the two men used to drink. Cartwright only called his bluff once. They had just begun to punch Alan when the law arrived.'

'What happened?'

Rogers laughed at the memory. 'They were up before the magistrate and sent down to the nick for ten days. They were also banned from the Eagles' Nest for life. That's when they started drinking at the Old

Windmill and on the very first night threatened a regular couple and Alan simply held up his phone. They left as quietly as dormice.'

James laughed. 'Thanks for the tea, Mr Rogers. It's been a pleasure talking to you.' They shook hands at the front door and James returned to his car to drive back to the garden centre. As he pulled into the car park he noticed that the police car had left and he went directly to Bernard Davies' office where he tapped on the door and entered without waiting for an invitation. Before Davies could react to the sudden intrusion James demanded to know who he had told about the chest.

'You've got a bloody cheek storming in here like this but if you must know I've already told the police,' Davies snapped.

'Then you can tell me.'

'If it's the only way I can get you off my back – it was Cartright and Whitey.'

'Whitey? That's your employee's name?'

'That's the only name I've ever known him by.'

'How can you register him as an employee if you don't have his proper name and National Insurance number?'

'They're only casual labourers and I pay them with cash at the end of each week.' Davies was clearly discomfited by James' line of inquiry.

'Did you tell the police how you avoid paying their National Insurance by not registering their employment?' James asked in an even quieter voice. Davies didn't answer. 'In which case I'll tell them if you don't tell me the whereabouts of your so-called employees right now.'

Davies winced and nodded. 'They're using a small cottage of mine on Fen Road close to the North Level Main Drain which is the main fenland drainage channel. You can't miss the cottage as it is the only one with a thatched roof and a red picket fence,' he mumbled. James stood up and left without saying another word.

As he drove across the fenland the only interruption on the low horizon was a line of dwindling electricity pylons and the occasional farmhouse. The road turned left abruptly but straight ahead, one hundred yards further on, he saw a small thatched cottage that had red fencing as described by Davies. He stopped and sat for a moment studying the front of the building until he detected a curtain twitch at one of the upstairs windows.

James left the car, went through the gate and strode along the flagstone path to the front door. Numerous layers of different coloured paint had been revealed by years of neglect. There was no doorbell button and the knocker was coated in a fine layer of corrosion. As he reached for it the door was violently opened and James found himself looking into the side-by-side barrels of a Russian Baikal. Although it was one of the cheapest shotguns you could buy it was no less deadly than the more expensive weapons.

The shock was too great to be suppressed by his daily Xyrem tablet and James immediately felt his legs grow numb before paralysis affected his whole body and he fell into a deep REM sleep. He collapsed on the muddy doorstep at the feet of an astonished Cartwright.

After only a few minutes James recovered sufficiently to open his eyelids. He had been dragged into an armchair before a wood-burning stove that was slowly toasting the soles of his shoes. A burly young man wearing a pair of work-soiled dungarees was seated opposite and staring at a mobile phone in his hand with indecision on his unshaven face.

'You're awake!' he exclaimed when James opened his eyes and withdrew his feet from the stove's searing heat. 'Who are you and what's wrong? Do you want me to call an ambulance?'

James looked around the room and saw the shotgun leaning against the wall by the door. 'I'm fine. It was looking down the barrels of that bloody weapon that made me faint,' James snapped with well-justified anger. 'What the hell did you think you were doing?'

'We're not used to strangers round these parts and there's been a few break-ins lately,' Cartwright mumbled by way of an apology as he put his phone down on a beer-stained coffee table.

James stood up and stretched his back. 'Are you Cartwright or Whitey?'

'Do I look like Whitey?' A confident sneer crossed the man's face and James took an instant dislike to him.

'I wouldn't know, what does he look like?'

'You can't miss Whitey, he's one of those albino chaps,' Cartwright sniggered as a kettle whistled in the kitchen. 'He carries his congenital disorder like a chip on his shoulder so I wouldn't cross him if I were you.'

'Where is he?'

Cartwright got up and leaving the room he shouted, 'As I said to the cops, he's disappeared. Whitey went to take a look at Oliver Cromwell and have a talk with Daniel Lightbody about getting the felling contract returned to Davies and I haven't seen him since. He might be down the Old Windmill,' he added slyly as he re-entered the front room.'

'Do you think he killed Daniel?'

'How the hell would I know, I was at the Old Windmill that evening and I've got a score of witnesses to say I was.' Cartwright's former arrogance had returned even though an old scar on his forehead had noticeably whitened and he pointed towards the door. 'I've just about had enough of your questioning. I suggest you leave before I throw you out.'

James nodded and opened the door. 'If you've given me false information you can be sure I'll be back.' He didn't wait for the man's response and left the cottage, slamming the door behind him. Cartwright frowned and immediately speed-dialled a number and spoke for a few minutes before returning to the kitchen to make fresh tea.

It started raining on his drive back to Margaret Lightbody's house and in the fading light the rain-soaked road seemed to vanish only a few yards ahead of the car. James had covered half the journey when the windscreen suddenly exploded, disintegrating into a thousand pieces. He instinctively jammed his foot down on the brake and felt the hire car slew sideways before skidding off the tarmac and into the drainage ditch running beside the road. The car struck the opposite bank and James' head was thrown sideways to hit the door pillar. As he slid into unconsciousness the car slid down the bank and into the water.

3

AT ABOUT MID-EVENING when the light was fading fast a local ploughman drove his tractor along Fen Road having finished the fifteen-acre field he had been contracted to turn over. From his high vantage point he spotted a blue car half-submerged in the drainage ditch. Switching on his hazard lights he climbed down and took a closer look. A man lay hard against the driver's door and up to his neck in freezing water. As he looked for any signs of life he noticed that the car was still sinking into the silt at the bottom of the ditch; the water level had now reached the stranger's chin.

    The ploughman hurriedly dialled the local fire brigade and ambulance service before returning to the tractor to collect a length of stout rope he had neatly coiled in the locker. He was unable to reach the man who was on the other side of the car but as the windscreen was gone he was able to fasten one end of the rope around the roof pillar. Scrambling up to the tractor he tied the other end to the hitch and climbed into the cab. He backed the vehicle until the rope was taut and breathed a sigh of relief when it held. He worked the controls to see if he could raise the car higher. The giant wheels lost their traction under the heavy load and as they spun he applied the handbrake and switched off.

    A faint wailing in the distance gave the ploughman a sense of hope as he stared at the unconscious stranger, praying that he was still alive. A fire engine came to a halt in front of the tractor with its lights still on full beam and when the siren died to a murmur suitably clothed and booted men poured from the cab. The fire chief quickly took in the situation and before the ambulance arrived the firemen already had the car tethered to prevent any further slippage. One of them pulled on a wetsuit as two others wrestled with the door that was facing up.

The ploughman could do little but watch the professionals handle a situation that frequently occurred on the farm roads after the pubs had closed. As the firemen applied the *Jaws of Life* and levered the door open he gathered up his superfluous rope and stowed it away in the locker. The emergency vehicles were now blocking the narrow road ahead and he was considering turning round when a police car arrived to block the way he had come.

After only a few seconds the fireman who had entered the car shouted, 'He's still alive!' A buzz of excitement rippled through the gathered men and a paramedic leapt down the bank, his white jacket and slacks were soon coated in mud but he smiled as he checked James' condition. 'No signs of any trauma apart from the possibility of concussion,' he murmured to himself. Nodding to the fireman they extricated the unconscious detective from the wreck and willing hands helped strap him into a cradle to slide him up the bank and into the ambulance.

As James was lifted into the back of the vehicle Sergeant Tanner leant over to take a look at the badly scratched face. 'I know this man and he's a bloody nuisance,' he declared. 'I'll need to interview him as soon as you get round to waking him.' The senior paramedic looked at him with shock on his face.

'Like hell. I'll not wake him up, Sergeant. He's been in a nasty accident. He's been injured and needs urgent medical care, not your questions and damned insults.' He shouldered policemen out of the way and slammed the ambulance doors shut.

Agnes was helping Margaret with the evening meal when the phone rang and she learnt of James' accident. The shock initially rendered her speechless but she suddenly snapped out of her daze and sprang into action.

'I must go to King's Lynn to see how James is but first I need to gather up a few bits of his clothing and a toothbrush,' she said in the normal brisk fashion that has made her so invaluable to the private investigator. The first thought that had entered her mind when the police sergeant said he would be visiting the cottage was to make sure James' personal effects were in order. She knew her employer closely logged every investigation and some of the details may need to be kept confidential so she slipped his small notebook into her purse and took the laptop to her own room where she placed it beneath a layer of cotton briefs and other essential items in her travel case.

With fresh underwear, pyjamas, toothbrush and safety razor neatly packed in a supermarket shopping bag she went downstairs to ask Margaret for the loan of her Mini Cooper. 'If a policeman comes and wants to talk to me you can tell him that I'm on my way to the Queen Elizabeth Hospital in King's Lynn,' she added as she left the cottage.

Traffic was minimal and although Agnes loathed driving at night she made good time and pulled into the hospital car park only forty minutes after leaving Newton. The receptionist was very helpful and directed Agnes to the ward where James had been taken. She scanned the room and saw that plastic curtains had been drawn around one particular bed. She walked over and whispered, 'Are you OK, James?' not daring to open the curtains.

'Of course I am, Miss Lightbody,' James answered testily and the curtain was whisked back. He was out of bed and fully dressed. 'They want me to stay for some unnecessary tests but I have better things to do,' he explained as he slipped on a jacket that was still damp and scuffed with green slime and mud.

'What happened?' she asked with her nose wrinkled in disgust while trying to pull the filthy jacket down in an attempt to return it to its former appearance.

'Someone took a pot-shot at me as I was driving from Cartwright's place to Margaret's cottage.'

'Who's Cartwright?'

'I'll explain later but right now my priority is to sneak out of this knacker's yard before they really find something wrong with me.'

'There must be something wrong with your head at least if you're not going to listen to the doctors,' Agnes said as she opened the door and checked the corridor for medical staff. Apart from one patient wearing a dressing gown and trundling his own intravenous drip, all was clear and they hurriedly left the hospital to Agnes' car. As James was still suffering from an acute headache Agnes insisted on taking the wheel with muttered comments about possible concussion.

James ignored the remark though he was touched by her concern. 'We need to go back to Cartwright's place,' he said as a fresh bout of pain played havoc with his frontal lobes. 'I have a nasty feeling that whoever wanted to silence me may also want to close that young man's mouth.'

'Just give me the directions and against my better judgement I'll take you there,' she muttered as they passed a police car just as they were leaving. 'Wasn't that the officer we saw at the police station?' she observed.

'Just keep going, Miss Lightbody, I'm not in any mood to talk to him yet.'

'I'm always telling you to use my first name, James,' she complained. 'We've been working together for some time now and been through a lot together.'

James didn't answer her and simply chuckled beneath his breath for although they have been through a lot together and become very close colleagues he still respected her like she was his own mother. They sped over the Great Ouse bridge and took off down the A47 at the roundabout. The road to Wisbech was clear and there were few headlights coming from the opposite direction. Agnes turned off the dual carriageway on the outskirts of the town and used the minor farm roads to Newton as though she had lived in the area all her life.

'Keep going along Fen Road until I tell you to turn off,' James instructed. He had fallen into a light sleep after leaving King's Lynn and only woke when they neared their destination. They swept through the sleeping village and out into the fenland that was criss-crossed by ancient drainage channels still keeping the land from flooding.

A full moon was casting a silvery sheen over the sea of crops covering the landscape. They passed the spot where the car went out of control and James noted that the police had left the car in the drainage channel and simply applied a *POLICE AWARE* notice on the side. When they reached the small cottage Agnes stopped the car to block the driveway as she had been instructed and James got out to study the four front windows. A light in one of the upstairs rooms was switched on and the net curtains glowed a dull yellow. James watched as a shadow flickered across the material. He took a gamble and walked to the front door half expecting to be confronted by the deadly-looking Baikal barrels again.

The hallway light came on and the door opened releasing a flood of light into the night. 'Now what do you want?' Cartwright demanded to know. His hands held the shotgun but this time the twin barrels were pointing harmlessly at the flagstone floor.

'Has Mr Whitey returned?' The question was accompanied by a smile to help put the man at ease but Cartwright wasn't that easily fooled.

'I told you last time, I haven't seen him since before going to the Old Windmill that night.'

The monotone denial immediately made James suspicious and he stepped up close to be in a position to prevent the shotgun from being levelled at him. 'He's here now, isn't he?'

'I told you no, now fuck off before I call the police.' The hand holding the Baikal twitched and James steeled himself for action.

'Did he tell you he tried to kill me earlier this evening?' James saw a brief flicker of surprise on the man's face. 'He blew out the windscreen of my car and sent me into a drainage channel. It was only the quick thinking of a farmer who was working late that saved my life.'

'I know nothing about that,' Cartwright declared with fear in the his eyes before he slammed the door shut.

'What now, James?' Agnes asked as he climbed into the car.

'That's one very frightened person,' he said as she started the engine. The curtain twitched again and James lowered his window and gave a mocking goodbye wave to the hidden watcher.

'Were both men there?'

'There was someone hiding upstairs. Whether it was Whitey or not is the big question. I think we should call it a day and return to Margaret before she starts to worry about you.'

Agnes checked her phone for a signal and speed-dialled the widow. 'We're on our way back and should be with you in ten minutes.' She listened and then raised her eyebrows in surprise. 'Margaret received a call from Mr Jackson, her neighbour, who said he had seen a young couple, a boy and a girl, leave Ravens' Wood on the day Daniel was killed.'

'Did the neighbour recognize the couple?'

'She didn't say.'

'We'll ask her when we get back providing she hasn't gone to bed,' James said with the familiar frisson of excitement when he could sniff a new line of enquiry. 'Those two youngsters may have seen something but are too frightened to come forward.'

The car sped across the fenland beneath the glittering stars with only the white blur of a hunting owl and the darting shadows of feeding bats disturbing the sky.

They went straight to the kitchen when they arrived where they found Margaret sitting at the table clutching a mug of tepid cocoa with both hands. Her eyes were red-rimmed and sodden tissues on the table betrayed the anguish she was feeling. A mournful looking Tammy was sitting at her feet.

'I think you should go to bed, Margaret,' Agnes said softly. James watched the two women leave the room followed by Tammy before filling the kettle. He knew a cup of coffee before bed was a bad idea for a narcoleptic suffering from insomnia but he felt the need to be alert and thinking clearly as he ran through the events of the day. He opened the notebook Agnes had returned to him in the hospital and began writing with the tiny pencil clipped to it. He was still writing when his secretary returned and switched off the boiling kettle.

'She fell asleep the moment her head touched the pillow,' she said as she took on the task of making two mugs of coffee. 'Tammy was also fast asleep beside her by the time I left the room.'

'Did she say anything before nodding off?' James looked up from his jotting with a look of hope.

'Her neighbour said he thought they were two teenagers. Possibly students from the Wisbech School of Modern Art.'

'How did he know that?' he asked as Agnes sugared his coffee with one precisely levelled teaspoon.

'He had seen them together in the Newton convenience store and although it had been dark he recognised them as they ran out of the wood.'

'Ran? They had been frightened by something?'

'Margaret didn't ask and I didn't want to tire her too much.' She sipped her coffee as James returned to his notebook and she knew he was in his own world. She put the half-drunk cup down, stood, yawned and left the kitchen to retire to her bed. It had been a very long day.

The big hand of the wall clock clicked onto midnight when James finished writing and laid his head down on his folded arms. He soon drifted into a light sleep and the only sounds were the ticking of the clock, his breathing and the light scratching of a lock-pick at the back door.

James was generally a very light sleeper at night and the unusual metal-on-metal scratching alerted him. He sat upright and listened to make sure but when Tammy appeared at the kitchen door, gave him an inquisitive look and then pit-patted along the hallway he knew it hadn't been his imagination.

The scratching continued and he took a flour-coated rolling pin and went to the utility room door where Tammy sat waiting with head cocked on one side. James switched the light off and waited until his eyes had adjusted to the darkness before going into the room and approaching the door leading to the garden.

He was halfway when his shoe collided with a mop and bucket. The clattering sounded like a thousand cannons in the silence and the scratching ceased immediately. The cocker spaniel began to bark and James rushed to the door. He could hear running feet outside and then the noise of a car door slamming. By the time he located the key and ran out of the house he could hear the vehicle accelerating away with spinning wheels. James ran up on to the road slowly followed by Tammy in time to see a dark shape with two faint red lights dwindling into the shadowy landscape.

Agnes, dressed in a quilted housecoat, was waiting by the open door when he returned. 'Who was it, James?' she asked with a nervous tremor in her voice. 'What on earth were they looking for?'

'I have no idea, Miss Lightbody, so I think the best thing is to try and get some sleep. Tomorrow's another day and I have a feeling it's going to be a very busy one at that.' He waited until Tammy had waddled back into the house then locked the door and checked all the windows. Taking his long overcoat from the hallstand he wrapped it tightly about himself before going to sit in one of the winged armchairs in the front room to wait for morning.

After a generous breakfast that Margaret insisted he ate as a guest under her roof he drove to Mr Jackson's flintstone cottage at the end of a *cul-de-sac* just outside Newton. A man who was small enough to match the minuscule house opened the door after the first knock. Like the landscape, his face was weathered and lined with age yet his voice was that of a young baritone.

'How can I help you, young man,' he resonated.

James liked the humour in his ice-blue eyes and immediately felt at ease. 'I'm investigating the death of Daniel Lightbody and I understand that you saw two school children leave Ravens' Wood on the night he died?'

Mr Jackson waved James into the house and led him into the living room where he took a bottle of Glenfiddich and offered him a drink. A shaggy Irish wolfhound was curled up fast asleep in front of the two-bar electric fire. He appeared to be the same age in doggy years as the old man.

'Thank you, sir, but it's a little too early for me and I'm driving.'

'Wise fellow.' The old man poured a generous tot for himself and sat in an overstuffed armchair with sun-faded material. 'In answer to your question, yes I did. It was a boy and a girl wearing uniforms of that arty boarding school in Wisbech.'

'The School of Modern Art?'

'That's the one. I was walking Henry along the north side of the wood where I'd seen foxes the previous night so that this lazy sod . . .' he nudged the dog with the toe of his boot 'could get some exercise.' He nudged the dog a little harder but Henry still didn't stir. 'Suddenly two kids dashed out of the trees right in front of me and took off like scared rabbits. They looked like sixth formers and fair startled me and Henry to death.'

'Did you see their faces?'

'Yes and I also saw that the girl's blouse was unbuttoned and the boy was busy closing his zip. That's when I knew what they'd been up to, other than listening to the nightingales.'

'Would you recognize them again?' James pressed and Jackson nodded vigorously.

'Of that you can be sure.'

James thanked Mr Jackson and took his leave to drive into town. Road signs directed him to the school which he found wasn't in Wisbech as the name implied but a good five miles to the south. A middle-aged woman with hard features and tightly pulled back grey hair opened the door as soon as he arrived as though she had been expecting him.

'I am Miss Standing, how can I help you, sir?' Her stentorian voice caught James by surprise. 'Are you a parent or making enquiries for children not yet attending?'

'Good morning, Miss Standing. I'm making enquiries about two sixth formers who may have been off the school premises at approximately eleven last Saturday night.'

'Are you a policeman?'

James explained who he was and why he was conducting a private investigation and the cool expression became positively frosty. 'I am not at liberty to give personal information regarding the pupils of this school to anyone except the correct authorities,' she snapped.

'Even if the pupils in question may have been witness to the horrific murder of a farm worker?'

'Murder?' The woman went pale. 'Are you saying that the man in Ravens' Wood didn't commit suicide?'

James nodded. 'The newspapers reported it incorrectly. His name was Daniel and he was almost beheaded with a chainsaw. As he was the cousin of my secretary I have a very personal interest in the circumstances of his death.'

The stiff shoulders slumped and her face softened. 'That's horrible but I should wait for the police before I give you any more information.'

'I'll pass on anything I learn from you to Sergeant Tanner.'

This appeared to satisfy Miss Standing and she said, 'Two of the children were caught climbing over the wall that night at about eleven forty-five and both were punished with extra studies and dismissal from the current school production of *Phantom of the Opera*.'

'Would it be possible to talk to them now?' James asked with his best smile and a beguiling tone of voice. Miss Standing held his blue-eyed gaze for a second, looked at her wristwatch and nodded.

'They should be at their lessons now. I'll get the piano teacher to bring them here,' she said and picked up the phone on her desk. As James idly studied some of the posters promoting the forthcoming performance there was a brief conversation before Miss Standing put the phone down.

'That's strange. Neither has been seen since lunchtime yesterday. Mr Williams, their tutor, had assumed that they had been sent home as part of their punishment.'

'But you know that they hadn't?' When Miss Standing nodded James felt a cold premonition and quickly took out his mobile and dialled the Wisbech police station. He reported that there were two missing teenagers and handed the phone to Miss Standing to supply the necessary information. She listened for a while and then returned the phone to James.

'They will be sending a police car to the school to interview students who were friends, take away photographs of them both and gather as much information as possible.'

'Can I have copies of those pictures for my investigation?' James asked hopefully and was surprised when a playbill was thrust into his hand. The playbill was for a school production and the names Samantha Fenton and Michael Robinson were beneath portraits of two good-looking teenagers in costume. The girl wore theatrical make-up and had green eyes and long blonde hair that hung over her shoulders like a gossamer cape. The youth had the promise of being handsome and his black hair was cut and styled to augment the character he was playing. The white mask covering one side of his face did little to hide his identity.

'His hair is normally dark brown,' Miss Standing explained as she looked over his shoulder at the opened leaflet. 'I do hope nothing has happened to them.'

'You believe they may be in some sort of danger?'

'No, but being in the woods after curfew can only mean they were up to something and the school will be held responsible if anything has happened to them.'

James nodded and then explained that he had to leave for another appointment when he really meant he didn't want another encounter with Sergeant Tanner so soon. He thanked Miss Standing and left before the police arrived. As he drove back to the cottage his thoughts returned to the attempted break-in and the reason why anybody should be so desperate to enter a house that was clearly occupied.

'It must be something Daniel had in his possession,' he murmured to himself as he turned into Fen Road and accelerated towards the cottage. 'Something that may lead to the identity of his murderer.'

4

JAMES' FIRST PRIORITY was to get Margaret's permission to search Daniel's possessions thoroughly. He found both women in the kitchen preparing a light lunch and looked expectantly at the teapot. Agnes smiled and filled the kettle.

'Any progress?' Margaret asked quietly as Tammy wandered into the room, sniffed James' ankles and, reassured, went to the warm comfort of her basket.

'The two youngsters seen running from the woods are missing and the police have been called in by the school principal.'

Both women gasped and Agnes voiced the thought running through their minds. 'Maybe they've seen Daniel's murderer and they're too scared to return to the school in case he knows they are there.'

'That may be the case, Miss Lightbody, but to help throw a little more light on the situation I need to ask Margaret if I can go through Daniel's things.'

The widow looked up from pouring the tea in surprise. 'Why do you need to do that, James?'

'The attempted burglary must have been connected with Daniel's death and the person breaking in was determined to find a specific object or piece of information.'

'While we were all here?'

'I don't think he knew that Miss Lightbody and I were here and believed he only had you to contend with.'

'Follow me, James,' she said and led him to a small study at the end of the hall.

'Do you know the password?' he asked as he sat at the open laptop on the mock Regency writing desk.

'You think the answer may be in there.'

'If Daniel found something of value in that old iron chest then he may have decided to do some research on the Internet.'

Margaret lifted the mouse pad and showed James the bright yellow note stuck to the bottom. James raised an eyebrow at the simplicity of Daniel's hiding place.

'I told him to memorize it but he didn't trust his memory and said that it made it easy for me to access our bank account when I needed to.' Her voice caught and she hurried from the room before the tears started to appear.

James tapped the keys and instinctively searched the emails first for any clues. It didn't take long to discover that Daniel had corresponded with Professor Stephen Calder, a Fellow and Director of Studies at the Cambridge Archaeological Unit. James studied the emails chronologically and learnt that ancient coins had stirred the professor's interest. So much so that a meeting had been arranged at Feeling Perky, a Wisbech coffee house, to discuss the matter further. More important was the fact that the meeting had been arranged for the Thursday, two days before the murder. A further check revealed that Daniel had explored websites on rare British coins, artefacts, metal detecting rights and the law on treasure trove.

So the chest did contain something of high value, James thought as he switched on the printer. He took a copy of the photograph he had found in one of the emails before logging off and returning to the kitchen.

'Did Daniel meet a Professor Calder on the Thursday before he died?' James asked as he sat opposite Margaret while Agnes put a cup of freshly brewed tea before him.

'Not that I know.'

'Daniel's latest emails were to an institute of archaeology in Cambridge and his enquiries were all about this old silver coin,' James said as he showed a picture of the coin to the widow.

'He never mentioned that to me.'

'I have a feeling that Daniel found something of value in that chest I found discarded in the nettles. So valuable that someone killed him for it.'

Both women were stunned until Margaret broke the leaden silence. 'Do you think this Professor Calder killed my husband for the sake of one small piece of worthless silver?'

'No, Margaret, I believe Daniel was killed for more than one. I think it was a chest full of silver pieces that he had found hidden in Oliver Cromwell. Whether Calder is suspect is a matter of conjecture at this stage.' As James was talking he had been checking directory enquiries on his mobile until he found and dialled a number.

'Professor Stephen Calder?' James asked. 'My name is James Goodfellow and I'm investigating the death of Mr Daniel Lightbody.' He paused to gauge Calder's reaction and then continued, 'I believe he was in contact with you concerning a silver coin he had found. Can you give me any information about it?' James listened for a while before thanking the professor and switching his mobile off.

'What did he say?' Agnes said eagerly.

'It would seem that there was a medieval hammered silver short-cross penny.'

'Whatever that is, it sounds bloody worthless,' Margaret stated.

'According to the professor it was far from worthless. He confirmed that it had been minted in Ireland by King John around 1216 and may possibly be one of thousands that were lost in the Wash on the king's fateful journey from Spalding to Bishop's Lynn.'

'Bishop's Lynn?' Agnes asked.

'That was its name until it became King's Lynn in 1537.'

'Fascinating as all that may be it's still only a damned penny,' Margaret grumbled peevishly. 'Surely Daniel wasn't killed for a single medieval penny or a chest full of pennies.'

'Margaret, that penny has an approximate value of £135,' James declared. 'Can you imagine how much several hundred or even thousands would fetch on the collectors' market?' The two women were speechless and James couldn't help grinning at their stunned expressions.

'However, the professor now claims that the coin he had been shown was a fake. He said thousands had been made over the centuries to perpetuate the myth that King John lost his wealth beneath a fast tide.'

THE KING'S CHARTER

'So there is no treasure?' Agnes asked.

'I did some research of my own and there are different points of view in the academic world. Some think that the whole treasury was diverted at the last moment and hidden, others that it was all lost in the race to outrun the sea.'

As James took a breath Margaret declared. 'But you think the coin Daniel found was real, don't you, James?'

He nodded his head. 'The chest and the hiding place suggests that whoever had put it inside Oliver Cromwell had put it there centuries ago because it had some value. I believe the coin is genuine and why the professor didn't confirm this is now a complete mystery to me.'

'So Daniel was murdered for an old piece of silver,' Margaret whispered as she unconsciously stroked Tammy's coat. Agnes put her arms around the woman and held her tight while James quietly left the room to use his phone.

Jennifer answered on the third ring and James outlined everything that had happened since his arrival in Norfolk. She remained silent until he had finished and then said, 'Aren't you going to ask me what my day was like?'

James laughed and the tension that had been building for the last two days disappeared. Eager for news he asked, 'How are you and what has Claudiu been up to?'

'You'd be so proud. Claudiu has made the swimming team at school. It means he has to train on Saturday mornings but luckily I've been able to move my shifts so that I can take him to the pool and bring him back.'

'And what about yourself, Jenny?'

'There's been very little of interest in the station and while you're out of town we're all keeping our fingers crossed that we won't need you to solve any of our crimes for us.'

'Funny, very funny, darling,' James chuckled.

'Mind you, it does sound like you've been busy enough in the hinterland of Norfolk.'

'And that's why I'm calling. I need a little help.'

'A little help?' she asked in a knowing tone of voice. 'Like illegally using police resources to help you with your case?'

'Just a little info on a Cambridge professor, a garden centre owner and any file that pops up on an albino man with the alias of Whitey.'

'You don't want much then?' The light sarcasm in Jennifer's tone was very clear and James felt like responding in kind until his wife suddenly calmed him with her typical kindness. 'I will do all I can, James. I can only imagine the hell Margaret must have gone through when she lost her husband and Agnes must have her hands full looking after her and you.'

James glanced towards the kitchen door to make sure it was still closed. 'Miss Lightbody is coping very well,' he whispered, 'considering Daniel was her cousin. She must be grieving herself but you wouldn't know it when you see how she is comforting Margaret.' He gave Jennifer as much detail as he could on the three subjects before they bid each other a loving goodbye. He then made a quick call to order a taxi.

The two women were still sitting at the table when James went back into the kitchen and announced his intention to return to the rental company in King's Lynn to fill in the required paperwork on the wrecked car and to pick up another if they were willing to let him have another.

The Newton taxi beeped outside the cottage within five minutes and James left after instructing Agnes to lock the door after him. When she frowned and silently mouthed 'why' he said that he wasn't sure if it was the man called Whitey who had taken a shot at him and if it was he might try to do so again. He heard the bolts being used as soon as the door closed and he climbed into the taxi feeling a little less concerned about leaving the women alone.

The rental company grudgingly loaned him the only Mercedes on the lot at a rate that would more than likely give Agnes kittens.

With the engine purring contentedly he made good time back to Wisbech and had set out on the road to Newton when his mobile chimed. James glanced at the screen and saw that it was Jennifer and he immediately pulled into a lay-by to answer the call.

'Professor Stephen Calder is a very ordinary sort of don,' Jennifer said. 'He's now lecturing at the same university that graduated him thirty-five years ago.'

'I knew that, Jenny. What I want to know is whether he was on police files for any kind of offence.'

'When he was an undergraduate he was arrested, along with a number of other students, for causing a public disturbance when they floated a Fiat 500 on four punts down the River Cam. They were nearly sent down as the car belonged to their history don. After graduating he took a sabbatical before his postgrad work and visited a number of archaeological sites around the world. It was in Peru that he formed a friendship with an archaeologist, a staunch communist called Juan Pablo Moran. Interpol investigations revealed that Moran was suspected of illegal trading in Peruvian treasures such as gold funerary masks, jewellery and various other artefacts. They also told me that Raul, his albino brother, was an active supporter of the Communist Party of Peru and belonged to a terrorist organization commonly known as the *Shining Path*. However, nothing could be pinned on the Morans at the time of a terrorist attack in Lima and they vanished off the map. Rumour had it that Juan went to Morocco to study Berber ceramic art in Marrakech. To our knowledge Calder didn't keep in touch with the Peruvian and returned to England a year later. He then gained his doctorate and has been tutoring in Cambridge ever since.'

'What about Bernard Davies at Green Fingers Garden Centre?'

'Went to Easton & Notley College in Norwich for eighteen months where he took the arboriculture apprenticeship. He gained top marks and a Level 2 certificate in forestry that enabled him to practise tree surgery professionally. He came into some money about three years ago when a distant cousin died which enabled him to set up his own garden centre. Four parking fines and two speeding offences was all I could find against him and I think he is clean unless he illegally imports seeds and plants for his business.'

'Whitey?'

'You saved the best till last, James.'

'Why, what did you find out about him?'

'Mr Whitey came up with a red flag against his real name which is, coincidentally, Raul Moran.'

'What!'

'Yes, Juan's brother, and he entered England on a forged British passport. Not only is he an illegal, wanted by the immigration authorities but Interpol also want him for art theft, grievous bodily harm and homicide. He shot two police officers during his escape from Morocco after being discovered with a roomful of stolen cellphones and laptops. Interpol believes that he was visiting his brother and decided to make a little money while he was in the country. I imagine all the gullible tourists surrounding him was too much of a temptation. The police were also unable to find Juan.'

James gripped the phone as his mind raced, piecing together the information that Jennifer had given him.

'If this Juan can't be traced in Morocco there's a good chance that they've joined forces here in England,' he said. Jennifer agreed, adding, 'And there's a good bet that it was Raul who took a pot-shot at you.'

James pulled out onto the road and put his foot down for he had suddenly thought of the two women who were alone in the remote farmhouse. He thanked Jennifer and they said their goodbyes as he raced across the flat landscape of fens and dykes. The muffled roar of the three-litre engine could hardly be heard beneath the hood and in no time he saw Margaret's house on the horizon.

However, the pretty whitewashed Norfolk cottage was now a blazing pyre, dulling the setting sun and James felt his mouth go dry with fear. He rammed his foot down even more and sped towards the flaming disaster.

Two fire tenders and three police cars were at the scene when the Mercedes screeched to a halt and James leapt out. He raced towards the house but was intercepted by a burly firefighter.

'You can't go in there, sir,' he said in a firm don't-even-think-about-it voice.

'James!' a voice cried out and he turned to see Agnes and Margaret standing by one of the police cars with Tammy in her mistress' arms. With a silent 'thank God' he hurried to hug them both.

'What happened, Agnes?' He stepped back to look at his secretary and only then noticed the black sooty streaks on her normal Pears-soap scrubbed face. Before she could open her mouth a familiar figure loomed beside James and gripped him by the upper arm.

'Well, if it isn't our smart-arsed detective from the south,' Sergeant Tanner mocked. 'You've certainly brought the heat with you. Who have you been upsetting this time?'

'What do you mean, Sergeant?'

'The fire chief tells me that this is a clear case of arson. A petrol can with a few milk bottles discarded beside it made it clear to him and anyone else with an ounce of common sense that this had been started deliberately.' He waved vaguely in the direction of the blazing house. 'A few Molotov cocktails through the windows and "whumf"! What do you know about it?'

'What could I know, I've only just returned from King's Lynn.'

'In style, too.' Tanner jerked a thumb in the direction of the Mercedes.

'The only car the rental company had free,' James said with a guilty look at Agnes, but her mind was elsewhere, too involved in the recent events to worry about protecting her precious petty cash.

'I assume you will be taking care of the ladies,' Tanner said and walked away to talk to the fire chief. The blaze that was now well under control rose like a billowing smoke phantom against the twilight sky. Acrid fumes from burning plastic and paint began to catch in their throats and James led Agnes and Margaret to the car and the comparative safety of the interior air filtration.

'What now, James?' Agnes asked when they were seated. Like Margaret his secretary was staring out at the gutted ruin with tears on her cheeks.

'I'll get us rooms at the Rose and Crown Hotel in Wisbech.'

'That'll cost us a pretty penny, James,' Agnes said and before she could suggest something cheaper Maragret came up with a solution.

'I have friends spending a month in Seville and I'll give them a call to ask if we can temporarily stay at their house until I sort things out with the insurance company. Then you can go and find the bastards who killed my husband and destroyed my home, James.'

'How will you know who did it?' Agnes asked as they glided through the fenland while Margaret used her cellphone.

'I'll start by asking Cartwright a few pertinent questions. I'm sure he knows a lot more than he let on last time we met. I will then drive to Cambridge and talk to the professor about his relationship with the Moran brothers.'

'You will be careful, James? These men sound like they could be extremely dangerous.'

'Don't worry, Miss Lightbody, I know what I'm getting into,' James said with a confidence that belied how he really felt. The Morans had a past history of extreme violence and they were not to be taken lightly.

'Jennifer would never forgive me if I let you walk into any kind of danger,' Agnes suddenly said.

James smiled as he stopped the car in a lay-by to await instructions from Margaret who had finished her long-distance conversation with an effusive thank-you.

'It's 27 Broad Street, James. I'll direct you.'

He automatically checked the mirror for signs of any followers before pulling away. The street appeared quiet when they arrived and he escorted the two women and the spaniel to the front door of a well-cared-for semi-detached house. Margaret took a key from beneath a terracotta flowerpot and as soon as she had opened the door James said goodbye and headed for the Green Fingers Garden Centre.

Although it was near to closing time Bernard Davies was still busily planting hyacinth bulbs on a bench laden with terracotta pots when he walked into the long greenhouse and asked to speak to Cartwright.

'Why do you want him?' he asked with suspicion. 'He's busy watering seedlings and can't be bothered.'

'One quick question, that's all I want to ask him, Mr Davies,' James replied calmly.

The man jerked a thumb over his shoulder. 'Down the back,' he grumbled. 'The seedbeds are by the statuary.'

James nodded his thanks and strode through the greenhouse and out into an area littered with concrete gnomes, nymphs and giant toadstools. He saw Cartwright at the same moment the man saw him and started running. James sprinted after him, leaping over large glazed pots and as the fleeing man turned to enter the greenhouse James brought him down with a flying tackle that sent both of them crashing into stacked rolls of turf. Cartwright tried to wriggle from beneath James' deadweight but was unable to budge an inch. James gripped the man by the back of his neck and squeezed until he squealed in pain.

'What do you want?' Cartwright pleaded. 'I told you I don't know anything.'

'Do you know where Whitey and his brother are?' James pushed Cartwright's face hard against the edge of the turf pallet. 'You certainly know where the two school kids are.'

'No I don . . .'

The King's Charter

James pulled the man's head back by his hair and slammed it down against the wood. Blood ran from a gash in the man's cheek and as his hair was pulled painfully for another assault Cartwright yelled out.

'OK, I'll tell you.'

James released the man's long greasy hair and got up off his back to let him turn over and sit up. He tossed the dirty rag Cartwright had dropped during the scuffle into his lap. 'Tell me everything you know or by God I'll smash your head with one of those bloody gnomes.'

Cartwright glared up at him as he wiped the blood from his face. 'I don't know where Whitey is but he's holding the children in one of the old disused pumping stations near Guyhirn on the River Nene.'

James grabbed him by the shoulder and pulled him to his feet. 'Right, take me there now.' He prodded Cartwright in the back with a gardener's craft knife that he had grabbed from a display unit. As they approached Davies he turned and expressed shock when he saw blood on Cartwright's face.

'What the hell have you been doing to Roger?' he demanded to know as he walked towards the pair, his callused hands curling into fists. Seeing the gardening tool pressed hard into Cartwright's back he stopped. 'Where are you taking him?'

'This man is going to take me to where the missing school children are being held captive and then I shall be taking him to the police.' James didn't pause and brushed past Davies as though he didn't exist. 'You had better pray that you were not involved.'

'Get behind the steering wheel,' James ordered Cartwright and went round to sit beside him. He handed the ignition key to the surly man and told him to drive to the pumping station. As the Mercedes drove out of the garden centre Bernard Davies was speed-dialling a number on his mobile phone.

James kept the knife down out of sight but Cartwright was fully aware of it. He took the road into the centre of Wisbech and then left the town on a minor road that followed the River Nene along the east bank before joining the busy A47. When they passed a signpost for Guyhirn, only two kilometres distant, he slowed the car and leaving the heavy traffic behind pulled off onto a farm track that zigzagged round the patchwork of farmland to a dilapidated brick building with a tall chimney.

45

'Is that the place?' James murmured and he received a brief nod. He studied the crumbling brickwork of the pumping station as they drew nearer and saw that the damage was only superficial. Victorian craftsmanship had stood the ravages of time. The car stopped at a rust-stained steel door that had been secured with a brand-new padlock that glinted in the twilight.

'They've been put in there?' James asked as he leant across and removed the key from the ignition before getting out of the car. Once more the answer was a sullen nod of the head. He gestured with the knife and Cartwright walked in front of James to the door.

'Open it and step inside first,' James snapped.

'I don't have the key.'

'Whitey?'

Cartwright nodded with a smug expression on his face and unable to stop himself James hit the man in the mouth. Cartwright jerked back and his head struck the door heavily. He collapsed unconscious onto the cracked concrete. James checked his pulse and then went through his pockets till he found a small notebook and a bunch of keys that seemed too small to open such a large lock. He flicked through the notebook but the names and addresses were meaningless. He slipped it into his inside pocket before taking a very illegal lock-pick from his breast pocket. Bending to take a closer look at the padlock he discovered to his horror that the keyhole had been filled with superglue.

Whitey had never intended to return to the pumping station and had left the two students to die.

James slowly circled the high walls but other than the steel door he could only see a row of tiny unglazed windows about fifteen feet above his head. Even if he could find a way of reaching them he would never be able to squeeze through. He looked round for a suitable tool to force the padlock and found an overgrown heap of discarded lengths of water pipe and rubble. He began pounding at the toughened steel with a brick until the red clay crumbled in his hand, leaving the padlock unscathed. James was turning to go and search for something stronger when Cartwright struck him on the side of the head with a piece of timber.

It was fortunate that the length of four by two lying within Cartwright's reach had been in the damp grass for a long time and had rotted.

The wood shattered and showered the area with splinters as James toppled onto his side and a familiar sensation began running through his body, rendering him incapable of any movement. The blow hadn't been sufficient to render him unconscious but the shock had led to a narcoleptic reaction, despite having taken his tablets.

Cartwright looked down at the prone man and thinking that he may have killed him his hands began to shake; with panic setting in he quickly retrieved the car keys and James' mobile phone and leapt into the Mercedes. Cartwright drove back to Wisbech where he abandoned the vehicle in a public car park.

As the luxury car raced back to town James began to stir and swiftly regained the use of all his limbs. Noticing that the car was gone his first thought was to call the police but he soon discovered that his phone too was missing. A deep sense of frustration overcame him, but any thought of walking to the nearest farmhouse was dispelled when he visualized the state of the youngsters locked inside the building. Without food or water they would be in a pretty bad condition and he hurriedly searched the ground around the pumping station for anything stronger than a brick. The ideal tool presented itself when James stubbed his toe against a heavy wrench lying half-hidden in grass and bindweed. The tempered steel tested his strength when he picked it up as it had clearly been intended for use on the larger bolts that held the big drainage pipes together.

James raised it up above his head and brought it down hard on the padlock. Nothing happened apart from a shivering vibration that shot into his wrists and arms. Ignoring the pain in his head he struck again and to his amazement it wasn't the padlock that broke but the heavily corroded sliding bar that the padlock held secure. The steel bar shattered and a shower of oxidizing metal flakes flew into the air.

James stepped into the inky interior and stood quite still to allow his eyes to become accustomed to the dark until faint shadows began to resolve into objects. Odd pieces of rusty machinery, their use a mystery to James, littered the concrete floor and he peered round in amazement at the vastness of the chamber where rhythmic pumps were once used to help drain the fens. A light whimper came from the furthest corner and he spun round and hurried through the debris to where two figures crouched against the wall. They wore identical school uniforms and James knew he had found Samantha and Michael.

'It's OK, you're safe now,' James said as Michael tried to shield the girl with his body. 'Can you walk?'

They both struggled to get to their feet and James noticed the lengths of thick cord that bound their ankles and wrists. 'Hold on, I've got a knife,' he said and bent down to slice through the tough nylon with the craft knife.

'Who are you?' Samantha asked nervously.

'My name is James Goodfellow. I'm a private detective looking for some answers that I think you may have but first we must get away from here and get some food and water into you.'

The students squinted as they went out into the fading light and staggered after James who had previously noticed a remote farmhouse on the flat-ironed horizon. They plodded across a field of Naturalo potatoes, the rich black soil clinging to their shoes. James could see that the lack of sustenance and their terrifying encounter with the kidnappers had left them drained. They may also have witnessed the horrific murder in Ravens' Wood.

'Not far now, Samantha,' James called out in a cheery voice despite his own weariness and the throbbing pain in his head. The lime-washed farmhouse was getting nearer but its colour was becoming grey in the weakening light. A welcoming light could be seen in a downstairs window and this seemed to give the students renewed energy to pass him and, with clods of soil impeding his progress, James was hard-pressed to keep up.

A tall, brawny man wearing thigh-high rubber boots and carrying a small crate of mixed vegetables stood waiting for the trio as they stumbled out of the field and entered the farmyard.

'This's private property, y'know?' he scolded in a broad Norfolk accent. There was the beginning of a scowl on his face as they approached him but his expression suddenly changed to one of concern when he saw the school uniforms. 'Hey, are you the two kids who've been on the news?' He put the crate down and strode to meet the odd-looking trio.

'They are and they need looking after,' James replied as he mentally put the responsibility for the students on someone else's shoulders. 'They need something to eat and I need to use your telephone, please.'

'Edgar Simpson,' the farmer offered, holding out his hand. 'Let's get inside and while you call the police I'll fry up some eggs and bacon.' He picked the crate up and tramped through the open door and into the warmth of the kitchen.

The thought of sizzling bacon perked the youngsters up even more and they eagerly followed the farmer.

'I'll help you,' Samantha volunteered.

Edgar grinned. 'You can make the tea,' he said and steered James to the landline phone in the hallway. James nodded his thanks and dialled the number he had memorized earlier; after the third ring tone a gruff voice spoke –

'Chief Inspector Cheswell, how can I help you?'

5

AGNES OPENED THE DOOR to the trio who had been dropped off by a cheery Edgar and her cautious expression changed to motherly concern when she saw the two students with James.

'Come inside and go straight through to the kitchen.'

Seeing that James was walking back to the garden gate she pleaded, 'Please come in, James.'

He paused before returning to the door. 'I'll linger for a while, at least until the police arrive, and then I have to go and ask some rather pertinent questions in Cambridge.'

'Isn't that a job for the police?' On getting no answer she gave another pleading look. Taking one last look around he went into the house and joined Margaret and the youngsters in the kitchen. Agnes also gave a brief look both ways and seeing that the road was totally clear she bolted the door and latched the security chain. As she entered the kitchen James was coming to the end of an abbreviated version of events that had taken place since he had last seen the two women.

'Now you must tell us what you actually saw that night in Ravens' Wood,' James said as he turned to the students.

Michael hesitated to speak and Samantha, being of stronger character, took the lead. 'We had slipped out of college as I had heard that the wood was the haunt of nightingales. It's something I've read about in romantic novels but had never heard.'

'It was a local boy who'd told her,' Michael interrupted with a light quaver in his voice.

'Let's be straight with each other shall we?' James demanded and Michael looked down at his feet sheepishly. 'You'd gone to the wood for a little billing and cooing of your own, hadn't you?'

Samantha frowned. Then she smiled, nodded and continued. 'We had followed the forester's trail a long way into the wood looking for a nice place to listen to the birds when we suddenly heard voices.'

'They sounded quite angry,' Michael interrupted.

'Oh do shut up!' The girl glared at him. 'We crept forward until we couldn't have been more than twenty yards from the people when we heard a terrible scream that stopped in a rather weird, frightening way. Then a chainsaw started up and that lasted for a few seconds only before it was switched off.'

'Oh my God!' Agnes murmured.

'I thought I'd try to see what had happened.'

'You were so scared you pissed yourself,' Samantha snapped, 'and while you stayed I crept closer until I was almost beside the old tree the locals call Oliver Cromwell for some weird reason. It was then that I spotted two men leaning over a dark shape lying on the ground. I think one of them was holding a chainsaw.'

The two women were listening to the girl in horror while James waited calmly, knowing what was coming next.

'I managed to get a little closer just as the moon came out from behind a cloud and I saw that it was a man on the ground and that there was a lot of blood coming out of his neck. I must have made a noise –'

'You screamed like a stuck pig,' Michael piped up.

'then one of the men turned and started walking towards where I was hiding. He had what seemed to be a knife in his hand and I leapt up and ran.'

James raised his hand. 'Are you sure that the man approaching you was the same man who later kidnapped you?'

'Absolutely. In the moonlight I could clearly see that he was albino and it would have been a fantastic coincidence if there had been two.'

'What about you, Michael, did you see the man standing by Oliver Cromwell?'

'No, but I knew by Samantha's scream that she had been seen and that someone was thrashing through the undergrowth after her and so I began running too.' Ignoring Samantha's flicker of annoyance he continued, 'I didn't waste time looking back to see who was chasing us.'

'And we didn't stop until we were safely back in the college,' Samantha added, smug at having had the last word.

'Oh, you poor dears,' Margaret said. 'The same man who killed Daniel must have kidnapped you and locked you both in that dreadful place. What a frightful experience.'

'You must also be very hungry,' Agnes added as she hurried to the gas stove to begin heating a frying pan before raiding the fridge. The students grinned at the obvious concern for their welfare but James smiled and held his hand up.

'No need, Miss Lightbody.' James turned to the students. 'What did you do when you reached the college?'

The students looked at each other for a few seconds before Samantha took the lead again. 'We decided we would have to go into hiding. I knew the man had seen my uniform and he would know where we were so we packed a few clothes, climbed back over the wall and began hiking towards Wisbech.'

'Hitchhiking?'

'Yes.'

'And a kindly man, Mr Cartwight, stopped to pick you up?'

Michael nodded shamefacedly and he bent to scratch Tammy who was leaning against him behind the ears.

'What happened, Michael?' James asked gently.

'He turned the car and went back they way we had come until his headlights showed someone standing by the side of the road. It was that awful albino and Cartwright stopped. The man was covered in blood and had a gun in his hand when he got into the car.'

'There was nothing we could do,' Samantha explained.

'They took us to that old pumping station and locked us in. They said they would come back and release us in the morning but they never came back.'

James turned to face them. 'You must stay on your guard until you have the protection of the police. At any time Whitey and his brother Juan could pitch up here and try everything they can to silence us all.'

Samantha blanched and Michael fell silent and sat down at the table. 'Do you really believe they would risk coming here? They must know that the police have been told of our release and who abducted us.'

'It could be that a lot of money is at stake, Michael, and having killed once I don't expect the brothers to back away from doing it again to get what they want.' James went to the window when a brief flicker of light outside caught his attention. He waited and then visibly relaxed. 'It looks like the police have arrived, Miss Lightbody, so I'll be off. I will stay in a hotel on the road to Cambridge tonight to get an earlier start in the morning.'

Agnes nodded even though she didn't accept that her employer was doing the right thing but before she could say anything there was a loud knock on the front door. Margaret stood, handed her car keys to James with a mimed 'thank you' and went to let the police in as he quietly slipped out the back door. Chief Inspector Cheswell and Sergeant Tanner entered the kitchen and they both gave audible sighs of relief when they saw the two students sitting at the table.

The constable who had been left outside was at a loss when he saw Margaret's car pull out of the drive and accelerate past him. The rear lights dwindled rapidly in the dark street and he decided to watch and wait for Sergeant Tanner to come out. His orders were to remain outside and 'watch for a bleached Peruvian lurking about the house with his llama.' He didn't dare ignore the formidable Sergeant Tanner even if he didn't fully understand the glib description.

James fixed his eyes on the straight road that all too soon faded to nothing in the darkness and flicked to full beam and cruise control. The acres of oil-seed rape lining the route were no longer their normal vivid yellow beneath the quarter-moon's feeble light. An occasional on-coming vehicle glared at him with eye-watering halogen beams and by the time he reached the small town of March he was in no doubt that he wouldn't be able to make it all the way to Cambridge without resting.

From the outside the Pig and Whistle seemed to be affordable and within the acceptable limit of Agnes' petty cash; he went in and chose one of the vacant rooms that overlooked the square where he had parked so he could check the vehicle from time to time and hopefully avoid any nasty surprises in the morning. Although he hadn't noticed anyone following him from the house he knew he couldn't take any chances.

James took a painkiller for his splitting headache and was soon fast asleep. This was a rare state of affairs as acute insomnia was a normal side effect of narcolepsy.

The next morning a bright shaft of sunlight slowly moved across the room to light up his face. James blinked and rose quickly to shave, shower, dress and pack his overnight case. The clerk yawned as he came on duty and was surprised to find a guest waiting at the front desk to check out.

'Breakfast is not until 7.30, sir,' he said morosely and James shook his head as he presented his credit card.

'I don't have the time.'

The small town of Chatteris and the magnificent Norman cathedral of Ely, 'The Ship of the Fens', had been left far behind by the time James reached Cambridge, turned into Downing Street at 8.30 and found a multi-storey in which to park the Mercedes. The archaeological department was only a few paces down the street and after asking to see the professor he was ushered into an office where a rather severe-looking woman was sitting, her iron-grey hair tightly pulled back from the face.

'My name is Miss Trindle and I'm Professor Calder's secretary,' she snapped.

'I believe he is expecting me,' James lied and when she picked up the phone he added, 'Tell him I wish to discuss the royal mint.'

After murmuring briefly into the phone the secretary led James to an empty anteroom. Tall lead-latticed windows and a mammoth French provincial desk relieved the sombre oak panelling covering every wall.

James sat in one of the leather club chairs standing near the desk and studied a huge oil painting in a gilt frame. Purporting to be a portrait of Darwin it showed a bewhiskered figure leaning stiffly on a silver-topped cane and clutching a copy of his earth-shattering book. On closer inspection James could see that the silver top was sculpted into the head of an ape.

'Wonderful, isn't it,' a voice said behind James, causing him to jump and at the same time give thanks that he had taken another Xyrem that morning. James turned and faced a tall, middle-aged gentleman in a three-piece suit that had clearly been tailored in a reputable part of London. A small terrier pattered along behind him on very short legs.

'Professor Calder?' James asked. 'I spoke to you on the phone yesterday. I'm James Goodfellow.'

'Ah yes, you're the private detective who was associated with the man who was killed.'

'Daniel Lightbody, my secretary's nephew.'

Calder went round the desk and sat in the winged chair to fix James with a penetrating gaze. The pale blue eyes lacked any sympathy and James found them a little unsettling. As the professor absently stroked his small moustache he flicked a diary open with the other hand and studied an entry.

'I have an appointment in ten minutes so, how can I help you any further than I did on the phone?'

'You could tell me why you thought the coin was a fake when it is clearly the genuine article. How do I know more than a Cambridge don? Simple, I sent it to a London University don who confirmed its legitimacy!' James lied.

'It's possible that I was in error. Mr Lightbody wanted a quick answer and snap judgements can often lead one astray.'

'Yet you thought the counterfeit coin was of such importance that you were willing to meet Mr Lightbody at the Feeling Perky coffee house in Wisbech to discuss matters further.'

'I was interested in researching the age of the coin, the metal composition and the stamping method used. Even counterfeits can have age. Many were cast in the seventeenth and eighteenth centuries and as I'm planning to write a dissertation on forged currency over the last three hundred years it was worth an investigation.'

'And you were going to ask Mr Juan Moran to co-author this important work?'

'Who?' Despite maintaining a straight expression it was obvious that Calder had been jolted by the name.

'Please, Professor, don't insult my intelligence. You met Juan Moran in Peru when you were still a student at this university.'

'That was a very long time ago, Goodfellow. How can you expect me to remember everyone I met in those days?'

James gave another lie. 'But you met his brother. I had you tailed.'

'His brother?'

'Mr Whitey or you may know of him as Raul Moran.' James had been studying every line of the man's face and was satisfied when he noticed the eyes narrow fractionally and the mouth tighten.

'I've never met anyone by those names and I insist that you leave this office now before my tutorial class arrives,' and Calder strode across the room to open the door.

James slowly uncoiled from the comfortable chair and sauntered past the professor. 'There will be other questions, Professor, but there's a good chance that I won't be the one asking them. Think about that for a while and then give me a call.' He slipped his business card into the top pocket of the pinstriped jacket. 'There's something else you might be interested to learn. The two students who had been kidnapped were found safe and well and are now under police protection. Good news, yes?'

'I don't know what you're talking about.'

James ignored the response and as he left the office door slammed shut with a loud bang.

Calder returned to his desk and speed-dialled a number. 'Raul? Good. I have a task for you, one you didn't have much success with the other day.' He paused to listen. 'The same man,' he answered and hung up.

The drive back to Wisbech was uneventful and none of the vehicles in his rear-view mirror seemed suspicious. When James arrived back in Broad Street armed policemen were sitting in a car outside the front door and they insisted on seeing James' identity before permitting him to knock on the door. Agnes gave a small cry of pleasure when she opened the door. Her eyes showed the affection she felt for him, reminding James of his mother when he came home from school with bruised arms and grazed knees. After being made to sit at the small table and offered a large glass of Merlot he told them what had happened in Cambridge.

'So you think this professor is one of the people involved in Daniel's death?' Margaret asked when he had finished.

James put his glass down. 'I'm not sure he was there at the time with Juan, but I have the distinct impression that he is in it up to his neck.

Unfortunately, we don't have any evidence to support his involvement or even any knowledge of the current whereabouts of the Moran brothers.'

'So what can we do?' Agnes sighed.

'I'll have to see of I can find a positive link that will convince the police that Calder was part of the conspiracy but I must first see if they've issued a warrant for the arrest of Raul Moran.'

'That must go without saying. Surely what the students have told them about their ordeal will put wheels into motion and start a countrywide search for the man?'

'I'll call Sergeant Tanner in the morning and ask what's going on. In the meantime, I'm going to book a hotel room for tonight and then I'm going back to Ravens' Wood to see if there is anything else the police have missed.'

'The forecast is for rain this afternoon. I don't think you'll be able to see much if it gets any darker,' Agnes said as she drew the curtain to look out at the lowering sky while sipping her wine. She turned away from the gloomy scene outside and as she bent down to place her glass on the table there was a loud bang and the window exploded into a thousand pieces.

'Down!' James shouted as he pulled Margaret off her chair and onto the floor. Agnes was only a split second behind them when the wall mirror disintegrated and a row of holes were hammered into the plaster above their heads.

The distinctive hammering of an automatic weapon outside and the chaos it caused inside had clearly attracted the attention of Constable Browning who was on duty outside. The door was opened with a duplicate key and Browning rushed into the room with an MP5 at his shoulder. He was unable to avoid the 4.6mm bullet that zipped through his body. He screamed as he was tossed to one side like a discarded soft toy and lay semi-conscious on the carpet. James rapidly crawled to his side and unbuttoned his jacket. Browning's shirt was speedily changing colour from pale blue to brilliant red.

Agnes appeared at James' side with a clean white petticoat and some linen. 'I'll staunch the bleeding with this while you get on the phone,' she said calmly as she tore the shirt open to reveal the wound. As James called emergency services he crawled to the doorway and looked both ways before shouting to the police officer who stood frozen inside the front door that he should call for back-up and remain where he was.

Agnes' organizational skills had leapt to the fore and while she leant with both hands on the makeshift pad she instructed Margaret to check the man's pulse and James to go and keep an eye on the corridor. 'The gunman may have entered the house through the back door to ensure he has had a kill,' she added.

'How can you be sure I was the target? It may have been aimed at Margaret or they may have thought that the students were still here,' James replied as he crawled back to the open door.

They waited ten minutes before two paramedics arrived and hurried towards the constable. He held up his hand to stop them. 'Wait while I check if it's clear for you to come in,' he shouted and crawled to the window. After studying the open area he rose to his feet. 'Come in,' he shouted.

Agnes sank back on her heels with a relieved sigh as she watched the professionals go to work. Drips were finally inserted into Browning's arms before they carefully lifted him onto a stretcher.

James was inspecting the destruction a few dozen rounds had wreaked on the property when Chief Inspector Cheswell stepped into the room with Tanner close on his heels.

'For Christ's sake, Goodfellow, when are you going to stop causing trouble and getting people hurt?' he demanded as he looked down at Browning who was being carried from the room.

'When you've put the Moran brothers in gaol,' James snapped back testily. 'Your search for them hasn't been very successful so far, has it?'

'What search. What brothers?' Cheswell was irritated by the investigator's attitude. 'We're not looking for anybody.'

'Haven't you spoken to the two students yet?'

'Of course not. They had undoubtedly been traumatized by their experience and needed to get a good rest back at the college without being pestered with questions. We'll formally interview them in the morning and that's when we'll ask them for a description of their assailants.'

James threw his hands into the air in exasperation. 'We know who they are and can give you descriptions and I'm surprised that you left your prime witnesses to a murder unguarded. The Moran brothers would probably start looking there next.'

'Murder, what murder are you talking about, Goodfellow?' Tanner mocked. 'They were kidnapped, not murdered.'

'Don't you understand? They were taken because they witnessed Raul Moran and another person kill Daniel Lightbody in Ravens' Wood. Cartwright was also involved and it was him I put pressure on to find the pumping station where the students were being held.'

The two officers stood in silence with mouths proverbially hanging open as they absorbed what they had been told them until Tanner exclaimed. 'Why didn't you tell me this when we were at the fire?'

'Because I assumed that as an efficient officer of the law you would have spoken to them already and have issued an all-points bulletin stating that Moran and Cartwright were armed and dangerous.' James turned away and Agnes could see the suppressed anger in his taut expression.

'This really means that Samantha and Michael are still at risk,' she murmured and James' head jerked upright with blazing eyes.

'You're right, Miss Lightbody. We must get to the school immediately.' James strode towards the door but was stopped by Sergeant Tanner's large hand on his shoulder.

'We're not stupid, Goodfellow,' he snapped. 'We have two armed men on guard at the college with relief every three hours and radio checks every ten minutes.'

'And you had two armed guards here, too,' James said in a quiet voice as he pointed to the open door where the stretcher had only just passed through. The point being made was clearly understood by both officers and Cheswell nodded at Tanner who immediately contacted his office.

'Sierra 5, Sierra 5 – Report.'

There was a loud static hiss and a disembodied voice answered. 'Sierra seven responding Sergeant. Sierra five has been silent for five minutes. Must be taking a leak. Out.'

'Sierra 7, check and report back.' Tanner switched off the irritating static and the room fell silent.

James was the first to speak and ignoring the officers he addressed Agnes. 'I suggest you and Margaret get bottles of water and whatever else you need and lock yourselves in an upstairs bedroom. I'll politely ask the sergeant for replacements to stand guard on the ground floor and outside your room.'

'That's enough of the sarcasm, Goodfellow. Sergeant Tanner will organize a protection detail until the crime scene officers arrive to question you on the attack before sealing off the area for a full forensic search.'

James nodded and sat down on one of the chairs that hadn't been showered with glass fragments and only then did he become acutely aware of a wet feeling on his leg and severe pain in his left palm. He opened his hand and saw a long glittering shard embedded in the flesh. As soon as he gripped the end it slipped out and blood began to flow from the deep cut; he picked up one of the unused pillowcases to wrap round his hand before looking down at his leg.

Cheswell became aware of what James was doing and swiftly crossed the room to help bind the knee. James was taken by surprise. The senior officer's kind demeanour briefly revealed a compassionate side that he didn't think possible.

'Thank you, Chief Inspector,' he said and then realized that he meant it. 'To save you troubling the teenagers I'll give you as many details as possible concerning Raul Moran and Cartwright.' Cheswell let his smartphone record every word and only became visibly excited when James related his visit to Professor Stephen Calder and his belief that he was involved in the hunt for the contents of the medieval chest.

'You think a top Cambridge don could also be behind this murder?'

'During our conversation I had the distinct feeling he was withholding some very pertinent information and his close relationship in the past with Juan Moran in Lima makes the whole thing stink.'

'What about Bernard Davies, the owner of Green Fingers Garden Centre. Do you think he's involved in this too?'

'Bernard Davies may have taken Raul Moran and Cartwright on as casual labourers to avoid paying their National Insurance but I think he would draw the line at murder and kidnap, which reminds me, your man hasn't reported back yet.'

Cheswell nodded and then dialled a number. 'Hello, Sergeant, I'm a little concerned about the men stationed at the art college. One didn't respond on the last check. I'm also sending you an audio file that has the descriptions of two men known as Raul Moran and Cartwright. I want you to contact Central Control and put out an alert to apprehend them. All caution must be exercised as they are very dangerous and . . .' he looked around at the shattered window and pockmarked wall '. . . possibly armed with fully automatic weapons.'

James held his hand up and Cheswell paused with one eyebrow raised.

'Raul Moran, the albino, is wanted by Interpol for murder and may be accompanied by his older brother, Juan,' James added.

'You've only been in Norfolk for a few days, Goodfellow, and already you're investigating missing treasure, a murder, kidnapping and a case of arson; are you always this industrious?'

'This is just a quiet day for my boss, Chief Inspector,' Agnes said as she walked back into the room with Margaret. 'He quite often has fraud, blackmail and a couple of lost kittens as well.'

Both men laughed until Cheswell's phone rang. As he listened to the caller his expression grew grim. 'That was Central Control reporting that they haven't been able to trace Cartwright or the Peruvians yet and a professor answering to the name of Calder left Gatwick Airport on a flight bound for Morocco.'

'Any news from the college?'

'We're still waiting for news from the back gate where the missing officer was stationed.' James felt a slight tingle as the hairs on his neck stirred.

'Did Calder check any luggage into the hold?' Agnes asked suddenly and the men knew what she was thinking.

'Only light hand luggage and therefore we can assume that none of the coins left the country.'

'Thank God,' James said. 'Now all you have to do is find the Moran brothers and we'll find the murderer and King John's silver.'

6

AFTER ABANDONING THE MERCEDES in a car park Cartwright began checking the vehicles parked in a quiet side street that had no CCTV. A five-year-old Fiat 500 was the first with a key still in the ignition lock; he looked around and quickly climbed in.

Some people deserve to lose their property, he thought to himself as he drove out of Wisbech and took the first road heading south to the cross-channel ferry port at Harwich. Now that he had outlived his usefulness, Raul Moran who was now a very rich man would include him amongst the witnesses to be silenced.

The little car had covered a mere fifteen miles along the fenland road when a light on the dashboard began flashing urgently. Without any warning the engine started to choke and splutter. Cartwright was able to pull into a lay-by just before the engine stopped and the car rolled to a creaking stop. The fuel gauge was reading empty. After pounding the wheel rim in an outburst of anger Cartwright cooled down and walked along the road, dodging into the hedgerow whenever he spotted an approaching car, until he felt he had put a good distance between him and the discarded Fiat. He decided to thumb a lift to the next town with the excuse that his girlfriend had driven off in a jealous rage and left him stranded.

When he was hiding from traffic there had been a car every few minutes but now that he was out in the open nobody seemed to be travelling his way on the billiard-table terrain. Many flashed past, in the opposite direction, some drivers peering at the strange sight of a man in a three-piece suit marching across a deserted stretch of Norfolk fenland.

The light was beginning to fade when Cartwright caught sight of a white family sedan going south. He stopped on the shoulder of the road and held up the traditional thumb, seeking pity from the driver.

The town of March was smaller than he had imagined and after thanking the young couple for the lift he entered the thatched public house and asked if there was a vacancy.

The room was low-beamed, cosy and tainted with the mingling smells of old tobacco and beer. Original thirteenth-century oak floorboards had cracked with age and the smoky environment of the public bar had filtered up over many years to saturate the timbers of the ancient inn.

The wallpaper had faded and a couple of strips were peeling and beginning to curl away from the wall close to the ceiling. Cartwright eyed the state of his room with disdain and after washing his hands went down to choose something to eat from the extensive blackboard at the end of the bar.

Avoiding anything that looked microwaveable he opted for the sliced ham, egg and chips and a large glass of mediocre red wine. Selecting a dog-eared paperback from the rack in the hall when he was finished he returned to his room and climbed into bed to spend the rest of the evening reading.

Cartwright had only just begun the first chapter when a slight movement in his peripheral vision interrupted his concentration. He turned his head and in the dark corner saw a piece of loose wallpaper moving in the draught that came from under the door. Recent strong winds had sufficiently lifted the thatch to let rain in and wet the wallpaper that was now giving off a musty smell. Cartwright went on reading but his pernickety nature wouldn't let it rest. Having noticed that the oilcloth lining the chest of drawers was held down with drawing pins he removed one and padded across to the offending corner. As he began flattening the damp strip of wallpaper another piece of paper that had been placed behind it was dislodged. Cartwright pulled it free to find he was holding a piece of water-stained paper that had been folded and sealed with a flattened blob of red wax. It was clearly very old for the paper was crumbling at the edges and the damp that had seeped through layers of wallpaper had stained it the colour of strong tea.

He gently edged a thumbnail under the ancient wax and with little coaxing it crumbled almost to powder to release its secret. Cartwright unfolded the paper and saw that it was covered with thin spidery handwriting that had blurred and faded over the centuries.

As he read the cursive script with some difficulty his pulse began to race. But for that storm of a few days ago and the fact that he had been given the last available room he would not have found this; he was holding the key that could unlock the whereabouts of treasure as old as the inn. The letter began with a stylized greeting and ended with a sad farewell to a list of family members.

> *To whomsoever finds my final words.*
>
> *God damn John for he will undoubtedly rot in hell for reneging on an oath made before righteous and just men of the realm. God forgive me for I am condemned a traitor for reading aloud in this hostelry the sanctified pledges of our King. This royal contract a rapscallion exchanged for a jug of mead has been hidden where all can see and know of the treachery of kings. I have always held sacred an oath above all else yet still I am to be taken from here to Norwich to meet my Maker. I go with head held high before it rolls at the feet of my executioner. May God have mercy on him and on my soul.*
>
> *Robert Brewer*
> *Hosteller of the Worshipful Company of Innholders*

Although Cartwright was a casual labourer who travelled the country his parents had put him through the best private school and paid his university fees until they died and the money dried up. He reverently put the paper down on the eiderdown and studied the room that had once been used as a holding cell for the condemned man before being taken and put to death. As he thought more about the luckless innkeeper and the name of the inn he came to the conclusion that the royal contract had to be the Magna Carta of 1215 or at least one of the few copies made at the time of the original. It had most probably been stolen from the man who originally hid the chest inside the Oliver Cromwell oak.

'Christ, that'll be worth a bloody fortune to the man who finds it,' he murmured as he looked at each wall, seeking some clues to the whereabouts of such a document.

It was drizzling with no let-up showing in the dark grey clouds that ranked from one horizon to the other when Cartwright went downstairs the next morning to the breakfast area in the bar. While waiting for his food he sipped the bitter Costa Rican blend and let his gaze wander over the interior decoration as though half expecting to see the medieval scroll 'hidden where all can see and know of the treachery of kings.'

Flocked wallpaper generously decorated with replica horse brasses and gleaming copper pans seemed to mock his search. When his food arrived he asked the friendly-looking landlady if the inn had always looked the same and was not surprised to learn that the ground-floor configuration had been changed many times during the long history of the building.

'It was once the village store until it went bankrupt and was bought by yours truly,' she revealed. 'And now it's a freehouse,' she added proudly before returning to her lecture on the history of The Royal Charter while Cartwright continued eating without saying a word.

'At one time, centuries ago, it was called The Red Rose but for some reason or another it was changed back to The Royal Charter. That only lasted for a year before being inexplicably changed back to The Red Rose. When I bought it I thought the old name was more original and would bring in more customers. Know what I mean?'

'Do you know why it was called The Royal Charter?' he asked as he laid his cutlery down and wiped his greasy lips with the paper napkin.

'Lord knows,' she said picking up the plate. 'Maybe some lord or even the king of that time was passing this way and the innkeeper wanted his business.'

So she doesn't know anything about the copy of the Magna Carta, Cartwright thought as he offered his credit card.

The light rain had cleared when he stepped out into the fresh morning air and he walked briskly towards the square where he had seen a bus stop the day before. An hour passed before a passer-by took sympathy on the frustrated man and informed him that there wouldn't be any bus until Thursday and that he should consider thumbing a lift.

Once more Cartwright found himself holding a thumb aloft while walking on a country road with flat farmland on all sides. Ten cars had rushed past, splashing him with road grime before a dark saloon slowed and came to a stop. Cartwright ran to catch up with the parked car.

'Could you take me to the next town?' Cartwright asked as the tinted window powered down and to his horror he looked into the muzzle of a large-calibre gun.

'Of course we can,' a familiar voice said. Cartwright bent his head and saw both the Moran brothers grinning at him with the dark dead eyes of tiger sharks. 'Get in,' Juan Pablo snapped, waving the barrel of the automatic and Cartwright climbed into the back where he cowered in the corner.

'How did you know where to find me?' he asked.

'That was simple, my friend. There are only two main roads going south from Wisbech and we were fortunate enough to take the one where we saw an abandoned Fiat 500. It was unlocked and as you kindly left the key in the ignition we soon found out that you'd run out of gas,' Juan sniggered.

'We checked all the hotels until the barkeeper at The Royal Charter said that a man without luggage had checked in. We took a room and waited until we saw you leave this morning,' Whitey added. 'Then we followed you to the square and waited until you started walking.'

'There are a few questions we want to ask you, my friend, about how the kids managed to escape,' Juan hissed.

Cartwright blanched and his pulse began racing even faster. 'I'm not sure I know what you mean.'

It was at that point that Whitey turned in his seat and fixed Cartwright with a cold look that foretold the terror that was to come.

James had said his goodbyes to Margaret and Tammy in Norfolk and Agnes had promised to be in the office before the end of the week. When he arrived home he kissed Jennifer as soon as she opened the door and she was so surprised that she completely forgot the acerbic greeting she had so carefully drafted in her head.

Claudiu burst out of the living room and leapt up to throw his arms about James' neck. For the next fifteen minutes he was bombarded by details of his son's daring exploits at the swimming pool. Jennifer finally brought his non-stop commentary to a halt by wrapping a scarf round his neck and putting his school bag under his arm.

'Let's go, little frog, or you'll be late,' Jennifer finally interrupted. 'You can tell Dad all about it when you get home from school.' Jennifer opened the door and turned to James. 'And today will be the last time I collect Claudiu,' she admonished with a wag of her finger. James laughed and watched them drive away before closing the door.

The phone rang as he passed the hall table and decided to wait for the recorded message. 'You've reached the phone of James Goodfellow. Please leave a message after the beep and he will –'

'This is Chief Inspector Cheswell. Call me as soon as –'

'What is it, what's wrong?' James interrupted, fearing the worst.

'The constable on watch at the back gate was found dead. He had been shot in the head at close range with a silenced heavy-calibre weapon.'

'The students?'

'They are safe. I took your advice and moved them secretly to my own home where they are being chaperoned by my wife. The constables were at the college simply to give the impression that the students were still there.'

'I'm so sorry the officer was murdered. Was anybody else hurt?'

'The night porter had been questioned rather brutally before being shot in the chest. He was taken to hospital in time to save his life but he was unable to say what the two men looked like as they wore ski masks.'

'The Moran brothers, I'd bet my life on it,' James remarked. 'And if they tortured the poor guy they'll know where to go.'

'No they won't because the porter didn't know my address. I have since moved the students and my wife to a safe house in –'

'Stop!' James yelled into the receiver. 'Don't tell me, Chief Inspector, just in case someone is listening on your line. Anyway I don't need to know, do I?'

Cheswell grunted his approval. 'The real reason I called was to warn you. If these men want to kill the students because they witnessed Raul Moran killing Daniel Lightbody then they'll want to silence you as a witness to Cartwright's role in the kidnapping; your testimony connects them all. I'll be asking the East Steading police to give you protection and I thought it best to let you know.'

'Thanks, but there was no need to do that, Chief Inspector. My wife is a detective sergeant at the local nick and she'll be talking to her superiors about this matter.' James felt profoundly grateful for Cheswell's concern and it strengthened his last opinion of the officer.

'Any luck in finding Cartwright yet?'

'Not at all. He seems to have vanished into thin air but we're still keeping a watch on all major roads, stations and the airport.'

'Good luck with the hunt.'

'A final warning, Goodfellow, we've just had a call from Mrs Lightbody to say that somebody was in the back garden. It could be that they thought you were still there and I was just about to order one of my men to go and investigate when I thought I'd better warn you first.'

'Thanks a lot, Chief Inspector.'

'Mind you, as a private detective with a police detective for a wife you're bound to be OK. I have to say that you're a very lucky man, James,' Cheswell remarked as he rang off.

'Possibly,' James murmured to himself. 'But I think Cartwright had better watch out for himself with those two animals still on the loose.' He entered the kitchen but the rigmarole of cooking a breakfast was too much to contemplate. He left the apartment and went downstairs, past his office on the first floor and down to the front door.

The entrance to the Forbidden City was the next one on the street and despite the early hour the door was open. He was hoping his friend, Feng Choi, could put together his favourite meal – bundles of minced shrimp and hearty egg noodles swimming in a fragrant wonton broth. He opened the door and entered but Feng was nowhere to be seen. Lin Lin, Feng's young daughter, beamed with happiness when she saw James and hurried across the restaurant to lead him to an alcove table by the window and take his order.

'I'll tell Father you are here,' she chirruped and hopped around the tables to disappear into the mysterious steamy environment that Jiao Choi, Feng's rotund and very jolly wife, ruled with an iron wok.

After renting the office and apartment above the restaurant and starting Goodfellow Investigations he had become good friends with the whole family and he had often enjoyed the culinary skills of Feng and Jiao before he married Jenny and was compelled to spend more time eating at home.

Feng had changed little since James last saw him. He emerged from the kitchen in a puff of steam like a fanciful genie and his light-footed trot and distinctive gait brought a smile to James' face.

'James, James,' he exclaimed clasping his hands together. 'Welcome! And breakfast is on the house.'

James warmly greeted the man who had once saved his life and whose daughter he had rescued and they sat to talk. Soon Lin Lin came skipping back followed by Jiao carrying a tray with a large bowl.

'Your wonton, James,' she announced as she placed the bowl before him and removed the lid. The fragrance arising in the steam that had been released made James unconsciously lick his lips to the delight of his small audience.

'*Xie xie*, thank you, Jiao, as always the aromatic fragrance promises a magnificent taste experience.'

Jiao blushed and backed away to flee back to the kitchen. Feng shoo-shooed with his hands and Lin Lin reluctantly followed her mother.

The restaurateur turned to face James with one shaggy eyebrow raised. 'Are you in trouble, James? Is there anything I can do to help?'

James lowered his fork. 'Thank you, Feng, but I don't need any help. As I clearly recall we experienced extreme danger together last year and the last thing I want is to involve you in my work again. I want you as my friend in this world and not the next.'

Feng studied the concern on James' face and nodded slowly. 'I appreciate that but I want you to promise that you will ask for my help if things ever get too rough.'

'That's a promise, Feng,'

Feng returned to the kitchen and James, relishing his rather unique breakfast, had just finished mopping up the last of the juice with a *mantou*, a light, cloud-like bun, when his mobile rang. He listened for a few seconds before switching off and waving to Feng who had emerged from the kitchen with a stack of clean napkins.

'I have to go, something urgent has come up.' James started to reach for his wallet but his friend stayed his hand.

'You know you never have to pay for anything when you're under my roof,' he said in reprimand. 'What you have done for my family in the past is worth more than any payment.'

James smiled, shook his friend's hand and rushed out to the car, disappointing Lin Lin who had come out of the kitchen carrying a dish of almond jelly.

He entered East Steading police station and found detective inspector Tilley and Jennifer in serious conversation by the duty officer's high desk and as he approached he caught the name 'Cartwright'.

'He's been found?' he called out in greeting.

'We've been talking about you, Goodfellow,' Tilley confessed as the two men shook hands. 'You're needed for a spot of identification.'

'If you've got Cartwright in custody why can't the two students or Bernard Davies of the Greenfingers Garden Centre identify him?' James asked. 'He's as familiar to them as he is to me.'

Tilley beckoned the couple to follow him to his office and closed the door. 'According to his secretary, Bernard Davies had decided to travel to Morocco for a short holiday and the two students are out of the question,' he said sombrely.

'Morocco!' exclaimed James as he turned to Jennifer. 'Didn't you say that Juan Moran had been in Marrakech studying Berber craftsmanship?'

'Yes, and Chief Inspector Cheswell told us that Professor Calder had also taken a flight from Gatwick to the same destination. That smells of complicity and creates two more possible suspects for Daniel's murder.' She paused to think. 'It's becoming very complicated, James. It's also far too dangerous for you to be involved.'

Ignoring her remark James continued. 'I agree that we have four suspects now but I still don't see why you don't want to involve the students.'

'Chief Inspector Cheswell of the Wisbech police asked us to contact you for a very special reason,' Jennifer said. 'I wouldn't ask you myself but time is of importance now if we are to catch up with the Morans.'

'Raul and Juan? I thought we were trying to catch Cartwright first so why can't the students help us with that? They were closest to him on a number of occasions.'

'Because Cartwright has been brutally slaughtered and shouldn't be shown to young people if it is at all possible.' Tilley switched on his computer and Cartwright's face, if it could be called a face any more, filled the screen. James gagged involuntarily; Cartwright had been pummelled with something like a metal baseball bat and his features were also burnt, almost beyond recognition.

As the camera pulled back James saw that the head was no longer attached to the naked torso lying on the stainless-steel autopsy table. Before he could warn the inspector paralysis overtook him and he collapsed over the desk.

'Damn,' Jennifer exclaimed. 'Sorry, sir, I should have warned him to take a second pill before he left the restaurant.'

'Narcoleptic attack?' Tilley had been the senior officer who had been duty-bound to enforce the detective constable's retirement because of his condition. He lifted James up off the desk and leant him back against the high-backed chair.

'I should have realized that this might trigger a response,' Jennifer replied as she stroked her husband's head. The camera had begun to drift over the muscular torso, focusing on the various cuts and burns the torture had inflicted.

'This was done over a long period of time so whatever information this man had must have been worth a great deal to the person who wielded the blowtorch and scalpel.' Tilley switched the screen off as James began to stir.

'That was Cartwright,' James confirmed as his eyes opened and stared fixedly at the blank screen. 'I could never mistake that small scar that is still visible on his forehead.'

'The Wisbech report says that a farmer found him in a dilapidated barn in the fens just outside a town called March. He had gone to tidy it up for a developer who was thinking of buying it.' Tilley shuffled some papers before finding the right page. 'Cartwright was tied to a chair, completely naked and decapitated. The police medical examiner stated that it was either the work of a surgeon or a sociopath who took pleasure in his handiwork.'

'Why a surgeon? Why that conclusion?' Jennifer asked.

'According to this report every cut had been done to slow the onset of death. Removing parts with a knife and cauterizing the wounds with a blowtorch would have slowed the bleeding to prolong life at the same time as causing the most unbearable agony. What the bastards wanted to know must have been vitally important.'

James sipped some water with a thoughtful expression on his face. 'This couldn't have been done to find the location of King John's silver coins. It had to be for something of far greater value.'

'Or purely for the pleasure it gave the sadist,' Tilley responded and shivered at the thought that anyone could be so perverted.

'Why March?' James murmured to himself.

'March?' Jennifer asked.

'Yes, why was he murdered outside a small village like March, apart from the fact that it's fairly remote and sparsely populated?'

'And what does the small scrap of paper signify?' Tilley mused aloud as he idly scrawled on the notepad he had taken from the desk.

'Paper?' James asked and sat up, fully alert. 'Where was that found?'

Tilley leant over his desk towards the screen. 'I forgot to mention that apart from being naked and in two pieces he was also gripping a tiny piece of writing paper in his left hand. It was no bigger than a fifty-pence piece and carbon dating placed it in the twelfth or thirteenth century.'

'Please switch the computer back on Chief Inspector. It was purely the shock that knocked me sideways last time,' James murmured. 'I'm ready now.'

Tilley touched the keyboard to begin running the clip that had been sent from Wisbech. James grimaced as the decapitation was revealed once more. The clip finally ended with a close-up of Cartwright's opened claw of a hand and a piece of material lying on the bloodied palm.

'It has faded marks on it,' James commented and Tilley nodded.

'We think it could be part of a bigger piece of writing and it's still being investigated at the Wisbech forensic laboratory. I doubt that we will receive any answers yet as the only reason Wisbech contacted me was to get positive identification on the body.'

Jennifer came in bearing a tray with three cups of coffee and she tossed a small box of pills into James' lap. 'Take one now, just in case you forgot this morning,'

James drove back to his office and when he reached the apartment he decided he couldn't leave the investigation solely to the police. The phone call from Wisbech about the intruder worried him and he quickly dialled Agnes.

'Hello James,' Agnes replied. 'Thank goodness it's you.'

'What's happened, Agnes?'

'Somebody has slaughtered Tammy and left her remains by the back gate. Unfortunately Margaret found her and she's still in shock. I will have to stay a little longer even though the police have placed a uniformed guard at the house.'

James went cold – the killer was still in Norfolk and he knew where the Lightbody ladies were living.

He phoned Jennifer to tell her of his decision to return to Norfolk and pursue the matter in Wisbech and the village called March. He spent the next few minutes arguing the pros and cons of such a foolish venture with his rather irate wife, especially as it meant that she would have to neglect her official duties to look after Claudiu full time while he was away. Eventually James won her over by promising that he would ask Agnes to return home and give Jennifer a hand until the case was closed.

'But you don't have a case, the police do, and Margaret has police protection,' Jennifer retorted. Somehow he found himself talked into taking Claudiu to Disneyland when it was all over.

'Yet another promise to keep,' James murmured after he had hung up and he went into the bedroom to repack his overnight bag with clean clothing.

7

IT WAS LATE AUGUST, 1992 when the *senderistas* descended from the highland regions of Peru. They travelled along dusty, dry dirt roads that wound between the steep slopes of sun-dried mountains. Mesquite, cactus, scrub and fodder grass randomly survived throughout this part of the rugged sierra.

They moved in small groups to avoid drawing too much attention to themselves as they passed through the small, impoverished villages. Their destination was Lima, the capital city and heavy machine-guns and rocket launchers had been carefully concealed beneath sacks of grain in scruffy donkey carts. They carried automatic pistols and compact Uzis beneath their winter coats in case they were stopped and questioned by one of the many police patrols patrolling the mountain roads.

They intended to ambush a police convoy transporting Durand, the leader of the Communist Party of Peru, as it left the courthouse. The party was popularly known as the Shining Path, a Maoist guerrilla insurgent organization bent on replacing the despised bourgeois government with a dictatorship of the proletariat. The organization planned to expand their political ideology with further revolutions, until they had converted the whole world to their ideal of the purest form of communism.

Raul Moran was a *senderista* hardliner and a dedicated follower of Oscar Ramirez Durand who was undoubtedly going to be condemned to a lifetime in jail. Durand was the son of a retired Peruvian General and had been a studious young man, gaining recognition for his academic excellence. He had assumed control of the Shining Path, the Maoist terrorist group, when the military succeeded in capturing Abimael Guzmán who had been sentenced to life imprisonment for his insurgent activities that had resulted in more than thirty thousand deaths.

Durand, otherwise known as Comrade Feliciano, had followed the same guerilla warfare strategy as Guzmán and civilians were deliberately targeted and killed in the most gruesome manner. He was eventually betrayed and captured by Lima police in a dawn raid.

Since Durand's arrest Raul had been working with his brother, Juan Moran. in actively planning their leader's escape. They had almost been caught at one time and had narrowly escaped the city-wide manhunt with the help of sympathizers. The brothers fled back into the mountains to continue terrorizing the peasantry opposed to *Sendero Luminoso,* the 'Shining Path'.

Five weeks later, while Durand was standing trial, Juan outlined a plan to a group of *senderista* officers who had gathered in his temporary headquarters in a hillside village they had 'liberated'. They agreed to pool their resources and work together despite the decline in morale since the capture and the loss of their supreme military commander.

Raul travelled with one of the small parties of nine *senderistas* and had assigned himself the task of walking ahead of the cart to check that the way was clear round every corner. If there was any encounter with the PNP, the Peruvian National Police, Raul's congenital achromia, a lack of pigment in skin, hair and eyes, would focus attention on him, giving the others extra time to produce weapons and open fire first.

Since primary school his condition had been ridiculed and each jibe was answered with violence; as a child he gained respect with his fists but as an adult it was his razor-edged machette that was feared the most.

The group comprised ten seasoned fighters and this included the three women who had amongst them cold-bloodedly executed twenty-two men, women and children suspected of collaborating with the PNP. They had left their own families when they were young and had chosen to live with strangers in the wild mountains, surviving primitive conditions and lying with any soldier who desired comfort. Two had even borne the children of fighters – the next generation of *senderistas* who were destined to carry on their revolutionary quest.

The party was taking a winding trail to bypass the town of Ate and the adjoining golf course when they ran into a small patrol of six policemen carrying Heckler & Koch MP7s. Raul saw them first but was unable to warn his group before one of the policemen shouted, ordering them to stop and raise their hands. All six machine-guns were levelled and Raul knew they would all be cut down when the PNP officers got closer and saw that they weren't ordinary peasants.

He smiled broadly and strode towards the officer with his hand held out. The officer in charge of the patrol noticed Raul's pure white hair and his violet-coloured pupils and he turned to his men with a vulgar comment. The other officers jostled closer and jeeringly joined in the laughter, their weapons forgotten and the barrels drooping to point harmlessly at the dusty path.

'*Campesino asqueroso bastardo*, farmer, filthy bastard,' the officer said as he held his nose and grimaced mockingly. Raul Moran did not let the insult go unanswered for an Uzi emerged from under his travel-stained poncho. The weapon on full automatic ripped the air like the sound of thick calico tearing. The senior officer was thrown to the ground, surprise still fixed on his face, and his men instantly followed him as the rest of the *senderistas* opened fire.

The deafening cacophony of weapons died away until only solitary pistol shots echoed around the hillside as the women administered the coup de grace to each fallen man. 'You don't laugh at a *senderista* and live to boast,' one sneered before pulling the trigger and shooting the writhing officer between the eyes.

The group rolled the dead into the shrubbery and continued down the hillside. They had to hurry as they had planned to rendezvous with the other five groups on the Avenida Paseo de la Republica at 4 p.m. precisely where according to an informer the prisoner would be taken under heavily armed escort from the Palace of Justice. The groups were to board buses arriving opposite the Museo de Arte Italiano exactly five minutes before deadline.

Juan's plan was simple: as the prison van left the courthouse they would use two of the bright orange buses to block the dual highway in both directions, effectively preventing any escape. The forty men aboard the buses would then storm the four police cars that the informer had told them would be escorting the prison van. Armour-piercing heavy machine-gun fire would kill the driver and guard and a light explosive charge would open the rear doors. Fast cars would be waiting with engines idling on the other side of the central reservation to carry their freed leader and the attack force away.

The perfect plan had one fatal flaw. An alert police officer on duty at the courthouse steps became suspicious when he saw the parked buses. He had also heard on his radio about the murder of a police patrol in the foothills. Casually using his radio he alerted senior officers and immediately after Oscar Ramirez Durand was sentenced to a life sentence he was whisked out of the building through a rear entrance to a waiting limousine. Crack police SWAT teams and commando troops that were garrisoned nearby were simultaneously briefed and put on standby.

Armoured cars turned into Avenida Paseo de la Republica at precisely the same time as the decoy prison van appeared and the buses were turning to block the highway. *Senderistas* poured out of the doors straight into a hail of steel that poured from rooftops on both sides of the double highway. The light went out for many Shining Path fighters in the first three seconds as SWAT snipers took their time to whittle down the groups of running men. The armoured cars then opened fire on the cabs, eliminating the bus drivers, and commandos raced in to lob grenades through the open doors and windows. The armoured cars used their heavy machine-guns to stitch the buses from one end to the other and to mow down any remaining *senderistas* running towards the prison van.

Sensing that something was wrong when the duty policeman used his radio before 'casually' disappearing into the courthouse Juan signalled to his younger brother to join him when he left the lead bus. Raul frowned but obeyed Juan who outranked him and followed him to where the two escape cars were parked. They remained standing by each of the cars as the attack force began their assault and all mayhem erupted. When they saw armoured cars appear at both ends of the wide avenue they looked at each other and opened the car doors. Juan shot the startled *senderista* driver with a silenced pistol and pulled him from behind the wheel while Raul did the same to his driver.

The slaughter before the courthouse was over in minutes and despite the slow, rubbernecking pace of the traffic the brothers remained patient.

Raul strolled to join his brother and they drove at the same crawling pace to avoid any unwanted attention.

'You know that the organization will believe we betrayed our own men and deliberately led them into that trap,' Juan said as he slowed to a stop for a red light. They could still hear sporadic firing behind them as the SWAT team moved from one wounded man to the next with handguns.

'We'll have to leave the city,' Raul growled.

'Leaving the country would be a lot safer,' Juan added and his brother reluctantly agreed. The original plan had been to take refuge in a shanty-town district called Villa el Salvador for a few days until things had cooled down. Instead, Juan changed direction and took the first main road out of the city on a three-hundred-kilometre journey to Chimbote in the north. They had a cousin there who owned a private plane that could fly them to Panama and an uncle working at the Miraflores visitor centre on the canal could arrange passage on a freighter bound for North Africa without any awkward questions being asked.

Forty-eight hours later the brothers had locked themselves in a cabin and were keeping quiet as the crew of the dry-cargo trading ship prepared for its long voyage. The crew was tight-lipped about the cargo although it didn't take long for the Morans to guess that it was illegally logged Brazilian ebony. A surly captain called Morales who constantly smelt of sweat and whisky controlled the ship with an iron fist. He spoke little at mealtimes except to grunt fresh orders at his Mate or ask the brothers to pass the bottle.

'When we reach Agadir I'll help you get ashore two kilometres from the port entrance and then you're on your own,' Morales informed them after they had been at sea for two weeks. It was the most he had ever said during breakfast and he said little more for the next two days.

At one in the morning the brothers were woken by rough hands and taken up to the captain who was waiting by the railing at the ship's stern. The number of crew gathered on the deck at that hour made Raul feel uneasy and he gave Juan a warning look. They both noticed that the engines had been slowed and the ship was making very little headway and beginning to wallow in the slight swell.

'On the starboard side you will see the lights of Agadir, gentlemen. They are roughly a kilometre away and with a little effort on your part quite possible to reach.' The captain threw two old-fashioned canvas-and-cork life vests at their feet. 'Put them on.'

'Why can't you take us ashore in one of your lifeboats?' Raul demanded ignoring the life vests on the deck.

'I do not have the time to spare and if we are caught dropping illegal immigrants off this coast the ship, its cargo and the paperwork will be impounded and closely inspected by customs and the Moroccan police. I'd rather not take that chance, thank you.'

'You were paid handsomely to bring us to Morocco and –' Juan began to complain.

'Enough! Payment was to bring you here not to put you ashore,' the captain interrupted angrily. 'Help them leave, Fernandez,' he ordered and six of the crew leapt on the two brothers before they could reach the weapons they had under their shirts and threw them overboard.

Raul and Juan fell five metres before plunging into the cold sea. They rose spluttering to the surface, the ship looming ominously over them as the two life vests were thrown in their direction. Suddenly a tumultuous churning of white water, illuminated by the full moon, appeared behind the ship as the engineer increased the ship's speed. The brothers could feel the pounding shockwaves against their bodies as the massive screws thrashed beneath the surface. They kicked hard to move away from the ship and the deadly cauldron churning behind it. As they rose up with each swell of the sea the ship's navigation lights dwindled as it steamed towards the port of Agadir.

Juan had kept his eyes on the life vests and without waiting for his brother he swam to retrieve them before they drifted too far away. It was an hour of hard swimming against a powerful current before they were able to pull themselves up on the beach. Moonlit ranks of empty sun loungers greeted them with a surreal stillness as they removed their life vests. Raul picked up two beach towels that had been left by errant tourists and tossed one to Juan. They quickly stripped and dried themselves before wringing out as much sea water as possible from their clothes before re-dressing. Their intention was to reach the main corniche and as they made their way between the brightly lit towering blocks Juan outlined their next move.

'At dawn, when the tourists are all hurrying down to the beach we'll use the facilities in one of these hotels before visiting my friend who lives in the Talborit district. He has been a very active supporter of our cause in Lima and has successfully completed more than a dozen assassination contracts for us in Peru, Cuba and North America. I often used his skills until a whore he had befriended betrayed him and he was hunted by the damned *rondas*. Like us, he fled from Peru with our cousin's help.'

Raul cursed when his brother mentioned the *rondas* for they were the government-supported peasant vigilantes who hated the Shining Path movement.

Juan nudged Raul to wake him and they quickly slipped out of the hut they had broken into the night before. Ignoring the strange looks the holidaymakers gave them they casually entered the hotel and walked up the stairs with the rolled-up towels under their arms.

As they reached the second floor a giggling couple with beetroot-red complexions left their room and hurried away to the bank of lifts. Using skills he had learnt in the slums of Lima Juan soon had the door open. While Raul used the bathroom he chose two pairs of lightweight slacks and shirts from an expansive wardrobe; fortunately the clothes were a good fit.

When they knocked on the door in the Talborit district their friend greeted them like long-lost brothers. He gave them the sad news that many Shining Path fighters had been trapped and slaughtered by the PNP in the Vizcatan region; this would have been the brothers' final destination if they had stayed in Peru to carry out the next step in their grand plan.

The Morans soon settled into their new way of life and within a few years had built a highly profitable export business in Marrakech. They dealt primarily in rare Berber artefacts that were ruthlessly appropriated from the wealthy living in riads and kasbahs in the city and in the Atlas Mountains that sprawled majestically across the horizon.

On a grey morning in Cambridge Professor Calder received a cryptic email which simply stated, 'Interested in a few trinkets?' He immediately knew that it came from Juan Moran, for although he had denied knowing him, they had become good friends when they were working together in Peru during an archaeological dig in Machu Picchu.

Calder was overwhelmed by the rarity and beauty of the pieces that were Skyped and dug deep into his grant to purchase them. The dissolute professor regularly flew to Marrakech and while staying with Juan he took advantage of the scantily clad young girls who constantly flittered about the riad to fill the rooms with seductive laughter.

The Peruvian's debauched lifestyle had gone to Calder's head like an excess of fine wine and he was reluctant to return to Cambridge and his dour wife. The works of art he had acquired were sold privately, quietly turning him into a wealthy man. However, after three years his life had become unsatisfactory for although he desired money he also craved fame as a respected leader in the field of archaeology. Silver chains, forehead diadems, gold daggers and fourteenth-century Berber ceramics were fast losing their allure and he sought something spectacular that would put his name on the New Year Honours List.

When an email from a Mr Daniel Lightbody with an accompanying image of an ancient coin appeared on his computer screen he suddenly felt the old frisson of excitement.

Calder instantly realized that the coin was one of those minted by King John and had to be from the hoard reputedly lost beneath a rising tide. Calder's hand shook as he tapped out a reply. He wanted to learn all he could from Lightbody for he was determined to be named as the one who had discovered the resting place of King John's treasury. Calder was prepared do anything, absolutely anything, to recover the original coins. 'This could mean a knighthood,' he murmured to himself.

As Calder was tapping on his keyboard Raul was slowly wiping the thin blade clean on Cartwright's tattered shirt before dropping it on a wooden crate. Despite being unconscious the man bound to the steel chair was still groaning with pain.

Juan was standing by the half-closed door and surveying the empty farmland for any signs of movement. 'Can he know any more than what he has already said?' he shouted.

His brother kept on pouring a can of cold water over Cartwright's head in an attempt to bring him round. Pools of blood were forming beneath the chair and the spilt water was streaked with red as it flowed towards the drain in the centre of the disused barn.

'He said the letter was a clue to a much bigger treasure than the old silver coins and I want to know what and where that is,' Raul growled as he tugged at Cartwright's hair to get a response.

'For Christ's sake, Raul, he doesn't know.' Juan walked across and checked their victim's pupils. 'I used to do a little of this in Lima and I know when a man has nothing more to offer. You're only doing it now for the pleasure it gives you. Let's just finish him and get out before anyone comes.'

'Once more, Juan, and then we'll go,' Raul said eagerly as he took the grubby piece of paper from his pocket and held it in front of Cartwright's face. The man began to wake and tried to focus through fluttering eyelids and a haze of agony inflicted by the knife and the cauterizing blue flame of the small kitchen blowtorch.

'What does this mean?' he shouted into the charred cavity that was once an ear. His words meant nothing to the man who was rapidly dying.

'Enough Raul.' Juan picked up the knife and pushed his brother away. He gripped Cartwright by the hair, wrenched his head back and cut his throat with one swift movement before striding out of the barn.

After a couple of minutes Raul emerged and closed the large corrugated steel door. Juan drove back the way they had come until they reached March. He found a suitable place to park in the main square and the brothers sat looking across the cobbles at the thatched medieval building. The regular customers were just beginning to arrive at The Royal Charter and cheerful greetings and banter filled the air. Interior lights became brighter as the shadows lengthened and when two spotlights suddenly illuminated the pub sign Raul grunted that they should make a move.

Once inside Raul asked for two glasses of Peruvian Malbec that had always been their favourite but settled for Merlot when told that it wasn't available. The chef's special was a beef stew. Raul made a point of sitting with his back to the bar and in the gloomiest corner to hide his face. They knew that if a countywide search was in progress they could easily be betrayed by his appearance even though a roll-down woollen cap covered his white hair.

Raul studied the other customers, typical farming and trades people, who were more interested in sugar-beet prices and low interest rates than in two strangers who clearly wanted to be by themselves. His gaze ran over the walls and the ceiling searching for any clues. No man could stand excruciating pain without eventually giving something up yet all Cartwright would say was that he had found the letter in his bedroom at the pub. The letter obviously referred to a contract made by someone of royal blood, which was now 'hidden in plain sight', but where?

He causally leant back to study the heavily beamed ceiling that had been stained a deep tan by log fires in the inglenook and centuries of clay pipes. Nothing seemed out of place and he began to scour the walls for the second time. Juan had noticed his brother's interest and leant forward with a questioning look.

'The condemned man mentioned in his note that whatever was hidden can be seen by everyone so it must be in this place where people are able to see it every day,' Raul explained in a low voice without pausing in his search for anything unusual. He ignored the replica horse brasses, muskets and grimy oil paintings that adorned every wall. Juan regarded the long wall before him until his gaze settled on one particular portrait of a heavily bearded man. Beneath the layers of soot and grease the paint was finely cracked and had begun to flake. He could see from the crude brush strokes and tonal values that the artist was a rank amateur. 'Well, I can't see anything here worth more than ten pounds in a flea market,' he observed as large plates of food arrived.

'That's worth a lot more than it looks, gentlemen,' the waitress said when she overheard Juan's comment. 'It's William Brewer, the great-great-grandson of Robert Brewer who was hung, drawn and quartered by King John for –'

Raul rudely interrupted. 'That painting is genuinely old?'

'If you can call 1332 old then I guess it must be. Bon appetite, gentlemen.' As the waitress returned to the bar the brothers kept quiet and ate in silence to satisfy their ravenous appetites. The room had become crowded by the time they finished eating and Juan went to the bar to enquire about a room for the night. When given the key to room No.12 he asked if the room overlooking the square was available and the manager reluctantly switched the keys, muttering that they were fortunate for the former guest had cut his stay short. Raul, knowing precisely how that guest had been cut, found it difficult not to smile as they followed the man up the stairs. Two single beds and a huge Victorian dressing table took up most of the space and when they were alone the brothers began exploring every inch of the room.

'This is where Cartwright said he found the letter,' Raul said as he gently peeled back the layers of loose wallpaper in the corner nearest the dressing table. Old plaster became powder beneath his touch and lightly dusted the deep maroon carpet. Raul pulled a little harder and a wax seal was released from a small cavity scratched into the daub. It hit the edge of the skirting board as it slid down the wall and broke into two pieces.

'This is interesting,' Raul said as he took the fragments and held them together to create a four-inch-diameter disc. 'It shows a seated man holding a sword in one hand and a stick topped with a cross in the other.'

'He's wearing a crown,' Juan added. 'It must be a royal seal.'

Raul carefully rotated the seal in the palm of his hand and studied the inscription running round the disc. *'Iohannes Dei gratia rex Angliae Dominus Hiberniae,'* he murmured.

'What does that mean?'

'From the Latin I picked up at college I would guess that it says *John, by the grace of God, king of England, lord of Ireland.*'

Juan's eyes widened and breath hissed from between his thin lips. 'If this was hidden at the same time as the old letter then they have to be linked.'

'Which means whatever Cartwright was looking for used to belong to this king and has to be worth a great deal of money. In fact, a lot more than the silver coins.'

'Even the wax seal has to have some value to a historian.' Juan looked up at his brother with gleaming eyes. 'If we can find what the seal was attached to and sell it we'll have enough money to return to Lima and arm our comrades with the latest weapons.'

'Then we'll break Guzmán and Ramirez out of that bloody hell-hole in Peru they call Lurigancho prison.'

'Just think, when our leaders are free we'll be able to rally new supporters to the communist party's cause. Guzmán, with our support, will kill thousands of bureaucrats and end the petty bourgeois democracy, giving our country the proletariat dictatorship that our cultural revolution hungers for.'

'But what can we do now?' Raul asked impatiently for he was familiar with Juan's often-repeated rhetoric. Since primary school his older brother had been his protector and mentor and had made every important decision for him and he still expected Juan to have all the right answers.

'We'll search this room for any more clues and failing that we'll employ that private investigator so that he can identify and find whatever was referred to on Cartwright's piece of paper.'

'How can we convince him to do that?'

'We'll use the same approach we used in Lima when we wanted a villager to give us some information.'

Juan grinned as he recalled the pleasure he derived from those times in the mountains.

'It would seem Goodfellow came to Norfolk to find out what happened to his secretary's nephew so we'll use that to ensure he does as he is told.' Raul's perfectly white teeth gleamed as a plan began to form in his head and he ripped the tired wallpaper from the wall with renewed energy. Juan began treating the opposite wall with similar disrespect and dust rose into the air making them both cough.

The revellers' voices seeping up from the bar below had diminished to mild murmurs by the time the walls had been bared to the original wattle and daub. Juan and Raul then carefully inspected each timber beam from one end to the other until they were satisfied nothing else was hidden in the room.

The thick-pile carpet and every piece of furniture lay beneath a thick coat of white dust and the brothers showered and brushed each other's clothing before going downstairs. Without bothering to glance into the near-empty bar they mingled with the departing regulars and strode across the square to the car. The screeching of rusting hinges drew the brothers' attention as the weather-faded signboard swung to and fro in the increasing north wind.

'I would now like to have a word with Mr Goodfellow,' Juan said to his brother as he started the engine.

On the outskirts of the village they took the moonlit Wisbech road back towards Margaret Lightbody's cottage.

8

MARGARET WAS PREPARING BREAKFAST when she saw her own car approaching the cottage and she sighed with relief when she saw Agnes behind the wheel. She had grown rather fond of the attractive, middle-aged secretary and her considerate ways and could understand why James relied so heavily on her services.

'Everything OK?' she asked as she and her tail-wagging companion led Agnes down the hall to the fresh tea she had been brewing in the kitchen.

'Yes, I dropped James off at the King's Lynn station and he should be in East Steading later this morning; I can leave my departure until late tomorrow afternoon to keep you company for one more night.'

While Tammy curled up in her basket the two women sipped their tea in silence, enjoying the light lemon-drizzle cake Margaret had baked to keep herself occupied while Agnes was away. It was a typical Mary Berry recipe and it seemed to slice itself without any help from a knife blade.

'Have you any idea what his next move will be?' Margaret asked as she wiped crumbs from the corner of her mouth. Agnes shook her head as she opened the back door to let her elderly pet out. 'I'm worried about her weight but I can't stop the tradespeople from giving her treats whenever they come to the door. Daniel didn't help either with all the tidbits he gave her from his own plate.'

Agnes smiled. 'I'm not surprised that people spoil her, she's such a sweet dog.'

Margaret poured them a second cup and cut two more slices of cake before going to the back door to look at the lush garden that was now glistening with rain. 'She's not normally this long when there's bad weather,' she murmured to herself and Agnes went to stand beside her.

'Off chasing a rabbit?'

'No, the poor old dear is getting too arthritic to do anything that active.' She took a waterproof from the hook on the door. 'I'll just pop out for a minute and see if I can find her. At her age she can't afford to get too wet.'

Agnes was about to lift her second cup when a scream stayed her hand and she rushed out into the cool morning air. Margaret was standing by an open gate at the bottom of the garden, and looking down in horror at a dark bundle lying by the gatepost. It was Tammy.

Agnes bent down to look closer and she could see the beloved pet was now a blood-soaked carcass. Tammy had been systematically butchered. Her silky little body hacked to pieces.

'Quick! Come away Margaret. They may still be around here,' Agnes shouted as she clutched the shocked woman's arm and dragged her back to the house. 'I'll tend to Tammy later but first we must get back inside and lock everything.'

When all the doors and windows had been sealed and double-checked a tearful Margaret phoned the police while Agnes called James to give him an update. She was relieved to hear that he planned to return immediately and that she should be ready to get back to East Steading to give Jennifer a hand. She was reluctant to leave her new friend when she was so distressed but knew it made sense to support James and Jennifer. Later that day the two women were just starting to cook the evening meal when the doorbell rang and their hearts stopped.

'Who could that be?' Margaret said with a tremor in her voice.

Agnes picked up the long fish-filleting knife and strode down the hall with a grim expression, ready to confront the devil himself. She opened the door an inch and was faced by a giant of a man in a police constable's uniform.

'Good evening, madam. I'm here on Personal Protection Duty,' Sergeant Tanner said in a deep, gruff voice as he showed his warrant card. 'Chief Inspector Cheswell instructed me to investigate the remains of your pet and then to stay in the house until relieved.'

Agnes gave a sigh of relief when she recognized the officer's uniform and without feeling any need to inspect his card or ask for his name she released the chain.

'You are a very welcome sight, Sergeant, do come in.' As he walked past her she noticed a white envelope lying on the doormat and picked it up.

After he had formally introduced himself the grim-faced sergeant went into the garden to inspect the dismembered body that had been Tammy. He hastily returned to the warmth of the kitchen where he thankfully accepted a hot cup of strong, sweet tea.

'Incidentally, Margaret, this had been dropped through your letter box,' Agnes said.

Margaret took the white envelope with a puzzled expression. 'That's strange. There's no postage on it and it's marked for the attention of Mr James Goodfellow,' she declared.

'I think I should take charge of that, madam,' Sergeant Tanner said as he took a clean handkerchief from his pocket and took the envelope between a forefinger and thumb. 'Fingerprints,' he explained needlessly as he placed it on the kitchen table. 'You can never be too careful,' Tanner added and used a knife and fork to open the lightly tacked flap and ease the single sheet of paper out before spreading it flat. The women looked over the sergeant's shoulder as he read the few words that had been typed in the centre of the A4 sheet of paper.

Dear Mr. J. Goodfellow

Unless you follow instructions you will find that the people you are fond of are very accident-prone. I will contact you soon to let you know what I want in the meantime do not attempt to contact the police or the first unfortunate accident may take place.

Yours sincerely
Mr. A. Cutter

Agnes was the first to break the silence. 'It is clearly obvious that his name is a subtle reference to his preferred method of killing.'

Margaret winced as she recalled finding Tammy's mutilated body. 'He's not very subtle, Agnes.'

Tanner refolded the paper and placed it with the envelope in a clear evidence bag. 'I'll hand this in for forensic examination the moment I return to the police station.'

The thought of getting as far away from Wisbech as possible suddenly had great appeal for Agnes; James' plan for her to care for young Claudiu, maybe occasionally taking him to East Steading park to fly his Tiger Moth motivated another great idea. 'Margaret, why don't you come and stay with me until those murderers have been caught?'

The younger woman wrinkled her forehead as she considered the invitation. 'Sergeant, do you think I should leave Norfolk,?' she finally asked Tanner.

'I would highly recommend it, Mrs Lightbody, provided you can leave here without anyone knowing where you've gone, otherwise they'll just follow you and carry out the threat.' The trio fell silent for a moment and then Tanner walked out into the hallway to use his radio.

'Any ideas, Agnes,' Margaret asked but before she could reply Tanner came back into the room, a secret smile hovering about his mouth.

'I think the sergeant has already worked things out,' Agnes said.

'Chief Inspector Cheswell believes that it would be best if you ladies left the area and he has accepted my plan of action even though it breaks all official rules.'

'And?' Margaret asked with one eyebrow raised.

'You will leave the house dressed as two policewomen. I have arranged for two of our officers and a driver to come here as if making a routine call. Mrs Lightbody will answer the door wearing the bright blue housecoat I saw hanging in the bathroom. You will all exchange clothes and you two will leave with the driver as though you had just paid a short visit. The officer wearing the bright blue housecoat will wave you goodbye. I asked them to bring a small briefcase which Mrs. Lightbody can use for a few basic items.' Tanner turned to Agnes. 'I assume that everything you need is duplicated in your own home?'

'Yes. I can leave what I brought here.'

'Good. Then I suggest you collect what you need now so that we are ready when the car arrives.' Tanner twitched the curtain as he spoke but apart from a mother with a pushchair the road was deserted.

Raul sat perfectly still watching the front door of the house. It was a hundred metres from where he had parked earlier that morning between two Volvo four-by-fours. After dropping the note through the door he had waited for any reaction but so far nobody had made a move. His cellphone vibrated on the dashboard and he picked it up.

'Anything?'

'Nothing,' Raul told his brother.

'Good. I'll leave it until the morning and then call Goodfellow.'

The line went dead and Raul settled himself for a long wait. His eyelids were beginning to droop when a police car pulled up outside the house and two policewomen got out. One was carrying an attaché case under her arm. A woman wearing a blue housecoat admitted them as soon as the taller officer had rung the bell.

'They must be doing a routine check,' Raul murmured to himself, now fully awake. He turned the ignition key on the off-chance that the two Lightbody women would decide to leave. Juan's instructions had been to follow them should they decide to run. The engine rumbled into life and he resisted touching the accelerator to keep the noise level down.

Ten minutes later it started raining and reluctant to switch the wipers on Raul was reduced to peering through the streaming windscreen. The front door opened and the two policewomen emerged. They kept their heads down to avoid the downpour and through the water rivulets he had a distorted vision of a person in a blue housecoat waving them off. The police car pulled away and was soon lost in the poor visibility. Raul switched the engine off and sunk back into his seat to await anything that seemed out of the ordinary.

Margaret regularly looked through the rear window of the police car but the road remained empty of any traffic until they were approaching the centre of Wisbech. To their amazement the driver ignored the police station and drove past without slowing and soon they were out of town and on the road to Norwich.

'Weren't we supposed to go into the police station,' Agnes asked as she removed the wet cap and placed it on the vacant seat beside her.

The constable briefly looked at her in his rear-view mirror before answering. 'My orders were to take you directly to Norwich station where you will buy tickets for London while I meet Mr James Goodfellow who will be arriving on the 18.30 Intercity train.' He said nothing for the rest of the journey until they had crossed the river and stopped outside the Victorian Grade II listed building.

'When you arrive at East Steading you are to take the uniforms to the police station. They will be expecting them and until then you are not to impersonate by action or word a police officer.' His voice was officious in tone and both women nodded timidly until he grinned, and they realized he had been teasing.

The glazed vaulted roof lit up the cavernous interior of the station as they approached the ticket office. Agnes took the lead and asked for two tickets to East Steading Station via London Liverpool Street station.

'Can I see your warrant cards?" the man said, his voice muffled by the glass partition between them.

'Warrant card?'

'If you're travelling on government business I need to see your identification,' he insisted as a queue began to form behind Agnes.

'Personal travel,' Agnes snapped in her best impersonation of a police officer.

'Full price then,' the clerk retorted and punched out the tickets.

Agnes paid by credit card and held her breath as the man studied the card details as though memorizing them before sliding the two tickets under the sheet of armoured glass. The two women quickly crossed the main concourse to the correct platform and while Margaret checked the information board Agnes looked round hoping to catch sight of James. The tannoy suddenly burst into life and the mandatorily distorted voice announced that their train was about to leave. Without catching sight of her employer Agnes joined Margaret who was hurrying through the ticket barrier.

James left the toilet facility in time to catch sight of Agnes trotting down the platform and boarding the London train. He smiled to himself knowing the women were on the way to safety. As he left the station a policeman took his elbow.

'Excuse me, sir. Are you Mr Goodfellow?' he asked and James nodded. 'I have been instructed to take you to the house where Mrs Lightbody was staying and to give you this,' he said handing James a photocopy of the note that had been dropped through the letterbox. 'The original is currently being examined by the forensic department, sir, and Chief Inspector Cheswell said he would forward any findings after they have completed the investigation.'

'I assume this A. Cutter will be contacting me at the address where you are taking me.'

'The general consensus is that he will do that as the note was delivered there,' the constable confirmed as he turned onto the A47 dual carriageway and took the vehicle to sixty-five before switching on to cruise control. When dusk approached the streetlights came on automatically and the driver kept the car in the fast lane, occasionally flashing cars ahead to clear the way so he could maintain a high average speed. He seemed at home and totally relaxed behind the wheel.

'You like driving, Constable?' James asked as he instinctively pushed his right foot hard against the bulkhead when a concrete-mixer truck appeared in their headlights. The officer expertly applied the brake and without pausing accelerated as the truck pulled over.

'Yes sir, I completed my advanced high-speed pursuit driving course with top marks three years ago. These days I normally patrol the motorway; you're a last-minute change to my duty roster.'

'I'll make a note to ask for you should the Moran brothers make a run for it. What's your name?'

'Stephen, sir. Constable Stephen Thompson.'

James nodded and put his head back against the headrest and allowed himself to relax and trust in the skilful hands of his driver. The journey was soon completed and as the police car braked outside the semi-detached house they were unaware of the eyes in the dark sedan that had suddenly become very interested in their appearance. Raul speed-dialled his brother and reported James' arrival at the house.

'So we now have all three in the same place. Bueno! I will join you in approximately thirty minutes,' Juan gloated.

Raul settled down and decided to take the opportunity to catch a little sleep; he closed his eyes and unknowingly missed something very important.

Inside the house James was introduced to the two policewomen who briefed him on Sergeant Tanner's ruse before they left with Stephen to return to their normal duties at the police station. After closing the door James began making some coffee while he called Chief Inspector Cheswell.

'Any more news about where Cartwright had been staying before he was taken to the barn and slaughtered?' he asked as he stirred in the sugar.

'Forensic scientists have been all over that barn and I'm allowed to inform you that there was a screwed up booking form in one of the old empty oil drums,' Cheswell declared in his normal authoritative tone. 'It was for a two-night stay at a pub in March.'

'March?'

'A small town that's fourteen kilometres south of Wisbech.'

'And the pub?'

'I don't know if I should tell you this bit Goodfellow, but it's called The Royal Charter. Two men, I'm assuming the Moran brothers, had left it in a bit of a hurry without paying their bill and not before they had thoroughly trashed the room. Forensics said that it looked as though they had been looking for something hidden behind the many layers of wallpaper.'

'Did they find anything?'

'Sorry, nothing that could tell us what happened next. It looks like Cartwright stayed there, found something and then, after being expertly tortured, someone took it before killing him.'

'But he didn't trash the place?'

'No, it appears it was done by the two men after Cartwright had checked out.'

'So there must have been another item that Cartwright didn't find and the brothers went to look for,' James mused.

'Current investigation results would support that theory.'

'Would you mind if I went and took a look around the place?'

'Be my guest but be warned, whoever did for Cartwright is still out there and is more than likely ready to kill anyone else getting close to what they are now after.'

James thanked the inspector and hung up. Soon after he went out to the garage to make sure Margaret's car still had a key in the ignition and re-entered the house to jot down some notes before retiring to the bedroom.

When the two policewomen left the house in the company of the police driver Raul had been on the verge of falling asleep. The engine noise woke him and he was startled to see two women in the back of the car as it rushed past his car. The house had been left in darkness and the lighting in the street was very poor but he was sure they were the women because one was still wearing a bright blue housecoat.

Raul decided to make sure and after doing a U-turn he tailed the car until it eventually pulled into the police station car park. He parked fifty metres further on and watched the occupants leave the car and walk into the building. The light over the doorway was extremely bright and as the woman in the housecoat walked beneath it Juan could clearly see that he had been fooled by a very simple trick; one that he and Juan had used many times in Lima to fool the security police. He cursed and quickly drove back to the house and rang the doorbell before hiding behind a hedge. The door opened and a man stood in the lit doorway and after studying the empty road for a few seconds he went back into the house leaving Raul cursing as he called his brother.

'The women have gone and I believe that only that damned private eye is in the house,' he reported and then winced as he listened to a string of abuse. 'Their disguise as policewomen was perfect and –' the obscenities in his ear ceased and he heard Juan laugh.

'I like a clever opponent. I wonder whose idea that was,' he chuckled to the amazement of his brother. 'However, this is good because if Mr Goodfellow isn't with the women then any threat to harm them will be more intimidating.'

'That's good. So what shall I do now?' Raul asked.

'You will take that copy of the old note I took from Cartwright and slip it through the letterbox. You will then stay parked there until he leaves the house in the morning and then you will follow him. If he values his friends he should be going to The Royal Charter in March.'

'What will he do there?'

'He'll use the words to solve the riddle and lead me to the treasure it refers to.'

'And what's that treasure supposed to be?"

'How the hell do I know, he hasn't found it yet.

James went downstairs with a sense of unease to answer the phone in the hallway. There was a long silence before a voice with a slight accent spoke.

'Mr Goodfellow?'

'Yes, who is this?'

'You received my note?'

'Is this Juan or Raul Moran?'

'So you are familiar with our names. Good. I will now tell you what I want you to do. You are a private investigator and I want you to find something for me.'

'Do you wish to engage my services?'

'In a manner of speaking, Mr Goodfellow.'

'If I refuse?'

'Then an accident may happen to one of your lady friends.'

There was a long silence until James rejected the threat. 'I do believe you're bluffing Mr Moran as my friends are not here in Norfolk.'

'I know precisely where they are: in East Steading, where you come from, and I will not hesitate to send my brother there to arrange something unpleasant.'

James felt his heart sink. 'Very well. What do you want me to find.'

'You will find a piece of paper by the front door. I wish you to interpret the words and find what it obliquely refers to. You will then call me on the number written at the bottom of the paper. Do not try to trace the number as it is an unlisted prepaid number.'

'And if I cannot find what you want?'

'That will be most unfortunate, Mr Goodfellow. Of that you can be sure.' The line went dead and James shivered at the icy menace in Moran's voice. He slowly replaced the handset and went to find the piece of paper on the doormat. Back in the kitchen he unfolded it and began reading softly to himself.

To whomsoever finds my final words. God damn John for he will undoubtedly rot in hell for reneging on an oath –

'My God, this is about the Magna Carta,' he exclaimed when he came to the end. 'And it's hidden where all can see it. What on earth can Brewer have meant by that.'

James reread the final statement of the condemned man and realized he had to follow Moran's instructions. His secretary and her family were in mortal danger. James was also motivated by the sheer thrill of the chase. To find a 1215 copy of The Article of the Barons, referred to now as the

Magna Carta, would be the ultimate prize for any private investigator. James knew that only four of the original draft copies existed – one was in Lincoln Cathedral, two were in the British Museum and another in Salisbury. A fifth copy would be priceless.

He folded the note and put it in his pocket, shivering with excitement at the thought that soon he would begin the biggest treasure hunt since Howard Carter searched in the Valley of the Kings for Tutankhamun's tomb.

9

IT WAS LATE in the morning and the sun's watery disc was still struggling to dissipate the lingering mist blanketing the fens. The car was running smoothly and James soon left the ethereal landscape to enter the main square in the heart of March. The whitewashed façade of The Royal Charter dominated the north side and James drove around until he found a parking space in the centre of the square. A phone call he had made shortly after breakfast had alerted the owner who was waiting to meet him when he entered.

'Mr Goodfellow?' she asked by way of a greeting.

James studied the brunette in the grey Yves St Laurent suit and was immediately struck by her proud bearing. 'Yes. As I explained on the phone, Ms Brewster, I'd like to take a look at the vandalized room and see if I can find what one of your guests was looking for. It is pertinent to the case I am on.'

'Please call me Gloria, and yes, you have my permission to search but I must caution you not to cause any more damage. The police have already looked at everything and I'm a little annoyed that they covered the whole room with a grey powder.' She held her hand out and James could feel determination in her firm grip. 'However, if you can provide me with any proof that the men who booked the room did the damage it would help because my insurance company has yet to be convinced that it's a legitimate claim.' She strode from the lobby and James followed her along the hallway and up the stairs to a room named *The Keep*. 'They seem to think I'm trying to blame my guests for the damage in order to get a room redecorated at their expense,' she said as she unlocked the door.

James walked in and was amazed by the atrocious condition the Morans had left the room in. 'They certainly did a thorough job of stripping the wallpaper,' he murmured as he strolled around studying each wall in detail. In many places their crude methods had dislodged large patches of daub and pieces of broken wattle.

'This is a listed building and it's going to cost a fortune to employ proper craftsmen to bring it back to a state that's acceptable to my guests and, more importantly, British Heritage,' she said as she idly nudged a piece of plaster with the toe of her black Ted Baker court shoe.

James sympathized with her dilemma as he continued to inspect the surfaces. It was clear that the brothers had been very exhaustive in their search and he realized that he would have to start looking elsewhere.

'What they were looking for, Ms Brewster, was evidently not here and I can only assume that whatever it is has been hidden somewhere else on the premises. However, you can use my name and tell your insurance company that this was deliberately done by your last guests,' James said reassuringly as he gave her his business card.

'This is a very old building and I cannot risk any more damage for the sake of something that may have no value whatsoever,' the owner declared strongly and James knew he would be unable to conduct a scrupulous search without causing further mutilation to the old edifice. 'I would like to stay and think through this problem, Ms Brewster. Do you have a vacancy?'

'I insist that you call me by my first name and yes, you can have the *Priest's Hole*.' Gloria led James out of the chaos and along the corridor to a room at the far end.

'Wasn't a priest's hole the secret hiding place used by Catholic families during the reign of Elizabeth I to hide their Catholic confessor? Surely this place is a lot older than that?'

'You're right, James. Only in this case it's just a name we've given a rather comfortable room with en-suite facilities. Despite the inaccuracy of three hundred years it adds to the character of the building and amuses the tourists.' She pointed to each room they passed and James saw various medieval names in gilt letters on the doors. Using her pass-key Gloria ushered James into a large room with panelled walls and a small four-poster bed. 'I believe you'll be more than comfortable in here,' she announced with a sweep of her arm.

'More than you can imagine,' James said gratefully as he eyed the soft downy bed for it was time for one of his regular daytime naps to diminish the chance of a narcoleptic lapse.

'Lunch is between 12 and 2.30 p.m. and until then you are free to look around the inn. You can search anywhere but I would advise you not to enter any of the guest rooms until I can be with you, which will be in the afternoon.'

'Thank you, Gloria, I look forward to that.'

As soon as the door closed James kicked his shoes off and climbed up onto the bed. Within minutes he was fast asleep and remained so for over an hour before a long-case clock in the corridor chimed midday. He called Jennifer and gave her the status report she had insisted on before he had left home.

'Agnes has arrived with Margaret who I really like,' she said excitedly. 'Not only that but they both love Claudiu and have promised to spoil him rotten until you return. When will that be?'

'After I have dealt with one more thing,' he said without giving her any more details that could start her worrying. 'I love you,' and then he hung up.

The buzz of conversation in the bar dropped a few decibels when James entered but he was unperturbed. The laid-back and relaxed environment boasted a mouth-watering menu and it was a few minutes before he was able to decide between pan-fried sea bass and the rack of lamb.

As he drank the smooth, well-kept ale his eyes swept around the room studying every detail but he could see nothing that would relate to the words in the ancient note. A few of the locals eyed him with outright curiosity and he gave each a smile to put them at ease and soon the conversation had risen back to its original level. Fully replete he went looking for Gloria and found her in a small room adjacent to the entrance that doubled as an office.

James complimented the chef's skill before asking, 'Please excuse me asking but aren't you rather young to be the owner of such a large inn?'

'That's rather personal, Mr Goodfellow,' she answered with a frosty edge to her voice.

'I meant no offence, Gloria, but running this type of business must be a huge task for only one person.'

Her expression began to warm. 'My father died two years ago and as The Royal Charter has been my home for twenty-nine years I think I know every trick to keep this business ticking over profitably.'

James felt suitably chastened and grinned an apology. 'Would it be possible to take a quick peek at the other guest rooms now?' he asked. She smiled back and took a bunch of master keys from a hook beside the letter rack.

'There are only five rooms in total and you've seen two of them,' she said while climbing the stairs. 'The others are occupied but I have the guests' permission for a brief visit. I said you were a health and safety inspector doing a regular check on fire exits, sprinklers and bathrooms.'

James nodded and entered the first door she had unlocked. It was named *The Armoury*, which belied the plush interior of the suite. He walked round slowly, tapping the walls and studying every architectural feature in the room before turning to Gloria and shaking his head.

'Without tearing down the panelling and ripping up the floorboards there is little else I can do to locate anything that may have been well-hidden many years ago,' he grumbled.

'Well, the other two rooms are exactly the same and you've already seen your own.'

'If what we're looking for is anywhere in this building then its hiding place has to link to the words in a note that was found by the men who stayed in *The Keep*.'

Gloria stepped back a pace in surprise. 'A note was found?'

'A very old message that purports to be the last words of a man called Robert Brewer.'

Gloria paled. 'Brewer?' she asked in a hoarse whisper.

'Yes,' James said with some concern when he noticed the effect the name had on the woman.

'Brewer was my family name until it was changed in 1748 by a snobbish relative who had no wish to be associated with the business of making ales. The family had sold this inn a hundred years earlier, during the Restoration, to escape the tyranny of Cromwell and that of Matthew Hopkins who was the Witchfinder General in this region. Unfortunately the family was too late to save Ma Brewer. She was made famous in the region for being dragged from this very inn and burnt at the stake in the square. Although the two witnesses to her so-called acts of heresy were later found to be liars and hung outside the inn and my ancestor declared innocent, the mud still stuck and the inn was shunned. It's said that the Brewer family was always under scrutiny as villagers looked for signs of witchcraft. Eventually they were forced to flee in 1649 in case a trumped-up charge was brought against them. They went to London and there they remained until 1932 when my grandfather, who had been researching the family history, bought this property and turned it back into an inn,' Gloria said as she finished a trifle breathless.

'Wow, it's amazing that you can trace your family history back so far,' James murmured, fascinated by what he had been told.

'The place was in a terrible state as it had been used as a stable, a store for winter vegetables, a shop and a private house before being converted back. Grandfather did a full restoration and gave it back its proper name.'

'Then whatever is hidden in this building will undoubtedly belong to you,' James declared as he thought of the brutal consequences of handing such a document over to Gloria. The Moran brothers will still want it and will go to any length to get their hands on it, James thought.

'I suppose you're right, James.' Gloria looked into his eyes and saw the mixture of concern and guilt reflected there. 'Do you know what you are looking for?' she asked nonchalantly but her tone implied that she knew he had some idea.

James baulked at telling her the whole story and said, 'I would only be guessing so I'd rather wait before telling you what's been rumoured.' He turned away before she could read the lie in his face. 'Can I have a look around downstairs?'

Gloria pouted at his evasive answer, shrugged and then pointed to the stairs. 'Of course you can, James, look anywhere you like but please don't get in the way of the chef and his team. They can be very possessive about their own spaces in the kitchen.'

James smiled his thanks and went down to continue searching. Gloria was right about the kitchen staff for he was scowled at on more than one occasion while he was studying the brickwork for anomalies and got in their way.

James spotted an old oak door with a sturdy padlock at the back of the preparation area and asked one of the chef's assistants what was behind it.

'Have a look for yourself, mate,' he said as he produced a key and opened it. 'I'm too busy to give you the Cook's Tour.' He laughed at his own joke and walked away. James smiled obligingly and stepped through the entrance. Pulling a cord hanging by the wall he switched the lights on and descended down a flight of stone steps into a large cellar of arching brickwork where a dozen casks were connected to the beer pumps upstairs by a labyrinth of plastic tubes. The air reeked of beer and corked wine that had been poured down a drain and the flagstone floor had a glassy surface, worn smooth by centuries of cellarmen's boots.

James walked through stacks of wine cases from far-off countries to the rear of the cellar that was dominated by two tall wine racks on either side of another closed door. This was only bolted and after wrestling with the stiff corroded hinges he went through into more darkness. James groped on the wall and tripped a wall switch which revealed a chamber packed with rickety furniture, doors, fittings and garden tools from bygone years.

An old wooden chest drew his attention. It was full of old hotel linen and even after rummaging to the bottom there was little else. Rotten doors and an old sign leant against the back wall and James turned his attention to the brick walls.

'Another dead end,' he muttered dejectedly as he finished his search after an hour and decided he needed some fresh air. The damp, musty atmosphere had caught in his throat and he coughed as he climbed the stairs and went through the kitchen. The chef and his assistants looked at him disapprovingly and James swiftly covered his mouth with his hand and left the inn to stroll in the late afternoon sun.

The temperature had fallen quite considerably which helped to reinvigorate him and he breathed deeply before turning to look at the other businesses lining each side of the square. Many were beginning to close for the day and The Royal Charter with its thatched roof appeared quaintly out of place amongst the more modern buildings.

The gentle creaking of the inn sign became an intermittent screech as it began to swing higher in the strengthening wind. James looked and once more was disappointed by the unimaginative design which consisted solely of the inn's name on a white background. He watched it moving back and forth and noticed how the newness of the hooks contrasted with the rusty rings on the oak beam jutting out from the building.

The King's Charter

'That sign is quite new,' he muttered to himself as he studied the sharpness of the lettering and then stood stock-still and slapped his forehead with the palm of his hand. 'What an idiot,' he shouted and dashed back into the inn. To the astonishment of the busy kitchen staff he rushed through without saying a word and leapt down the steps.

The rich heady odours assaulted his senses again but he ran through to the storeroom and moved the door panels to find the old sign.

The colours had long since faded to a whisper of their original brightness and the crudely painted image of King John's head was almost unrecognizable but the name of the hostelry was still clear. James lightly ran his fingers over the cracked paint as he slowly spoke the words 'The King's Charter'. He rummaged in his pocket to find the copy of the old message and silently read – *This royal contract, which a rapscallion exchanged for a jug of mead has been hidden where all can see and know the treachery of kings* – James now knew what Robert Brewer had meant. The document had been hidden in the sign and held up high for all to see as they approached and entered the inn. The Red Rose sign had been changed and teasingly advertised the presence of the charter. James fingered the rotting board and peeling away some of the pitch that sealed the edges he saw that the sign comprised a clever lamination of two pieces of well-seasoned hardwood.

His heart was beating like a trip hammer as he rapidly chipped away at the centuries-old pitch until he was able to clear a few inches. Taking a rusting chisel from an old toolbox he hammered it in and levered the two surfaces sufficiently apart to enable him to put an old cork between them. He then worked on the top edge until with a resounding crack the ancient pitch gave way and the sign came apart to reveal a shallow cavity.

James stared at the sheet of calfskin that had been undisturbed for eight hundred years and a familiar sensation ran through his body. He fell to his knees and then onto his side as the paralysis took effect. Despite taking a Xyrem tablet that morning the shock of finding a priceless copy of the original Magna Carta was too much and he fell into a deep sleep. The board containing the sheet of vellum toppled to lean against one of the old doors and there it stayed for ten minutes until James awoke.

The tablet was hard to swallow without water but he forced it down and waited a minute or two before turning his attention back to the document.

He held the vellum sheet up in order to read the fine writing of the long-dead royal scribe by the dim light of a single bulb. The 3,500 minuscule words in Latin that outlined the original 62 clauses were still as sharp as the day they were penned and James was in awe as he held it in his hands. The 1215 charter concerning the medieval relationship between the monarch and the barons had formed the basis of all freedoms and continued to be an important symbol of democracy in the twenty-first century.

He knew that the Moran brothers wouldn't be interested in the history of the document, only its value, and James vowed to protect it. 'I'll make damn sure they don't take this national treasure out of the country and sell it to the highest bidder,' he muttered.

Touching the ragged edge he could feel that the skin, protected in its airtight container, was still as supple as the day it was inscribed and he tentatively rolled it into a tube. He slipped it under his jacket and did the buttons up before hiding the sign behind one of the doors. He wanted to keep his find a secret until such time as he had worked out a plan to defeat the Peruvians.

James went to his room without anyone noticing the bulge beneath his jacket and he packed the precious parchment in his overnight bag before returning to the bar. It was almost deserted apart from two businessmen in the far corner who were in deep discussion. Gloria was talking to a customer at a nearby table and he ordered a reviving gin and tonic and sat on one of the few bar stools.

'Is everything OK, Mr Goodfellow?' she called out and by her formal address James knew that the florid-featured man she was talking to must be an occupier of one of the rooms he had searched.

'Fine. All clear and top marks to you and your staff,' he called back and turned to sip his drink while he waited for Gloria to finish her conversation. It was clear that she wanted to talk to him for she soon wound things up and crossed the bar to sit on the stool next to him.

'Did you manage to find anything?' she inquired in a low voice and James decided to be totally honest with the attractive woman. 'It's a long story, Gloria,' he began and then related the complete history of the case from the murder of his secretary's cousin to the threat made by the Moran brothers. They had both finished two more drinks before he finished talking and he studied her face for a reaction.

'Are you saying that you've found a copy of the Magna Carta in my inn and that international murderers are blackmailing you for it?'

'You have it in a nutshell, Gloria. Would you like to see it?'

Her eyes lit up at the prospect. 'I'll get George to stand in for a few minutes.'

With George behind the bar they went upstairs and into James' room where he slowly unrolled the vellum on the bedspread. Gloria leant over his shoulder with a look of wonder in her bright eyes.

'Can it really be eight hundred years old?

'Yes. It was safely preserved in a chest before being sealed in the pub sign; being cured animal skin it was able to survive better than any paper of that time.'

'What will you do with it?

'That's the problem I now have to solve.'

'Legally you should return it to the owner,' her eyes twinkled briefly with mischief before she suddenly frowned deeply. 'These men plan to kill your friends and your family, James. You only have one option and that's to give them the Magna Carta copy.'

James heard the sincerity in her voice and if it wasn't for the love he had for Jennifer he knew he could easily fall for this woman. 'That's more than generous and I promise that you will be given what is rightfully yours as soon as this is all over.'

'They've got you over a barrel, how can you say such a thing?'

'As they say in the movies, they will have to be terminated.' James held the gaze of the frightened woman without the hint of any humour in his expression.

Gloria placed her hand on his. 'That would be murder, James. I can't let you to do such a thing just to give me that silly piece of animal skin that even the barons denounced after a year.' Her soft voice trembled at the thought that James might commit two murders. 'I'll burn the damned thing.'

'That would be a horrendous act, almost like murder, and it wouldn't stop the Morans from carrying out their threat. They'd believe I was bluffing and still insist on me handing it over.'

'Burning that silly relic may still be the only chance of saving lives and preventing you from killing.'

James frowned. 'It's silly old relics like this that keep us safe and free from the tyranny of depraved people such as the Morans. I have to go ahead; you may consider it rough justice but nonetheless it will be justice.'

Gloria's hand remained on his. 'God be with you, James, for I cannot be there if you go ahead and kill those two men,' she murmured sadly.

'If I can think of a way to turn them over to the police and the courts to mete out justice then I will,' James said candidly. 'You can be sure of that, Gloria.'

There was a sudden rapping on the door and James raised a warning finger to his lips.

10

RICARDO VARELA, a GEIN agent arrived from Lima in the small hours of a drizzly morning and travelled to the Peruvian Embassy in London to meet with Zamaras, an old colleague. *Grupo Especial de Inteligencia* had a small operation in London that liaised with MI5 on matters of terrorism and Ricardo had been sent to help Zamaras.

The red-brick building in Sloane Street with a new Peruvian flag hanging from a balcony was a welcoming sight to Ricardo who was of Mestizo descent. Spanish blood in his veins could be seen in his handsome aquiline features and with head held high he walked down the street with the grace of a *marinera* dancer.

The front door opened automatically as though he had been observed approaching the embassy and Ricardo stepped into the warmth of the large lobby. The man who stood before him was very different for he was a *tusán*, a Chinese Peruvian. He was a lot shorter and had a much rounder face with distinctive Asian eyes.

'Welcome to London, Ricardo,' Zamaras said extending his arms and the two hugged with a familiarity that came from having shared dangerous times before. 'I hope you've brought some decent weather.' Ricardo laughed and put his small travel case on the marble floor as his friend took the wet raincoat from his arm. 'I'll try to do my best but first, what have you got for me?'

The friends went up the grand staircase and entered a small conference room where two men were waiting. Ricardo immediately recognized the Peruvian Ambassador but the bearded man sitting beside him was a stranger.

'Your Excellency, may I introduce Ricardo Varela who is a much decorated captain in the Grupo Especial de Inteligencia,' Zamaras announced with a flourish in his voice that would have done justice to visiting royalty. 'He was party to the capture of Abimael Guzmán and Oscar Ramirez Durand. He will be assisting me in the termination of Shining Path's latest plan.'

'And what would that plan be,' the stranger muttered.

'An assault on Lurigancho Prison to release Durand and start a new revolution,' Ricardo stated, turning to the man and fixing him with a challenging look.

The dark eyes beneath the heavy forelock stared back. 'They have the money and enough men to carry out such an assault?'

'My contacts in MI5 and Zamaras' friends in Scotland Yard informed us that the anti-terrorism force have been following an interesting case that involves two men we know very well. One is Raul Moran and the other is his brother, Juan Moran. A few years ago CCTV cameras showed they were both involved in the attempted rescue of Durand at the Palacio de Justicia in Lima. GEIN managed to forestall this and killed or captured most of the Senderistas but these two men managed to slip through our net and flee from the country.'

'Shoddy work,' the bearded man exclaimed scornfully. 'Can't you people in GEIN get anything right?' Ricardo bristled at the jibe but remained silent as the ambassador leant to whisper to his aide.
Zamaras' eyes narrowed as he controlled his anger. 'Seventy-three out of seventy-five is an excellent result, sir.'

Ricardo spoke calmly. 'And we're on the trail of those who slipped through the net, the Morans, who are now in this country. They left Marrakech one step ahead of the Moroccan police after clearing their bank accounts and transferring considerable funds to an offshore account in the Caribbean. We also have reason to believe that they killed an Englishman in Norfolk to gain something of great value for the same cause. This attracted the attention of a private detective who is presently on their trail. A chief inspector, called Cheswell, at the regional police headquarters is keeping us informed and we'll take over the moment either of the Morans show themselves.'

'Then I suggest you get on with it and get this situation under control before they make enough money to return to Lima and cause trouble at the prison.' The bearded man's bluntness left the two agents in no doubt that he had to be a senior officer in the secret service. They bowed respectfully to the ambassador and without acknowledging the bearded man they left the room. Zamaras apologized for the man's behaviour with outspread hands as he led Ricardo down to his basement office that was more reminiscent of a janitor's broom cupboard than a senior GEIN agent's office.

After cups of Café Quechua had been poured Ricardo sat facing his colleague in the tired-looking club chair. 'Tell me a little about this cop called Cheswell. How does he fit into the frame?'

'I had a tip from a 'friend' at Scotland Yard. It seemed someone had wanted background information on Professor Stephen Calder who you may recall had been a friend of the Morans in Lima quite a few years back. After a little encouragement I was told about a small police headquarters in Norfolk –'

'Norfolk? Where is that?'

'In the top part of East Anglia with the North Sea forming its coastline.' Zamaras walked to a large road map of Great Britain pinned on a corkboard and placed his finger on Wisbech. 'This is where Cheswell operates and I asked my friend to get me an introduction. To cut a long story short I visited the chief inspector and he informed me that a private detective had also become involved in trying to solve the murder of a local farmer.'

'He gave official data to a stranger who can hardly speak English, just like that!'

'I showed him my credentials and told him that I wanted to apprehend the brothers as they had committed atrocities in Peru and he was overjoyed to get help. He wants a quiet life and since the Morans and a meddling private detective have been on his patch there's been nothing but trouble.'

'So, the chief inspector wants to end it?'

'Fast.'

'Who is this detective?'

'His name is James Goodfellow and he started his own investigation on behalf of a client who was related to the dead man.'

'And you're sure this has something to do with the Moran brothers?'

'The chief inspector is convinced that Raul was the murderer and that the motive was a medieval chest filled with hundreds of unique silver coins.'

Ricardo raised one eyebrow and chuckled to himself. 'Do you honestly think Raul can use old English money to recruit and arm Senderistas in the Huancayo district?'

'No. However, I believe they could sell the coins for quite a large sum of money and add that to what they have already accumulated in Morocco and safely banked offshore. The coins represent millions but it would seem there is something far more valuable that interests the brothers.'

'What makes you think that, Zamaras?'

'It's likely that they already have the coins in which case why would they linger any longer unless it's to find something of far greater value. They should have left the country three days ago, instead, the chief inspector reports that they have tortured and murdered yet another man and ransacked a hotel as though looking for something completely different.'

'How can you be sure it was them?'

'Cheswell showed me post mortem pictures and they were similar to Raul Moran's method of torture in a village called La Oraya. It's as though extracting information is of secondary importance to the man. Inflicting pain is his principal pleasure in life.'

Ricardo grimaced for he too had witnessed scenes where the Shining Path had punished villagers. 'What do you suggest is the best strategy for nailing the bastards?'

Zamaras smiled. 'You and I will consider a nice holiday in the White Lion which I've already booked and is quite close to Wisbech. Then I will take you to meet the rather sad-looking chief inspector.'

'He'll be happy enough once we've terminated his problems.'

Both men grinned at each other and Zamaras went to open a securely locked steel filing cabinet. A rack of high-powered rifles and CZ Scorpion semi-auto pistols shone in the dark interior; he chose two 9mm Glock 17 automatic handguns and gave one to Ricardo along with a well-greased shoulder holster.

'It is obvious that you came through British Customs unarmed so that should rectify the situation,' the moon-faced agent said. 'We'll also put two of these hunting rifles in the car as the territory we'll be operating in is open and as flat as my grandmother's old flat iron.'

The weapons were the ultimate in hunting rifles: CZ 550s chambered for .300 Magnum cartridges. The Valdada scopes with illuminated reticles delivered accuracy exceeding a third of a mile.

'Looks like we're starting a war,' Ricardo commented as he weighed the Glock in his hand.

'That's what the brothers are going to do in our homeland if they can finance their plan to free Abimael Guzmán and Durand.'

Both men fell into silent thought as Zamaras used the coffee dregs to top up their cups. A number of documents were strewn across Zamaras' desk; Ricardo idly scanned one of the red-flagged reports and immediately noticed Calder's name at the top.

'Yes, he's of special concern at the moment,' Ramaras said when he saw his colleague's interest. 'He fled to Marrakech last week and a man from our consulate has discovered that he is staying in the riad that was used by Juan Moran before police pressure forced him to leave the country.'

'Why special concern?' Ricardo put his cup down.

'When questioned about Calder's disappearance a university postgraduate said that he had seen his professor putting an old metal box into the boot of his car in Cambridge. That could mean that the Morans don't have the silver yet and that Calder has hidden it somewhere to retrieve when the dust has settled.'

'The coins are somewhere in Cambridge then?'

'Or Norfolk. I don't know, we'll just have to get one of our agents to trick Calder into believing that the Morans are getting too close to the chest and he'll soon be scuttling back to England. In the meantime we'll be looking for Raul and Juan in Norfolk.'

The Intercity train made short work of the journey from London to King's Lynn where the agents hired a dark Ford saloon for the drive to Wisbech. A clock was chiming one o'clock as they entered the fenland town and drove past the Clarkson Memorial spire with its statue of the eighteenth-century abolitionist. Ricardo followed the instructions of the sexy sat-nav voice and drove on to the police station.

Cheswell's mood had not lifted since speaking to the man from the embassy as he normally went to the Tandoori restaurant at that time to meet Akira, his mistress, who never liked to be kept waiting for the trinkets and sexual pleasure he gave her.

'What can I do for you, gentlemen,' he demanded as Ricardo and Zamaras were shown into his office and the agents introduced themselves.

'You're a busy man and we won't keep you away from your work for too long,' Ricardo said in a silky voice. 'We just want to know more about this hotel you said had been ransacked.'

Cheswell shuffled some papers on his desk and glanced at one piece that only had a few short paragraphs. 'It's called The Royal Charter, gentlemen, and is located in the town of March which isn't very far from here'.

'And where is the man called James Goodfellow? You mentioned he was trying to locate the killer of his secretary's nephew,' Zamaras said.

'I was about to say, before being interrupted, that Mr James Goodfellow is staying at the hotel and looking for leads even though my forensic team had thoroughly inspected that room and found nothing, not even a fingerprint or stray hair.'

Ricardo looked down at the sheet of paper Cheswell was resting his hand on and the chief inspector held it out for the GEIN agent.

'Take a look for yourself. I can assure you that's all there is.'

Zamaras grunted and stood up. 'Thank you for your time, Inspector, but we must go.'

Ricardo held his hand out and shook the puzzled policeman's hand briefly before following his colleague out of the office and the police station. 'What now?' he asked.

'The Royal Charter and Mr Goodfellow,' was the curt response. Ricardo nodded his agreement and not having asked the inspector how to get to March he thanked God for the dulcet sat-nav voice.

They made good time on the busy road and soon Ricardo was parking in the square. They entered the hotel and went into the bar where Zamaras ordered two pils lagers from the attractive woman behind the counter. He smiled as she bent to retrieve the bottles from the cool cabinet and was rewarded with a scowl when she caught him looking down her blouse. Gloria took the note, slammed the change down on the counter and turned away to place wine glasses on a shelf. Zamaras mumbled a gentlemanly apology and went to join Ricardo in the far corner.

'Nice-looking woman?' he said.

Zamaras gave a noncommittal grunt and as they sipped their beers they watched the woman leave the counter to sit with a large ruddy-faced man wearing a tweed jacket, moleskin waistcoat and a bright red bowtie.

The King's Charter

'Your oriental looks are definitely not to that lady's liking, Zamaras,' Ricardo chuckled for he had noticed the barmaid's rebuff. He studied the ruddy-faced man more closely. 'I wonder if that's Goodfellow,' he mused.

'He certainly doesn't live up to my idea of an English private investigator. For starters he's not wearing a deerstalker.'

Ricardo laughed. 'I think you're right, Zamaras. He's more likely to be Doctor Watson or one of the local farmers.'

The two had gone back to discussing the Moran brothers when a tall, lean man entered the bar and perched on one of the barstools. The woman called out to him and Ricardo caught the name 'James'. His ears pricked up and he looked at his friend as Gloria left the bluff-looking character and went to sit next to the newcomer.

'Mention the Devil and he appears,' Zamaras murmured in Spanish and like Ricardo he tried hard to overhear their conversation whilst pretending to be absorbed in what his partner was saying.

Gloria suddenly began talking in an animated manner as though excited by whatever James had told her. After a few minutes Gloria spoke to the man behind the counter and she and James left the bar. The two agents watched them go up the stairs and Ricardo mentally timed their progress before following them with Zamaras close behind.

They slowly walked along the uneven first-floor corridor until they heard muffled voices behind one of the doors. There was a torn piece of blue-and-white police tape on the carpet and Ricardo rapped on the hardwood with his knuckles. The voices stopped and the agents waited in the ensuing silence until the door opened suddenly.

James frowned when he saw the strangers. 'Can I help you, gentlemen?' he asked, his tall frame tensed to react to any sign of aggression from either of the two men before him.

'We are agents of the Peruvian National Police and we wish to question anyone who has been in contact with Mr Juan Moran or his brother Raul.' Ricardo slowly reached into his breast pocket and produced his identity card.

James studied the card and then nodded. 'You and your colleague had better come in, Mr Varela.'

Gloria had retreated to the far corner of the room but when she saw James welcome the two men she relaxed and sat in one of the two armchairs. They formally introduced themselves and politely shook Gloria's hand before stepping back.

'Chief Inspector Cheswell led us to understand that you met Juan Moran,' Ricardo said, addressing James who was now sitting in the other chair.

'I didn't exactly meet him. I received a note and only spoke to him on the phone."

'What were the circumstances at the time?'

James studied the agents for a few seconds before deciding to trust them and he told the complete story, beginning with Daniel Lightbody's murder and ending with the vandalism of the room in The Royal Charter.

'So, you believe they have a wealth of silver coins that date back to 1211?'

'Correct,' James said without mentioning the theory that Calder had misappropriated those for himself and that a copy of the Magna Carta was in existence. He had decided that these details should remain a secret until the brothers were finally apprehended.

Zamaras fixed James with his dark eyes. 'What do you think they could have been looking for in the walls of this public house? Surely not more coins.'

'That's a mystery that can only be solved when we catch and question them.' James felt a slight shiver in his calf muscle that was always the prequel to a seizure when he lied. Fortunately he had taken two Xyrem tablets that morning and after a few seconds the sensation passed.

'Would you have any idea where they might have gone, Mr Goodfellow?' Ricardo asked. 'We have a suspicion that they plan to buy enough men and weapons in Peru to free two leaders of the Shining Path. That would be a disaster for our country as it would throw us back into a full-blown civil war.'

'And send us back to the dark ages,' Zamaras added.

'That would be awful,' Gloria murmured.

'Indeed madam,' Zamaras concurred. 'That's why it's imperative we catch them before they can arrive in Lima.'

'I appreciate the dilemma, gentlemen, but brothers' whereabouts is completely unknown to myself and the police.' This was the truth and James didn't suffer any onset of paralysis.

Ricardo handed James his business card with a temporary cellphone number scrawled across the old Lima number. 'Please call us if you hear of anything that can assist us in finding those two terrorists.'

James nodded and slipped the card into his top pocket as the agents bid farewell with a casual wave and left the room.

'They were nice,' Gloria said as soon as the door closed.

James put a finger to his lips and went to the door to place his ear against the panelling. All he heard were the fading footfalls of the two men and he went back to sit in the armchair.

'Why didn't you tell them about the Magna Carta?' Gloria asked suddenly.

'All men, including special government agents, can be affected by greed and although I couldn't give tuppence for all the silver coins in that chest I definitely wouldn't take a risk and lose the most precious artefact that's been found this century.'

Gloria nodded and went to the door. 'If there is any way I can help you to save your friends then do not hesitate to ask. However, never use me as an excuse to commit murder.'

It was James' turn to nod and she left, closing the door quietly behind her. He took the scrap of paper from his pocket and read the telephone number before tapping the screen of his cellphone. The call tone went on for a few seconds before the connection was made.

'You have found something, Mr Goodfellow?' a familiar voice asked gently.

'I have.'

'What is it?'

'A copy of an old document written on vellum.'

'Very old?'

'Yes, it is dated 15 June, 1215.'

'Valuable?'

'Not being an antiquarian I wouldn't like to hazard a guess.'

'I wish to see it,' Raul demanded. 'I shall judge for myself if it is worth the lives of two women in East Steading.'

'Where do you want to meet?' James asked, his brain working at high speed to find a solution.

'I'm not a fool, Goodfellow. We'll never get together that easily. Instead, I want you to go to the Brundall Bay Marina on the River Yare. It's located on the other side of Norwich and there you'll find a cruiser that has been hired under your name. I want you to take it downriver to Reedham and moor outside the Ship Inn and there you will wait for new instructions.'

'I understand. Brundall Bay, Reedham, Ship Inn and then wait.' The line went dead and James tossed his cellphone onto the bed. As he sat pondering the strange instructions it suddenly dawned on him why they wanted him to use a boat. The River Yare wound its way through Reedham to where it became the River Waveney that flowed into Lowestoft Harbour and on into the North Sea. The Moran brothers had never planned to leave the country by air but by ferry across the sea to Amsterdam.

James took Ricardo's business card from his pocket and considered phoning the agent but then put it back. He had to come up with a plan that would enable him to retain the vellum document without risking the lives of his family or his friends.

James packed and went downstairs to check out. Gloria gave him a quizzical look as she processed his credit card.

'Are you sure you know what you're doing?' she asked, trying to learn what he was planning to do next. She had grown rather fond of the attractive brown-eyed man and even though she knew he was married there was a desire to get closer to him.

'I've been given my instructions by the Morans and I will go along with their demands until I have the opportunity to turn the tables on them.'

'You will take care, won't you?' The card and receipt was placed in his palm and her fingers lingered a while, maintaining a bond that she feared might be severed by violence.

'You can be sure of that, Gloria. Thank you for all your help and understanding.' James picked up his overnight bag and left The Royal Charter without looking back. He had a strange premonition that it would be the last time he saw the hotel and its charming owner. The car started first time and he pulled out of the square and set off on the A47 leading to the Norfolk Broads and Brundall Bay Marina.

He had a journey of 140 kilometres to work out what to do.

11

JAMES DROVE INTO THE MARINA and after getting directions to the boat hire office from one of the men stripping the upturned hull of a boat he parked near a clapboard shed and was greeted by the warm smell of tarred rope and teak oil.

The boatyard owner was a heavy-set, elderly man with a firm grip and James immediately felt comfortable in his company. An old Aladdin paraffin heater was warming the room, accentuating the mixture of smells that included the reek of strong shag tobacco coming from the old man's pipe. He took a business card from under his blue Breton sweater and James read the name Ted Rackham.

'Good morning, Mr Rackham, I understand you have a cruiser booked in my name, James Goodfellow. I would like to use it for the whole day and then leave it later this evening at the Reedham moorings. Two colleagues of mine, called Moran, will be returning it here tomorrow morning.' A shiny pate flashed in the neon lighting as the balding fisherman nodded.

'You'll have one of my finest, Mr Goodfellow,' Ted Rackham said as he took a key from the board on the wall behind him. 'Despite her size you'll find the Empress very easy to handle just as long as you keep her under the speed limit.'

'How would you like me to pay you?'

'No trouble sir, the charter has been paid for up to midnight tomorrow by people who said they were your friends. Now that I have confirmation that they are called Moran we can go out to the boat. I've made sure the tanks are full,' he said as he led the way out of the office and across the boatyard to the quay where three large cruisers were moored. A small group of herring gulls took off as they approached and voiced their displeasure at being disturbed with shrill cries.

'The Empress is the one on the left and I'll give you a hand with the casting off. You are familiar with a craft such as this?'

'I took a Birchwood 33 from Oulton Broad to the Hook of Holland last year.'

'Then you'll find this a bit of a breeze, sir.'

James jumped onto the deck and then stopped dead when he saw the expression on the old man's face. 'Is something wrong?' he asked and then followed Rackham's gaze down to his shoes. Oh, damn, he thought.

'My apologies, I didn't bring any soft shoes with me,' he explained as his face coloured with embarrassment – to forget the first rule of boarding any craft was unforgiveable.

'Size nine, I reckon,' the old man grumbled. 'I think I've got an old pair you can use. Just leave them in the locker when you've finished with them and make sure you warn your friends.'

James smiled his gratitude and when he returned he handed him a generous tip in exchange for the stained pair of plimsolls. 'I'd like to buy you a drink, Mr Rackham.'

'If this is for a drink then my name is Ted,' he replied slipping the twenty-pound banknote into the top pocket of his denim shirt. 'If I see you round these parts again you can be sure I will reciprocate.' He untied the front line and walked towards the stern.

James inserted the ignition key and the engine instantly rumbled into life. He gave the old man a wave as he gently eased the throttle forward and manoeuvred the cruiser into midstream before turning it to follow the current.

'Fair weather to you,' Ted called out with an arm raised before he turned and walked back across the yard to his office.

James pushed the throttle until the speed registered the legal maximum of 6 mph and only then did he begin to consider his options. He knew he had to hand over the vellum to the Morans but how could he retrieve it without them knowing? The problem had been nagging him since leaving Wisbech and he still hadn't come up with a solution.

The fields on both sides of the river were now as level as a coastal salt plain. There were very few trees to break the monotony of the landscape and wispy cirrostratus had spread evenly from horizon to horizon. This cloud ceiling was broken by two dark cumuli from which a misty grey curtain hung. He studied the approaching clouds and smelt the onset of rain before the first fine drops struck his face.

Ted Rackham had anticipated the turn in the weather as old sailors can and he had placed a rolled-up Pac-A-Mac on the gunwale alongside the wheel. James slipped it on and zipped it right up to the chin just as the misty drops became a driving downpour. He slipped the hood up until he could hear nothing but the plastic reverberating under the ferocious assault.

It was a short-lived squall and within five minutes it had become a light drizzle. James looked round and noticed a small red speedboat travelling in his wake. A protective cover, not unlike those found on old-style prams, had been pulled over the cockpit and he was unable to see who the occupants were.

James had not seen any other craft when he left the marina and he assumed that the powerful boat had exceeded the speed limit in order to get so close to the cruiser. It was now maintaining a distance of about one hundred metres. James kept checking without alerting them and moved the throttle up one notch. The gap between the two vessels began to grow and then shrank again as his shadow accelerated to keep the same distance between them.

Without giving any warning James yanked the throttles back against the stops and the engine died to chuckle softly as the Empress slowed to match the pace of the sluggish current. The speedboat was taken completely by surprise; the gap was closing rapidly and to avoid passing and being recognized the driver of the speedboat was forced to turn sharply to the right. At that point the river wasn't wide enough to complete a full U-turn and before the man at the wheel could react the prow was embedded in the soft riverbank.

The current swung the stern towards James and he could see that there were two men aboard, both of them strangers. One shook a fist at him and James laughed as he increased the Empress' speed back to the legal limit. A bend in the river hid the stranded speedboat from view and within fifteen minutes the cruiser was approaching the attractive town of Reedham.

The rain had ceased by the time James throttled back to moor at the Ship Inn, a large red-brick public house covered in ivy. A few families were sitting at the teak benches overlooking the river but James couldn't see any men that could possibly resemble Peruvians. He cut the engine and jumped ashore with a line in his hand and when securely moored he went on board again and went below to pour himself a drink and await events.

A light thump above his head and a sudden movement of the cruiser alerted James that someone had come on deck and he quickly went to the gangway. A dark silhouette blocked the light. 'Yes, can I help you?' James said as he squinted up at the figure confronting him.

'Will you be using the hotel's facilities, sir?'

As his eyes adjusted he could see that it was a young woman in a blue skirt and a white blouse with the crest of the hotel embroidered on the left pocket.

'I'm sorry sir, but the mooring is for Ship Inn guests and those stopping for a meal only,' she added pleasantly.

'I will most certainly be eating here. You have been highly recommended.'

She gave a relieved smile as telling visitors to move on often led to a heated response. He's rather dishy, she thought to herself as she thanked him for the compliment before stepping ashore to inform her manager that the Empress would be dining.

As James slipped on his jacket the smartphone rang. The beautiful image of his wife appeared in the window and he pressed the receive button.

'Any news, James?' she asked and he sat down again before relating every detail of what had transpired since arriving back in Norfolk.

When he finished there was a moment's silence before she said, 'So you're sitting on a boat in the middle of nowhere waiting for two killers to come and take the Magna Carta from you?' Sensing the concern she had for his safety despite the sarcastic overtones he quickly reassured her and then asked her to take Claudiu to temporary accommodation as the Moran brothers knew his home and work address in East Steading.

'James, why should I be concerned about them coming here unless you're planning to go back on your word?'

'I've got it covered, Jenny,' James soothed, using his most reassuring tone of voice with a smile she couldn't see. 'Just make sure you are both somewhere else later today. Can you also contact Miss Lightbody and tell her to be on the lookout for any strangers in the vicinity of her home and to leave the office right now and not to return until I give her the all clear.'

'God, you make me worry James, especially about you. Why can't you simply contact Chief Inspector Cheswell, put the document in his hands and then let him provide you with police protection until the bastards are safely behind bars?'

'Two reasons. Firstly, I don't know whom to trust and secondly, I made a promise to Miss Lightbody that I'd catch the murderer of her nephew.'

'You can do that by talking and trusting the right people and –'

'And right now I don't know who they are,' James interrupted and before it could develop into a serious argument he rapidly changed the subject. 'You said Claudiu had a swimming contest. How did he do?'

There was a moment of silence before Jennifer replied. 'He came third in his age group. I took him for a celebratory pizza and you're ignoring my point about calling Cheswell.' The chill in her voice could be felt and James felt grateful for the cellphone's sudden warning ringtone.

'I've someone holding, Jenny,' he said. 'I'll call you later today and let you know what's happened. Bye for now. Love you.' He switched to the incoming call without waiting for her reply.

'Welcome to Reedham, Mr Goodfellow.' The familiar voice had a gleeful tone that irritated James. 'I shall now give you your final instructions for the handover.'

'Where? When? And were you following me just now?' James snapped.

'Following? No we have always been well ahead of you every step of the way.'

'Then either you or I should start worrying.'

'What's meant by that?' the man asked, clearly rattled.

James was pleased that he had taken the wind out of the man's sails and replied rather smugly.

'Two men in a red speedboat and wearing dark suits were following me and are now moored fifty yards upstream from where I'm sitting. Friends of yours?'

'It's only your imagination, Mr Goodfellow, so listen very carefully. You will go to the Berney Arms windmill that is five kilometres from the Ship Inn. You cannot miss it as it's seven storeys high and the tallest drainage windmill in Norfolk. Once there you will moor on the north bank, walk to the mill where you will find the door unlocked. Enter and place the document in the leather bag you'll find leaning against the wall beneath a diagram of the building. You will then climb to the top level and wait until I phone to say you can leave.'

'When do you want me to make the drop?'

'Be there at five o'clock precisely.' A sudden click and James was left holding a dead line. He checked his watch and saw that he still had time for a bite to eat in the inn. He soon discovered that the steak-and-ale pie lived up to its reputation as being the best in Norfolk and after two coffees he was replete and ready for the next step.

The Empress rumbled into life and the craft continued its lazy journey on the slow-running river beneath clouds that seemed to have been taken from a Constable painting. After about thirty minutes James spotted the sails of the scheduled ancient monument and fifteen minutes later he was throttling back to pull alongside the low piling that stopped the bank from collapsing at high tides. Taking two steel rods he leapt onto the shore, hammered them into the spongy turf and moored the Empress fore and aft. As he climbed aboard to fetch the document a glint of light caught his eye and looking back up the river he caught a glimpse of the little red speedboat pulling into tall reeds on the south bank. James waited a moment but could detect no sign of life and with an uncomfortable feeling he went ashore.

The entrance to the tower mill, an English Heritage site, was twenty-paces from the river. and signs advertised that it was under the care of English Heritage. An elderly couple walking their greyhound on the footpath running parallel to the river and flood embankment passed him with a cheery hello and he waited until they were out of sight before descending to the mill. With extreme caution he pushed the door open and stepped inside.

Although there was little wind and the sails had been locked to prevent them from turning, the mill was still filled with the sound of creaking timbers. The leather bag was where it was meant to be and he carefully put the document in it and closed the top. He glanced around the ground floor but it was unoccupied, as were the other levels when he climbed the old wooden ladders. The distinctive aroma of mildew permeated the mill and little light penetrated the small grime-covered leaded windows. James was wheezing when he finally arrived on the top floor and stood amidst the complicated mass of wood and metal machination that turned the scoop wheel to move water from the fen to the river. The sound of wood bending, straining and stretching had become more pronounced and the air passing through the stationary sails created a low mournful whistle.

James went to one of the tiny windows and rubbed it vigorously with his hand to clear some of the filth. He was amazed at how far he could see across the fenland. Going to a window on the opposite side he looked down on the River Yare just in time to see the Empress slowly going past the Waveney junction and maintaining a steady course on the Yare. The Morans had taken the document, the cruiser and James for a ride. 'My God,' he said softly, 'they had no intention of driving down to Harwich and taking the car ferry. They've stolen the Empress to make a sea crossing from Great Yarmouth to Holland.'

He quickly climbed down and gasping for breath he emerged from the mill as a deafening red blur went past. The speedboat was on full throttle and was throwing up rooster-tail plumes that rose high into the air. A light wind swept the spray over the flood embankment to dampen James from head to toe.

So much for the speed limit, he thought as he climbed the wooden steps to the top of the flood barrier just in time to see the craft vanish round a bend in the river. He politely stepped back to allow a man in a soaked Macintosh hurry past. The man was towing a terrier that had been reduced to a pathetic jumble of wet fur and the comical sight briefly distracted James.

The sound of the fading speedboat abruptly ended as though the throttles had been jerked back and this refocused his attention to the bend in the river. There was a strange sound not unlike distant fireworks on bonfire night. As he watched, the Empress re-appeared to continue on down the Yare at the mandatory six miles per hour. James saw one figure at the wheel but was unable to identify him. I should have brought my binoculars, he thought as he began walking towards the Berney Arms to inquire about local taxi services.

He was about halfway along the towpath when two cars sped by on the rough access road to the inn, one seemingly chasing the other. As they drew level with him he could see only one occupant in the lead car; the second car passed before he had a chance to study it in detail but the tow occupants were dressed in a similar fashion to the men he had briefly seen in the speedboat.

'So, Raul creates a diversion and goes to Holland by sea whilst Juan disappears with the Magna Carta,' James murmured to himself. 'But *who* was the diversion for and who are the two men who had been shadowing me?' He idly noticed a mud-spattered Volvo slowly driving away on the same road and he caught a brief glimpse of a driver in a water-stained mackintosh. This would have meant nothing if the sudden appearance of a dog's head at the rear window hadn't immediately conjured a clear image of an oak-panelled office in Cambridge.

The dog barking silently behind the glass was the rare Dandie Dinmont terrier he had seen there and again minutes ago on the footpath by the mill. The driver was even more 'rare' for he was last seen boarding a plane to Morocco. James started running towards the small parking area and peered through the windows to find a vehicle that still had keys in the ignition.

Two burly fishermen, making the pints in their hands look like half measures, started walking towards the suspicious-looking character.

'Looking for summat, pal?' one inquired and James looked up to find himself confronted by two man-mountains wearing bright red and green waterproof waders. They stood before him like a pair of impassable traffic lights.

James couldn't go anywhere anyway because of the tingling sensation that had started in his calf muscles. How can that be, he thought before his legs buckled and he collapsed onto the cobbled courtyard. The two men looked down in surprise at the unconscious stranger and the taller of the two knelt down to feel James' pulse.

'Well, we didn't kill him, he's still alive,' he said. 'Do you think we should try a bit of mouth-to-mouth resuscitation?'

'I'm not kissing the bugger,' the other replied as he took a step back. 'We don't know what that mouth has been up to.'

'I agree. Let's get him inside where it's warmer and we'll ask Jeremy what to do.'

They picked the prone man up and carried him into the bar where all conversation immediately stopped.

'Where did your mate do his drinking, Eric, 'cos I ain't served him a drop 'ere and he ain't getting a drop from me,' the barman said leaning over the counter and looking down at James.

'He's not our mate,' the one wearing red wellies said. 'He's a stranger we caught lurking in the car park and when we asked him what he was up to he just dropped at our feet.'

'What do you think we should do?' his pal asked after taking a long swallow from his glass.

There was a groan from the floor and all three men looked down as James opened his eyes. His body rapidly resumed its normal functions as he struggled to his feet. James now accepted that excessive activity, such as climbing water mills and running to public houses were too much for Xyrem and he resolved to have his prescription changed for a stronger drug.

'I hope I didn't frighten you guys,' he said calmly as he brushed himself down with the palms of his hands.

'You did at first 'cos we thought you were trying to nick one of the motors out there.'

'I'm no thief!' James snapped. 'A friend I'm supposed to be meeting here didn't tell me what car he was arriving in and I was looking for clues.' He could see that he hadn't quite convinced them and chose a different approach. 'I'll go and see if he's in the other bar.' James casually walked between the two scowling mountains and went through to the saloon bar. Their looks of suspicion gave way to puzzlement when James made a big pretence of studying everyone in the room before asking the equally huge man behind the counter if he knew of a Professor Calder.

'You should have said something earlier 'cos you've just missed him,' the man called Jeremy said with an apologetic grimace. 'The gentleman had booked to stay for one night but left in a big hurry a few minutes ago, leaving a small case behind.'

'Oh darn, how disappointing,' James said. In a clear voice that carried to the two fishermen he added, 'However, I can return the case to him if you like as we will now have to meet tomorrow at his office.' They visibly relaxed and left the bar to resume collecting the empty fish crates that were stacked outside in the yard.

Having been relieved of all responsibility Jeremy nodded enthusiastically and asked James for his name and address and then gave him the telephone number of a local taxi service.

James received a complimentary beer, albeit only half a pint, while he made the call and had just put down his glass when a miserable-looking man entered the bar and loudly announced there was a 'cab for Mr Goodfellow'. James thanked Jeremy for his help and the drink, took possession of the leather overnight case and left the inn.

During the long drive back to the house in Wisbech James was subjected to a non-stop diatribe against Norwich for paying a ridiculous transfer fee of £27.25 million for a West Ham United striker. James nodded sympathetically in the appropriate pauses and gave a silent sigh of relief when they pulled up outside 27 Broad Street.

In the privacy of the living room James called Chief Inspector Cheswell and told him that Juan Moran was in possession of an English relic and was last seen driving towards Norwich. When the inspector questioned him about the relic James pleaded ignorance to what it actually was but suggested that it may be linked to the missing chest of silver coins.

'I'll alert the senior officers in Norwich,' he said.

'And in Cambridge.'

'Why Cambridge?'

'Because Calder has returned to England and it's a good bet that he could even now be on his way back to the university to collect the last of his property before disappearing again.'

'Thanks for the tip, Goodfellow. It sounds like you've been rather busy. Would you care to tell me what you've been doing?'

'Another time, Chief Inspector,' James said and hung up. He went to the bathroom and took two more Xyrem tablets before calling Jennifer on her smartphone.

'What's happening,' were her first words.

'All's well. I gave the damned document to the brothers and therefore the pressure should be off you and me and Miss Lightbody. You can take Claudiu home.

'Nice to know that, James, but you needn't have called as we never left. I'll not be frightened out of my own home by a couple of Peruvian terrorists.'

James felt a brief chill when he heard those words but couldn't help a feeling of intense pride in his wife. 'That was rather foolish, Jenny, and a very dangerous move on your part.'

'You forget that I'm a detective sergeant, James, and it wasn't too much of a risk as I had your father's old service revolver which I wouldn't hesitate to use on your foreign playmates.'

'Don't let Inspector Tilley know you said that. He has a thing about police officers using unregistered firearms.'

They both laughed but it was tinged with unease for they both knew that the case had now become an extremely deadly game.

12

BEFORE JAMES ENTERED the tower mill as instructed Juan Moran had preceded his brother over the embankment and after checking that the path was clear he used his picks on the door lock. It was a simple Yale and the door swung open within seconds. Raul entered the mill and placed the leather bag under the wall chart while Juan gave instructions to Goodfellow on his cellphone.

When they left Juan taped the tongue of the lock back and closed the door. Going round the watermill they sat on the ground with their backs against the black wall to wait for Goodfellow's arrival.

The sound of an approaching cruiser made Raul check his watch. It was two minutes to five and he guessed it was Goodfellow. They kept their eyes on the man in a raincoat who was walking his dog on the river path. He could clearly see the Morans and gave a surreptitious nod to indicate that James had entered the mill. Juan raised his hand briefly in acknowledgement and the brothers crept round until they were at the doorway. When they heard feet climbing the old steps Raul slipped inside and collected the bag, taking care not to make a noise.

The two brothers climbed the flood barrier and descended to the moored Empress. Raul released the ropes from the iron rods driven into the bank while Juan, seeing that the key was missing from the ignition, used his picks again with a dexterity born from practice in the slums of Lima. The engine roared into life and Raul leant across his brother and pushed the throttle forward with an impatient shake of his head. The cruiser had exceeded the speed limit by the time it went round the bend to where the river had widened into a lake dotted white with water birds and gulls.

Raul edged the cruiser towards the bank where they had parked their dark blue car on the rough surfaced road. They were both surprised to see another car parked behind theirs and Juan gave his brother a nervous look.

'Just a fisherman, I expect,' Raul presumed. 'I'll meet up with you at the usual place in two weeks' time, Juan.' The elder brother leapt from the boat clutching the leather bag and gave a small wave as he trotted to their car.

Raul was cruising out across the river when a throbbing sound suddenly grew louder and a red speedboat planed into sight and sped towards the bank where Juan was in the act of unlocking the car door. A .300 bullet smashed through the car door close to his leg and he leapt into the car and started the engine. Juan was accelerating away when the second bullet hit him.

The speedboat turned to pursue the much slower cruiser and the high-sounding report of the CZ 550 echoed across the water again. The Empress' instrument panel exploded and sent a shower of fibre-glass into the air. Raul ducked low and rammed the throttle forward. He reached across the cockpit to pick up the Turkish Huglu shotgun that he had placed on the gunwale in readiness for any unforeseen circumstance.

The kick against his shoulder was like the sudden embrace of an old friend and he fired the second chamber to better effect. The speedboat's clear Plexiglas windshield shattered and one of the figures jerked back clutching at the superficial cuts in his cheek. The speedboat veered away and slowed to a halt before the engine screamed again and raced to the spot on the riverbank where the mysterious car was parked. Raul punched the air and gave a shout of victory before realizing that the two men were now hurrying to what had obviously been their car parked behind Juan's. The strangers' aim was very clear, they intended to chase and catch his brother.

'Faster Juan, make sure you outrun the bastards,' he muttered as he replaced the shells in the shotgun and stood it close by his seat. He was completely ignorant of the fact that the second bullet, distorted by its passage through the passenger door, had crudely torn through Juan's cheek, shattering teeth and jawbone before exiting messily through the other cheek and out through the window.

Juan's mouth was filling with blood as agonizing pain shot through his skull yet he was able to maintain control of the car on the rutted dirt road and he kept his foot down. Glancing into the driver's mirror he nearly choked at the ghastly sight that stared back.

The nearest hospital was in Yarmouth, and he was still three miles from the first tarred road and then it would be another ten miles before he would receive any medical aid. Juan knew it was tantamount to giving himself up to the police but it was preferable to falling into the hands of the men he knew were close behind. He knew who they were and that they would be catching up fast.

He was relieved when he was able to pause briefly beside the parked sedan and throw the bag through the open window before accelerating away. Calder had been visibly shocked by Juan's appearance but nevertheless he waited until Juan had driven off before forcing himself to drive on at a deliberately steady pace.

The wounded man, his eyes fixed on the road surface ahead, didn't see the black limousine race past Calder with horns blaring and compelling him to pull over. The senderista only knew it was there when he heard strange popping sounds over the noise of his engine.

Deadly 9mm rounds began hitting the car and Juan was mortally hit, despite hunching down. One bullet drilled a neat hole in the rear window and the side of his neck. He flopped forward onto the steering wheel and the car swerved off the track and careered across a newly tilled field before stalling and coming to a stop.

Ricardo braked and the two agents ran with weapons at the ready. When they reached the car they were astounded to see how much damage they had inflicted on the Shining Path terrorist. Juan moaned as blood spurted from his neck and Ricardo stepped back, astonished that the man was still alive.

'We should put him out of his misery,' Zamaras muttered as he placed the muzzle of his automatic against the dying man's temple and pulled the trigger.

Juan flopped sideways and the agents had just reholstered their Glocks as an old Volvo drove past, startling them both. Ricardo raised an eyebrow and looked questioningly at his colleague.

'I don't think the driver could have seen us shooting as he was too far behind. Besides, he couldn't have seen our faces at that distance,' Zamaras said. 'To make sure we'll get rid of the car in the next public car park.'

They drove off without a single backward glance at Juan's car and its grisly contents.

Two whole days had passed before three teenagers cycling on the same stretch of road saw the car in the field. They were tempted to see what they could recover in terms of CD players and satnav equipment but when they reached the vehicle they got nothing except recurring nightmarish images of the dead man's staring eyes.

'Juan didn't have anything with him at all,' Ricardo mused as he drove. 'Why do you think he and Raul went to that watermill?'

'It must have been a drop. They went to give or pick up something that had to be kept secret and therefore was of great importance.'

'Or value, knowing those two. I think Raul is the one who has whatever they recovered,' Ricardo added.

'Do you think Raul will head straight for Amsterdam?'

Ricardo thought about it for the next kilometre before answering. 'I have a feeling he will want to be somewhere safe until he makes his next move. He knows the police are looking for him here and he can't stay still for any period of time in Europe before he is picked up so I think he'll head back to the rat hole he came from.'

'But the Moroccan police have him on their books as well and are looking for him,' Zamaras protested.

'I doubt that. It has been far too long. Anyway, the latest Islamist attacks in Tunisia combined with their search for jihadist sympathizers will be keeping them very busy. He'll not be spotted at the passport check, not unlike our security scanning in Lima. I think our best bet will be to check out that place in Marrakech where he had stayed last.'

'That was a hotel and you can be sure the manager will report him to the authorities the moment he shows his face after what Raul did to the reputation of his business.'

'Not there, but where his brother was staying. That scruffy nondescript riad that's tucked away in the old Medinah.'

'A perfect hole for rats,' Zamaras growled.

Ricardo grinned and dialled an unlisted number to get their controller's permission and funds to travel to Morocco as official rat-catchers.

Calder was jubilant. He now possessed the hoard of silver coins as well as the precious copy of the Magna Carta, each providing sufficient provenance for the other. When he learnt about the existence of the document he had intended to recover it and bask in the academic kudos that would undoubtedly have followed. However, recent events had rendered the priceless piece of English history worthless for he would never be able to show or sell it without becoming involved in a police enquiry. I'll have to dispose of it privately and preferably not in England or any other country with an extradition treaty, he suddenly decided.

As he took the ring road to avoid the centre of Norwich he thought of all the possible options until one clearly stood head and shoulders above the rest. Calder slapped his forehead. 'Marrakech!' he said aloud and grinned. 'I can target the right buyers who ask no questions by using the Internet there and nobody can touch me.'

Keeping an eye on his mirror for any police pursuit Calder took the main A11 road and soon arrived in a village called Six Mile Bottom where he rented a small cottage in one of the private lanes for secret liaisons with his female students. He also used the unusually dry cellar for storing a number of small archaeological artefacts he had taken from digs he had been on. There were even some from the university archives that he had appropriated over many years; he thought of these as his emergency pension as the total value when sold to private collectors would exceed one hundred thousand pounds.

The small chest of King John coins could also be hidden there to be retrieved before the authorities uncovered any paper trails or put pressure on one of the many dissolute youngsters he had 'entertained'. If the illicit love nest was disclosed a quick search would uncover more than his passion for carnal affairs. 'A more thorough search would uncover my greatest secret of all,' he muttered grimly.

After James had hung up he thought about his next step with a certain amount of nervousness for Agnes Lightbody would severely chastise him for raiding the petty cash without her permission. She would veto any expenditure that had no chance of being recouped and he knew that flying to Morocco offered no guarantees whatsoever. However, he stood no chance of retrieving the Magna Carta by looking for the Moran brothers in England – there was a very good chance that they had left the country already.

The three-hour drive to London Heathrow was long and tedious and James was drained. It was only as he was buying a ticket for an Air Maroc flight that he called Jenny and told her where he was going. He grimaced as she gave him an earful. James gave a wan smile and the ticket clerk grinned as she handed him the paperwork. He had an hour to waste before checking in and he spent a good deal of this time explaining to his irate wife, who was suddenly a very officious policewoman, his reasons for leaving the country. Knowing how stubborn her husband could be, Jenny became the caring wife instead and chastised him for not changing his prescription before firmly instructing him to take enough Xyrem tablets and to take no risks whatsoever.

'I'd rather see that bloody piece of vellum burnt to ashes than have you harmed by those ruthless terrorists,' were her parting words and James' cheeks warmed and turned pink with guilt. He knew he was taking a terrible risk in confronting the Peruvians. What he didn't know was that one of the brothers had been killed and that Professor Calder now had both the document and the coins and was heading for the same North African destination.

The flight was called and James boarded with little idea how he was going to trace the Morans. Marrakech was a large city and he had scant knowledge about the language or culture of the Moroccans. Apart from the hotel where Raul stayed and Juan's hideout in the old Medinah, he had little to go on. Jenny had acquired these addresses when she was sourcing the professor's background.

The Moroccan police may have stumbled upon a link between Raul's business in stolen electronics at the hotel and Juan's presence in the souk but because Professor Calder was the legal owner of the riad the authorities were unable to confiscate it and hadn't bothered to put any surveillance on the address. James was now gambling that Juan and his brother would return to where they had felt the safest after fleeing from Peru.

Ricardo abandoned the car in a Norwich car park after wiping every surface he and his colleague could possibly have touched. With a small torch he inspected the seating, headrests and floor mats for any loose hairs before locking the doors and dropping the keys down a drain. While he had been wiping and dusting the vehicle Zamaras had recovered their bags from the cheap lodging where they had been staying. They met up, as agreed, at the mainline station.

The agents stood waiting on the concourse until Ricardo received the green light from their senior officer, Colonel Diego Rosales, who was based at the embassy in London as one of the cultural attachés. The gravitas in his voice when talking to Ricardo emphasized the importance of apprehending Raul.

'With the money he'll raise from those stolen items he'll become a bloody awful headache in Peru,' was the Colonel's closing comment before slamming the phone down.

Zamaras bought through tickets to Heathrow and they boarded the first Intercity train to Liverpool Street Station and took the London underground to Paddington for the Heathrow Express.

A consular secretary was already on the phone booking two business-class tickets that would be waiting at the Royal Maroc information desk whilst Colonel Rosales phoned three oridinary-looking 'businessmen' with instructions to look for Raul at any airline check-in desk that had flights to Lima and Marrakech. Like Ricardo and Zamara these men were members of the elite Grupo Especial de Inteligencia and because the foreign office disapproved of foreign embassy employees carrying arms they were trained in deadly hand-to-hand combat.

Each of the three men were very familiar with Raul's appearance and they spread out to sweep the departure hall making sure to cover all five airline check-in points. They continued searching for five hours until all the scheduled flights for the day had left and then reported back to the colonel.

They were unaware that Raul had instead gone by boat, crossing the North Sea to Zandfoort in the Netherlands. Once there he ran the cruiser ashore near a well-known beachfront restaurant and simply walked away to the amazement of a few people exercising their dogs and early staff members who had just arrived to raise the shutters.

Amsterdam Schiphol Airport was only twenty-five kilometres distant and Raul hitched a ride in a baker's van. Within forty minutes he was buying his ticket to the pre-arranged rendezvous and used his forged British passport to board the Air Maroc flight to Marrakech. As it took off he sank into the soft calfskin of the first-class seat and sipped from the champagne flute, not knowing that his nemesis, the GEIN agents, were making a similar journey.

Raul's progression through immigration, security and customs at Menara airport went without incident. The retouched passport photo was only marginally different so that it tallied with official records and also raised no suspicion from the immigration officer.

'Eduardo Wilson?' he asked holding the rubber stamp ready to deface a whole blank page.

'My mother married an English diplomat.' The lie had been well rehearsed and *thump* the stamp came down and the passport was returned.

'Have a nice vacation.'

'Thank you.' Without any bags to retrieve Raul bypassed the baggage carousel and sauntered through customs at a casual pace until, with a slight sigh of relief, he was able to blend into the bedlam of the main hall. Dodging taxi touts who tended to accost every tourist emerging through the automatic doors he hurried across the service road. The early morning warmth already shrouding the city closed in on him as he went straight to one of the white, air-conditioned limo taxis. The driver of the more expensive form of transport nodded his head when Raul barked the address. He looked forward to being reunited with his brother but he had one stop to make before going to the dilapidated riad in the old medinah.

With a tap on the driver's shoulder Raul stopped the car fifty metres from the entrance to a pink-coloured building. Ten Palms Hotel was definitely not a salubrious venue despite being on a scenic street lined with heavily scented orange trees. It's clientele came primarily from the poorer end of the market.

Raul asked the driver to wait and stepped into the dark foyer. He was reluctant to remove his dark glasses in case someone recognized him and he waited for a few seconds until his eyes had adjusted to the gloom. He was familiar with the ground floor configuration and a quick glance towards the tiny reception desk showed that it was untended. The foyer was deserted and Raul quickly went up the stairs until he had reached third floor and a door with the plastic numbers 302 glued to the grimy surface above a cheap spyhole.

There was no immediate answer when he rapped on the door and he was just about to use his knuckles again when the door was suddenly jerked open and he was confronted by a man of medium build wearing a dazzlingly white thobe.

'*Shoo esmak?*' was all he managed to say before a lightning-fast fist crushed his larynx. The hotel guest fell back from the force of the strike and as he writhed on the carpet with gurgling sounds issuing from his crushed windpipe Raul swiftly stepped into the room, closed the door and ran into the bedroom. A Berber woman who lay on the bed sat up in surprise, clutching the sheet to hide her nakedness. Raul crossed the room and struck the same blow. As she fell back clutching at her neck he gripped her forehead and crushed her skull against the headboard. Raul went to finish the man who had fallen silent but found he was already dead, asphyxiated.

Raul hastily pulled the carpet in the corner of the room to one side and removed three short pieces of floorboard he had previously fashioned so he could retrieve the contents: two 9mm Steyr semi-automatics with a box of ammunition, a block of Semtex-H with appropriate detonators plus two double-edged combat knives. There was also a small folding sports bag containing a thick roll of US dollars into which he packed the weapons and after a quick glance down the hallway he went down the stairs.

The limo driver was still waiting for him and he gave an address close to the ramparts of red sandstone that circled the old town for twelve miles. In a dark, narrow lane in a poor district close to the wall Raul asked the driver to stop the car. As soon as the vehicle rolled to a stop he cut the man's throat with one of the combat knives and entered the medinah on foot to meander like a tourist in the maze-like warren of heavily crowded streets.

He kept to a leisurely pace to avoid drawing attention to himself and merged with a group of tourists whose shopping bags overflowed with perfumes, sandals and assorted ceramics. Craftsmen carrying cured leather hides for shoemaking, sheet metal for turning into Berber souvenirs and boxes of sweet-smelling oranges completed the orderly confusion of the medinah and was the perfect cover for a man who had just slaughtered three people.

Raul paused to watch a sandal maker at work while the group moved on. When they were lost to sight in the crowd he turned down an alleyway that was even narrower than the one the tourists were following until he reached his destination.

The riad had only a few windows on the outside and they were all latticed. Raul pulled the wrought-iron lever next to the sun-bleached door hung with decorative iron hinges and the sound reverberated within the building. He turned his back on three curious children who had come out of the shop-front behind him. Footsteps sounded in the riad followed by the metallic sound of bolts being drawn. The person who opened the door stared curiously at the Peruvian.

'You must be Raul,' Professor Calder said genially. 'Although you are albino you resemble your brother.'

Raul was stunned for he had expected his brother to greet him when the door opened.

'Do come in old chap before the whole medinah and the Moroccan police force know you're back in Marrakech.' Calder waved him in and the *senderista* followed him down the passage to the central courtyard. Calder threw himself down on a cane daybed and picked up a condensation-streaked glass of gin. The splashing of water in a small fountain was the only sound in the silence that had fallen.

'Where's Juan?' Raul managed to say as he slowly sat on one of the cane seats facing Calder.

'How the hell would I know? I'm not your brother's keeper.'

'He should have been here long before me.'

'With the document?'

'Yes.' Raul was looking a little bewildered.

'And all those lovely silver coins,' Calder added as he looked at the Peruvian over his glass and studied the bewilderment that fleetingly flickered across his face. 'Do you think he's kept it all for himself?'

Raul cursed the professor in his own Quechuan language and made a dismissive gesture. 'Juan wouldn't do that; he is dedicated to our cause and it is our intention to free General Abimael Guzmán and Oscar Ramirez Durand from Lurigancho Prison as soon as the sale of the coins and that damned document is completed.'

'But first you need Juan to do that,' Calder smirked and took another sip before ringing the tiny silver bell that stood on the coffee table. Instantly, as though she had been waiting behind the bead curtain, a young woman in a pale blue chiffon creation entered the courtyard and knelt subserviently before the professor who pointed at Raul. 'We have a guest, Asmae, bring some light refreshments and a new bottle of gin.'

'And pisco,' Raul added. 'I happen to know that Juan kept a stock of our national spirit here.'

'Of course, my friend,' Calder said as he dismissed at the *sharmuta* with a wave of his hand.

'You have more like her in the house?'

An evil glint appeared in Calder's cold blue eyes and then he grinned. 'There are four to cook, clean and keep me company when I have the need.'

'You must have plenty of money to afford so many whores like her?' Raul grunted, a harsh edge betraying his suspicions.

'I emptied my savings account and cashed my investments when I left Cambridge. I have enough to keep me comfortable for the rest of my days,' Calder said in an even voice as he watched the senderista with an unblinking stare. 'Incidentally, that woman you called a whore is my private researcher.'

Raul ignored the caustic remark. 'What happened after those men started shooting at the boat?' he demanded to know. 'I saw very little after Juan got ashore because I had troubles of my own to contend with before I could take the cruiser downriver.'

'Nothing. Juan managed to escape in the car and I stayed and watched to see if anyone followed.'

'And did anyone?'

'No.' Calder omitted to mention that Juan's car was in the middle of a freshly ploughed field and that two men had gunned him to death. He was about to elaborate on his story when the girl returned carrying a silver tray. Both men watched her in silence as she placed it on the small table between them and poured the drinks. She looked knowingly at Calder who fondled her in a familiar manner, then she smiled brazenly at Raul and left without saying a word.

Calder offered a plate of sweet pastries but Raul shook his head and sipped the chilled pisco. Memories of the street bar in Lima where he and Juan planned their futures together were brought back vividly by the sharp bite of the spirit.

'What are your plans now?' Calder asked.

'Wait for my brother, sell everything and then return to my homeland to begin a just revolution.'

'And where the hell do you think you'll sell a priceless document that was written in the twelfth century and is an irreplaceable part of English history?' He paused before saying, 'Perhaps to one of the snake charmers in the Jemaa El Fna market?'

Raul didn't fail to spot the sarcasm and he slammed the lead crystal glass down on the inlaid table, spilling half the contents. 'I'm not a fool, Calder.' He leant forward and fixed the professor with a cold look. 'I'll use the internet to invite offers from all the leading universities and museums in the world.'

'For God's sake, why advertise what you have and where you are when I have private collectors who insist on total secrecy and are willing to pay up to four million sterling?'

'But you don't have the old document.'

'I forgot to mention that Juan had a suspicion that he was being shadowed and when I caught up with him he gave it to me before driving off.'

'Where did this happen?

'King's Lynn.'

'And then you brought it here, to Marrakech?'

'It's here and my buyer will be arriving at the Hotel Sofitel with an expert authenticator and a banker's draft tomorrow morning.'

'And where is Juan?'

Calder finished his drink and calmly told the Peruvian that he didn't know as they had gone in different directions. He had hardly finished talking when he found himself looking down the barrel of a Steyr semi-automatic.

'Did you kill Juan?' Raul demanded and the coldness in his voice warned Calder that he was within seconds of his own death.

'No. The last time I spoke to him he was healthy and said he would be catching a flight to Morocco the following day.' The barrel was unwavering and Calder began to sweat despite the air-conditioners and fountain that kept the courtyard pleasantly cool. 'He told me to bring the document to Marrakech, to this riad, where he would be waiting and I'm still waiting.'

'Did he give you the silver as well?'

'No. He said he had a foolproof way of shipping such a vast number of metal coins out of the country without being detected.' Calder picked his glass up before remembering he had emptied it. 'I couldn't have brought them with me on the plane as they would have been detected immediately,' he added.

The semi-automatic was lowered and Raul put the weapon back in the sports bag on his lap. 'You'd better be telling me the truth or I'll use it next time. Now tell me about this buyer you've found for my Magna Carta.'

Calder jerked upright to protest and then sank back when he saw that Raul still had his hand inside the bag. He knew the man wouldn't hesitate to kill him and he undoubtedly would the moment the banker's draft was in his hand.

13

THE AGENTS FAILED TO spot Raul but one standing close to the Air Maroc check-in desk recognized James as he was walking away towards passport control. The agent revealed his identity to the ticket clerk and asked for the time of James' flight and his seat number. He alerted the controller who passed the information on to Ricardo and Zamaras.

'Goodfellow will be in Economy so we'll wait until everyone has boarded and the curtains have been drawn between the cabins before we enter the plane,' Zamaras said as they went up the escalator and into the terminal building.

'Do we follow him when we get to Marrakech?'

Zamaras nodded. 'It's clear he knows something we don't and I want to keep as near to him as possible until we have learnt everything.'

'Such as?'

'Why did Raul Moran choose Morocco when we know he wants to stir up trouble in Peru. Is it being used simply as a safe bolt-hole or for a more sinister reason?'

It was Ricardo's turn to nod. 'Good point, and I'd also like to know why Goodfellow is going to such lengths to catch him. What Raul does in Peru can't be of any importance to him and it can't be to seek revenge for the killing of his secretary's cousin. He could have told the police where Raul was and they would have picked him up before he had taken two steps beyond passport control.'

'Not if he didn't have any hard evidence against him.'

The agent on surveillance duty was waiting by the check-in desk as they approached with passports in hand and Ricardo briefly told him to inform the team to keep a sharp lookout for Raul Moran. The agent used his throat mike while his superior officers collected their boarding passes.

Two espressos and an almond croissant later they passed through security and walked briskly to the departure gate. The two men quickly surveyed the remaining few passengers having their boarding passes checked but were unable to see James Goodfellow.

'He's on board,' Zamaras muttered unnecessarily.

Ricardo grunted and then smiled at the flight attendant as she returned his passport with the boarding pass tucked inside. As soon as they were seated in business class Zamaras nudged Ricardo with his elbow and indicated with a slight inclination of his head the familiar person sitting only three rows ahead of them.

James had been pleasantly surprised to find that he had been upgraded to the front of the aircraft in order to balance the passenger load on the under-booked flight. He was the first passenger in Business class and when the flight attendant started talking to some new arrivals he glanced over his shoulder to see two men in dark suits being seated. They both wore dark glasses yet James was sure he had seen one of them before.

Ricardo noticed the man turning to look at them and he tapped Zamaras on the knee and put a finger to his lips.

'He's seen us,' he whispered in his colleague's ear. 'I don't think he recognized us but just in case let's keep anything we have to say down to a whisper.'

'I don't think you need to do that, gentlemen,' a voice said and Ricardo looked up and saw James standing right beside his seat. He lowered himself into the empty seat across the aisle. 'Do excuse me, but could you satisfy my curiosity about something?'

'How can we help, sir?'

'Weren't you the fellows I saw exceeding the speed limit on the river Waveney yesterday, and again later when you were driving a car in the very same part of the county?'

There was a long silence during which the trio was asked by the pretty Moroccan flight attendant to buckle their seatbelts in preparation for take-off.

'I think you must have mistaken us for someone else,' Zamaras said apologetically as he leant across his partner to make himself heard above the rising engines. 'We're returning from a three-day conference on brush sand-barriers as a solution to desertification in Saharan regions.'

James wasn't convinced by Zamaras' story and without saying a word kept looking into the agent's face in an effort to place him at the scene or get him to say something that would jog his memory.

'We've never used a boat on the River Waveney or the River Yare or driven a car in Norfolk, sir,' Ricardo said confidently and smiled broadly – an expression he normally reserved to charm attractive women.

'And yet you knew the Waveney was in Norfolk and that it joined the River Yare.'

'I think there must be many people who know that,' Zamaras said with irritation creeping into his voice.

'Local people, yes, foreign conservation engineers, no.'

The last word was like a starting gun for the taxiing aircraft had reached take-off speed and was leaving the ground, thrusting them back into their seats as it climbed steeply with the tarmac falling away at an alarming rate.

They had reached an impasse and remained silent for the rest of the flight apart from responding to the flight attendant's questions regarding refreshments and meal choice.

The flight was thirty minutes ahead of schedule and was being held in a holding pattern until it could be cleared to land at Menara Airport. James looked down on the snow-capped peaks of the Atlas Mountains as they passed over Jebel Toubkal, the highest mountain at 4,167 metres, and marvelled at the almond tree blossoms that seemed to flow down the lower valleys like rivers of white foam.

As the plane banked again lush farmland came into view and the green fertile plains stretched as far as the eye could see. The two strangers across the aisle appeared oblivious to the wonder unfolding beneath them and James turned to draw their attention but stopped when he saw the front page of a broadsheet paper being read by the man closest to him. *Peruvian Shot in Norfolk* read the main headline and James went cold when he saw the subheading: *South American Terrorist Found Dead in Potato Field*. It could be the man who tried to kill me, James thought. The paper was suddenly folded and he found himself looking into the stranger's blank expression.

'Would you like the paper?' Ricardo asked in a polite tone of voice as he glanced down at the headline.

James hesitated before answering, 'Yes, thank you very much.' He took the proffered paper and made a pretence of opening and reading the inside pages. The story was more detailed on page three and he was convinced that it had to be one of the Moran brothers, which raised two questions. Which brother had been killed and who were the two men sitting across the aisle?

He lowered the paper and looked at Ricardo's handsome Latin profile. 'Why are you following me?' he said boldly.

The blunt question took Ricardo by surprise. 'What gave you the impression that we're following you, sir?' he stuttered.

'I know it was you in the red speedboat.'

There was a long silence that was broken by the sudden whining of the landing gear being lowered. 'We are special agents of the Peruvian anti-terrorist agency and we have been given the task of taking the Moran brothers back to Lima to face charges of killing police officers.'

'Moran brother,' James said quietly.

'I beg your pardon?' Ricardo asked as a puzzled expression crossed his face.

'You assassinated one of the brothers in Norfolk and now you wish to do the same to the other one.'

Ricardo ignored the accusation. 'And why are *you* following Raul?'

He now knew that it was Juan who had died in Norfolk but he still wasn't prepared to reveal his true reason for being on the plane; however he had to say something. 'I believe he callously murdered someone close to me and I plan to take him back to England to face charges. So, it looks like we have similar reasons for wanting to capture and transport Mr Moran, albeit to opposite sides of the planet.' His glib answer seemed to satisfy the two agents and when he felt the sudden numbness in his feet he fumbled in his pocket for one of his tablets.

James turned his head away when an unconvinced Ricardo asked him how he planned to capture Raul and spirit him back to the Old Bailey and true justice. He swallowed the little pill as the paralysis began spreading up his legs and his eyelids became extremely heavy.

The King's Charter

Ricardo asked again but the way the Englishman had slumped back into his seat indicated that he had fallen asleep.

'Looks like the fool has nodded off,' he said to Zamaras in Spanish. 'Nevertheless, we'll follow him and see where it leads.'

His partner nodded as the seat-belt sign lit up and the plane began its rapid descent towards the runway.

The sudden thump of rubber on tar was sufficient to wake James and as the tingling effect in his limbs faded he sat upright and looked askance at the Peruvians to see whether they had noticed the incident. They were deep in conversation that he was unable to follow and he looked out of the window to see the Menara terminal swing into view.

Clearance through the passport and customs checks was trouble free and James soon emerged into the stifling humidity of Marrakech. He checked the address on a scrap of paper he had fished from a pocket and showed it to the taxi driver. The old Berber shrugged and waved his hand at the paper, a clear sign he couldn't understand what was written on it.

'Ma ke nifhimsh,' I don't understand, he said impatiently.

James carefully pronounced the hotel name a number of different ways until the man's dark eyes opened wide and he thumbed the OK sign. James had a fleeting glimpse of a grin in the rear-view mirror before he was thrown back against the seat as the taxi accelerated away.

The skill of his driver became apparent the closer they came to the city perimeter. Streams of suicidal students, traders and office workers on scooters were forced to give way as he sped undeterred towards the old medina in the muddling stream of traffic. They followed the nineteen-foot high red mud wall that surrounded the old city for two miles before eventually turning into a narrow street that headed into a poorer district of Marrakech where the buildings showed considerable neglect.

Constantly checking behind him James soon realized a taxi that had also been ranking at the airport was now tailing them. He had noticed the registration number at the time as it contained Jenny's birthday. Without even seeing the passengers he was ready to bet that they were the Peruvians from the plane and, without doubt, they were using him to find Raul.

Suddenly the taxi jolted to a halt and a muffled curse came from the driver who was pointing ahead. Two police cars with flashing light bars were blocking the road and traffic was being directed to turn right or go back the way they came. The driver briefly shrugged and raised his palms before beginning to turn down a side street and James had a brief glimpse of his destination.

The Ten Palms Hotel was only a few metres past the roadblock and James tapped the driver on his shoulder to stop the car. Like most Englishmen on holiday he spoke slowly and a little louder than usual. 'Please wait, I will only be five minutes,' he said as he held up five spread fingers and then tapped the face of his watch.

Ever since his cousin had been mistaken for a thief and shot by an off-duty officer the taxi driver had been nervous of anybody in uniform. He watched James walk back to the corner of the road but the moment his fare turned out of sight he put the car in gear and drove away without a single thought for the safety of the foreigner he had left stranded in an unknown part of the city.

James shouldered his way through the small knot of 'neighbours' who had gathered to argue noisily about what may or may not have happened and started walking along a rough footpath on the opposite side of the road. Three heavily armed officers were standing guard on the hotel steps and as he passed he could see another group inside the lobby. He was now approaching the second roadblock and a heavy-set officer blocked his way with a vicious-looking weapon slung around his neck. *'Jawaaz safar!'* he barked but James was unable to understand.

'Jawaaz safar!' Passport, the officer repeated.

'I don't understand,' James said spreading his hands and the officer placed a hand on the butt of his weapon, clearly losing his patience.

'Papier!' he shouted in French. This time James understood and immediately reached inside his jacket for the little blue book. In one fluid motion the officer unslung the sub-machine gun and with a finger on the trigger put the muzzle against James' chest.

'Papier,' James said calmly as he slowly withdrew the passport. The edgy policeman snatched the document and with the weapon still trained on James he flicked through the pages, pausing briefly at the entry stamp before lowering his gun and handing the passport back.

'You go now,' he ordered as he pointed down the road and away from the hotel. 'You go, nothing see here.'

James nodded and walked slowly away but not before he noticed the two Peruvians standing behind a group of locals who were still arguing. The two men were both staring in his direction but were unable to follow without running the risk of being interviewed by the same very nervous police officer. Finding Raul in the Ten Palms Hotel was now out of the question; something had obviously happened there to justify a formidable police presence.

Small children trotted beside him and he was soon lost in the concentration of small dusty streets. The sun was now much higher and he slipped his jacket off and carried it over his arm while keeping an eye open for anything resembling a taxi.

A beige municipal petit taxi was standing outside a small grocery shop that was selling everything from lavatory seats to washing powder. Barrows heaped high with fresh oranges lined the entrance and James breathed in the strong scent and stepped inside. He waited briefly for his eyes to become used to the deep gloom and soon identified a coffee shop at the rear of the establishment. Two men seated on rickety tubular steel chairs at an oilcloth-covered table were alternating between sucking on shisha water pipes and sipping from tiny cups of jet-black liquid. James ignored the older of the two who wore a traditional Berber robe and made straight for his companion dressed in a rakish western suit. His chair was tipped back in a rather precarious, nonchalant manner and he was undoubtedly the driver of the taxi parked outside.

The young man looked up with one well-trimmed eyebrow raised as he studied the stranger's face and then his clothes. 'Do you speak English,' James asked politely. The man nodded but said nothing.

'Can you take me to an address in the medinah?'

A well-manicured hand was raised with thumb and forefinger rubbing together.

'I'll pay you ten US dollars to take me to Place Jemaa El Fna.' James said in answer to the gesture.

'I cannot drive into the square but I can take you as far as Place Foucault which is one hundred metres from the main square.' His English was perfect with only a hint of an Arabic accent. Seeing the surprise on James' face he explained that he had attended the London School of

Economics thanks to his father's generosity. At this point the old man, who had been stroking his long beard while listening to his son, spoke. 'I myself have a science degree but choose to live here to help my own people.'

'My father teaches at the school nearby,' the young man added as he stood up. 'My name is Jamal and ten dollars is far too much. I'll only accept five,' he said and then led the way out into the brilliant sunlight.

The modest limousine boasted air-conditioning and the two men rode in relative comfort and silence for most of the journey until James said, 'If I wished to hire you for the duration of my time in Marrakech how much would you charge me?'

'Thirty US dollars would put me on standby for a twelve-hour day and fifty would give you a twenty-four-hour service. You would only need to call this number,' Jamal said as he passed a business card over his shoulder. 'You have a mobile phone?'

'Thank you, Jamal, I do.' James leant forward and dropped a crisp banknote onto the passenger seat. The young man glanced down and then took the money.

'What is your name,' he asked as he tucked the note into his breast pocket.

James leaned forward and tucked his business card into the same pocket. 'Now you have it, habibi.' He sensed the young man was smiling and found it infectious. They drove through the Bab Er Rob gate and entered the medina. 'I should warn you that I am looking for a dangerous man who has killed at least two people and the last thing I want is for you to be added to his tally.'

'You need not concern yourself, sir,' Jamal said looking at James in the rear-view mirror as he slowed to a standstill in the Place Foucault. 'I did my military service and can take care of myself.' He removed James' card from his pocket and read it. 'You are a private detective?'

'Investigator.'

'Are you armed?'

'Only a small number of police are armed in Britain which, having lived there for a few years, you undoubtedly know.'

Jamal winked and then opened the glove compartment and took out a bundle of cheesecloth. 'If the man is as dangerous as you say he is and he's hiding in the old souk you may need this.'

James slowly unwrapped the bundle to reveal a 9mm Beretta with a spare magazine. 'Thank you Jamal but I cannot take this. I've always tried to solve things without resorting to firearms.'

'You're entering a very dangerous environment and if the man you seek has friends in the souk then they are either thieves or killers hiding out there. They're the sort who, for a few dirhams, would rather cut your throat than look at you.'

'Your knowledge of colloquial English is very good, Jamal.'

'That's all due to my misspent youth watching American gangster movies. Now put the weapon in your pocket before someone looks into my taxi and sees it.' Jamal gave a broad grin. 'And put my number on your speed-dial before we get out.'

When James refused to take the weapon Jamal shrugged and put it inside his jacket before getting out of the car. James looked at him over the roof of the car with one eyebrow cocked.

'Do you have the exact address?' Jamal asked.

'Yes.'

'Do you know how to get there?'

'Not yet, but I can ask people.'

'That's not good. You may ask the wrong type of person and as I know the souk intimately it is better that I go with you and show you the quickest way.'

The determined look on the handsome face told him it would be a waste of time to argue and he handed him the slip of paper. Jamal glanced at it, nodded and then started walking purposefully. 'Follow me.'

They strode together down the avenue to the expansive central plaza of Jemaa El Fna where they dodged snake charmers' touts, orange juice and tea vendors and row after row of fruit and vegetable stalls, repeatedly having to say *la shukran*, no thankyou, to the harassing souk guides.

Entering the narrow alleys of the souk the number of traders wanting to sell something seemed to increase but following Jamal made progress easy. They turned left, right and then right again until he was completely disorientated and had to place all his trust in the young taxi driver. After ten minutes they paused outside a ceramic shop where the potter was using an ancient kick wheel to throw very delicate pots. The regular slap of his bare foot on the wooden rim was soothing and despite what might lie ahead James started to feel the rhythmic pulse of the city and he began to relax.

'We are getting very close to the address you gave me so we must go very carefully,' Jamal said as he pointed to the entrance of a very narrow alley. 'Does the man you are looking for know what you look like?'

'Yes, on those times he saw me he was trying to kill me.'

Surprise crossed Jamal's face. 'Then staying behind me will reduce the chances of him spotting you too soon.' He slipped a hand inside his jacket and, holding it there, turned into the gloomy alley. At first, James stayed close behind and was unable to see the building they were approaching very clearly, but then he stepped forward and took the lead.

"I cannot allow you to take any more risks,' he said as he used the brass pull beside the crude iron-decorated door. There was a faint jangling of bells inside the building followed by the approaching slip-slap of sandals on stone. James held his breath unable to think of his response if confronted by Raul himself. They heard a chain rattle and a key turn before the door opened a fraction and James could see a young woman in a dark blue burkha peering out. Her eyes were carefully made up with black kohl, pale blue shadowing and expensive lash extensions. Her dark eyes grew big with curiosity when she saw the two handsome men standing outside.

'Can I help you, sirs?' she asked in English. Her low, sensuous voice reminded James of chocolate slowly melting on the tongue.

'Is your master at home,' James asked, mistakenly assuming she was an expensive *sharmuta*, prostitute.

'Who would that person be, sir.' Once again the sound of her voice fascinated both men.

'Monsieur Raul Moran.'

'Who should I say is calling?'

'James Goodfellow.'

The eyes blinked twice and the door was opened wide to let them in. After closing the door she led them into a cool courtyard that was open to the sky and filled with exotic plants of complex leaf patterns and colour.

The woman pointed to the cane furniture. 'Please wait here while I announce you.' She floated out of the room through the bead curtain, the hem of her long burkha swishing on the stone paving. Jamal sprawled on the long daybed and James chose a cane armchair that faced the bead curtain. He nodded his head toward the two glasses and a bottle of yellowish spirit standing on the inlaid coffee table; the label was in Spanish but he knew that pisco was a Peruvian brandy.

'Looks like Raul has had a visitor.'

'He could still be here,' Jamal replied.

'Do you know the boy scout's motto, Jamal?' he asked softly and the Moroccan smiled, reached into his jacket and withdrew the semi-automatic. He flicked the safety off and placed it on the daybed out of sight of the doorway.

'Three years in London's East End teaches you to always be prepared,' he whispered as they tensely waited for someone to enter the courtyard. The woman came first and she was now dressed in a blue chiffon dress that clung to a figure of such perfection that James and Jamal were momentarily distracted and did not immediately notice the man entering behind her.

'Welcome to Marrakech, Mr Goodfellow,' Calder said cheerfully as he chose a chair facing both men and waved a hand at the young woman. 'Coffee for my guests, Asmae,' he demanded and she left as silently as she had entered.

'And who is this?' Calder asked glancing at James' companion.

'You needn't know his name,' James said.

Calder shrugged. 'It is a long while since we last met in Cambridge.' He smoothed down the white Omani ankle-length jabbah he had adopted as his normal attire since arriving back in Morocco. The long cord with its tassels hung free from his neck when he leant forward to offer them local *Anfa* cigarettes from a box of carved *thuya* wood; Jamal took one but James declined and waited for Calder to open the conversation.

'I can only assume that you followed me here for a particular reason. Maybe you would be kind enough to tell me what that could be.'

James studied the man's face before speaking. 'Actually, I was following a murderer to this address but as you are here you can make my trip really worthwhile and return the king's charter and the silver coins to me.'

Calder contrived surprise. 'My dear fellow, I don't have those items with me.'

'You wouldn't have left them in England when you came here.' Ignoring James' correct assumption Calder replied with feigned interest. 'You said there's a murderer here? And who might that be?'

'I think you know him, Professor.'

'Enlighten me.'

'Raul Moran, the killer of Daniel Lightbody in Ravens' Wood.' As James spoke he saw the bead curtain move slightly and he leapt to one side as a gun fired, shattering the back of his cane chair with a heavy-calibre bullet.

'Jamal!' James warned as he rolled across the stone floor to the daybed. 'Get down!'

The young man had already sensed the danger and had slipped off the daybed and onto one knee to adopt a professional two-handed grip on the Beretta. He fired twice into the curtain sending glass and ceramic slivers in every direction as the beads were shattered. Jamal rolled into a new position and fired once more but there was no response from the other side of the swinging barrier.

'Was that Raul?' James called out to an unruffled Calder who had remained seated during the exchange of gunfire. 'Was it,' he repeated and the smirking professor shrugged.

'Whoever it was seems to have gone,' Jamal said without lowering his gun.

'Is there a rear entrance to this building, Calder?'

The professor looked at James crouching on the floor and smiled. 'How else would the staff and general garbage leave this place?'

'Then I can assume the garbage was Raul and that he's now left. Where would he go?'

'Is that all you want from me, Goodfellow?'

'I would also like that thirteenth-century document that is in your possession,' James said watching for any reaction on Calder's face. 'The King John coins wouldn't go amiss either. I presume the Moran brothers gave you both items to get them out of the country.'

'You are almost right in your presumption.' He watched Jamal walk to the curtain and jerk it aside.

'Nothing,' Jamal reported and disappeared to investigate further.

Calder turned to look at James. 'I have the copy of the king's charter but the silver coins are still in a very safe place in England.'

'Give me the charter now and tell me where the coins are hidden,' James demanded as he walked to stand over the professor. There was a sudden burst of gunfire in the passageway and bullets burst through the beaded screen.

'It seems the garbage wasn't put out after all,' Calder sneered.

James leapt to one side with his back against the wall; conscious that Jamal was in serious trouble he darted through the curtain. The gloomy passageway was barely lit by red-shaded wall lights but his vision improved as he ran from one room to the other. His new friend was sitting on the black and white tiled floor in a large bedroom and slumped against a king-size bed. He was clutching his side with blood oozing from between his fingers. Jamal was still loosely holding his pistol and he looked up and managed to smile even though bouts of pain stabbed him in the side.

James dropped to his knees and ripped the shirt open to get at the wound. Jamal briefly moved his hand to show the damage and James could see the leaking hole and, on shuffling round, the ragged exit wound.

'It's a through and through that's only nipped the waist. I'll live,' Jamal declared with a brave grin and James felt a jolt of guilt for having exposed the young man to such danger.

'I'm sorry, Jamal. This is precisely what I wanted to avoid.' James stripped the bedspread and was tearing the thin cotton sheet into strips when the chiffon-clad woman appeared at the door. She hurried across the room and took one of the strips to stem the bleeding.

'I will help you get to a doctor but that is all,' she said in Arabic as she bound crude pads over the wound and kept winding the strips around his body until Jamal winced. 'My sincere apologies,' she added when with James' help they got him to his feet.

They had reached the door when she said, 'There is a dead man in the back corridor. I have friends who will help me to dispose of his body but I am telling you in case he is your friend and you want to see him before we leave.'

Jamal leant heavily on the beautiful woman and looked into her dark eyes. 'I have no friends in this place except for the man I came with and a beautiful woman who will take me to a doctor,' he flirted despite the pain in his side and was rewarded with a shy smile.

'I will go and make sure it's Raul and then get some information from that man Calder,' James said as he slipped from under Jamal's arm and went to locate the dead man.

It wasn't Raul.

The body sprawled awkwardly in the corridor was one of the Peruvian agents, the one called Zamaras. A heavy 9mm bullet had made a mess of his head but James still checked for any sign of life. He fished around in the dead man's pockets and found his passport and a smartphone.

'He's not the man I came for,' was the first thing he said when he caught up with the others in the courtyard. 'Raul must have been lying in wait for us when he was surprised by someone coming in the back door.'

'He must have killed that person and then shot at me in the passage before I could duck back into the bedroom,' Jamal said. 'I don't understand why he didn't follow me and finish it.' He winced with pain as Asmae checked the crude dressing.

'He panicked after killing the agent and made a run for it,' James speculated.

'The man we were talking to in the courtyard has also disappeared,' Jamal said.

'Mr Calder owns this place,' the woman exclaimed in Arabic. 'He has the right to stay here whenever he visits Morocco.'

'Somehow I don't think he'll be returning,' Jamal said and then translated what the girl had said.

'Which means I've lost something of great value to my country.' Jamal gave James a puzzled look.

'The man had stolen one of the very few copies of a historical document signed by a king of England,' James explained.

'King John?'

'Looks like you picked up some of our history when you were in London, Jamal,' James said with a humourless laugh.

'Well, let's see if we can pick up your lost Magna Carta after I've picked up a few stitches.'

They left the riad and Asmae led them to a place where she had friends with medical training.

14

RICARDO AND ZAMARAS WATCHED in frustration as the Englishman showed his passport to the police guard and then strolled on. They had been tempted to follow but knew the Moroccan police would want to know why two Peruvian agents were present at what was clearly a major crime scene. They couldn't risk showing their passports and returned to the taxi to ponder their next move.

'I suggest we take a chance and go directly to the medina,' Ricardo said. 'I have a feeling that whatever happened here is closely connected to Raul and his only safe house now is where Juan lived.'

'A place in the old souk?'

'Correct.' Ricardo leant forward and instructed the driver to take them to Jemaa El Fna and when he leant back Zamaras tapped him on the knee.

'And how the hell are we going to find this safe house?'

'Simple, we get to the square before Goodfellow and then follow him to the address he clearly has in his possession.'

Zamaras shrugged. 'And if we don't see him in the crowds, or even more likely, Goodfellow doesn't know where the bloody house is either, what then?'

'We sit in the square drinking orange juice until our luck changes.' Ricardo playfully thumped his colleague in the bicep. 'Don't worry yourself, Englishmen always stand out because their faces are either white or scarlet.'

'Or peeling,' Zamaras added and both men chuckled.

The driver drove through the arch in the city wall and then told them it was against the law to go any further. He stopped in Place Foucault and the two men walked to one side of the square where there were a couple of restaurants with seating outside. Ricardo chose a table set far enough back to remain discreet without limiting their visibility. After ordering the mandatory glasses of freshly squeezed orange juice Zamaras pointed to the corner of the square where a terraced restaurant could be seen on an upper level.

'That would give us a much better vantage point,' he said and Ricardo nodded. They left money on the table and hurried to the other restaurant. Having climbed a dingy staircase to a large open area they chose a canopied table by the balcony that gave them the best view of the whole square and ordered two vegetable tagines and Casablanca beers.

'If we have to split up for any reason we'll use our phones and GPS bugs to find each other.' Ricardo handed a small silver button to Zamaras who nodded and dropped it into his top pocket. They both used their GEIN smartphones to double-check each other's location.

The sun had reached a point directly above them when they finished the meal and simultaneously spotted James threading his way amongst the throngs of traders and tourists. Ricardo waved to the waiter and asked for the check but the man only waved back and continued taking orders from a large table of tourists.

'You go on, Zamaras, follow him and keep me informed of your whereabouts by phone.'

Zamaras nodded, checked James' position in the square and hurried down the stairs and out of the restaurant while Ricardo grabbed the menu and began adding up what they had had to eat and drink. He looked down and saw that Zamaras was only fifty yards behind Goodfellow. Then he saw the second man who was obviously accompanying, possibly leading, their man across the square and into the souk. He had the appearance of a young Berber yet wore western clothes and was clean-shaven.

'That's not a licensed guide,' he murmured as he glowered at the waiter who was explaining in French to a German lady tourist what *makouda* and *kefta tagine* was. Ricardo waved a fistful of dirhams at the waiter and tossed them on the table before rushing after Zamaras.

The tiny open-fronted shops lining the narrow passages were attracting scores of people like butterflies to buddleia and low-hanging baskets and rainbow-coloured woven hats provided perfect cover when Zamaras saw the couple stop before a tiny alley. He pretended to admire the handiwork until the shop owner emerged from the darkness to begin his customary sales spiel. Zamaras shook his head and moved off when he saw James and his companion go into the alley. He approached slowly and briefly ducked his head round the corner in time to see them being shown into a riad. He tried to use his cellphone to call Ricardo but the hundreds of tiny businesses surrounding him blocked any chance of a signal.

Feral cats scattered with aggressive hisses as Zamaras walked cautiously to the end of the alley and saw that there was an even smaller, darker passage that went round the riad to end at a rear gate. With one hand on the wall guiding him and the other holding a handkerchief over his nose and mouth to reduce the vile stench that rose from rotting garbage littering the path he slowly made his way to a wooden gate.

It opened easily and he entered a small yard that was stacked with wooden crates and cardboard boxes. The entrance to the riad was invitingly wide open. Ricardo went in and on turning left he peered down a long corridor in to a brightly lit room beyond a bead curtain.

A man emerged from one of the side rooms and stealthily crept up to the curtain. As Zamaras could not readily recognize him in the poor light he held the automatic by his side and waited to see what would happen. A woman wearing a blue dress came and went without acknowledging the man who took a long-barrelled gun from inside his jacket and pointed it at someone beyond the beads.

Zamaras held his breath and the man fired twice. As the harsh sound echoed up the corridor another gun fired and a bullet ricocheted from wall to wall, narrowly missing him. The man spun round and began running towards Zamaras. In that split second he recognized Raul. He stepped into view, raised the Walther and repeatedly pulled the trigger until Raul returned his fire with a single shot.

The Peruvian agent was killed instantly and Raul had almost reached the open door when a gun sounded behind him and he felt a searing pain in his forearm. Seeing a young Berber running towards him Raul fired from the hip, his random shot hitting the young man who tumbled through a doorway. Raul raced from the riad and was soon lost in the maze of crowded alleyways and passages.

Ricardo was following in Zamaras' footsteps when he saw James emerge from the riad supporting a young man who was clutching at his side while a woman, wearing a full burkha, was walking ahead of them. He was of two minds whether to follow them or investigate the riad where his smartphone was still showing Zamaras' location. Choosing the latter he approached the old house slowly, studying the latticed windows for any signs of movement. The door was slightly ajar and after a quick look round to make sure he wasn't being observed he entered and closed it behind him.

Experience had taught him to be careful whenever there was a suspicion of nitrocellulose in the air and he could distinctly smell the aftermath of a gun discharge in the empty courtyard. He took a Walther that Zamaras had procured from his jacket and slipped the safety off. The bead curtain was moving slightly in the draught and the stone paving was littered with the colourful glitter of glass splinters.

Ricardo parted the curtain with the barrel of his gun and looked down the gloomy corridor. The pungent smell was much stronger and he moved cautiously from room to room with every sense tuned for danger. In one room he found signs that somebody had been shot but no sign of a victim. He assumed that it was the man James had led from the riad. At the end of the corridor he briefly checked round the corner with his gun hand leading and found his partner.

Zamaras lay in an unnaturally crumpled manner with a large pool of dark blood around his head. Ricardo knelt beside him and checked for any sign of life but the damage done by the bullet was evidence enough that his partner was beyond any help. He genuflected before checking the pockets. Zamaras' passport and smartphone were missing.

'The killer is going to regret he took that phone,' he murmured as he made the sign of the cross over his friend and stood up. There was the sound of men's voices coming from the courtyard and Ricardo stepped outside and waited behind the wall. The voices drew nearer until one very close swore volubly in Arabic when he examined the body. Ricardo then heard the sound of a heavy zip and the heavy crackling of plastic before the Moroccans stumbled away down the corridor and the riad was silent once more.

Ricardo looked round the door frame and immediately saw that his partner's body was no longer lying in the corridor; only a large pool of blood remained to tell the story of his colleague's demise. Using the smartphone he brought up a street map of Marrakech and tapped in the code for Zamaras' phone. Almost immediately a small green dot began to pulsate.

I've got you now, Raul, he thought.

Supporting the wounded Jamal as best he could James followed Asmae along the winding streets thronged with shoppers, many of whom noticed Jamal's bloodstained shirt and quickly looked the other way. Eventually the young woman stopped at a small shop with boxes and wooden barrels spilling out into the street. Most were heaped with aromatic ground spices, sticks of cinnamon and large chunks of rock salt.

'A spice shop?' James exclaimed. 'What's going on?'

Asmae put a finger to her lips and went inside, beckoning the men to follow. The shop was lined with shelves stacked high with baby products, cosmetics and common medical products. Asmae murmured something to an elderly man whose back was curved by advanced osteoporosis. He glanced at Jamal and picked up an old telephone. After a few seconds of rapid Arabic in a painfully creaky voice the door behind him opened and a young man appeared. He introduced himself as Tony before leading them into a room brightly lit by a dozen neon tubes set in the ceiling. The door closed and a middle-aged man wearing a white jacket and black *taqiyah* skullcap invited Jamal to sit down.

'Asmae said you have been shot, monsieur?' he asked in French as he slipped on surgical gloves before gently removing Jamal's hand from his still bleeding side. 'This may hurt you, sir,' he advised as he unwound Asmae's handiwork and from a small vial poured liquid on the blood-soaked pads before peeling them away. As he examined the leaking wounds he spoke in Arabic to the younger man. James watched him as he crossed the room and noticed for the first time that floor-to-ceiling shelves filled with jars of all shapes and sizes surrounded them.

'We have everything for most complaints,' the pharmacist said when he noticed James' interest. He pointed to the lower shelves. 'Those are beauty creams for all skin types and those are different argan oils to apply and ingest.' He opened the large box Tony had brought for him and took out an assortment of medical instruments. 'Apart from selling natural medicines my son and I also do favours like this for our friends.'

Jamal groaned loudly and jerked his torso as both wounds were doused with a bright yellow liquid. Asmae took his hand and he gripped hers tightly when a stainless steel probe was inserted.

'I'm sorry, sir, but I must make sure that no fragments or soiled material from your clothing have been driven into the wound.' He gave a grunt of satisfaction and poured more liquid into a kidney dish containing needles and suture. 'This will also hurt,' he added with a grim smile and professionally began to close the larger exit wound with very small stitches.

Thirty minutes later James helped Jamal to his feet and when he saw his reflection in a full-length mirror the taxi driver grimaced, realizing that he couldn't go into the street wearing ripped and bloody clothing. Recognizing his plight the pharmacist sent his son to fetch one of his old thobes.

'We will wait a little until Tony returns from our home and while we do so I would like to revitalize you with one of my special herbal teas.'

'It will help you to recover, Jamal,' Asmae murmured.

James had noticed the secret glances being exchanged between Asmae and Jamal since they had left the riad and he smiled to himself. Maybe something good will come out of this whole mess after all, he thought.

The tea was delicious and when the young man returned Jamal managed to slip into the long white thobe and discard his slacks without too much embarrassment. He also transferred the automatic from the slacks to a thobe pocket without the pharmacist or his son noticing.

As they prepared to leave James offered one hundred dollars to Tony and was surprised when it was refused.

'Thank you, Mister James, but I have known Asmae when we were both at Cambridge and since then she has been a very good friend to me and my father; taking your money for helping a friend would bring shame on this house.'

When James looked at Asmae she answered his unspoken question: 'I studied archaeology at Newnham College in Cambridge; we are Sunni Moslems and it's one of the few suitable women-only colleges. On my return home two years ago Professor Calder offered me a part-time position in Marrakech as his private researcher and as Tony and I used the same mosque it was inevitable we would meet again and continue our friendship.'

'He's just a friend?'

Asmae smiled to herself. 'Yes, just a friend.'

'And that's what you were doing today, just researching for the Professor?' Jamal asked.

Asmae frowned. 'What did *you* think I was doing at the riad?'

The young man was at a loss for words and James quickly interrupted. 'I suggest we get Jamal home and you too, Asmae, before we get into any more trouble.'

'My home is in Rabat where I live with my grandmother. My parents died last year in a road accident.'

'I'm so sorry for your loss. So how do you get to and from home each day?' Jamal asked tentatively.

'I don't,' Asmae snapped. 'I stay at the riad during the week and go home on the weekends and before you ask another silly question, I was only doing the Professor's work. My bedroom door stayed locked even though some of the other women were inclined to stray.'

James smiled as he led the offended woman through the door. 'Well you can't stay at the riad tonight. As Calder has decided to disappear you have no employer and we'll have to find somewhere else for you to stay tonight. You can travel home tomorrow.'

Asmae smiled back before covering her face with the burqua mask.

Jamal shook the pharmacist's hand before following the others out into the shop; to his horror Ricardo was standing amongst the spice barrels with a deadly-looking Walther PPQ pointing at James, a look of hatred in his eyes. Jamal touched the automatic through the light cotton of the thobe but James imperceptibly shook his head.

'Which one of you killed my partner?' Ricardo shouted and the barrel moved from one to the other. The pharmacist's father remained quite still on his chair and then made a small sign for his son to do the same as he came out from the back room.

'None of us shot him,' James said. 'It was Raul Moran and he almost killed my friend at the same time, too.'

'I can attest to that, sir, as I've just cleaned and closed two holes in the young man's side with ten stitches,' the pharmacist said calmly and then flinched as the gun barrel swung round to point in his direction.

Ricardo stared long and hard at the pharmacist and then lowered his gun. 'You say it was Raul?' he repeated and James nodded. 'Then why have you got his smartphone?'

'I have his passport as well as I didn't think you'd want the authorities to identify him too quickly,' James answered. 'This buys us some extra time in which to track down the bastard.'

The agent quickly saw the logic and replied, "It was probably the best course of action at the time.' He held his hand out and James took the smartphone and document from his pocket.

'How did you know I had your partner's phone?' he asked.

'There are tracker devices fitted into every GEIN smartphone which can be activated by one agent dialling another using a unique code; that's what led me to this place.'

'Now that's what I call a really smartphone,' Jamal said.

'How do you plan to find Raul?' Ricardo said, ignoring Jamal. 'The hotel has been compromised by an unusual incident and the riad is a no-go zone after the shooting there.'

'I'll put the word out,' Jamal suddenly said. 'The killer still has to move about and he'll most probably do it by taxi. I'll put a general call out to as many taxis working this area as possible.'

'Good idea, Jamal, they might be able to give us the lead we need,' James said with a renewed feeling of optimism.

'I disagree,' Asmae cried out and the men fell silent and looked at her, surprised by the anger in her voice. 'Jamal has been shot and has lost blood; he needs to eat and rest.'

James silently agreed with her and realised that he'd been selfish and neglectful. Asmae had reacted in the exact same way Jenny would have done and this reminded him to call his wife before she started using official channels to alert Interpol.

'To get home I still have to get to my car and once there using the radio won't be too tiring,' Jamal countered and Asmae's face fell. 'You have a driving licence?' Asmae nodded. 'Then you'll be able to drive me home while I take it easy beside you and then I can ask my mother if you can stay the night.' Asmae's eyes flashed alarmingly and Jamal hurriedly went on. 'She can make up the bed in the guest room on the other side of the house.'

Her eyes softened and he inwardly gave a sigh of relief. Ricardo and James looked at each other and turned away to prevent their grins from showing.

For Jamal's sake the walk back to the parked taxi was taken slowly. The setting sun cast an orange glow as day traders, snake charmers and tooth-pullers departed and the square became a hive of activity once more as restaurant stalls were erected in preparation for another evening of feasting.

Asmae soon became familiar with the car and following Jamal's instructions she drove to the small shop while he used the radio to contact his fellow-drivers. He finally put the microphone down and lay back in the seat, wincing with every pothole.

'What next?' Ricardo snapped impatiently.

Jamal made a calming gesture. 'I will be listening on the shortwave radio I have at home for any messages about strangers leaving the souk dressed the way I described but you have to understand that thousands of tourists pass through every day. Being able to isolate one will be very hard indeed.'

A disconsolate air settled on the occupants of the taxi.

Jamal's father was still sitting where they had left him. Introductions were made and then made again as Jamal's mother entered and asked what had happened. She eyed the young woman in the burqua with suspicion as the events of the day were unfolded but when it came to the part where Asmae had helped her injured son she burst out crying and hugged Jamal so tightly he had to warn her about the stitches. Alarmed, she let go and stepped back with concern wrinkling her lined face even more deeply.

'It's all right, oummi, Asmae was a wonder and knew exactly what to do,' Jamal said with a laugh. 'She's a researcher working for Professor Calder, the English archaeologist we met at the riad.'

Ricardo looked up suddenly, his eyes narrowing. 'He's the man who helped the Morans,' he growled.

'He was there when we arrived,' James said, 'but when the shooting began he fled with a valuable artefact that doesn't belong to him and should be returned to the rightful owners in England.'

'What's the bet they're together somewhere.'

'Because there's a lot of money at stake I won't take that wager, Ricardo,' James warned and there was a long awkward silence that ended when the elderly parents suddenly stood up and took charge. Asmae was whisked away by oummi to be shown the guest room while *baba*, Jamal's father, showed James the spare bed in his son's room. When he returned Jamal was sitting before his hissing short-wave radio and Ricardo had left.

163

'Gone back to his hotel to send a report to London,' Jamal said.

'Anything yet?' James asked and when the young man shook his head he continued, 'I'm sure it's too soon so I'll go to the bedroom and call my wife. Do let me know if anybody makes contact.'

'*Inna sawf*, of course I will, James.'

James speed-dialled and the warm familiar voice that always made him light up inside answered. They spent thirty minutes bringing each other up to date, from meeting the Peruvian agents and attending a PTA meeting to events in the riad and a pickpocket arrest in East Steading high street.

'I know I've said it before but it sounds like things are getting far too dangerous, James,' Jennifer said towards the end. 'Don't you think you should call it a day, talk to the local police and come home? I'm sure Agnes would agree with that course of action in a flash.'

'I can't, Jenny. It's not so much Raul Moran but Calder. I have to find him and recover the Magna Carta copy.'

'It's not worth lives, especially yours, darling.'

'Hundreds of men were slaughtered on battlefields to make King John sign that charter which makes what I'm risking nothing by comparison.'

'It's everything to me.'

James felt a welling up of love and he hastily finished the call before his voice betrayed him and he rashly promised to return home on the next flight.

That evening, after *Salat al-Isha* prayer, they sat as a family round the large table made of native thuya wood while Jamal's mother brought in bowl after bowl of lightly spiced food. James was exceptionally hungry and his stomach protested loudly, much to his embarrassment.

'Now that's something my wife can rectify,' the old man said and laughed out loud as he took James' plate and began ladling generous helpings of each dish until it was almost too difficult to hold with one hand. Asmae giggled and she helped to pass the plate to James. She had shed the burkha and was wearing her blue chiffon dress with a white headscarf which complemented the dress and accentuated her natural healthy colour.

They had just finished the *b'stilli*, an exquisite Fez-styled pigeon pie spiced with saffron, when there was a burst of hissing from the corner of the room and an Arabic voice called for attention. Jamal leapt up after a brief apology to his parents and using the earphones he listened for a while, nodded vigorously and said *naam*, yes, two or three times before calling off. Jamal turned on the swivel chair to face the others with excitement in his eyes.

'That was my friend, Mohamad, who is the doorman at the Mamounia Hotel. He'd spoken to the taxi drivers ranked in the hotel drive –'

'Someone has spotted Raul?' James interrupted.

'No, not Raul but I had mentioned the other man –'

'Professor Calder?'

'Let me finish,' Jamal declared loudly and James raised his hands apologetically. 'Yes, I had described Calder as well as Raul and a man matching the description of the professor entered my friend's hotel and took a single room for one night.'

'Is he still there?'

'I imagine he would be because he asked the porter if he could have a quiet word. At first the man thought he was going to request a *sharmuta* for the night but instead he asked where he could hire a car without too many questions being asked.

The porter went to Mohamad because the request sounded highly suspicious; moreover, the man arrived at the hotel completely out of breath as though he had run a long distance – tourists don't run in Marrakech unless they want to suffer heatstroke. He checked with the drivers but none could recall such a man.'

'That takes us back to square one,' James said.

'Not quite, Mohamad came up with a fabulous plan that would enable us to check the identity of the man; the porter will tell the guest that the doorman has a car of his own that he is quite prepared to hire out but he can only take him to it early in the morning.'

'How does that help us to know if it's Calder or not?'

'Mohamad told him that on the way to his home he has to stop briefly at his cousin's shop. He'll stop right outside here at 8 a.m. and that's when we can get a discreet look at the passenger.'

'Your friend is a genius,' James declared and clapped his hands in appreciation.

Jamal grinned. 'That's when we can grab him and get the Magna Carta?'

'No. I believe he will lead us to where Raul is hiding and if we follow him we can catch two birds with one stone.'

Jamal looked at James in puzzlement. 'What birds?'

James couldn't help laughing and the whole family joined in without knowing why.

15

Ricardo strolled into the shop at 7 a.m. precisely when James and Jamal were sipping cups of strong coffee accompanied by *chabakeya*, syrup and rose water covered pastries and cinnamon buns hot from the oven.

'Salaam alykum, Ricardo,' Jamal called out and beckoned him to join them at the table.

'Have you heard from your friends,' was the first thing he asked as he sat and helped himself to one of the buns while James poured him a small cup of coffee.

'Yes, I did, and in one hour precisely we will see whether we have a definite lead to where Raul is hiding,' Jamal answered.

Ricardo was confused. 'What do you mean, in one hour?'

'That's when Jamal's friend will stop outside in a taxi and come in here,' James said. 'The man will remain in the car and we'll get a good look at him through those net curtains at the window. Hopefully, it will be Calder in which case we'll follow him because I believe he'll lead us to your man.'

Ricardo nodded and without another word began the serious task of breaking his fast. Asmae strolled into the room wearing a long beige dress that had been loaned to her while the chiffon creation was being cleaned. Her black hair was partially hidden by the same white scarf.

'Bonjour, monsieurs,' she called out cheerfully as she sat beside Jamal. He was instantly bewitched by her perfume – jasmine with gardenia and mimosa – and was lost for words while the other men greeted her with easy banter and grinned at him. She wore no make-up and the unadorned beauty of her green-blue eyes and naturally curly lashes revealed her Rif heritage. Eventually he managed to mumble a welcome and was about to offer her some coffee when a vehicle stopped on the pavement right opposite the window.

James checked his watch. 'That's most probably Mohamad.'

James indicated that Asmae should disappear while he and Ricardo went to a corner table and sat with their backs to the door. Jamal casually sauntered out of the café area and into the shop when the door opened and a man in a splendid red cape, white fez and gloves entered. He greeted Jamal with kisses on both cheeks and gave him a bearlike embrace.

'He's outside in the back,' he said quickly and then spotting the display of buns in the café he released Jamal and hurried across to help himself.

Despite the netting the men had a perfect view of the back seat and the pompous figure sitting there with arms folded and impatiently tapping his fingers on his forearms.

'No question about it, that's Professor Calder,' James muttered through clenched teeth.

'It's him alright,' Asmae confirmed having crept out of the kitchen to peer over James' shoulder. 'And he owes me two months salary.'

'You'll get it back, don't worry,' James promised as Mohamad approached him happily chewing a cinnamon bun with one hand while balancing a cup and saucer in the other.

'Mohamad, will you please say you have to wait for a parcel to be wrapped for your wife while we go out the back way to Jamal's taxi.'

'Can I have some of these in the parcel?' Mohamad requested and held up what remained of his cinnamon bun. He strolled out and climbed into the taxi to speak to Calder. While Jamal led the group to the back door he gave his mother, who was still baking bread for the neighbours, a quick kiss and brief instruction before leaving.

Having expressed concern for Jamal's wound Asmae got into the driver's seat and drove down the narrow lane and into the main street where she parked fifty metres behind. The back door of the taxi suddenly opened and Mohamad jumped out to meet Jamal's mother who handed him a small paper parcel. He took it with effusive thanks, bid her farewell and the taxi pulled away.

'Let the hunt begin,' James murmured to himself.

Mohamad's home was only a kilometre from the shop and Asmae parked at the end of his dusty road so they could watch him instruct Calder on the many quirks of an old red Citroen 2CV. Calder was clearly becoming impatient with the doorman's unending list of do's and don'ts. Finally Mohamad made a point of carefully counting the notes Calder had given him before handing the key over. After a couple of grinding gearbox clashes the professor smartly drove off in a cloud of dust. Jamal waved to the concerned-looking Mohamad as they passed him and started following the rust-stained deux chevaux.

After they had driven in silence for thirty minutes across a bleak plain dotted with old mud-baked buildings James ventured to ask where they were going.

Jamal pointed ahead at the impressive range of mountains that dominated the whole horizon. 'It looks like Calder is planning to meet his nasty pal somewhere high up in the Atlas Mountains.'

James was awed by the magnificence of the vista confronting them. The road seemed to run to a vanishing point in the foothills and looking up he could see that the remains of winter were still colouring parts of the mountain slopes white.

'As we're on the N9 highway I think he's going to take that poor old car through the Tizi n'Tichka Pass,' Asmae commented as the scrubland changed and they began driving through an area of lush greenery. 'This will soon end and as we gain altitude the road will become very dangerous until we reach the pass which is the highest in the country.'

'You should be a tour guide,' Jamal teased.

'If you think you know these mountains better then why don't you tell James what we can expect,' Asmae scolded.

The car returned to silence and all eyes were focused once more on the tiny red car as they began the ascent. Soon the air temperature had fallen considerably and the car was on a winding road with precipitous drops first on one side and then on the other. The young woman expertly dodged the occasional rocks that had tumbled down onto the tarmac.

'Where does this whatsit pass lead to?' Ricardo asked. It was the first thing he had said since leaving the shop and James looked round in surprise. 'If Raul were here where could he possibly hide out without freezing to death.'

'There are villages and small towns that cater for tourists; people who like to climb these mountains,' Jamal said. As if to confirm his words they suddenly saw scores of dun-coloured houses on the opposite ridge. The small gardens sloped at perilous angles and when James looked further down into the valley he saw the almond orchards he had first seen from the plane at ten thousand feet. The trees were all in blossom and as before they gave the appearance of a white-water river rushing down the valley.

'Beautiful,' James murmured softly.

'That's because you're now in Berber country, my homeland,' Jamal announced proudly as he gazed at the mountains still rising about them and the lowlands so far below.

The little red car was occasionally glimpsed ahead of them as they turned corner after corner with the engine straining. James wondered out loud how the old Citroen coped with the altitude and patches of snow. He shivered even though Asmae had switched the heater on and set the fan to warm the whole car.

'I'm guessing he's heading for the Kasbah of Tifoultoute,' Asmae observed. 'It has a hotel and restaurant and may be the perfect rendezvous for Calder and Moran.'

Ricardo suddenly spoke again as he peered at a small road map in a hotel travel guide. 'It gives them the option of driving either to the coast to leave by sea or to the nearby airport at Ouarzazate to fly out of the country.'

Within a matter of minutes they caught sight of the Kasbah. The ancient fort rose like a golden stack of children's play blocks in the lush vegetation of an unexpected oasis. Beyond was the sprawling town of Tifoultoute.

'According to this guide there are quite a few hotels and bed- and-breakfast establishments in the area. How will we know which to check first?' Ricardo grumbled.

'They'll want to keep as far away from crowds as possible. All we have to do is check the car parks of the more isolated hotels for the red deux chevaux,' James rationalized.

'Good thinking, lets do it,' Ricardo said.

'Which one first?' Asmae chipped in.

'According to the map there's one called Kasbah Zitoune and it's just before we cross the wadi and enter the town.' Ricardo closed the guide with a self-satisfied flourish.

They were no longer climbing steeply and driving had become easier even though they were still surrounded by the magnificent cragginess of the Atlas Mountains.

'Turn right here,' Jamal said. 'I know this part quite well.'

Asmae left the main N9 and after a few more twists and turns two red pillars with the name of the hotel in bold letters on a gold arch between them appeared. The driveway meandered between mature palms until they reached an attractive red sandstone hotel. Asmae followed a sign for car parking and cruised along the rows of cars.

'First time lucky,' James cried, pointing towards a rusty red deux chevaux that was parked at the far end. Asmae went to a vacant bay that was hidden from the car by an ornamental red azalea.

'What now,' Jamal asked.

'I'll go and find Raul, that's what I came for,' Ricardo said as he opened the door.

'He's all yours but I need to talk to Professor Calder and get him to give me the document,' James said as he got out with the Peruvian. 'Try not to use your weapon when you find your man, Ricardo. Hoteliers are a little touchy about tourists firing guns and killing each other in their hotels.'

'If the first thing he does when he sees me is to pull a gun I'll have no other option but to stop him.' Ricardo strode away without looking back at the group.

James turned to look at the couple. 'I want you both to stay here,' he instructed. 'It's not your fight and I could never forgive myself if either of you were hurt.' When they both agreed he strode after the agent.

The hotel lobby felt warm after the cool mountain air and James saw Ricardo talking to the efficient-looking receptionist.

'Any news?'

'This lady told me that a man who introduced himself as Professor Calder asked if Moran had checked in. She told him that he was in room 104. It's in the south wing on the ground floor.'

'We are friends of the gentlemen and would like to surprise them,' James said to the receptionist. 'May we go to their room without you calling ahead to tell them we're here?'

Her handsome face creased into a wide smile. 'A surprise? Certainly, sir,' and she pointed with a red-lacquered finger. 'Just cross the courtyard and take the corridor on the right. Room 104 is at the end.'

When they reached the room Ricardo pushed the doorbell before James could stop. James had spotted the spyhole and he pushed Ricardo to one side a split second before the oak panelling was splintered by a 9mm bullet at chest height. Ricardo nodded his thanks and a weapon appeared in his hand. The closed door had muffled the sharp report of the gun and James doubted that anyone could have heard it.

'What now,' Ricardo hissed.

'Calder, I just want to talk to you,' James called. 'Put the gun away before someone gets killed.'

'Tell that to my brother, Goodfellow,' a faint voice replied.

'Shooting can't help you, Raul,' Ricardo shouted and a door opened behind them. The agent spun round with his gun at the ready and a portly middle-aged woman in the open doorway of room 101 stepped back with a hand to her mouth. Fear showed in her eyes and James quickly reassured her that they were friends of the men inside and that they were just fooling around. The woman's eyes flicked back to the agent's weapon.

'Put it away, Ricky,' James said cheerily and the agent slipped it back into his pocket. 'It's just a toy gun we bought in Marrakech.' The woman gave a doubtful smile and closed her door.

'She'll be calling reception right now so we'd better think of another way of getting them to open the –'

There was an explosion of splintering wood as Ricardo kicked the door. The flimsy lock didn't stand a chance and was torn from the jamb. Both men crouched instinctively before the agent rushed into the room with his gun levelled in a two-handed grip.

There were two quick shots and James rushed in to find Ricardo standing over the prone figure of Raul. He looked round quickly and checked the bathroom but Calder was nowhere to be seen. An open window suggested his escape route and James rushed to look but nothing stirred in the well-tended colourful garden.

'He shot first,' Ricardo said to justify the large hole in the centre of Raul's forehead. James pointed to a framed print with shattered glass on the wall. 'He missed, I didn't and my job's done.' Ricardo turned and walked out of the door with James following closely behind.

'What shall we do about that?' Ricardo asked jerking a thumb over his shoulder.

'About what?'

'One look in 104 and the police will have an all-points bulletin out for us all.'

The receptionist was on the phone and she gave them a strange look as they walked past. She's undoubtedly talking to the woman in 101, James thought as they hurried across the forecourt and into the car park. The red deux chevaux was gone but they breathed a sigh of relief when they saw the young couple was OK.

'What happened?' Jamal asked as they got in. 'Did you see Raul? We saw Calder who came running round from the back of the hotel, climbed into Mohamad's car and left as though the devil was right behind him.'

'And he will be when Asmae gets this car going as quickly as possible,' James growled.

Asmae immediately started the engine and they left the car park at speed to drive back the way they came. 'I assume he'll want to get to the airport as quickly as possible,' she said as they approached the junction to the main highway.

'But which one?' Jamal was confused when they stopped and looked both ways. 'He may have previously made a reservation at Ouarzazate airport which is only twenty-five kilometres from here or he may be returning to Marrakech and taking his chances on booking a flight at Menara.'

James had a sudden thought. 'Did you notice if there was a document or a collection of coins in the hotel room, Ricardo?' The agent shook his head and James continued, 'Then he'll be heading for Marrakech and the Menara airport.'

'What makes you so sure?' Asmae queried.

'The weight,' James said simply. 'He couldn't have taken the document and all those coins when he fled from the riad which means they must still be there or –'

'– he didn't arrange for the coins to be brought to Morocco in the first place which means they must be still in England,' Jamal added confidently.

Slightly confused Asmae said, 'But surely Ouarzazate airport would be a lot closer if he needs to return to England?'

'I happen to know there are no flights to London Heathrow and Gatwick today, so he'll have to go to the Menara airport; and should the coins be hidden in the riad he'll still need to go there first.' Jamal waved his hand indicating that Asmae should turn left and when James agreed she shrugged and started the long drive back to Marrakech.

'Would he have the document on him?' Ricardo murmured as he replaced the used round in the magazine from the small supply he always kept in his jacket pocket.

'There's no doubt about that,' James said with uneasy certainty. 'It is more precious than the coins and when rolled is easy enough to transport but Calder is a greedy man. He'll take a chance and try to return to Cambridge to retrieve the coins. When I spoke to him at the university he struck me as being a passionate archaeologist so my guess is that he kept the medieval chest as well.'

Ricardo grunted and snapped the magazine back into the butt of the pistol. 'Worth quite a lot of money, I suppose.'

James turned to look into the man's dark eyes but saw no guile there. 'I don't know the exact number of coins but I would guess by the size of the chest that there were two or three thousand.'

'And their worth?'

'Approximately £130 each,' James said and there was a collective intake of air as everyone began doing rough calculations in their heads.

'Could add up to six million dirhams! That's a lot of money,' Jamal commented and as the taxi wound down the mountain and through the pass a silence fell upon the occupants until Jamal added, 'That's the coins but what's that old document worth?'

'Approximately 45 million dirhams to a crooked collector,' was the short answer which drew further gasps from his companions.

'So, do we go straight to the airport?' Ricardo asked. 'My job is over but I would like to find out who the clean-up crew were.'

'Clean-up crew?' Asmae asked.

'My partner was taken from the riad by people who specialize in the disposal of bodies. My partner is owed the respect of a decent burial than bening dumped on a landfill site.'

James nodded for more recent events had driven all thoughts of Zamaras from his mind. Once more little was said until Jamal's taxi was parked in the street close to the Place Jemaa el-Fna. As the sun sank low they had caught no sight of Mohamad's red car. Even when they left the mountains and headed across the barren plain all they saw was their road running on into a hazy redness.

As the sun disappeared beyond the medinah walls the evening food stalls were being readied for the hungry diners and the muezzin was calling the *Maghrib* prayer. They hurried across the square and entered the souk. To their surprise there were no police on guard or barriers to keep the curious away when they approached the riad.

'Seems like nobody heard the shots or maybe they didn't bother to report them for fear of reprisals,' Jamal said as they grouped before the door.

James tried the door but it was firmly locked. 'We'll try the rear door,' he whispered. The narrow alley forced them into single file with James leading and Asmae at the rear. The back door was closed but not locked.

Ricardo placed a hand on James' shoulder to restrain him. 'He was my friend, I'll go in first,' he whispered and took the automatic from his pocket as a precautionary measure.

Thankfully the door opened on silent hinges and Ricardo disappeared inside with James close behind. Asmae was about to follow when Jamal stopped her, drew his own gun and putting his lips close to her ear whispered that they should wait for the others to declare it safe. The light jasmine scent of her hair stirred him and he drew away before he did something he would regret. Asmae had noticed his reaction and smiled secretly for she was starting to find him appealing the more she learnt about him.

In the gloom of the corridor Ricardo studied the clean spot on the stone floor where Zamaras had fallen. Despite the smell of the cleansing chlorine memories of the many times they had eaten, drunk and wooed beautiful women together went through his mind. The rare instances when they argued, competed and fought for the same girl were forgotten; he could only remember the good times.

James slid his shoe over the floor and shattered his reverie. 'Your own cleaners have already been, I see.'

'I had taken the opportunity to phone my local contact at the embassy when we were at Jamal's place.'

'They give a fast and thorough service; there isn't a drop of blood to be seen.' James went into the passage and checked the bedroom where Jamal had stumbled and collapsed and that was also spotless.

'At least you now know he'll have a proper burial in Lima.'

Ricardo gave a contented grunt and then asked, 'If Calder had the coins you mentioned where would he have hidden them?'

James shook his head. 'Lord knows. We need to identify and search his bedroom: look for a hidden safe, test for loose floorboards there as it's all stone-flooring down here and then check all the other rooms.'

'I'll get the others to help us,' Ricardo suggested.

The evening *Salat al-Isha* prayer was being called when James called a halt and checked his watch. 'It is quite obvious that the coins aren't here. Either he got back here before us and took them or, as was suggested earlier, they never left the shores of England.'

'Menara next?' Ricardo asked.

'Yes, but you needn't come with me as you've achieved your mission and the terrorists have been stopped before they could cause any trouble in your country.' James thanked the agent profusely for his help and once more extended his condolences on the death of his friend.

'I shall go to the embassy and make sure that Zamaras was picked up by my own people and sent home.' Ricardo spoke softly with an edge to his voice that promised trouble for anyone who hadn't accorded his partner the respect he deserved.

James nodded and turned to the young couple. 'I would also like to thank you both for everything you've done for me.' He grasped Jamal's hand. 'Especially you, Jamal, for you risked everything and came very close to being killed.'

Jamal grinned with embarrassment. 'It has been the most exciting time of my life and one I will always remember.'

'It had better not be,' Asmae murmured, putting an arm around his waist and Jamal's grin grew wider.

James smiled. 'C'mon Jamal, you'll have plenty of time later to get to know Asmae better. Right now you have to get me to the airport in time to catch Professor Calder before he catches the last flight.' He turned to speak to the Peruvian and discovered he had disappeared.

'I saw him wave when he went out the front door,' Asmae explained.

Bon voyage, my friend, James thought.

The airport was virtually empty when Jamal dropped James at the terminal building. They shook hands for the last time and Asmae kissed his cheeks lightly and murmured, *'Shokran, James, ma as-salaamah.'* Thank you and goodbye, James.

As the taxi pulled away James felt a brief emptiness that was instantly filled by thoughts of Jenny and as he strode through the terminal to the ticket office he speed-dialled home.

'You took your time, what happened,' were his wife's first words. James felt a flush of guilt and immediately apologized for being so remiss before giving her a detailed account of everything that had happened in the Atlas Mountains and in the riad.

'I told you to take care and instead you came pretty close to being killed while a Peruvian special agent *was* killed and your taxi driver was wounded. You're risking too much for that copy of the king's charter, James.'

'I'm OK, darling, and you can help end this thing by notifying the police at Heathrow and Gatwick that Professor Calder is on his way back with the Magna Carta. Once they've taken him into custody I can come home and plan that holiday we promised Claudiu.'

'My superiors will be informed immediately,' Jennifer said briskly and then added. 'I have also been concerned about the effectiveness of the Xylem tablets and when I mentioned this to our doctor he told me something very interesting.'

Knowing he had fallen asleep more often lately James' interest was instantly aroused. 'What did he say?'

'The pharmaceutical company has been doing a lot of testing over the last year and one particular drug was rated far more effective than Xyrem. It's called Zenzedi and is a schedule 3 drug, unlike the milder one you're using now, which means you cannot refill a prescription willy-nilly or touch any alcohol.'

'Apart from the last point it sounds ideal,' James said eagerly.

'I thought you'd say that so the doctor gave me a prescription which I will send by courier; what is your address in Marrakech?'

'It can be sent care of the Air Maroc information desk in Menara airport.'

There was a sigh and Jenny went on in a softer voice. 'Come home James, come home as soon as you can; I miss you so much.'

The couple exchanged loving goodbyes and James broke the connection as he reached the ticket desk.

A middle-aged woman in a pristine Royal Maroc uniform was pulling down shutters. 'Could you tell me if Mr Calder has bought a ticket to the UK?' he asked.

'I cannot possibly give you any information about our passengers, sir,' she said apologetically.

'Can you at least tell me the time of the last flight tonight?'

'That left ten minutes ago, sir,' she said in the same mandatory apologetic tone. 'The first flight tomorrow is 9.30 a.m. Would you like to reserve a seat?'

James nodded and after paying the fare and receiving his ticket he asked for the most convenient accommodation close to the airport. Glad to have something positive to say she directed him with a smile to the Sofitel that required only a fifteen-minute journey. James thanked her and with the sound of the final shutter clattering into place he left the terminal. There was only one taxi waiting and Jamal and Asmae were standing beside it.

Jamal grinned broadly. 'It was when we were on our way back to Marrakech and saw a plane climbing above our heads that I looked at my watch and realized how late it was.'

'Jamal knew it was the last flight out of Menara and that you'd have to return to the city for a hotel,' Asmae added with a broad grin.

'So, after I've dropped Asmae at her home you're more than welcome to stay with me and my parents.' Jamal opened the back door and James ducked inside to prevent the youngsters from seeing the tears gathering in the corners of his eyes.

Despite the horrors that had occurred since his arrival in Marrakech James knew that he had gained new friends who would stand by him through thick and thin. Two generations of traditional pharmacists and an elderly couple whose son, a perfect stranger until two days ago, had bravely helped him achieve what he couldn't have done alone.

James felt honoured to have known them and he was happy that such a frightening adventure could transform into a love story for two charming young people.

16

THE FLIGHT MADE GOOD TIME. After touching down at Heathrow and completing the immigration and customs formalities James went to one of the cafés and as he sipped an espresso and nibbled on a warm croissant he put a call through to East Steading police station.

'Are you home, James?' was Jennifer's opening question when he was put through to her office.

'Yes, I'm at Heathrow and will be with you fairly soon. Thanks for sending the Zenzedi; I picked it up this morning in Menara.' He mentally crossed his fingers while watching the rain make cat's paws on the window. 'Has Calder been apprehended?'

'I'm sorry James but I checked when I arrived at the station this morning and it seems he gave everybody the slip. Arrangements hadn't been made by the time he landed and he sailed through immigration. Despite an APB alert this morning nobody has caught sight of him or even knows where he went after entering the country.'

'Damn and blast!'

'I took a risk with my boss and made my own inquiries with the coach and taxi companies that were on duty last night but one man and a walk-on case is not something people easily remember; it means he could be anywhere.'

James chewed at a hangnail for a few seconds. 'That's all right, Jenny, I think I know where he might be heading,' he said and then added, 'It'll be Cambridge or somewhere very close.'

'Why would he return to where he'll be recognized so easily?'

'I'm making a wild guess when I suppose that the silver coins were too heavy and too noticeable to take with him to Morocco which means he has hidden them in the area he knows best.'

There was a long silence. 'Are you going to Cambridge before coming home, James?' she asked. 'After you promised?'

'I won't be gone that long, darling,' James pleaded before the storm broke.

'You *do* know Claudiu will be *very* upset.'

'As am I, darling, but I'm sure you can let him down gently when you explain that Daddy had to do a bit more work and that he'll be –'

'I know what to tell our son, James,' Jenny snapped and the line went dead. James sighed, picked up his bag and headed for the Heathrow Express station.

The journey into Paddington and then onward to Cambridge took James two and a half hours and it was lunchtime and raining heavily when he stepped from the train, left the station and crossed the road to the car rental office. The Ford Mondeo was smooth to drive and he soon reached the professor's college. James climbed the stairs in the archaeological unit and entered the oak-panelled office. Calder's secretary was sitting where he had last seen her.

'Can I help you, sir?' she asked in an officious tone. She studied the man in jeans and roll-neck sweater as though he were a gatecrasher at the dean's garden party.

'Is Professor Calder here,' James asked politely.

'Do you have an appointment?'

'No, and I'm sure he isn't expecting me but –'

'I'm sorry. You cannot see the professor without an appointment.'

'Let's cut the crap,' James ordered. 'We know he's being hunted by the police and other interested parties so keeping up with this pretence of normality is of little value.' James paused for effect before asking, 'Is he here?'

The woman glared icily before her face seemed to soften and then collapse. She unexpectedly burst into tears. 'I don't know where Stephen is,' she sobbed. 'I gave him twelve years of service and he left without saying a word. I don't know where he is even though the police didn't believe me when I was questioned by them.'

'I believe you, Miss Trindle,' James said softly, suddenly remembering the secretary's name from his last visit to the college. 'I saw him in Morocco yesterday and I have reason to believe he has returned to England.'

'And you thought Stephen might come here?' There was a note of optimism in her voice.

'It was an outside chance. Now I have to try and work out where the professor could be.'

'He may be with his friend,' she volunteered. 'I tried calling last week but I was told he hadn't heard from Stephen in ages.'

'Who is this friend?'

'Bernard. They've been good friends for many years,' she said dabbing at her eyes with a small embroidered handkerchief.

'Bernard Davies? Owner of the Green Fingers Garden Centre?'

'Why yes, do you know him?'

James blew Miss Trindle a kiss and ran from the office and down the stairs. Why on earth didn't I realize that those two knew each other a lot better than they let on, James thought as he hurried to the car park. The rain had become torrential by the time he drove out of Cambridge and took the Wisbech road. As he approached the gates to the garden centre James reviewed how he could enter without alerting Davies. It was possible that Calder had used his friend to hide the coins and that they were still on the premises. If that was the case then Davies could be very dangerous as he had met James and knew what he was looking for.

He slowed the car one hundred yards from the entrance and then pulled onto the grass verge to stop. Three cars left and two entered the centre as he walked to the gates. Turning his coat lapels up and using the new arrivals as cover he slipped into the curved glass-roofed showroom. James immediately spotted Davies talking to a customer by the electric lawnmowers and he ducked behind the shelving stacked high with horticultural pesticides, fungicides, garden hoses and secateurs while he made his way to the door at the rear marked *PRIVATE*.

It opened easily and James stepped inside and closed the door behind him. The office was empty and he quickly scanned the papers on top of the desk for any evidence that Calder had been in contact. Using his handkerchief he opened each of the drawers without any success before noticing the red light flashing on the landline phone. There were three calls on the answerphone and James turned down the volume and switched to play. The first was an enquiry about purchasing ladybirds, the second on signs of elm disease but the third stopped James from rifling through any more papers.

'Bernard, I'm back in the country and staying at the old place. Make sure you come tonight.'

Click. The sound was instantly recognizable and it was right by James' ear. 'I would be justified in shooting you as a burglar, Goodfellow,' Davies said. 'Especially if you're armed.'

James raised his arms and turned. The wrong end of a 12-gauge shotgun was levelled at his face. He knew his head was within a finger pressure of being blown apart but was unprepared for the weapon being used as a club to deliver a knock-out blow with the stock and he fell to the floor.

'However, I could be prosecuted for using an unnecessary act of violence on an unarmed man. You are unarmed, aren't you?' Davies asked as he kicked James' foot. He received no response from the investigator and Davies kicked him harder. 'Fainting after a mere tap on the head, some detective you are,' he muttered. 'I don't know how Stephen could think a big girl's blouse like you could represent a threat,' and he kicked again to create another bruise.

'There's a strange man lying on my office floor, Doris,' he said as he passed the cash payment desk. 'Chuck him out when he comes round.' She nodded and continued checking out the hydrangeas. The Range Rover left the garden centre and within minutes was heading for Wisbech.

When James awoke he was lying on a mud-stained mat beside a dull grey steel desk and a puzzled middle-aged woman was looking down at him. She was holding a small trowel aloft as though it would give her confidence when the stranger sat up.

'Don't try anything, sir,' she said timidly and waved the trowel as though brandishing a claymore. 'Mr Davies said that I have to ask you to leave the premises.'

James groaned, held his head and then felt his side where the owner had been playing football. 'I will if you'll tell me where he went,' he said with a grimace of pain that was intended to be a reassuring smile.

'I'll phone the police if you don't go.'

'Just tell me and I'll be off,' James said as he slowly stood up to tower over the diminutive woman.

She took a step back. 'He keeps a boat on the Nene,' she squeaked. 'Now go.'

'Where exactly, madam, it's a very long river.'

'It's quite close to Guyhirn.'

James managed to smile as he left the office, followed at a discreet distance by the trowel-wielding woman. He went through the main gate and returned to his car still holding his aching side.

He checked the satnav for Guyhirn and as he drove off he could see in his rear-view mirror that the woman had followed him out of the main entrance and was jotting down his registration number.

After ten minutes of fast driving across the flat farmland he reached the bridge crossing the Nene to Guyhirn. James entered the village and parked opposite the church. Using the steps cut into the high river embankment retaining the river he reached the top and instantly spotted a solitary white boat moored about seventy-five metres from where he stood. There were no signs of life and James strode to a small gangplank to study the vessel. It was a twenty-foot, two-berth Viking with an inboard engine and the curtains were drawn on all the windows.

The Viking was motionless in the water and James tentatively put his foot on the gangplank. It creaked a little and the boat moved as he put his full weight on the treads. There was still no movement within the boat and he took a chance and stepped down into the cockpit area where he stood perfectly still for a few seconds.

James listened as the gentle wind soughed through the longer grass and down the river to lightly slap water against the hull. He was mildly startled by a formation of low-flying geese and he decided to get a move on. He went to the small door, cautiously opened it and descended to the lower deck, passing between a kitchenette on his left and a toilet cubicle on his right before entering the lounge area.

Professor Calder was sitting on the couchette with a cigarette in one hand and a tumbler of whisky in the other. He looked up at James with a self-satisfied smile on his face. 'This is the end of the road for you, Mr Goodfellow,' he said. James was too late to notice the second glass standing on the small formica table and Calder's eyes briefly flicking over his shoulder. Before James could fully react the pickaxe handle was already swinging and it struck him a glancing blow at the base of the skull. Once more he collapsed at the feet of Bernard Davies who tossed the handle to one side and picked up the second glass of whisky.

'He'll be out for quite a while,' he said as the fiery spirit warmed his throat.

'Have you killed him?'

'I don't know but I believe we should make sure.'

'Not in here,' Calder said vehemently.

'Of course not, I'm not an idiot,' and Davies tapped the side of his nose knowingly. 'The next time something hits him hard it will be in the dark and on the road.'

Calder gave him a puzzled look.

Later tonight we'll pour whisky in his mouth and on his clothes, lay him out on the darkest part of the A47 and let the next truck do the job for us.'

Both men laughed and Davies gave James another bruise with the toe of his shoe.

High clouds were scudding across the moon's face, darkening the land and reducing the road to a ribbon of black with only the occasional glare of lights as vehicles rushed past the two men. Calder had pulled James from the back seat onto the verge and was waiting for Davies to come from his car to give a hand.

'Have you got the whisky?' Calder asked as his partner squatted beside him. Davies nodded and proceeded to pour the alcohol down James' shirt. Calder forced the unconscious man's mouth open and Davies poured in a generous shot and quickly turned his head sideways to prevent him from choking.

'That's enough, is anything approaching?'

Davies checked the road both ways before grabbing James by the legs. 'It's clear, Stephen,' he said and the two men swiftly carried the unconscious man to the centre of the road and put him down. They arranged his body as though he had passed out while crossing and sprinted to their cars to return to the boat and decide on their next plan of action.

'I'll drive to Harwich and take the ferry to the Hook of Holland while you return to the garden centre as though nothing has happened,' Calder dictated when they were in the Viking's lounge.

'And the coins and the charter?'

'I'll take them with me and start negotiations with my contacts.'

Davies glanced at his partner with more than a touch of suspicion. 'And when will I get my share?'

'When they're all sold and the hullabaloo has died down.'

'It's fifty-fifty, right?'

'Less expenses such as my time in Morocco and Holland.' Calder leant back and took a leisurely sip from his tumbler.

'We'll call that three thousand, shall we?'

Calder looked up and stared at his friend for a few seconds before lowering his gaze to the tumbler. 'Sure, that'll just about cover it,' he murmured as his mind raced. 'So your share now totals one million, less three thousands pounds.'

'You're going to be paid more than four million for the charter and the silver which means you'll have to pay me two million less three thousand pounds sterling,' Davies said in a low ominous tone as he slipped his right hand into the jacket pocket.

'If you insist, Bernard.'

'I do.'

The lounge descended into an uneasy silence as they drank the whisky, smoked Turkish cigarettes and eyed each other with obvious suspicion.

Calder suddenly banged his tumbler down on the table. 'Goodfellow's car,' he exclaimed. 'He must have parked it near the boat. We must move it close to his body so the police think he staggered out of it in a drunken stupor and passed out in the road,' he concluded. He stood up and the two men hurried out of the boat to look for James' car. It was about seventy-five metres away on the embankment.

'Shit!' Davies cried when he reached the driver's door. 'We haven't got the keys.'

'Where are they?'

'In his bloody jacket where he put them, I would guess.' The sarcasm in Davies' voice was unmistakable as he yanked at the door handle without any success.

'Then we'll have to go back to where we dumped him. We'll use your car.' Calder didn't wait for an answer and they were soon speeding back.

After ten miles Calder tapped Davies on the knee. 'Haven't we gone past the place already?'

Davies checked the odometer and shook his head. 'Another mile to go, by the drainage channel that feeds into the River Nene.' He suddenly jammed his foot down on the brake, pulled into a convenient lay-by and pointed straight ahead.

Red and blue lights were flashing up ahead and when Davies cut his lights they also saw orange lights flashing on the road behind them and heard the unsettling sound of an ambulance siren.

'Well, we can't move the bastard's car but at least the job's done and we can relax a little,' Calder said unemotionally.

'We could smash the window and short the ignition wiring,' Davies suggested as the ambulance swept past them and rushed towards the scene of the accident. They could see by its powerful headlights that two police cars and a giant articulated lorry blocked the road.

'He must resemble a hedgehog after being hit by that,' Calder murmured with a frisson of pleasure running the length of his spine. Davies chuckled and started back to Guyhirn to park behind James' vehicle. The cricket bat made short work of the window on the driver's side and it took him a further ten minutes to remove the dash molding and locate the right wiring.

When the engine came to life Calder said, 'We'll leave it as close as we dare to where his unfortunate "accident" took place and then we'll pick up the coins at your garden centre. I'll then drive to Harwich and take the ferry to Rotterdam.'

The mortuary was naturally cold and the medical examiner, Daphne Sampson, shivered as she looked at the well-toned naked body before her. She recognised the face and was saddened by the task confronting her.

Chief Inspector Cheswell entered through the swing doors and approached the stainless-steel post mortem table. 'I rather liked the fellow,' he said softly as he studied the face. 'Somehow I can't believe that he would ever be drunk enough to wander across a road in the middle of nowhere and be hit by a truck.'

'He wasn't, Inspector,' the medical examiner said as she pointed at the bruising on the torso. 'I've only just started but it's obvious what caused those marks.'

Cheswell moved closer to study the bruises. 'Bloody hell, you're right. The one on his chest is the shape of a boot and I wouldn't mind betting that the marks on his side were made by the cap of the same boot.'

While the inspector leant in closer to look at the purple bruises the medical examiner turned James' head to reveal the damage at the base of the skull. 'Blunt force trauma,' he conjectured and Daphne nodded.

'There are some fragments of something. Take some samples for analyses,' she instructed an assistant.

'Do you think he was first kicked and then killed by someone hitting him with a blunt object?' Cheswell asked.

'I do but until I get some results back from the lab I cannot say what for sure, Inspector.'

'Then I'll leave you while I go and pass on the bad news to the widow,' Cheswell said with a heavy heart and left the mortuary.

Daphne nodded and wondered who had the more onerous task: herself for having to dissect the body of someone she rather liked or Cheswell who had to talk to the grief stricken wife. The lab assistant had taken his swabs and left and Daphne sat on the high stool and contemplated the still figure lying before her. She had only spoken to him a few times but he had struck her as being a strong, compassionate person who cared about people and was driven to seek justice. The face wasn't overly handsome yet showed strength. His eyes were closed but she remembered how much life was in them as she reluctantly climbed down from her stool and went to the instrument trays. Reached for a scalpel she stepped up to the table.

'For God's sake, no!' Cheswell shouted as he burst through the swing doors.

Daphne, scalpel poised inches from the breastbone, looked round in shock.

'Don't cut him,' the inspector panted breathlessly, 'not until you've carried out a number of tests that the paramedics were unable to do.'

'Why?' Daphne stuttered and the scalpel clattered loudly as it was dropped in the instrument tray.

'I gave the bad news to Goodfellow's wife and asked if she could come up to Norfolk to identify her husband. Naturally, she was extremely upset but she told me something that scared the hell out of me. Goodfellow is a narcoleptic and can go into a very deep REM sleep. This depends on the type of shock he receives and when he last took a Zenzedi tablet. I said I would ask you to do a thorough check and that's when I remembered that you were planning to conduct the post-mortem now.'

'Thank heavens you stopped me, Inspector. I was on the point of opening him up.'

The doors opened again and the lab assistant hurried in with a sheet of paper in his hand. 'Excuse me, Inspector, but I've had the results of the substance found in the victim's hair. It's simply linseed oil, plain and simple.'

'Such as used on a cricket bat?'

'Yes, and the fragment was a minute splinter of willow.'

'So he was knocked for a six by an unknown assailant,' Daphne murmured.

'Which makes it murder,' the inspector added.

'But only if he's dead.' She began to make preparations for the tests, excitement lighting up her whole face. 'Wouldn't it be wonderful if he's still with us?'

The men nodded and the inspector made his apology, asked to be kept informed about James' condition and left the room to begin the investigation into what could either be a murder or a case of grievous bodily harm with a deadly weapon.

17

THE SUN WAS JUST showing above the horizon when a community support constable driving from Wisbech to March stopped alongside the abandoned car on the grass verge. Seeing the broken window and damaged dashboard he called it in to have the registration checked and the car rental company supplied March with all the information they required; this was then shared with Wisbech and King's Lynn police stations.

Sergeant Tanner tapped on the open door and stepped into the office carrying a sheet of paper. 'Message just in, Chief, the car Goodfellow hired has been found on the A47 and had been vandalized, suggesting it's been used by joy riders.'

Cheswell looked up from a witness report about two men who had helped a drunk cross the road late the previous night. 'I don't think it was kids out for fun, Sergeant,' he muttered. 'An old man was cycling back from his local when he spotted two men carrying an unconscious man away from a car and onto the road.'

'And?' Tanner had a puzzled look on his face. This didn't surprise his superior as he wasn't the brightest copper in the purse.

'He claims that he didn't see them completely cross the road before suddenly driving off.'

'Do you think they were carrying Goodfellow, sir?'

'What do you think, Sergeant? For God's sake man, our witness was at exactly the same spot that Goodfellow was found. If that lorry driver hadn't just started his shift and was wide awake and alert Goodfellow would have been reduced to strawberry jam.'

'He's still a corpse, sir.'

'That we don't know yet –'

The phone interrupted what he was going to say and after listening for a few seconds he jumped up and left a rather bewildered sergeant sitting alone.

Cheswell ignored the irritatingly slow lift, rushed down the stairs to the basement and burst dramatically through the swing doors and into the mortuary.

'What's new, Daphne?' he called out as he crossed the room. The first thing he noticed was that the examination table was empty. Secondly, the medical examiner was sitting at the office desk with Goodfellow who was wearing little more than a towel round his waist; they were both sipping coffee as though enjoying a perfectly ordinary domestic moment.

'My God, you're alive!'

James looked up at the officer and grinned broadly despite the searing pain in his head and side. 'I hope I haven't disappointed you, Chief Inspector,' he said.

'I had only just begun to prepare the tests when he simply woke up, sat up and asked for a cup of coffee. However, I still need to make sure there are no fractures in the skull,' Daphne said. 'I'm taking him for an X-ray now.'

'I'll also need replacement clothes for those you removed with your dangerously sharp scissors.'

Daphne grinned and left to get a hospital gown from the stores.

'What happened exactly?' Cheswell demanded as he drew up a chair and sat facing the half-naked investigator.

'I was caught unawares by Calder and Davies.'

'The garden centre owner?' Cheswell frowned. 'Are you claiming Davies has been working with the Professor all the time?'

'I wouldn't say working together but forming a rather uneasy alliance until they've retrieved something Calder left behind.'

'The Magna Carta copy?'

'No. Calder already had that in his possession. He came back to England to retrieve the silver coins.'

'He never took them?'

James shook his head. 'He clearly hid them somewhere in the Cambridge area and my bet is that they're with Davies.'

'So it wasn't academic glory but greed that compelled him to take a chance and come back.'

James nodded and winced as a dagger of pain shot through his head. 'I also believe that he had given them to Davies to hide somewhere until his return; he would then collect them to take to a buyer.' More pain raced through his head and a numbing sensation began to affect his limbs. 'Tablets . . . in my jacket . . . I need my . . .' To the astonishment of the inspector James collapsed across the desk.

Cheswell made sure the unconscious man was safe and hurried from the cold room to alert Daphne or any other member of the medical staff. As he turned a corner he ran into an attractive woman and they both tumbled to the floor.

The inspector scrambled to his feet and helped the young woman up. 'My sincere apology, miss, but there's an emergency and I need to find a doctor or a nurse,' he said as he visually checked that she hadn't come to any harm.

'Then you'd better hurry along,' she replied as she smoothed down her skirt and jacket. Cheswell gave a smile of appreciation and handed her the blue handbag she had dropped before running on. He found Daphne leaning over a large cardboard box and pulling out a number of embarrassing backless items humorously referred to as gowns. He explained what had happened and they both ran back to the mortuary.

'It could be a blood clot,' she conjectured as they went through the doors and saw a strange woman sitting beside James. She had pulled him upright in the chair and was gently patting his cheeks while murmuring something in his ear.

'Who are you and what on earth do you think you're doing with my patient,' Daphne exclaimed as she tried to restrain the woman's hand.

'My name is Jennifer Goodfellow and I'm in the process of waking my husband,' she answered, unperturbed by the angry tone in Daphne's voice.

'He may be experiencing a brain haemorrhage and needs urgent medical attention.' Daphne punched a large red button on the wall beside the desk and Cheswell mentally kicked himself when he saw the sign *Use In An Emergency Only*.

'All James needs is a Zenzedi tablet. Where are his clothes?' Jennifer asked as she looked around the large room.

'That must be what he was saying when he passed out,' Cheswell said and continued when he saw the question in the women's eyes. 'It was something like, I need my, and then he was out like a light.'

'It's his tablets. James is narcoleptic and shocks, pain and even humour can trigger a reaction,' Jennifer explained as she had done so often. The medical examiner immediately crossed to a large wicker hamper on castors and delved into the pockets of a blood-stained jacket to withdraw two small boxes.

'Discard the old Xyrem tablets and use the stronger Zenzedi pills that I couriered to him last night,' Jennifer said.

The doors crashed open and a crash-cart team led by a middle-aged doctor streamed into the room. Daphne held her hand up. 'My apology, doctor, but although I still need to X-ray this man the reason he collapsed may be due to a narcoleptic attack.

The doctor frowned as he took James' wrist and checked his pulse. 'What brought him here?' he asked.

'Hit on the head with a blunt instrument and kicked in the side,' Daphne said as James was quickly examined. 'I won't be happy until I see the results.'

'I agree. Let's get him moving now,' he ordered the three accompanying nurses and James was carefully lifted from the seat and laid on a gurney. Jennifer stood to go with them but was restrained by the chief inspector.

'I know you want to go with your husband but don't worry, he'll be fine and I would like you to answer a few questions for me. You're a detective sergeant at the East Steading police station?'

'Yes, sir.'

'Tell me, how long has James had this condition?'

'It started when he graduated from college as a microbiologist and became a researcher in forestry conservation. He resigned after an attack caused him to fall from a tree, breaking two ribs and his collarbone. Soon after James also had to resign from the police force.'

'He was a copper?' Cheswell said with raised eyebrows.

'A good one too; made detective constable within a year but unfortunately his condition worsened and the pills he was taking let him down and he started falling asleep on the job.'

'Wow, I've heard of sleeping policemen to control traffic but that's taking things too far. So he resigned?'

'He was retired on medical grounds but because his dream to be a detective was so strong he decided to start his own investigation agency. He has been doing this for two years now and has solved some tricky cases.'

'Such as?' The inspector was intrigued by James' life and encouraged Jennifer to go on.'

'He exposed and ended an organization that kidnapped and brainwashed children for experimentation purposes in East Berlin before and after the Wall fell.'

'I read about that at the time.'

'He also solved the murder of a Chinese man in London and recovered a vast treasure of ancient artefacts from the Yakuza.'

'James certainly gets around, doesn't he?' Cheswell murmured as he stood up and invited Jennifer to join him in the waiting area. James had been taken to the radiology department and Daphne joined them there to explain the procedure to Jennifer.

'I can tell you that your husband has recovered and was able to explain that it was a head pain that started his relapse. He didn't take a pill this morning due to being knocked unconscious last night and as a consequence he was very vulnerable to another narcoleptic attack. As well as giving him a shot of Zenzedi I will be checking for any fractures or blood clots.'

Daphne noticed the concern deepening in Jennifer's expression and quickly went on. 'The procedure is quite straightforward and I expect to have results in a few minutes' time. In the meantime I suggest you go to the hospital restaurant for a cup of coffee and a sticky bun. They're quite nice actually, and I'll come and join you as soon as I have any news.'

Jennifer thanked the medical examiner and after shaking the inspector's hand she went to the restaurant where people were talking in the guarded tones one expected in an establishment that primarily dealt with unpleasant matters. One reasonably tasting coffee from an automatic machine was followed by a second before Daphne weaved her way between the tables and chairs to reach Jennifer.

'Your husband must have a skull as hard as steel as there's no sign of any cracks, hairline or otherwise, and apart from the bruising his ribs are also in good shape,' she reported as she sat opposite a very relieved Jennifer.

'We've given him an extra box of Zenzedi and some painkillers and he should be able to leave with you in approximately thirty minutes.'

Barely twenty minutes later James appeared in the restaurant wearing a borrowed sweatshirt promoting Children In Need and a pair of Theatre Blues disposable trousers.

'Ooooh, sexy,' Jennifer murmured with a wink and James blushed before giving his wife a hug and a lingering kiss.

'Can we go and get some proper clothes, darling,' he grumbled as they left the hospital. Chief Inspector Cheswell was trailing behind but as he had exhausted his supply of questions he bid them goodbye and returned to the station to coordinate a national hunt for Professor Calder and Davies.

James checked the travel case Jennifer had brought with her and was able to change on the backseat of her car with the necessary amount of discretion before getting behind the wheel.

'Home now?' Jennifer asked.

'Uh-huh, I want to check the Green Fingers Garden Centre to see if my "friends" have dared go back there.'

'But surely they must know they're being sought by the police and therefore wouldn't go anywhere near that place?'

James grinned mischievously. 'They think they've killed me and that nobody knows of Davies' involvement or Calder's presence in Norfolk. They'll be feeling very self-satisfied which means I will be a bloody big disappointment to them both.'

'That could be dangerous, James,' Jennifer warned, a deep frown creasing her forehead.

'It will only be dangerous for them, darling, only for them.' He drove out of Wisbech and took the road to Newton.

Davies drove fast to keep up with Calder who had elected to lead the way back to the Green Fingers Garden Centre. Everything was in darkness when he stopped beside Calder's car in the driveway. The padlock was removed, the gates opened wide and they drove straight to the showroom.

'Where did you hide them?' Calder asked as Davies unlocked the door. The man simply smiled and led him past the lawnmowers and on to a hothouse devoted to specialist orchids. He tapped the rheostat on the outside and used a Yale key.

'Close the door behind you, these plants are very fragile and a drop in temperature can affect their performance.'

Calder slammed the door behind him and then coughed as he took his first breath of the exceptionally humid air. 'It's like trying to breathe under water in here,' he gasped.

'Like being in a tropical jungle where pirates used to bury their treasure, you mean.' Davies laughed and pointed at a promotional display amongst the exotic plants. A multicoloured showcard, decorated with a skull and crossbones invited customers to take part in a treasure hunt within the garden centre. The object of the hunt was to track down plants marked with a pirate's flag stuck in their pots which would give them a mystery discount when the silver panel was scratched at the checkout. A leaflet dispenser, explaining the rules, stood beside a half-buried chest from which spilled scores of dull, corroded coins.

'Are they what I think they are?' Calder said disbelieving his eyes as he took one of the discs from the moss and bark composite.

'The perfect hiding place,' Davies declared smugly. 'Right out in the open where everyone can see them.'

Calder suddenly realized that the half-sunken chest was also the original that had been found in the tree. 'Weren't you afraid a customer or kid would take one or more of them as a souvenir?'

Davies pointed up at a CCTV camera mounted six feet above their heads.

Calder nodded and began the task of excavating the chest and putting the spilled coins back in it. When they were sure they had traced every piece and the lid was closed the professor got Davies to carry it out to the parked cars. Using both hands the garden centre owner staggered out leaving the hothouse door open. Damn the orchids, I won't be coming back, Calder thought.

'Put it in the boot of my car and then we'll discuss how to dispose of them in Holland.' Calder didn't wait for an answer and walked back inside to wait at the office door.

'When did you last check the monitors?' Calder asked after Davies had unlocked the door and switched on the lights. He looked around, trying to find them.

The King's Charter

'I did just now,' Davies said as he sat in his swivel chair and took a piece of card from his inside pocket. 'I used the cheapest deterrent I could afford, a fake camera. Nothing works except for the little red light and that runs on a single AA battery. However, I check if anything has been taken with this,' and he flicked a crisp photograph of the display over the desk to Calder. Every coin that had spilled from the chest could clearly be seen.

'Any pilfered coins would be missed instantly by a simple comparison with the photo. Every time someone went into the orchid house I, or my assistant, would go in with that picture when they were about to leave.'

'No tapes, discs or recordings at all?'

Davies rocked back in his chair and laughed; it was the last sound he would ever make for Calder took a semi-automatic from his pocket, pointed it at his right eye and pulled the trigger. Davies was pushed back by the impact and a crimson spray coloured the seed catalogue posters on the wall behind him. Calder wiped the gun clean and using his handkerchief placed it on the floor beneath the dead man's dangling arm. After checking every surface he may have inadvertently touched he switched the lights off and left the garden centre. The clock on the dashboard showed 3 a.m. and the road was empty as he drove out through the gates and took the road to Wisbech. From there he would head south for Harwich.

James slowed down as he approached the entrance to the garden centre at 7.30 a.m. and was surprised to find the gates wide open. He drove in and after instructing Jennifer to stay in the car he went to the showroom. The sun was streaming through the glass panels in the roof and illuminated the displays of hose reels, forks, spades and potted monkey-puzzle and fig trees.

The place was deserted and James moved slowly through the building until he spotted that the indoor hothouse door had not been closed. Curiosity compelled him to investigate and although the temperature had dropped a few degrees the humidity was still cloying. He walked amongst the jasmine and passion fruit climbers and briefly admired the various orchids until he reached what appeared to be a display area. A square hole in a raised bed and moss scattered on the pathway were evidence that something had been hurriedly wrenched from it. James raked through the soil with his fingers and found a single metal disc. He held it up in the light and immediately recognized it as one of the silver coins.

James looked round the hothouse for any other signs but finding nothing he went out, considerately closing the door behind him as he pocketed the coin. He crept towards the frosted office door which opened silently and jumped in to find Davies staring at him with one sightless eye, his right eye a black cavity that had trickled blood into the stubble on his cheek. James didn't have to go any closer to know that Davies was dead and he returned to the car.

'I think Cheswell will be interested in what I found,' he said as he sat down beside Jennifer who looked at him with raised eyebrows. 'There's been a falling out of thieves and Davies lost.'

'He's dead?'

'Just one shot in the head, execution style.'

Jennifer was already dialling as James spoke to report the incident to Cheswell.

'Cheswell says we have to stay until he turns up with the crime scene team.'

James settled back in his seat and wearily closed his eyes. 'I'll try to get some shuteye,' he informed his wife and she nodded. 'Why don't you check how Miss Lightbody is getting on with Claudiu?'

Jenny started to say something but when she saw that James had already fallen asleep she speed-dialled Agnes. After five minutes she had a complete rundown of what Agnes and Claudiu had been up to while she'd been away. Agnes was relieved to hear that James was OK and asked Jennifer to get him to call her when he woke up.

Another thirty minutes passed during which Jennifer turned away three prospective customers who, on seeing the gates were open, assumed the centre was too. Jennifer felt relieved when she finally heard the familiar wail of police sirens. Two cars screeched into the driveway and stopped in a cloud of gravel that rattled in the wheel arches.

James woke up and holding his side he went to greet the disgruntled officer.

'For God's sake, Goodfellow,' he exclaimed. 'Every time I see you it's because there's been more carnage. I ought to lock you up for disturbing the peace; my peace.'

'Sorry, Chief Inspector, but it looks like our nice, quiet university professor has become a raging psychopath.' James led the way to the office and stood back as the inspector entered with the crime scene investigators. 'Have you apprehended Calder yet?' James called out only to be answered with a noncommittal grunt. 'I take it that means no.'

Cheswell came out with a grim expression. 'He could be anywhere by now,' he grumbled. 'Heading for one of the ports, Norwich airport or just lying low in another nondescript cottage until all the rumpus has died down.'

'And then slip away to sell his ill-gotten gains in Europe?'

'That's an old-fashioned way of putting it,' Jennifer said as she passed the two men and entered the office.

'That *is* a crime scene, Mrs Goodfellow,' Cheswell bellowed after her. 'You can't go in there,' and he made as if to follow her.

'Jennifer's a detective sergeant, Inspector, as you well know,' James said quietly and grinned as he laid a restraining hand on the officer's arm. 'She knows the proper drill and isn't likely to contaminate the scene.'

After another grunt Cheswell turned to James. 'Where do you think the professor has gone?' he muttered.

'God knows,' James said with a sigh as he handed the piece of silver to the officer. 'What I'm certain of is that he's got all the silver coins with him.'

'Except for this piece,' Cheswell said.

Both men stared at it as though it might give them a lead to the professor's whereabouts.

18

CALDER HAD PASSED THROUGH Colchester with its ancient Roman remains and taken the Stour road shadowing the river to Harwich, a large ferry port. Golden light was spilling across rooftops and large herring gulls were wheeling noisily overhead as he drove down the main street towards the foreshore. The chest of coins meant Calder had to forego flying and instead take the car ferry to Rotterdam. The earliest sailing time was ten o'clock and using a reliable alias, for which he had a passport, he made a last-minute booking. He now had a two-hour wait and he pulled into an all-night supermarket car park to satisfy his hunger at the first seaman's café that was open for business.

A substantial bacon-and-tomato toasted sandwich and two cups of strong tea soon passed the time and as he prepared to return to the car he overheard the conversation of two uniformed crew members from one of the cross-channel ferries.

'The immigration and boarding officers just received red alerts,' a bearded man said in a conspiratorial tone.

'What's it about this time? Just another bloody exercise I expect; they're a fucking waste of time.'

'Not this time, mate. Our First Officer told me that there's a fugitive who could be trying to get to the continent on one of our ships.'

Like a gundog his companion suddenly sat up. 'Dangerous is he?' he inquired and then drained the last few drops of tea.

'We've been warned that he's armed and should be approached with extreme caution.'

The weight of the automatic in Calder's jacket seemed to grow as he listened. He quickly paid for his meal and left the café feeling as though the eyes of everyone present were on his back.

The car did not appear to be under surveillance and Calder left the car park and the town as fast as he could. All chances of reaching Rotterdam by sea were quashed; somehow the police had found out that he was in the country. There were no paper trails leading to Davies or the Green Fingers Garden Centre and he had been careful about using his alias when he returned from Marrakech.

How on earth could the bastards know I was in England and wanted to leave again? The only person who knew of his connection is now lying dead in Wisbech mortuary. It must have been CCTVs at Heathrow, he thought as he left the built-up area surrounding Harwich and headed back across the flat farmland to the main road and Colchester.

As he drove his mind ran through all the options there were for a man on the run in the United Kingdom. He could return to the college and attempt to bluff it out, saying he had taken a short break in Morocco to conduct research for his next paper on North African artefacts, or he could risk renting a house in a remote village.

His final option was to leave the country but how could he when all the legitimate methods of travel were now being watched. He had driven past the old roman castle and was taking the northerly route out of the town when he thought of the only solution open to him.

Keeping safely within the speed limit Calder entered the small coastal village of Walberswick on the River Blyth after fifty minutes. He drove past a traditional pub called the Bell Inn to the end of the road with a car park on each side and a motley collection of boating sheds ahead. Calder parked and walked on until he stood on the banks of the wide river. To his left it wound its way into the countryside and to the right it flowed tidally into the North Sea.   Looking across the river towards Southwold he could see the ramshackle sheds that the fishermen used to store and sell their morning catch. Each sign proclaimed its fish to be the freshest and the moorings were filled with an eclectic fleet of vessels. The majority was salt-stained, designed and fitted for commercial fishing, but dotted amongst them were smaller, spotless leisure craft.

Calder ran his eye over them until his attention was drawn to a small and rather old Beneteau fishing boat. A weather-resistant tonneau stretched from the roof of the small wheelhouse over the open rear deck to the stern indicating that it had been closed for a lengthy period or possibly for the season. It was imperative that he selected a craft whose absence would not be noticed for a few days if he were to reach the continent without shipping and aircraft keeping electronic eyes open for him. Calder noted the Beneteau position and walked back past the car park to the public house and ordered an early lunch. He hardly noticed the flagstone floor, curved settle and roaring open fire for he was deep in thought, planning how to steal the boat and sail to Rotterdam.

The hearty home-cooked meal sat comfortably beneath his belt as he sipped a malt whisky and very soon he began to doze. He was startled into wakefulness by a harried barmaid who gathered up his plate and cutlery with deliberate clattering. Seeing his eyes opening, she asked if he wanted anything else. He thanked her, paid without leaving any gratuity and left the pub that was beginning to fill up with holidaymakers to seek the solitude of his car.

After checking that the chest and the large cardboard tube containing the charter were still in the boot Calder made himself comfortable on the back seat and once more fell into a deep sleep. Dusk was approaching when he awoke with a stiff neck and a painfully dry mouth. He took a drink of water from a bottle he had purchased earlier and strolled down to the river to check on the Beneteau. Nothing had changed and he could see that no lights had been switched on in the wheelhouse or cabin below; he was ready to go as soon as it was dark enough.

The sheet of used blotting paper on Davies' desk had sparked some interest but at the time Jennifer had dismissed it. It was only when they had returned to the hotel that the impression a ballpoint pen had made in the soft paper came back with crystal clarity.

'Zalmhuis,' she exclaimed excitedly as James emerged from the bathroom towelling his wet hair.

'And what's that supposed to mean?'

'A name was impressed in the blotting pad in Davies' office and it definitely read Zalmhuis.'

'Sounds German.'

'No. Dutch. I think it means salmon house. It could be where Davies had planned to rendezvous with Calder.'

James leapt onto the bed to hug Jennifer. 'You're right, darling. All we have to do is find out where on earth this salmon house could be located in a country of thirteen thousand square miles.'

Jennifer ignored her husband's negative wit, switched on her smartphone and began searching the websites. James switched on the television and caught the tail-end of the regional news about the death of a local businessman. Davies' murder had been leaked to the media and although it was only a scant press release there was a clear picture of professor Calder. The fugitive would have to take flight and leave the country before he was spotted. James was suddenly nudged by Jennifer's elbow in his side and she held her smartphone up as a Google map of Rotterdam appeared on the screen. She activated the zoom button to highlight a building that was close to the Van Brienenoordbrug over the river Nieuwe Maas. Jennifer keyed the street-level view and he was looking at a contemporary building with a terrace, canopied tables and a large sign on the roof that read 'Zalmhuis'.

'It's a very classy restaurant overlooking the river, James.'

'Looks like a good meeting place for someone who hopes to come into a lot of money.'

'Enough money to order a lobster dinner as they perused their Magna Carta?' Jennifer said with a broad grin that was instantly smothered by a kiss.

'England's Magna Carta,' James corrected. 'You've cracked it, Jenny,' James added as he held her face between his hands and kissed her again. 'I don't have to worry about how Calder gets there as I only have to wait for him to arrive.'

'How can you be so sure that he will arrive?'

'Why else would Davies have scribbled the name on his blotter? That's where they were to meet their prospective buyer. Calder reneged when he realized he didn't need a partner once he had recovered the coins from wherever Davies had been hiding them.'

'A professor who teaches archaeology at a Cambridge university college stoops to murder? He has certainly moved from the sublime to the ridiculous. It doesn't seem to make sense.'

'It does when you consider the man was driven into bankruptcy by his wife when she divorced him last year. She stripped him of all his investments, a large percentage of his income and claimed virtually everything else including the house that she promptly sold. She then disappeared with his highly prized 1929 Morgan Aero car.'

'Men and their cars,' Jennifer mocked.

'It was worth £58,000 and it is most probably in the South of France now or, as others claim, at the place she bought on Lesbos.'

'I take it all back, she's a bitch and –' Jennifer was interrupted as James began making passionate love to her. She eagerly responded and it was late when they finally sank into an exhausted, dreamless sleep.

James' smartphone buzzed and warbled before dawn and he quickly switched it off, rolled away and got out of bed as carefully as possible so as not to disturb Jennifer. He did a web search in the bathroom and found that there were three flights to Rotterdam from Norwich. He had just started to make a booking when the door opened and Jennifer, stark naked, stood before him holding her hand out. He showed her the screen with an embarrassed grimace.

'So, you planned to leave me here while you traipsed round Holland chasing that damned professor and the charter?' she said as she snatched the phone from him and began tapping on the screen. 'Leave the little woman at home to do the cooking and care for the children while you have all the adventure? Like hell!' she scolded as she handed the phone back. Jennifer had booked two seats and he shrugged in defeat. 'OK, we go together but we have to hurry as the flight leaves at midday. I'll call Miss Lightbody and tell her what we're doing.'

'Poor soul, she deserves a raise.'

James laughed. 'And she'll get one as soon as we get back.'

'Just out of interest, James, why don't we simply notify the police? With the help of the Dutch authorities they could very easily apprehend Calder. It would save Agnes' precious petty cash the cost of two air tickets.'

'I don't trust the police to be careful when retrieving the document and I'll talk to Miss Lightbody when we return.'

'You'd better pray she understands.'

James was about to respond when Cheswell rang. 'How can I help you, Chief Inspector?'

'Good morning, Goodfellow. You may be able to help the police if you have gained any information since yesterday regarding the whereabouts of Professor Calder.'

James hesitated. 'I can't help you Chief Inspector but could you tell me why you're calling me about this so early in the morning?'

'In carrying out our investigation we discovered that the professor had another residence, a small cottage in a tiny place called Six Mile Bottom.'

'I can only assume he wasn't there otherwise you wouldn't be calling me.'

'No, he wasn't there, but his wife was.'

'After suing her husband for every penny he had I thought she left to live in France or Greece.'

'Mrs Joan Calder would have found it difficult to travel, Goodfellow, because she was found in the basement of the cottage under two feet of earth and a thin layer of newly laid concrete. Are you sure you don't know where he is?' There was a touch of suspicion in the chief inspector's tone and on quick reflection James decided to give him some information.

'I can only guess that he's going to try for Holland, possibly Rotterdam,' he admitted without mentioning the Zalmhuis restaurant.

'And why would you think that?'

James thought rapidly. 'You've got the airports and ferries well covered so he would have to use either his own boat or a stolen one to cross the Channel. Calais is the narrowest stretch of sea but due to the heavy sea traffic all ships and boats are closely monitored by the coastguard radar so I think he'll leave from where he's least expected to make the crossing which could be somewhere on the East Anglian coast to the Netherlands. Crossing the North Sea is a lot more dangerous but his only option.'

'You seem to make sense, Goodfellow. However, we've gone through all his personal papers and bank statements and nowhere can we find any purchase or mention of boats capable of making such a sea journey.'

'Which gives you more reason to keep checking for any theft of a vessel along that stretch of the coast,' James said. 'Not owning one means he'll be forced to try his hand at stealing one.'

'There are thousands of boats he can choose from –'

'Concentrate on powered boats,' James interrupted. 'If he's never had a yacht I doubt that he'll trust himself to sail single-handed across the North

Sea; he's more likely to rely on an engine and a vessel big enough to handle safely in the open sea.'

'I'll put out the call now,' Cheswell said and hung up.

The police shift of focus to the east coast posed no immediate threat to Calder. According to some of the friendly locals in the public bar of the Bell Inn, the owner of the old Beneteau was taking his annual vacation in Florence. They also told him that the boat was called Maria II after the owner's wife.

Calder had taken a room for the night, paid in advance, so that he could leave at two in the morning. The waxing moon threw sufficient light on the beaten earth track as he made his way on foot down to the riverbank. He stared across the still water at the small fishing boat until he was sure there was no life on board and returned to the car. He took out the large heavy backpack that 'chinked' healthily when dropped, recovered the tube from the boot, locked the car and went up-river to cross the long footbridge and make his way to where the boat was moored.

A few gulls lifted their heads to watch him as he passed their roosts on the mooring posts and then tucked them back under their wings. Gravel crunched loudly beneath his feet and he moved off the path and onto the grass until he reached the short jetty.

Maria II gently rocked with a light slapping of small waves on the hull as he went on board. He looked up and down the row of vessels but there were no signs of life and he used a heavy screwdriver lying on the transom to lever the lock on the wheelhouse door. There was a loud crack of splintering wood that reverberated across the water and he froze. Calder waited without moving a muscle until he was sure that nobody would be coming to investigate before slipping inside. He placed the backpack on the deck by the wheel and stowed the cardboard tube in one of the lockers.

There was enough light to check the instrumentation and search the single drawer for the ignition key. Like many boat owners this one had relied solely on the security of the door lock and the surrounding boats. Calder found a small bunch of keys, one of which fitted the ignition lock. He gave it a half turn to switch on the instrument lights and gave a sigh of relief when he saw that the fuel tank was full. He then went outside to check for any movement before releasing the bow and stern lines.

Calder hurriedly went back into the wheelhouse, turned the ignition until the engine fired and steered Maria II away from a large fishing boat that was moored on the same side of the jetty. The rumbling of the Volvo engine rolled across the water and he checked each of the buildings and shacks he passed for any signs of life. With the engine at quarter throttle Calder slowly headed down-river and out to sea.

The headwind had increased by the time he was five miles from the coast and the swelling waves beat against the bow to throw spume over the wheelhouse windows. Calder had switched on the navigation lights and was keeping a close eye on the compass as he ploughed further into the North Sea. He had worked out his route from one of the simple charts he had found in the overhead locker and now his full attention was fixed on gripping the helm and ensuring the Maria II didn't drift off course.

After covering thirty-five nautical miles Calder's arms were beginning to ache and he let the boat have its head while he used his mobile phone. The number rang for a long time before a very irate voice answered.

'Do you know what fucking time it is, you moron?' bellowed his contact in Rotterdam bellowed in a broad American accent.

'This is Calder and I can tell the time,' he snarled back. 'And if you still want what we talked about then I expect you to be a little more civil, especially when I'm fighting a heavy sea in a ridiculously small fishing boat.'

There was a long moment of static electricity before the voice spoke again. 'You have it with you?'

'I do. We can meet where we agreed at lunchtime tomorrow.'

'I'll be carrying a folded Albert Heijn shopping bag.'

'Just be there.' Calder closed his phone and stared into the darkness. He still had over sixty miles to cover before choosing where to beach the Maria II – taking the boat into a port would be a clear invitation to curious immigration and customs officials. His main problem would be to avoid the patrolling Netherlands coastguard vessels.

Calder switched on the radio and tuned it to Radio 4 to wait for the shipping forecast which was due in an hour. He half listened to the talking heads while focusing on the darkness beyond the bow. The broadcast was regularly interrupted by static hiss as the bow dipped into each wave, sending white foaming water up and over the railings to splatter against the glass.

The programme finished and a familiar voice began reading. Calder waited patiently until he heard *Humber ... Thames ... north veering north east ... showers ... good ...* He finally switched off with a satisfied expression. As if to corroborate the report light rain began to pitter-patter on the top of the wheelhouse and the wind lessened in intensity. He checked the compass, inched the throttle forward to take advantage of the smaller waves and relaxed back in the leather seat as Maria II increased her speed.

With luck, he thought, I should make the coast by nine o'clock which will give me four hours to make the rendezvous. Calder suddenly realized there was a time difference. 'Damn it,' he exclaimed aloud. 'I'll only have three hours.' Without any regard for the engine Calder thrust the throttle hard against the stop.

He had been making steady progress for about an hour when a chance turn of his head made him aware of the ominous silhouette of a ship behind him. The vessel still glittered with lights and he was able to recognize the 240-metre StenaLine ferry. It was two miles distant and catching up fast, dwarfing the 7-metre Beneteau. Calderwell watched as the ferry altered course and within minutes, after giving infuriated blasts on its horn, it swept past his boat. The bow wave rushed out towards Maria II and Calder spun the wheel to present his bow to the wall of water racing towards him. With a resounding thump the bow went skyward and then dropped again, seawater cascading over the foredeck. The professor grinned for the ferry had shown he was on the right heading for Rotterdam and he brought Maria II round to follow the massive vessel. Even though it was already dwindling in size it was plotting a perfect course that he could follow for at least fifteen minutes.

The sun was just clearing the distant coastline when Calder caught sight of the oil terminal squatting by the mouth of the Nieuwe Waterweg. He turned the wheel and veered towards Visserhaven knowing that there were long stretches of soft sand that were ideal for the Maria II. The hull had been designed to be beachable and as he held the boat steady to follow the coast he scoured the sea for other vessels. Although the ferry would have been a large radar target for the harbourmaster it had also provided cover for Maria II which would have shown on the screens as a tiny anomaly, a shadow of the ferry. Having moved from cover he would be revealed as a separate target and he knew he had to get ashore as soon as possible.

The sky was clearing and a light drizzle had left the upper deck gleaming in the rising sun. Calder briefly checked that the fastenings of the large backpack were secure and put the stout cardboard tube on the instrument console in readiness for going over the side.

He passed a short parade of high-rise apartments and a long pier and he checked for watchful eyes before spinning the wheel and heading straight for the deserted shore. Maria II seemed to sense what was coming and the engine misfired in protest before resuming its normal smooth beat. Only then did Calder notice that he had arrived during high tide and that the exposed beach was only a narrow strand. He braced himself as the vessel struck the shelving sand and kept going for another five metres before the screw jammed and the engine expired.

Calder swung the heavy pack over his shoulder and slipped his arms into the straps. Taking the tube he climbed over the side and lowered himself into the sea which rose no higher than his knees. He had reached his goal and a glance at his watch showed that he had two and a half hours to make his appointment.

Jennifer was the first to notice the board for Mr & Mrs Goodfellow being held high above the meeters and greeters outside the customs hall and she pointed to the grim-faced man holding it.

'Chief Inspector Cheswell, what a pleasure,' James said holding out his hand and the officer shook it grudgingly before doing the same with a smiling Jennifer. 'Who told you we were coming to Rotterdam?'

'My colleagues at Norwich Airport had your picture as well as Calder's. I had an idea that you would keep chasing the money.'

'Not the money, Cheswell, England's heritage,' James corrected as they walked across the concourse. 'I'm trying to prevent a genuine copy of the 1215 Magna Carta from falling into the hands of a private collector who will keep it solely for his own pleasure.'

'And I'm after a murderer. That takes precedence over your precious piece of paper,' Cheswell declared as he opened the door of a taxi for Jennifer.

'I hope you catch him, Chief Inspector,' James replied as he got in after her and wound the window down. 'But whatever you do to apprehend him please try not to damage the document.'

James closed the window and asked the driver to take them to the Hotel Novotel which he knew was closest to the Zalmhuis restaurant.

Cheswell waved to the unmarked police car parked on the other side of the road. 'We don't have to follow them as I luckily overheard where they're going, Inspecteur,' he said as he got in. Thin wire-framed glasses caught the sun as the slightly built man sitting beside the driver turned round and raised one eyebrow. 'It's the Novotel in Brainpark,' Cheswell added. 'We could lunch there while we wait for the Goodfellows to make their next move.'

Inspecteur Adriaan Peters nodded. 'Are you sure Professor Calder is here and that the Goodfellow couple will lead us to him?'

'I'm quite sure that they know something we don't and the man has his own agenda for not telling me what it is.'

'We'd better be right or I'll get it in the neck from Hoofdinsinspecteur de Graaf.'

The BMW X5 pulled away smoothly and was soon crossing Rotterdam on the E19 *autosnelwegen* until sweeping off on the slip road to circle the hotel and enter the parking area. The three plainclothes police officers entered the reception and went directly to the restaurant where they chose a table in a far corner.

'Is this such a good idea, Chief Inspector?' Peters asked. 'Wouldn't the Goodfellows choose to eat here too?'

'We'll take that corner table behind the latticed screen. That way we can keep an eye on them and we'll have some protection should Calder turn violent.'

'You do understand that any action you take will be solely your responsibility. If it breaks Dutch law I will have to counteract any orders you give to my men or myself. Only then will the Dutch government be culpable for anything that happens to the Goodfellows.'

'We agreed this point on the phone, Inspecteur, and I assure you nothing will happen to them as a result of what I do,' Cheswell said as he picked up the menu card and perused the a la carte. Trips to the continent with expenses paid were few and far between for a regional Chief Inspector and he intended to have an excellent lunch at the very least.

The King's Charter

Cheswell had almost decided on a mouthwatering list of dishes when he was nudged by the inspecteur. 'There they are,' the Dutchman muttered as he watched James and Jennifer cross the spectacular atrium to the automatic glass doors and leave the hotel. 'The Goodfellows.'

Cheswell lowered the large menu in time to see the couple disappear and with a silent curse he leapt up. Unfortunately he collided with a passing wine waiter who, grabbing wildly at the table to regain his balance, sent the cutlery flying and the water jug toppling into Cheswell's lap.

Apologizing profusely the waiter began retrieving the silverware from the floor as Cheswell replaced the unbroken jug back on the table.

'I think we've lost them,' Cheswell said before realizing that the waiter was now attempting to use a napkin to dry his crotch in a most embarrassing manner. He pushed away the awkwardly fumbling waiter and asked for the menu he had dropped.

Peters returned with a long face. 'We'll have to wait until they return to the hotel and then we can question them.'

Cheswell nodded and as he ran his eye down the dishes thoughts of the Goodfellows slowly faded; despite the damp, uncomfortable sensation below his waist Cheswell wasn't going to forego this rare opportunity to enjoy an excellent lunch paid for by Her Majesty's government.

A taxi was depositing two guests as James and Jennifer came out of the hotel. They asked the driver to take them the short distance to the Zalmhuis and gained a nod of approval. It was clear that the restaurant had a good reputation and they looked forward to trying the food. Luckily James had phoned from their room to make a reservation and they were warmly greeted at the door.

La Grande Salle in the Zalmhuis was indisputably jaw-dropping. Stained-glass ceilings soared metres above the tables and the large windows offered a magnificent view of the river with ships silently gliding past. They were led to a window seat and politely left to peruse the gourmet menu and wine list.

Jennifer chose a whole gilt-head bream and a large glass of Chardonnay while James settled for a dry-aged sirloin steak and a tall cold glass of Grolsch. The waiter had just left with their order when Calder entered the art deco-styled salon and walked across to the bar to be greeted by a large man who was in his late thirties and elegantly dressed in a blue pin-striped suit. His hair was cut close to the scalp and he had a long scar that ran from his left eye down to the jawline.

'Don't look, but he's here,' James whispered as he leant across the table. 'That must be his contact for the sale.'

Jennifer removed the headband and swung her hair free giving her a quick glimpse of the two men standing fifteen metres away. 'Calder looks very tired,' she observed and James nodded slowly.

'I'm surprised he got here at all.' He kept his eyes fixed on the men who had their heads close together and were discussing something quite vehemently. 'And he doesn't look happy with what the other guy is saying.'

The drinks arrived with fresh bread and small bottles of sparkling Ogo water. James studied the professor's salt-stained trousers and creased jacket and immediately pictured the journey he had made. There was no sign of the king's charter or the coins which clearly meant Calder didn't trust the man he was meeting. This presented James with a new problem: how to follow Calder back to where he had stashed both items. They would have to rely on a taxi being available when the professor left.

Jennifer had her back to the bar and there was little chance she could be recognized by Calder but James ran the risk that at any moment the professor would look his way. He sidled over onto the seat closest to the window and hid behind the floral centrepiece to give himself some cover.

The meals were delicious and they unashamedly cleared their plates. As they were sipping the last of their wine James noticed that Calder was showing signs of terminating his discussion with the stranger.

'Time to go, Jenny,' he murmured and signalled to the waiter for the bill. As they waited anxiously for him to return Calder shook hands with his contact and started to walk away. James' frustration had reached its peak and he was about to go after their quarry when the waiter returned. A quick Mastercard transaction and they were able to rush out. As they passed the stranger who was still lingering at the bar he gave them both a quick glance and James felt some unease.

They stepped out into a light drizzle and suddenly Calder was standing beside Jennifer. He had obviously been aware of James all along and the hand in his jacket pocket was clearly holding a weapon of some description.

'Don't say or do anything, Goodfellow, or your wife will be shot first,' he muttered. The door opened behind them and the big man emerged to stand beside James. Up close he was a lot bigger than James had imagined. As he looked up into cold, emotionless eyes James sensed the man could be more dangerous than the professor from Cambridge.

'We're going for a small drive and I advise you to behave yourselves or Vos will break your wife's neck. Do I make myself clear?'

Calder whispered as he jerked the hand in his pocket in the direction of a dark green Volvo parked close by.

James nodded and kicked himself mentally for leading his wife into such a deadly confrontation.

19

VOS SAT IN THE BACK with Jennifer and James was forced to sit beside Calder. They drove past light industry factories lining a small tributary until Calder suddenly slowed the car and turned into what at first seemed to be a scrapyard. Old sailing yachts, motor cruisers and barges were lined up at the water's edge like a poor man's regatta and the Volvo went to the far end and stopped by a rotting hulk. It was half out of the water and the ancient timbers were covered in green slime.

'Out!' Calder ordered and the couple were taken aboard and led to a deck hatch that Vos threw open to reveal steps descending vertically into darkness. There was a strong smell of oil and stagnant water and Jennifer screw up her nose in distaste despite her fear.

'Down, both of you,' Calder said and Vos gave James a shove in the back making him stumble and fall into the void. He landed on his back in two feet of oil-slicked water, his back badly bruised and hurting. Jennifer cautiously descended and in the weak light from the hatch above she saw James lying in pain in the filthy bilge water. She jumped down and lifted his head clear just as the hatch closed with a slam and everything went black.

They heard the sound of a lock turning and footsteps passing above their heads before fading to a deathly silence that was broken only by their heavy breathing and water lapping against the timbers.

Something scuttled in the darkness followed by a splash; whatever it was had jumped into the water and Jennifer shivered as she suspected it was a rat, one of her pet hates. James struggled to stand upright in the cold water, finding the submerged deck littered with rubbish and steady footing was made difficult.

'What now James, they've locked us in.'

'No doubt to die,' James added. 'This is a tidal river and judging by the feel of the marine growth up the ladder the sea fills this hold completely.'

'Cheerful thought.'

'Before that happens, my darling, I intend to find a way out of this rat trap.'

'First things first.' Jennifer felt in the dark and put a hand on James' shoulder to restrain him. 'Have you any Zenzedi on you. Take one just to be sure."

He felt in his damp pockets and found the small plastic tube containing five tablets that he kept for emergencies. He swallowed one wishing he had a glass of pure water and then slowly climbed the steps to the hatch. One hard push told him it was fastened well and he felt around until he found a soggy edge and was able to prise a piece of the rotting wood away. As the small splinter of wood came adrift a chink of light appeared. He tried to pull more of the timber away but without success.

'Lacking tools this could take days, Jenny, and we only have until the turn of the tide. That's if we don't die from hypothermia first.'

The sound of splashing water started beneath him. 'There's a lot of junk under the water. We may be able to find something a workman has discarded,' Jennifer said as she groped in the dark for something solid.

James climbed down and found that the water had noticeably risen and now almost reached his thighs. 'We'll have to find it fast, darling,' he remarked as he began shuffling his feet around. Pieces of debris moved and with each discovery he submerged himself in the brackish water to retrieve the object. He had discarded an eclectic mix of metal and plastic objects when Jennifer suddenly spat oil from her mouth and squealed with excitement.

'I think I've found a large screwdriver,' she called out.

'Where are you?'

'I don't know.'

'Just come towards my voice,' James instructed and he began counting slowly until something bumped against him. He put his arm around Jennifer and squeezed her tight as she pressed a large wooden handle into his hand.

'Well done, Jenny. I'll start chiselling away with this while you try to find something else that can help.' James went back up the steps and began attacking the section of the hatch where he had created the original crack. He could hear Jennifer moving away and winced every time he heard her duck under the water to reach for a possible tool lying on the bottom.

The gap had widened sufficiently for James to see a tiny fraction of the leaden sky when he heard Jennifer call out again. He turned round and saw that the opening had sent a small shaft of light down upon the water's surface.

'I've found a hammer, James,' she called out. 'I can see you.'

James descended and Jennifer placed the shaft in his palm. Holding it up to the beam of light he could see that it was a heavily corroded club hammer. The handle had been broken at one time or another and was half its original length.

'Beautiful, darling, absolutely beautiful.'

Jennifer had moved slightly and the beam of light illuminated part of her face. He grinned at the oil-and-rust-smeared image and couldn't help feeling a powerful wave of love welling up. James bent down and kissed her on the tip of her nose.

'Tide waits for no man to kiss his wife,' she said.

James quickly set to with both the screwdriver and the heavy hammer. The soft wood stood no chance and he had soon chiselled a hole large enough to put his hand through and locate the padlock and hasp screwed to the hatch. Sweat poured from his hairline and trickled down his forehead and into his eyes as he used the screwdriver to apply leverage to the hasp.

With a teeth-setting screech the screws were wrenched from the old oak and James heaved upward with his shoulder. The hatch gave way and was thrown open. Cool, fresh air flooded his lungs and the sky rewarded his efforts with a refreshing shower of rain. He reached down and lifted Jennifer out of the water and she climbed the few remaining steps to join him on the deck of the derelict boat.

As they walked to the stern and climbed onto the riverbank a police car stopped on the road running parallel to the scrapyard. Two *hoofdagents* strolled towards them with thumbs hooked in leather belts close to their holsters with a certain amount of suspicion on their faces.

For a few seconds they studied the filthy, oil-streaked couple from head to foot before the taller of the senior constables spoke. '*Wat heb je gedaan de laatste tijd?*' – 'So what have you been doing?'

James didn't understand and took a chance that one of them knew some English. 'We're tourists and we were kidnapped and locked in that hulk.' He jerked a thumb over his shoulder and then began brushing small rust flakes from Jennifer's hair.

'You were kidnapped?' the shorter officer said with a heavy accent. 'You must come with us.' They were wrapped in large towels produced from the boot of the police car and made to sit in the warmth of the vehicle while one rattled off a report to his controller. They were instructed to go to the nearest hospital and the car pulled away, accelerated rapidly and was soon racing through the streets with sirens wailing. Ten minutes later they arrived at their destination and the driver slowed down to cross speed bumps.

'Why are we here?' James asked and the driver shrugged his shoulders and replied in broken English that he had been instructed to make sure the two tourists were thoroughly checked by doctors.

'But we're not hurt,' Jennifer exclaimed. 'Why don't you take us to the Novotel Hotel where I can get cleaned up?'

'You must be checked for water contaminants,' the officer explained. 'That river has many factories and is not very healthy.'

The conversation came to an end and they allowed themselves to be taken into the hospital where the taller officer had a brief conversation with a doctor that neither of them could follow. They were taken to adjoining examination booths and after being fed a number of pills, given tetanus injections, inspected for rabid rat bites and asked to sign a form they were declared fit to leave. The police officers took them to a room along the corridor and asked them to wait.

After ten minutes a nurse rushed in, gave them cups of strong, heavily sweetened tea and left just as swiftly. Another fifteen minutes elapsed before the door burst open and Chief Inspector Cheswell strode in with a senior Dutch police officer following him.

'What the hell have you been up to, Goodfellow?' Cheswell bellowed as he sat down on the black leather couch. 'This is Chief Superintendent de Graaf,' he added as though he was an afterthought. 'We received a strange report that you'd been kidnapped and locked in an old rotting barge by a river.'

'To be accurate it was an old rotting barge *in* the river with the tide rising fast,' James corrected with a grin.

'Who took you there?' de Graaf asked and Cheswell frowned at being interrupted.

'Who do you think? It was Calder, Hoofdinspecteur,' Jennifer chipped in as she pointedly directed the answer to de Graaf. 'It was him and a tall chap in a dark grey suit; he had a crew cut and a long scar down his face.'

The hoofdinspecteur spoke first. 'He sounds familiar to me, would you be able to recognize the tall man again?'

'Yes,' they both replied.

Cheswell sniffed.

'I would like you to come to the station and go through some pictures; would you help me?' de Graaf asked politely.

'Provided we stop at our hotel on the way so that my wife and I can have hot showers and put on a change of decent clothing,' James responded. De Graaf nodded with an understanding smile. The foursome went to the Novotel hotel in a police car that on arrival raised the doorman's eyebrows.

Champagne-pink clouds were drifting slowly westward when they independently identified the thug in the dark suit as Vos Xander.

'I thought it was Vos whom you had described. He is an exceptionally dangerous man,' de Graaf summarized. 'He is the right- hand man of Berendzen, a particularly nasty gentleman whose real name is Piet van Rijn and who heads up a large penose organisation.'

'Penose?' James asked.

'It's a colloquial term for the organized criminal underbelly of our major cities. Van Rijn runs a prostitution racket in collaboration with the Snakeheads, a Chinese gang that smuggles young girls into the port of Rotterdam but we've been unable to find any evidence that links him to the gang.'

'Is he a local man?' Cheswell asked.

'He was born and raised in the Schilderswijk district which is one of the poorest neighbourhoods and not one we're very proud of. Van Rijn dropped out of school and started his career as a pickpocket before moving on to petty theft, burglary and pimping. It was after both his parents died under mysterious circumstances that he told everyone his name was Berendzen and that he had royal blood. He then disappeared for a couple of years and reappeared in one of the wealthiest districts called Hillegersberg with a fortune that some said he made from selling arms during the collapse of the Soviet Union. Just for a joke a close friend started calling him Count which van Rijn liked and it stuck.'

'You've never been able to pin anything on him at all?' James asked incredulously.

'He's a clever bastard and does all his dirty work through subordinates and unaffiliated companies who import harmless products such as children's toys from the Far East. We have a dossier of unsolved murders that we'd like to attribute to him but he always has alibis supplied by a ring of close associates. Vos Xander joined him two years ago and is the heavy muscle that van Rijn uses when irritated by those who interfere in his business affairs.'

'Apart from being big what sort of man is Xander?' Jennifer asked as fresh coffee was brought into Ernst de Graaf's office.

'Three words sum him up: sadistic, homicidal and maniacal. He kills for pleasure and when let loose he is like a bull-mastiff; nothing stops him until his target is food for worms.' De Graaf turned to look hard at James and Jennifer. 'If it *was* Vos Xander who locked you in the barge and he hears that you've escaped you can be certain he'll make sure of you the next time you meet. So be warned, Mr Goodfellow.'

'And these are the men who are helping Calder,' Cheswell commented with a wry expression.

De Graaf smiled then gave a light chuckle. 'I don't think that partnership will last very long, Chief Inspector. Xander also has a nasty habit of disposing of people he can no longer steal money from.'

'A silver lining at least,' James murmured. 'Small, but nevertheless it's silver.'

'Like the coins Calder is going to lose,' Jennifer added.

'But how on earth did a Cambridge professor latch on to these thugs to sell the charter?' Cheswell mused.

'The Count has a genuine-looking website that promotes his royal bloodline and proclaims himself a connoisseur of fine art, antiques and historic artefacts,' de Graaf answered and then shrugged. 'I can only assume Calder was fooled into thinking he could make a quick sale at the price he wanted without any questions being asked.'

'My feeling is that the Zalmhuis will be used as a rendezvous point and that we should keep an eye on it in case Calder turns up to make contact with his buyer.'

Calder was at that moment dining on *stamppot* and *rookwurst* sausage in a discreet restaurant that was for the exclusive use of penose members. Vos Xander sat opposite Calder with another man who had long grey hair hanging over his Cerruti-dressed shoulders and had been introduced as Count Berendzen. Calder assumed that he was sharing the table with a man of high breeding and said respectfully, 'My dear Count, do you now say you can only give me €1,000,000 for the Magna Carta?'

'That is correct, Professor. Considering its dubious provenance it's a fair price for an item that cannot be sold on.'

'But you offered me €4,000,000 for the document during our telephone conversation three days ago.'

'Not at all, Professor, you asked for three million sterling but I didn't exactly say that I would give you that much.'

Xander hadn't said a word during the meal and had simply fixed Calder with an unblinking stare like a black mamba eyeing a bushbaby.

'Then I must find another buyer, Count,' Calder said as he threw his napkin onto the table.

'I can assure you, Professor, there isn't another buyer who would dare top my offer and I will make quite sure that you will be unable to leave Rotterdam alive,' Berendzen said in a cold voice.

Xander slammed his knife into the table to punctuate his master's words.

Calder sank back into his chair. 'Then, whether I like it or not it's a deal,' he mumbled as his mind raced. He would have to make an excuse to leave them and then make his way to Brussels where he knew of two people who would also be interested in the charter.

'Where it the charter, Professor Calder?' Berendzen asked softly.

'It's in a safe place. I will take it to wherever you want us to meet.'

'Vos will accompany you.'

'That's not necessary, Count –'

'I believe it is *very* necessary,' Berendzen interrupted sharply. 'I do not trust you to return as I have the distinct feeling that you are foolishly planning to back out of our agreement.'

Calder looked into the man's ice-blue eyes and then at Xander who was leaning over the table to bring his face close to Calder's.

'Very well.' He sighed inwardly as he realized €1,000,000 would be the most he could expect and he would have to find another buyer for the coins if he wanted a realistic market price for them.

Berendzen signalled for the bill that appeared almost instantly and it was torn in half and left on the small plate with a €50 tip. They left the restaurant in a tight group that gave Calder no leeway to make a break and run for it. A large black Mercedes with tinted windows drew to a halt before them and the driver got out to open the door for his employer.

'I will not see you again, Professor,' the count called from the dark interior. 'Vos will collect the Magna Carta and give you the money. He will then bring it to me to put in my private museum. Vaarwel.'

Vos pushed Calder towards a dark green Audi and indicated that he should get into the driver's seat. Neither man noticed the deep blue BMW X5 that was parked at the corner of the street.

'Take me to the document,' Xander curtly demanded as Calder started the engine.

'Where's the money?' Calder asked.

'I have been given a certified banker's cheque by the Count and it has been made out to you for the sum of money that you have just agreed. Now take me to the place where you have hidden my master's property.'

Calder pulled away and drove past the unmarked police car without seeing James or Jennifer huddling down on the back seat. The BMW slowly began to follow, lingering as far back as Inspector Peters dared risk. Once on the motorway the mini convoy sped swiftly towards the professor's hotel.

'Berendzen left in his own car and headed south,' Peters observed. 'It looks like Vos is going with the professor to fetch the document.'

'And once he has it –' Cheswell muttered.

'He'll dispose of Calder.'

Jennifer shivered at the finality in the inspector's words and James felt her hand grip his knee.

'I'll call for armed support as soon as we know what their destination is.'

James turned to face Jennifer. 'I need you to go home, Jenny.'

'I can't leave,' she exclaimed. 'As a police officer it is my duty to see this case through to the end.'

'And as your senior officer I'm telling you to return to your own turf,' Cheswell ordered and glared over the back of his seat at Jennifer. 'This never was your case. You were invited to come to Norfolk to identify your husband's body, which in the end proved unnecessary, and you have no official directives from your senior officers in East Steading to investigate Professor Calder.'

Jennifer sank back into the seat and James could feel her wilt with disappointment. 'Think of Claudiu, Jenny. You've been away from home for days and he'll be missing you big time.'

She nodded and fell silent. James took her hand and squeezed it in a pathetic effort to remove the glum expression on her face.

'As soon as Calder stops I'll get one of the support team to run Mrs Goodfellow back to the hotel to collect her things before taking her to the airport,' Peters said in the ensuing silence.

'My rank is Detective Sergeant, Constable,' she said petulantly.

'Yes, ma'am,' Peters said respectfully.

Suddenly Calder took an off-ramp and they held back as the speed level dropped considerably. They entered a district that was decidedly run down. Dutch women with care-worn features mingled with others wearing hijabs as they made their way in and out of shops that reeked of exotic spices while men lounged outside bars and coffee shops, sipping tiny cups of strong coffee and drawing deeply on shisha pipes.

'It looks like he chose a cheap and not so cheerful place to stay,' James observed.

'This is an area of mixed nationalities where people don't ask questions and strangers are generally ignored completely,' Peters said. 'It's a place to hide as we rarely patrol these streets.'

'If it's so rough surely you would have cause to come here more often than anywhere else,' Cheswell commented.

'The penose organisations have their own methods of policing which are generally brutal and occasionally lethal,' Peters said. 'They can be cruel to the innocent and generous to the loyal but overall they mete out a strange even-handed justice that keeps the whole district under control. If you choose to live here you must forget the law and live by penose rules.'

'How are these organisations structured?' James asked.

'There's the mafia as well as the Turkish, Chinese and Russian penose and also the Ndrangheta who aren't traditional penose but are highly active in the underworld. They are generally a mix of Surinamese, Antillan, Moroccan and Ambonese ethnic groups.'

'Quite a cosmopolitan part of the city,' Cheswell muttered.

'They're not all in this one district,' Peters replied. 'If they were their individual interests would clash violently and World War III would start.' The lights changed and the traffic moved on; Peters continued to shadow Calder.

'Which groups rule here then?' James said.

'There is a huge Moroccan community here who are primarily involved in trafficking marihuana; many have families cultivating the weed and hashish in the Rif region. Some have expanded to providing cocaine and managing prostitution rings as well as organising the occasional armed robbery.'

'That explains why Calder was attracted to this place,' Cheswell interrupted with an abrupt cynical laugh. 'Somewhere to hide.'

'Where does the pseudo Count Berendzen fit in?' James asked.

'Van Rijn is a major crime lord and exports cocaine and imports cannabis and very young girls from Eastern Europe. He sells the girls to brothels in the Netherlands and Britain and uses motorcycle gangs to distribute smaller quantities of heroin countrywide.'

Calder suddenly pulled up outside a tenement block and Peters warned the couple to duck down as he cruised past to park fifty yards further on.

The big brute of a man that they now knew was Vos Xander got out first, closely followed by Calder, and the two men entered the vestibule of a scruffy rooming house five storeys high.

Peters was using the car radio to summon the support team as James prepared to get out of the car.

'Where do you think you're going, Goodfellow?' Cheswell demanded to know. 'We all stay put until the SWAT team are in place and even then they will be the ones who go in first. I also want your wife well away from here and out of harm's way. My chief constable would flay me alive if he thought I had put a fellow police officer from a Norfolk division in any kind of danger.'

This time it was James' turn to look glum.

Calder entered the vestibule and led the way to the old service lift. It was slow and reeking of ammonia and Calder was conscious of Xander's stare all the way to the fifth floor. When it stopped with an abrupt jerk Xander stepped out and waited for Calder to join him in the dimly lit corridor.

'Number?' Xander growled and Calder pointed to a door that had a plastic number 6 hanging upside down by one Phillips screw. They entered the dank-smelling apartment and Calder led the way down the short corridor while Xander checked the bathroom and kitchenette as he followed more slowly. The lounge had a Juliette balcony that dared anybody to rest his or her elbows on the heavily corroded railing.

'Where is it?' the big man demanded as he sat on the settee and sent glittering dust motes flying into the air. Calder simply climbed onto a flimsy chair in the middle of the room, pushed a panel up and retrieved the cardboard tube from a ceiling cavity and passed it down to Xander. As the big man turned his back on the professor to face the light filtering through the curtains Calder stepped down and swung the chair hard with all his strength. Xander stepped aside but not quite fast enough. One of the heavy legs caught him a glancing blow behind the left ear and rendered him unconscious. Calder hit him once more on the head and satisfied that he had killed the man he climbed onto the chair again to retrieve his heavy backpack of coins from the same cavity.

He replaced the charter in the safety of the tube and searched the man's pockets thoroughly but as he expected there was no certified bank cheque for €1,000,000. Calder wiped every surface he had touched before leaving with the precious coins and charter. He pocketed Xander's automatic and then disposed of the dirty cloth, the only thing that might have his DNA, down the lift shaft before taking the stairs without touching the handrail.

Calder knew the BMW X5 would still be waiting outside and continued down to the basement and the rear entrance. It was a few steps up to the backyard and he was soon hurrying amongst discarded cardboard boxes, oilcans, bathtubs and shattered toilets to a small gate leading to the private service road. He kept walking for about ten minutes, breathing heavily through his open mouth, before he felt he was a safe enough distance from any police trap.

The professor now faced two problems: the police manhunt *and* van Rijn's vengeance.

20

THE ARMED SUPPORT TEAM arrived in their black van with sirens muted and took up their positions after being briefed by Peters. The commander was given a detailed briefing before he positioned Kevlar-protected officers with silenced VSK-94 sniper rifles on either side of the building. Although Cheswell was a senior police officer he had no legal power in the Netherlands and was asked by Peters to remain behind the van until the situation was declared safe.

On a signal from Peters the commander and his team started to close in on the entrance. Suddenly Xander staggered through the doorway and collapsed heavily onto the pavement.

One sniper kept his crosshairs fixed on the motionless figure while another shifted his focus to the inky doorway. Peters moved in slowly with his Walther P5 fixed on Xander. He studied the man until he was satisfied that both hands were visible and held no weapons before kneeling to place two fingers on the side of the man's neck. He then signalled that the man was still alive and two officers rushed in to fasten Xander's hands with *Tuf-Tie* handcuffs.

Once Xander had been secured four officers with semi-automatic weapons at the ready trotted into the building and up the stairs, checking the lift indicator lights for movement at every level. On the fourth floor they spread themselves along the corridor, alert for any movement.

Once the team leader was sure his men had him covered he darted into the apartment and ran down the corridor checking the rooms, shouting *veilig,* safe, after each. When he reached the living-room he stopped, pushed it open with his boot and cautiously entered with his weapon tucked into his shoulder. He had just called out *veilig* again when he spotted the small pool of blood on the carpet by the settee.

'Calder's disappeared,' the commander shouted after listening to the team leader's report on his earpiece. 'My men will search the rest of the building but my guess is that he's flown the coop.'

'Damn!'

'Well at least we've got Vos Xander,' Cheswell said. 'With your testimony, Inspector Peters, you will be able to charge him with kidnap, assault and attempted murder. That should put him out of circulation for a few years at least.'

Peters nodded and beamed with satisfaction.

All conversation ceased as an ambulance arrived with its blood-chilling siren. The paramedics leapt out and under the poised muzzles of automatic weapons set about checking the state of the unconscious man.

'They couldn't find the Magna Carta,' James added glumly as he rejoined Jennifer in the car. 'Calder got away with the charter.'

Peters got in the car and used his mobile to update Chief Superintendent de Graaf. The rapidly changing expressions on Peters' face and his involuntary wincing said it all.

Peters turned round to speak to the couple. 'With Xander in custody we'll be able to apply for a legal warrant to phone-tap Berendzen, a known associate of his,' he said optimistically. 'Up until now I've only been able to instruct my men to use directional microphones to pick up snippets of information through any open window at that man's house. This has occasionally alerted us to the arrival of new drug shipments at the docks but not much more than that.'

'He's a more important fish to fry than Xander, isn't he?' Jennifer asked.

'Right. He controls large parts of southern Holland. Working with the Snakeheads he is responsible for thousands of young girls being brought from the Far East and Asia to become innocent slaves in massage parlours and brothels across Western Europe and Britain.'

'Berendzen ships girls across the channel?' Cheswell asked.

'Yes, but we can't prove that the vessels occasionally stopped by the coastguard are owned or leased by any of his companies.'

'He deals in drugs, too,' Cheswell said tonelessly.

'Big time.'

'Tell me, Inspector, what the hell would a man like that be doing with an old human-rights document?' Jennifer added. 'It seems he has no respect for anybody's rights for it to be of interest to him.'

'He has always made a point of projecting his 'aristocratic lineage' as well as his love of art and collecting fine and rare antiquities. We have a strong suspicion that he has many stolen pieces that he keeps hidden for personal gratification.'

'You mean he has a secret room where he goes and sits to simply salivate over his own art collection?' Jennifer said scornfully.

'And you're gambling that Calder knows this and would still want to sell him the charter?' James added.

'It's a slim chance otherwise we will have to monitor every road, station and airport which would be a financial and logistical impossibility.'

'But won't it take time to get the phone-tap warrant?' James protested. 'Calder could be phoning right now.'

'The taps are being put in place as we speak.' Peters gave a weak smile. 'I suggest the driver takes you and Mrs Goodfellow to the hotel now and when you've packed to drive you to the airport. I would like you, Chief Inspector, to accompany me to the police station to await further events.'

Cheswell agreed. 'However, I should point out that I will have to return to Norwich tonight,' he added.

Peters' phone sounded and when he answered his face lost all colour.

'What is it, Inspecteur?' his driver asked.

'Xander has escaped!'

'How on earth could that happen?' James exclaimed. 'There was an armed guard in the ambulance and two paramedics.'

'He overcame them all. My officer and the paramedic had their necks broken and the driver was shot in the back of the head with his own weapon. Xander is now armed and hunting for Calder and possibly for you again. The ambulance was found only three blocks from here. It had crashed into a delicatessen and only one of the witnesses dared admit that he had seen Xander run from the scene.'

'He's that well-known and feared?' Jennifer asked.

'In this area he is virtually a god.' Peters explained morosely. 'Let me put it this way, Mrs Goodfellow, I definitely wouldn't like him on my trail.'

Calder's phone needed recharging and he decided to catch a bus to the shopping centre he had visited before. The T-Mobile was still open and he went in to get enough charge for two calls.

An extremely pallid-faced youth of Celtic origin but with greasy dreadlocks beneath a bright Rasta hat took the outdated phone with a sniff of indifference and disappeared into a back room. Calder put the heavy backpack on the floor and rubbed his chafed shoulders while he stared through the plate-glass window at every passing pedestrian. Occasionally a policeman wandered past but the professor was well hidden.

A police car rushed by with siren warbling and Calder, struggling to curb his impatience, waited another five minutes before leaving the shop for a brief check outside. The police car had stopped at the far end of the road and officers were showing photographs to pedestrians as they slowly made their way in his direction. Calder went back into the shop just as the self-styled Rastafarian returned from the workshop.

'How much,' Calder asked as he took the phone.

'Five Euros, or you can have the charge free if you consider upgrading to something a little less Stone Age from our range of models.' His cheeky grin rapidly became a surly scowl when Calder threw a single note onto the counter and picking up the backpack strode out without saying a word. He quickly made two phone calls. First he dialed a boat owner he had dealt with previously and then he dialed Berandzen. When he answered Calder simply said, 'Gouda. Don't try any tricks this time.'

The police agents were on both sides of the street and only fifty yards distant. Calder began striding away in the opposite direction and flagged down a cruising taxi. He asked the driver to take him to Hoge Gouwe in Gouda and then dialed a number.

The driver took the E26 highway and when he located Hoge Gouwe on his satnav he followed the attractive tree-lined canal until Calder tapped him on the shoulder. Calder paid the fare plus a generous tip and then made his way to a neat, white launch that was moored exactly where he had seen it six months earlier. As he stepped onto the deck a distinguished-looking man emerged from the main cabin and greeted him with a broad smile. '*Goedemiddag Wetenschapper* Calder,' he said in a cheery voice. 'It is so nice to see you again,' and he held out a key for his esteemed client. 'As before, she is fully fuelled and there is fresh milk, cheese, sliced ham and four bottles of beer in the refrigerator, with my compliments of course.'

Calder thanked the man who then stepped onto the canal bank and after a brief wave he strode down the avenue towards the restaurant where they had met during happier times. The professor went below deck, stowed the backpack and put the tube in an overhead locker. He helped himself to one of the Carlsberg pilsners and sat on the bench seat to await Berendzen.

The sun was beginning to set and the avenue was filling with workers going home when an S-Class with tinted windows rolled to a stop alongside the launch and the familiar figure of the ersatz count emerged. Calder waited until Berendzen's gaze was in his direction before raising his arm to attract his attention. Berendzen strode across the cobbles to be waved aboard and as he followed Calder into the main saloon two more men climbed out of the car to follow their employer. The professor spotted them through the large window in the saloon as he sat facing the door. Berendzen sat on the opposite side of the fold-out table and placing his elbows on the polished walnut he steepled his fingers and stared at Calder with unblinking eyes.

'If those men attempt to board I will shoot you dead,' Calder said calmly as he took Xander's automatic from his pocket and rested it in his lap with the barrel pointing at Berendzen's genital region.

'Don't come any closer, stay on the road, Lucas,' Berendzen said as he spoke into an almost undetectable microphone without taking his eyes off Calder. Realising that his visitor could communicate with his men Calder said, 'Throw your earpiece and microphone into the canal,' and he pointed at the open window beside the count.

'They are rather valuable electronic devices.'

'Do you not consider your life just as valuable?' Calder said with a sneer and watched as the earpiece and microphone were dropped out of the window. Only the tiniest of splashes marked the loss of a few thousand dollars.

'You're not carrying anything else?'

'What do you think I have on me, a weapon of one kind or another?'

'No. I expect you to have €1,000,000 in cash!'

'I have never carried that amount of cash on my person. It would be inviting trouble and on that subject, I would like the exchange to take place in my car where the money is. In other words, somewhere I cannot be shot the moment you have the money in your hands. And I will insist that one of my men is present. You may remain armed and keep pointing that damned silly thing at me as long as you don't mind Lucas pointing his weapon at you.'

'Sounds fair, Berendzen,' Calder said and he stood up to retrieve the cardboard tube from the locker. 'When we get outside you will walk in front of me and instruct the other man and your driver to walk to the far end of this avenue and not return to the car until they see this launch passing under that bridge.' Calder pointed in the opposite direction towards the pedestrian footbridge and Berendzen grudgingly nodded his agreement.

Berendzen passed on the instructions as they went ashore he climbed in first, closely followed by the levelled automatic in Calder's hand. Lucas got in the front passenger seat and turned round to point a lethal Makarov with a laser sight attached at Calder. He had no need to switch the powerful beam on as the range was almost point-blank. Calder kept his weapon jammed into Berendzen's side as the man opened the cocktail cabinet before him and took out a small package of brown paper sealed with red wax.

'That's one million?' Calder asked incredulously.

'It's surprising how little space Round Brilliant diamonds occupy.' Berendzen said and laughed at Calder's expression. 'Each F- classified two-carat stone has a clarity of VS1. They also have excellent symmetry, no fluorescence and an estimated market value of £20,241 per stone.'

'That totals over one million in sterling,' Lucas explained and added with a low chuckle, 'You'll be getting the few thousand as a bonus.'

'And what the hell am I going to do with bloody diamonds?' Calder said angrily and jabbed the barrel harder into the roll of fat round Berendzen's waist. Lucas shifted the aim of his own weapon to Calder's right eye and the professor turned his head in case Lucas decided to switch the laser sight on.

'That's an easy question, Professor. Sell them, of course. You'll find they're the finest form of currency anywhere in the world and unlike most things they don't depreciate in value.'

Calder reached for the package but it was held out of reach.

'The king's charter first.'

The tube was passed over and Berendzen opened the end, slid the document out and unrolled it carefully to study the fine calligraphy. He grunted, nodded and gave the package of diamonds to Calder who took it, broke the seal and opened it carefully in his lap with one hand whilst keeping his weapon pressed against Berendzen's side.

The collection of stones blazed gloriously in the diminishing sunlight. He picked one stone up and held it within a beam of light to study the clarity and beauty of the flawless diamond.

'We have a deal?' Berendzen asked smugly as he slowly rolled the charter and slid it back into the tube.

Calder agreed and refolded the brown paper. 'Now we'll both get out of the car.' Lucas kept his gun aimed and watched as Calder led Berendzen back to the launch, his weapon kept discreetly out of sight as they crossed the road. Lucas rested his arm on the car roof with the automatic's laser sight switched on. The little red dot remained fixed on the centre of Calder's back as he climbed aboard the launch.

'Untie all the moorings and stay on the bank in plain sight,' Calder instructed Berendzen. The launch moved away from the bank and Calder started the engine and spun the wheel to head the boat towards the distant bridge. Ignoring the red dot on his chest he jerked the automatic when Berendzen attempted to move back to the car. Everyone froze until the boat was far enough down the canal.

Berendzen ran across the road to the Mercedes and beckoned the two men further down the avenue.

'Where can he go from here, Lucas,' Berendzen snapped as he carefully laid the tube on the armrest between the rear seats. 'I want all of those bloody diamonds back and that bastard dead as soon as possible. I have a cash customer in Amsterdam for that package and he doesn't like being kept waiting.'

'If he turns left at the first junction he could take the canal running beside the Turfsingel road which would give him access to the Hollandsche IJssel,' Lucas said, referring to the main waterway as he consulted the map of Gouda on his smartphone.

'And then what?' Berendzen exclaimed.

Lucas scrolled the map. 'He'll eventually arrive in Rotterdam and feed into the Nieuwe Maas which will take him to the Hook of Holland and the open sea,' Lucas said lamely.

'Is that boat seaworthy?'

'No, not at all. I would say by what I saw that it was built for canal use only and he'll have to change to something with a deeper draught and a more powerful engine to deal with tides and strong currents if he wants to take his chances on the open sea.'

'Good, then you'll be able to get him at one of the bridges he has to pass under. Failing that you take him out when he abandons the launch to find something bigger.' Berendzen sat back and interlaced his fingers on his belly and his men looked at each other with nervous expressions.

'He's armed, sir,' the stocky chauffeur said. 'It won't be easy to confront him without drawing fire and police attention to ourselves.'

'I'm aware of how difficult it will be, Claude. Just do it.' The car accelerated on the cobbled street and raced towards the first bridge.

Calder watched the men running towards the Mercedes as he passed under the pedestrian footbridge and headed for the next bridge and the canal junction further on. The launch was responsive to a light touch and he kept to the centre as he went under the bridge that was designed for private cars and light commercial vehicles. Fortunately there was little canal traffic as he approached the junction and instead of following the route Lucas had anticipated he spun the wheel and turned right, avoiding the Turfsingel canal and heading in the opposite direction. He was now travelling on a large horseshoe-shaped canal that ended abruptly at a sluice.

He was unaware that he had put himself out of sight of his pursuers who were now crossing the canal and heading the other way and he kept the throttle open as far as the waterway law permitted. The launch puttered on, spouting engine-cooling water as it passed scores of moored canal craft and attractive houseboats decorated with potted tulips that blazed colourfully on their decks.

Calder soon saw the *Kleiwegplein* bridge where he intended to abandon the vessel and he eased the throttle back and pulled over to the bank. As the launch slowed to a standstill he slipped the backpack on and leapt ashore. Without a backward glance he started sprinting and turned left when he reached the bridge. The momentum of the launch caused it to nudge the bank before drifting aimlessly in the middle of the canal.

One of the Gouda mainline stations was roughly three hundred yards down the tree-lined avenue and soon he was turning into *Stationsplein* and approaching the main entrance. At the ticket office he kept his face turned down and bought a single to The Hague. He planned to take a Sprinter train to Rijswijk where he had a contact, a wealthy coin collector he had used as a research source when writing papers for the university.

He had fifteen minutes to wait for the next train and he went into the Kaldi coffee shop for a leisurely Americano and a warm almond croissant with pastry so fine and flaky he was tempted to purchase a second to eat on the train. Calder was boarding when he noticed a pair of police officers walking slowly along the platform. They were making a point of studying every passenger and he had the distinct feeling that they were searching for someone in particular. He quickly walked the length of the carriage, slipped into the toilet and locked the door.

The carriage jerked in the couplings and he sat down to eat the croissant and wait for the train to increase its speed before opening the door. Looking out he could see that the police hadn't boarded the train at all. He took a window seat that overlooked the main highway running beside the tracks and as he idly watched the traffic he noticed a familiar-looking black Mercedes with tinted windows.

The train continued to accelerate and after a few minutes it had left the big car far behind. Calder relaxed and closed his eyes for it would be another fifteen minutes before he arrived in The Hague. As the train raced towards the seat of government he guessed that there would be just enough time to purchase a Sprinter ticket and be on his way before his hunters could reach the station concourse.

21

JAMES ACCOMPANIED JENNIFER BACK to the hotel and helped with packing her things before giving her a passionate kiss and waving her off to the airport. Her favourite perfume was still lingering in the room when he returned and in a mood of frustration he took two miniature bottles of whisky from the minibar and threw himself onto the bed where he proceeded to finish them both.

He had criss-crossed the counties of Norfolk and Cambridge and large parts of The Netherlands over the last three days and yet he was no closer to finding the king's charter and the silver coins or solving Daniel Lightbody's murder. James seriously considered terminating his search and cutting his losses when the landline phone rang.

'We've got a lead on Professor Calder,' said Inspector Peters. 'Our officers were making a street-by-street search when a salesman in a T-Mobile shop told them that there had been a man acting in a rather suspicious manner. When they showed him Calder's picture the salesman confirmed that it was our man.'

'Why did he go into the shop?'

'Calder told him he had very little time and that he wanted sufficient charge for his phone to make two local calls. While this was being done the curious salesman checked the phone's call history and when the name van Rijn came up he decided something wasn't quite right and mentioned it to the officers.'

James was becoming excited. 'Did he say where Calder may have gone?'

'He could only remember Calder turning right on leaving the shop and we checked at the nearest taxi rank in that direction, and guess what!'

'He took a taxi,' James teased.

'Yes, but the fare wasn't to an address in Rotterdam but in Gouda. Local officers were asked to keep an eye open and reported that they had found three witnesses on the opposite side of the Hoge-Gouwe canal. They had seen men pointing guns at each other and two had boarded a canal launch while the others stayed with a large Mercedes that later suddenly drove off.'

'Are they sure it was Calder?'

'The witnesses were shown some photos and they confirmed that one of the men was Calder and the other van Rijn; van Rijn got off again and returned to the car to join his friends as the launch set off in the direction of the Kromme Gouwe industrial park.'

'Are you chaps following this up?'

There was a long pause and James sensed he had offended the officer who sighed and said, 'We are doing everything possible to trace the launch as well as the Mercedes. I believe the two had rendezvoued at the launch to make an exchange.'

'My apology Inspector Peters,' James said. 'So, you think that van Rijn, alias Berendzen, now has the Magna Carta copy?'

'Undoubtedly.' It was Cheswell's voice, sounding rather hollow, and James knew that he had been listening on speaker mode. 'We've just located the owner of the launch who has also confirmed that it was Calder and that he had been carrying a large backpack and a stout cardboard tube.'

'The king's charter!' James exclaimed.

'I've just received a report that local officers have found the launch drifting near the *Kleiwegplein* bridge. It was deserted, which isn't surprising as it's only a ten-minute walk from the mainline station,' Peters added.

'Where can he go from there?'

'Rotterdam, The Hague and any station in between,' Cheswell said. 'Officers are now on their way to check with the booking clerks to see if anyone can recognize his face but I don't know why I'm telling you this. You're just a private citizen and shouldn't be privy to any official information concerning a manhunt –'

'Chief Inspector, after everything he's been through I think he has the right to know what was happening,' Peters interrupted firmly. 'Goodfellow, I suggest you come to the station as you could possibly help us in predicting what he might do next.'

James sprang from the chair and grabbed his jacket. The chase was still on and the quarry was running and he was determined to run him to earth; there'd be no slip-ups this time. He ordered a taxi and in his hurry forgot his Zenzedi tablets.

Within a matter of minutes he arrived at the police station on Prins Frederik Hendrikstraat where he found Cheswell and Chief Superintendent Ernst de Graaf drinking espresso coffees and poring over a street map of The Hague in Peter's office.

Cheswell greeted James and said, 'The booking clerk in Gouda said a man of Calder's description bought a one-way ticket to The Hague.'

'We're now waiting for any news from the officers who have been checking every train arrival,' Peters added.

'If he's arrived already then shouldn't they also be questioning the drivers at the taxi rank?' James asked innocently.

'We're not incompetent, Goodfellow,' Cheswell snapped.

'What about the station booking clerks?'

The three officers looked at James blankly.

'He may only have bought a single ticket to The Hague but that could have been done deliberately to put them off his trail. He may have planned to travel further to his real destination.'

Peters was already murmuring into his phone before James had finished his hypothesis and de Graaf was nodding thoughtfully as he put his cup down.

'Taking the train to another destination makes a lot of sense when you consider how intelligent Calder is. He's the sort of man who wouldn't leave a clear trail. The Hague has an exceptionally busy airport which would enable him to slip onto a flight before anyone realized he was gone.'

'And he knows that we're aware of that and would be planning something totally unexpected, Hoofdinspecteur,' James added.

'Exactly, James. He'll be seeking an alternative escape route believing we're fully focused on the airport.'

Peters' landline gave a strident ringtone and after a few seconds' listening he put it down with a grim expression. 'Your theory is correct, James,' he said. 'Calder bought a ticket for Rijswijk and there's a train every twenty minutes with one expected to arrive at his destination now.'

'He's undoubtedly been in contact with someone there who can help him to dispose of the silver coins.'

Calder did leave the train at Rijswijk and with the heavy backpack straps cutting into his shoulders he walked across *Piramideplein* and took a taxi to Steenvoorde and one of the small terraced houses on Nanenstraat.

Ferdi van Vliet opened the door on the second long ring of the doorbell and when recognizing Calder's face from his articles in *World Archaeology* he stepped to one side and invited him in with a broad smile on his lined face. As a member of the Professional Numismatists Guild the elderly coin dealer had also spoken with Calder on issues concerning the discovery of antique coins. It was a pleasure to finally meet him in person.

Their hands clasped and van Vliet smiled, revealing gleaming white teeth that had clearly been capped.

'You mentioned that you had a few silver coins you wished to sell and that they had been minted by King John in 1211?' the dealer said when the initial pleasantries had been concluded and they were seated in a small yet comfortable living room. 'A great deal of research has been done to resolve what happened to that monarch's treasure. I myself was involved in a ground-penetrating radar search in the River Welland area when I was younger and a lot better-looking but we found nothing and neither has anyone else.'

'You're right, Ferdi,' Calder said as he took a sip of coffee. 'However, a number of coins were stolen before the king's baggage train was lost beneath the spring tide. The thieves hid the coins in an old oak tree.' He paused for effect. 'After eight hundred years I managed to find the chest and cut it from the living tree. It contained a great many coins, the ones I described to you, and a copy of the Magna Carta.'

'*O mijn God!*' the dealer declared, his bright eyes opening wide. 'That is something I would be very interested in buying from you.'

'You're too late, Ferdi, I was obliged to sell it to Count Berendzen.'

'That thug! How did you manage to get mixed up with a man like that?'

'You know him?' Calder asked.

'Know him, no. Know of him, everyone does. He's always in the newspapers posing as a great philanthropist and connoisseur of the arts but there have been back-page stories that cautiously imply he is linked to organized crime and drug trafficking.'

'I only discovered that after I met him,' Calder growled. 'Now what about the business at hand?'

'You should have declared what you found as treasure trove, Stephen,' van Vliet said with a broad grin and waggled an admonishing finger.

'And received a paltry finder's fee. You must be joking, Ferdi. I have exactly 2,157 coins in this bag and at a value of £130 each I estimate the total to be €280,410.'

Van Vliet eyed the backpack and made a gesture for Calder to open it. Socks neatly stuffed with coins toppled out onto the carpet and the elderly man took one sock and loosened the tie. Dull grey metal discs poured out into his hand. He held one up and studied it closely with the loupe he always kept in his waistcoat pocket.

'It appears to be genuine but I must be sure before we talk business.' Van Vliet flicked the disc with a yellowing fingernail and it gave a bell-like ring. He stood with some difficulty caused by his rheumatic joints and went into the small kitchen where he took a cube of ice from the freezer. He placed it on the coin and watched closely as the frozen water began melting faster than normal room temperature would allow. Calder had followed van Vliet into the kitchen and was watching him test the metal. The expert then took a bottle of bleach from under the sink and after drying the coin let a small drop of the acid fall on the king's head.

'A powerful oxidizing agent such as this will tarnish silver very quickly,' he explained and to support his words the coin began turning black. He flicked it into the sink and ran the tap to wash it clean.

'Surely you have proof enough?' Calder said with impatience creeping into his voice.

'One more and I will be satisfied, Professor,' van Vliet said as he opened a drawer and removed a small bar of dark grey metal. He placed the coin on one end and slowly tilted the bar until the coin began sliding down its length.

'I'm satisfied now,' he said. 'This is a rare-earth magnet made out of neodymium. Silver is paramagnetic and has a weak magnetic effect; if this coin had stuck strongly it would have proved that it could not be silver. Fortunately, the coin passed all the tests so I can say with some authority that it is very close to pure silver.'

'Can we now get down to the real business,' Calder said as he returned to the living room and sat down.

'Of course we can, Professor, however I must say straightaway that I cannot pay you the figure you asked as the coins are undeclared and therefore can't be sold in the open market.'

Calder sat forward with eyes narrowing suspiciously.

'I'll give you eighty thousand pounds sterling and I believe you'll find that it's a very fair price given the current circumstances.'

'You're cutting the price by two hundred thousand!' Calder stuttered, not believing his ears. He walked to the window to gather his thoughts and vaguely watched as a car parked across the street and a rather large man got out.

'For security reasons I don't normally keep that much money in the house but as I am about to make a cash loan to my grandson who is buying his first house I can let you have sixty thousand now and the other twenty when we go to my bank.'

Calder was only half listening for the man by the car appeared familiar. He turned to look both ways as though searching for someone and then he looked across the street and Calder was staring at the scarred features of Vos Xander. He backed away from the lace curtains and went to sit facing van Vliet. 'I'll take it now, Ferdi,' he requested. 'Could you make it as quickly as possible, as I have to leave immediately to catch a train.'

Van Vliet looked at Calder with a puzzled expression and crossed the room to an inset Chubb wall safe behind a heavily framed Jozef Israëls print. He tapped in the code, removed two small stacks of brand-new Euro bills and placed them on the coffee table. 'There's €82,000 at the current exchange rate and if you can wait a little I'll make out a receipt for you to sign and a promissory note for the remaining €27,500.'

Calder snatched up the notes, rammed them into his pockets and offered his hand. 'I'll sign whatever you like when we go to the bank,' he said. 'Is there a back way out of your house?'

Van Vliet looked at the professor and frowned. 'Are you in some sort of trouble?' he called after a fleeing Calder who was running down the hallway, through the scullery and leaving by a small gate at the bottom of the garden.

Calder had already gone through the gate and was sprinting along the narrow lane running behind the long terrace of houses by the time van Vliet reached the hallway. He had the distinct feeling that he would never see Calder again. Someone rapped violently on the front door and van Vliet went to open it.

'*Waar is Calder?*' the big man shouted the moment the door opened. Van Vliet was lost for words and stumbled back as Xander pushed his way into the house and slammed the door behind him. '*Waar is hij?*' he repeated, pushing the man ahead of him and into the living room.

Xander's quick glance around the room revealed the backpack and stuffed socks that had been spilt on the wool carpet. He pounced on one and tipped some of the silver into the palm of his hand.

'So, he has been and now he has flown,' he said as he pushed the protesting coin collector into a chair and dropped the coins into his lap. 'You paid him?'

Van Vliet nodded vigorously as the scarred face and cold eyes moved in close. Xander detected the inadvertent flick of the old man's eyes towards the painting on the wall and stepping back he gripped a thin arm to pull van Vliet to his feet.

'Open it now!' Xander demanded as he pointed at the Jozef Israëls. While van Vliet hobbled to the safe the big man knelt and repacked the socks of coins in the backpack. He swung the bag onto his back as though it contained little more than goose feathers and van Vliet meekly stepped away from the gaping safe. Xander ignored the small bundle of Euro notes in a bank wrapper and concentrated on a number of soft felt bags. He untied one and poured five large coins onto the palm of his hand. Even with his limited knowledge he could tell that they were very old.

'What are these?' he demanded of the old man.

'You're holding two 1517 Dutch *guldens* and three 1680 silver *guilders*; the Pallas Athena coin shows her holding a spear.'

'Damn the bitch, are these two solid gold?' Xander barked as he held up the two guldens and slipped the others into his pocket. Van Vliet nodded and Xander walked back to the safe and removed the remaining soft pouches. 'These all contain gold and silver coins?'

'Yes,' van Vliet said weakly as he watched the giant rob him of his life's savings. 'Will you leave me nothing?' he pleaded.

'What do you think?' Xander slammed the safe door shut, gave a guttural laugh and taking a block of perspex with an encapsulated 1849 gold dollar from the mantelpiece he struck the old man on the side of the head. Van Vliet was instantly rendered unconscious and he collapsed into the armchair with blood trickling down his face. Xander tossed the perspex block aside and proceeded to search the rest of the house for any signs of James before boldly leaving by the front door and driving away.

Calder was winded by the run from Ferdi's house and after briefly checking the pocket road map he had bought at the station he reduced his speed to a brisk stride. Using small byroads he crossed a piece of wasteland and then the busy A4 motorway to reach the expansive woodland that was used as a recreation area. With the constant humming sound of traffic all around Calder slowed his pace and stopped to sit on a damp bench and catch his breath.

Having seen no signs of pursuit he followed a small footpath past some swings that were being used by a young child and her father and spotted a car park through a gap in the dense foliage. There was a number of cars and all appeared to be unoccupied. He stepped out onto the open tarmac and casually went from one to the other until he found an unlocked Volkswagen with a bunch of keys hanging from the ignition lock.

The car started immediately and he was soon on the motorway and the start of a smooth eighty-kilometre run to Amsterdam where he hoped to exchange the diamonds for cash.

Calder had a vague knowledge of the Amsterdam Diamond Centre in Dam Square and the complicated legal processes involved in selling a quantity of large, cut diamonds. He planned to split the diamonds into small packets to avoid any suspicion; visiting a number of less prominent dealers in the area would help to keep a low profile. His credibility as a highly respected professor at Cambridge would circumvent any reservations concerning the stones' provenance and he checked that he had enough business cards to hand out.

As he drove towards the city his one concern was the scarred man and what his next move might be. How he had survived the blow to his head was a complete mystery.

22

HOOFDINSPECTEUR ERNST DE GRAAF sat back in the leather chair and glared at the men before him. Cheswell was quietly murmuring into his mobile phone while Inspector Peters shuffled papers in a file that lay on his lap. Constable Cobus Westhuizen leant against the wall by the door and James waited impatiently for someone to suggest their next steps.

'What are you planning to do now, Peters?' de Graaf finally demanded to know and was abruptly interrupted by the door flying open and Sergeant Cas Mesman entering.

'Sorry to disturb you, sir, but we've just got a result from the van Rijn phone tap.' James looked from one man to the other for a translation and Peters obliged as Mesman continued. 'Van Rijn received a call saying that Professor Calder had escaped their net –'

'And ours,' de Graaf interjected.

'– and he wanted to know what he should do. Van Rijn told him to stay where he was until further orders. The voice sounded very much like Vos Xanders but the call was too short for us to get a fix on the bastard, so we're remaining on watch.'

'Good work, Sergeant,' Peters said. 'Let us know as soon as you've got him pin-pointed so we can all go and get us a cop killer.'

The sergeant saluted with a grim expression and left hurriedly.

'I suggest we all take a break and get something to eat and a brief rest,' Peters announced. When de Graaf nodded there was a rumble of agreement around the desk and they all left, apart from de Graaf who stayed behind.

James tagged along beside Peters and Cheswell as they they took the lift down and left the building. They all checked their phones and James found that he had three messages, two from Jennifer and one from Miss Lightbody who chastised him for travelling to Europe without telling her, draining her petty cash on trivial matters and not having a client to compensate for the company losses; he grinned and trashed the message. Jennifer's first note was to let him know that she had arrived home safely and that Claudiu had sent his love and the second was a reminder to take care and return home soon.

'Do you fancy *Lust*?' Peters suddenly asked the two men; startled from their individual reveries they stopped to give him very confused looks.

'Err hummm,' Cheswell responded, as much at a loss as James.

'*Drank & Spijslokaal Lust* is a great bar two blocks from here that serves up a fabulous tapas for only €21 and the beer is the best in South Holland,' Peters said as he looked at the two men with a bemused smile on his face.

'Sounds great,' James said and Cheswell simply grinned like a Cheshire cat.

The two officers and private investigator were soon perched on comfortable bar stools at a 60's retro counter and tucking into a host of small dishes and tankards of chilled lager. They had almost finished their *stoofvlees* and tortilla chips when Peters' mobile rang.

'Great news, gentlemen,' he announced, he face alive with excitement. 'As we anticipated, a second phone call instructed Vos Xander to go to a specific address in Rijswijk. Police presence at the railway station has been doubled and local officers are preparing to go to the house right now.'

'I trust they've been warned that Xander is a very dangerous suspect,' Cheswell said.

'They know that Xander has already killed one of our comrades so I think they'll know how to handle the situation,' Peters remarked in an icy tone that made it quite clear what he meant by handling.

'If Calder is still in the house when Xander gets there we're going to have another murder on our hands,' James muttered as he signalled for the bill.

Peters shook his head. 'This is on me,' he said taking the slip from the waitress who had given him a winning smile earlier. James raised an eyebrow and the inspecteur grinned. 'Her name is Gretha and she's my wife. She took over the running of this business when her father retired which is why I suggested we come here in the first place.' James chuckled and put ten Euros in the tip bottle marked *Dankjewel*. Although his expression was far from appreciative of James' generosity Cheswell felt obliged to follow suit.

They gave a cheery wave to Gretha and hurried back to the police station. The desk sergeant informed them that a report that had come in from Rijswijk was on Peters' desk. The lift seemed interminably slow but eventually they arrived and read the report.

'Xander or Calder had visited van Vliet, the coin collector who lives there, and one of them left him in a critical condition,' Peters said as he read from the single sheet of paper. 'Xander was seen pushing his way into the house and when he left he was wearing a backpack. I can only assume that Calder had sold the coins to van Vliet and Xander appropriated them.'

'When you say critical, is he likely to die?' James asked.

'He had his skull cracked with an unpleasantly heavy ornament and doctors have given him a fifty-fifty chance of survival.'

'And what about Xander?' Cheswell asked as he stood up and paced the office impatiently. 'Didn't any of the local officers manage to apprehend him?'

'They arrived too late and he had gone. However, the neighbour who had seen him leave said he drove away in a dark-coloured Ford Taurus but she was unable to remember the number.'

'So we're back to square one,' Cheswell sniffed and sat down again. 'I'm beginning to think this chasing about is getting us nowhere fast.'

'Not quite, Chief Inspector, the second phone tap fortunately gave us a positional fix which turned out to be a brothel we didn't have on our lists. The woman running it was reluctant to cooperate with us for fear that Xander would return and take his revenge. We then checked and found that most of the girls were under the age of consent and we threatened to throw a whole library of statutes at her unless she was more forthcoming with information about Vos Xander and his employer.'

'She had the car number?' James asked hopefully and Peters nodded.

'Xander took her car. She also told us that the property was part of one of the many companies owned and run by van Rijn. That now gives us probable cause to search his house and those premises we have reason to believe are being used to house illegal immigrants for the purpose of sex services. We've applied for a number of search warrants.'

'When you say illegal immigrants you mean young girls who fled from poverty and terror, thinking they were going to be offered employment and a safer way of life?' Cheswell said with eyes narrowing in anger.

'That's correct, Chief Inspector. We may only affect a tiny percentage of the trafficking but it will make a big difference to the lives of many girls controlled by van Rijn.'

'Wait till I get my hands on the bastard,' Cheswell growled.

'And Vos Xander,' James added.

'We have Highway Patrol monitoring all main roads for the Taurus,' Sergeant Mesman said when he entered the office. 'We've also put a call out for a Red Volkswagen Polo that was stolen from *Wilhelminapark* which is only a short distance from van Vliet's house.'

'When was it taken?' James asked.

'The owner had only just parked and was pushing his daughter on the swings when she felt ill; he carried her back to where he had parked the Polo but it was gone.'

'But *when* was it taken,' Cheswell asked.

'We've worked out that it must have been shortly after the neighbour saw the big man leave the house and drive away in the Taurus,' the sergeant concluded. After a nod from Peters he withdrew from the office to check for any incoming reports.

The four men remained silent for a while before James spoke. 'Calder has sold the coins and the king's charter, which we can assume are in the possession of van Rijn and Xander. He will definitely be looking for a fast escape so where will he be driving to?'

'He needs to evade Dutch police and cross a border fast,' Constable Westhuizen murmured.

'He'll also know that any official border crossing will be the first place we'll watch like eagles,' Peters added. 'If I were him I'd lose the car and then myself in one of our cities for a few weeks until I was sure that the hunt had cooled down. Only then would I leave the country for one that had no extradition treaty with Britain or the Netherlands.'

'You've put your finger on it, Adriaan,' James exclaimed. 'He'll do precisely what he did last time.'

The police officers looked at James with renewed interest.

'The bastard will go back to Marrakech. He has the money now to live the life of a sheikh if he got the true market value for both items.'

'And what would be the black market value?' Peters asked.

'A lot less than the four million I estimated for the charter and the coins as he's been forced to sell in a hurry, but it will still be a great deal of money.'

Peters stroked his chin thoughtfully. 'I think it'll be a great deal less than you believe, James, for two reasons. Firstly, he sold the charter to van Rijn and that's a man who prefers to take before he pays for anything and secondly, a coin collector doesn't keep fortunes in his wall safe for one obvious reason, burglars. I doubt that Calder got more than a few thousand Euros for the coins. He would have been in a bit of a panic and wanted to offload the coins as soon as possible. Van Vliet is a serious businessman and would take advantage of that and pay the very bottom rate.'

'He *was* a serious businessman,' Hoofdinspecteur Ernst de Graaf corrected as he entered the room. 'We've just received a report that van Vliet died without recovering consciousness twenty-three minutes ago. There was also a very old coin found in the kitchen sink which I believe could be one of the hoard Professor Calder was carrying. The crime scene team said there were signs that someone, possibly van Vliet, had been testing the metal for silver content.'

There was a collective sigh and Peters grimaced. 'Xander has a lot to answer for.'

'I want you to focus all your efforts on gathering as much evidence as possible to bring van Rijn to justice on a number of charges that his expensive lawyers will not be able to repudiate. Too often that pseudo count has wriggled off the hook to continue his filthy business as usual,' de Graaf concluded.

'With your permission, sir, and the help of your Highway Patrol, I'd like to track Calder as he's the main reason I'm in your country,' James said.

Despite Cheswell's objection that he was a civilian and had no authority to apprehend felons James' request was granted.

'Officers will assist you whenever and wherever they can and you'll be issued with a letter of authority that enables you to practise as a private investigator on Dutch soil,' de Graaf said and instructed Senior Constable Westhuizen to take James to the traffic control centre.

The large room, eerily lit by giant screens lining the walls, could easily be mistaken for being a Bond film set. Traffic analysts sat before individual desktop screens covered with graphs and charts while monitoring agents studied the wall screens that showed the streets of the whole city and the motorways leaving it.

'This is Sergeant Brouwer's kingdom,' Westhuizen said with a cheeky grin as a middle-aged officer approached with a 'what the hell are you doing in here' expression on his weathered face. 'Nothing moves in or out of Rotterdam and the major motorways without him knowing about it.'

'And I also control *this* traffic centre. What do you want Westhuizen?' the sergeant demanded in a rasping voice born from a lifetime of smoking as he studied the slender, handsome man in civilian clothing.

Westhuizen made the introductions and then added de Graaf's instructions to assist Goodfellow in his investigation.

'As a civilian you're very honoured to have de Graaf rooting for your cause, Meneer Goodfellow. It can only mean you've been giving him a lot of help in a major case.'

James immediately relaxed and felt more optimistic.

'We've already been tracking the two car numbers we were given but lost them on the E19 heading for Leiden,' Brouwer said as he led James to a large console that showed a still picture of a Ford Taurus on a three-lane motorway. Sergeant Brouwer touched a key and the picture zoomed until James could clearly see Xander scowling at the traffic ahead of him.

'That's the really nasty one,' James murmured, impressed by the technology being used. The sergeant tapped another key and James was looking at Professor Calder through the windscreen of a red Polo.

'The Taurus was approximately five kilometres behind the Polo and that particular road is the fastest route to Amsterdam.'

'If they enter the city we've lost them,' James said suddenly feeling glum.

'Not necessarily, I have already been in contact with my colleague in Amsterdam and we now have an automatic visual link via the street cameras. The screens you see on that end wall have been allocated to our pursuit in Amsterdam. I have a special team tracking both cars every minute and the moment they settle, like butterflies, we'll net them.'

Brouwer led James across to the wall and pointed at one screen showing a busy junction packed with cyclists and a red Polo. The car pulled away when the light changed, turned left and accelerated beyond the range of the camera.

'That's the Rijksmuseum, isn't it?' James asked as he caught a glimpse of the large gothic-and-renaissance building designed by Pierre Cuypers.

'Correct, and if we wait a few seconds our suspect will be picked up by the next camera.' True to the sergeant's words the screen flickered black and resolved to show a different perspective of the red Polo as it came into view and went past. 'We'll be following the same procedure for the Taurus which has yet to reach the outskirts of the city.'

'This is the most exceptional tracking system I've ever seen,' James declared much to the delight of both officers. 'I now need to get to Amsterdam as soon as possible,' he said as he and Westhuizen went back to Peters' office where Cheswell was already waiting.

'Why Amsterdam, James?' Peters asked. 'We'll soon be picking them up and bringing them back to Rotterdam to face charges.'

'And I don't want you rushing off ignoring police protocols in countries other than your own, Goodfellow,' Cheswell added.

James thought for a moment and then accepted that he couldn't contribute anything positive by being in Amsterdam.

Calder turned left at the museum and drove towards Jansen Diamonds, a reputable diamond merchant. He went down a number of small streets until he was sure there was no camera surveillance and parked the car. He took the diamonds and divided them into four, tore the tissue paper into squares and wrapped each sample before walking the two blocks to the showroom. At every street corner he studied the buildings for security cameras and only proceeded when he was sure it was 'clean'.

A very elegant-looking woman sat in the reception area and he was greeted cordially and asked if he had an appointment. Calder presented his card and asked if he could see someone about selling a few quality diamonds. The woman gave him a penetrating look then smiled and went to a door that opened silently on her approach as though someone had been watching.

Calder looked around the plush surroundings noting the three cameras that covered every part of the reception and finally chose a red satin chair near the front door. He didn't have to wait long before a lightly tanned gentleman in a dark blue suit came through the same inner door and approached him.

He bowed politely. 'If you would be so kind as to follow me, sir,' and he led the way into a small room where an armed guard stood by yet another door. He was wearing full Kevlar armour and carried a fully automatic machine-gun across his chest.

'Please leave your weapon on this table, sir,' Dark Suit said with a smile that didn't touch his eyes.

Calder remembered Xander's weapon and realized that he must have been scanned for weapons when he entered.

'Of course,' he replied cordially and slowly took the automatic from his pocket and laid it on the table. 'With diamonds I don't like to take chances,' he added.

The guard stepped forward, took the weapon and tucked it into his waistband. 'The item will be returned on your departure, sir.'

Calder was first taken into a hallway with a number of identical doors and then into a starkly lit room that had the dimensions of a large cubicle. Three fluorescent tubes provided the light. An elderly Hasidic man in a long black jacket and peyot side locks was already sitting on one side of a small table and he stood to shake Calder's hand before indicating that he should also sit.

'My name is Klaas van Jansen and I am the owner of this establishment. I understand you wish to sell some cut diamonds, Professor Calder,' he said in perfect English with only the smallest hint of an accent.

Calder saw that his card was already lying on the table and so he took one of the small packets from his pocket and laid it reverently on the table before the man.

'Not the most professional presentation,' the diamond trader observed dryly as he slowly unfolded the torn scrap of paper. Six stones glittered beneath the lights and he used a loupe to study them one by one. Minutes ticked by as the trader clicked his tongue and made faint despairing noises. Finally he put his loupe away in his waistcoat and refolded the paper before sitting back and crossing his arms.

Calder was the first to break the long silence. 'They are all F classified two-carat stones of VS1 clarity with no fluorescence. I was told that the estimated value would be £20,000 sterling each.'

The air was suddenly charged as van Jansen tilted his head to one side and gave a small smile. 'You have an expression in English that says, you must be joking. I don't know where you got these stones from my friend and who gave you that ridiculous figure. They are certainly two-carat in weight but unfortunately they are only WS2 with barely standard symmetry. I would value these quite fairly at £6,900 per stone.'

'What!' Shock prevented Calder from saying anything else and he just stared at the owner with his mouth open.

'My apologies, Professor, but to use another of your quaint English sayings, take it or leave it. I cannot pay more if I am to make the smallest of profits from the transaction.' Van Jansen pushed the small packet towards Calder who had decidedly paled.

'That's the best price you can offer?'

'It is indeed, Professor Calder, if that is your real name. I have to consider that you have offered me no provenance for the stones which means I have the expense of cutting them and converting them into jewellery before I can place them on the open market.' Van Jansen pushed a small button under the table. 'You should be pleased that I don't call the police and have you charged with fraud or attempting to sell blood diamonds.'

Calder jumped to his feet, his face suffused with anger. 'How dare you accuse me of doing anything illegal. I am a respectable archaeologist, a Professor at Cambridge University. Those who gave me the stones should be arrested by the police, not me.' He clenched his fists and as he leant forward in a threatening manner the door flew open behind him and his arms were firmly pinned to his sides by the security guard.

'I would like you to leave now, Professor, and to take those with you.' The packet was poked towards him by the man's dismissive forefinger. The guard released the fuming man and Calder snatched the diamonds and stalked from the room. At the security door he turned to the guard and held his hand out. His automatic was returned with the magazine removed. The receptionist glared icily at the professor as he stormed out of the showroom and hurried down the street. Her phone rang and van

Jansen instructed her to notify the police of Professor Calder's visit and attempt to sell what was possibly stolen diamonds. 'E-mail a head shot from the security footage just in case the police know him,' he added.

Calder strode back to where he had parked and was about to turn the corner when he spotted two police cars waiting in the street. The red Polo had been boxed in and two constables were casually leaning against their vehicles and smoking as they waited for the forensic team to arrive. Calder hurriedly retraced his steps until he was close to the Rijksmuseum. He had been checking all the parked cars but without the same good fortune he had experienced in Wilhelminapark.

He walked through the museum and began scrutinizing the few bicycles leaning against the railings. The majority was immobilized but finally Calder spotted a man's model that wasn't chained. Reliving his earlier days in Cambridge he cycled confidently along Boerenwetering to Beatrixpark where he started looking for a car in five cul de sacs. He struck lucky in the third and propping the bicycle against a hedge he slipped behind the wheel of a bright-green Smart. He had never driven such a small car before and it took a few hundred yards of neck-jerking leaps before the two-seater settled into a smooth and nippy ride. Calder was soon clearing the city and setting out on the road to Utrecht.

He knew the police would have the fastest highways covered so he decided to go to Utrecht on minor roads and then use much smaller country lanes to meander back to the Hook of Holland.

Thank God for sat-nav, he thought as he began programming his route.

23

XANDER HAD TRAWLED MOST of the roads in Amsterdam's diamond trading area when he drove past two police officers who were inspecting an abandoned Volkswagen Polo. The officers hardly took any notice of him and he kept going knowing that the professor had lost his mode of transport; Xander was now looking for a pedestrian. He had just passed the Rijksmuseum building, scanning the street on both sides, when one of the policemen guarding the Polo recalled the description of the second suspect. The alert went out and the police net tightened on the area surrounding the museum.

When Xander reached the major crossroad outside the museum he realized what a hopeless task he had been given and decided to return to Rotterdam and give the coins to van Rijn. Pure chance enabled him to pass through the cordon and leave the city but cameras soon located his position on the motorway.

'We've got Vos Xander back on the map,' Westhuizen said excitedly as he burst into Inspector Peters' office.

'Where?' Cheswell asked.

'He's just passed through Schipol Airport on the E19 and is heading in this direction in the same Ford Taurus.'

'Current status?' Peters asked.

'One Spyker C8 Spyder has been instructed to join the motorway at Leimuiden as soon as Xander passes and another will join the same road at Nieuwe Wetering at approximately the same time. Together they will sandwich the bastard in and bring him to a standstill. They have been advised that Xander is armed and exceptionally dangerous.'

'What is a spyker,' Cheswell asked.

'It's a luxury sports car. Our C8 Spyders from the Spyker line-up are the fastest chase cars we have,' Westhuizen said proudly. 'They can accelerate to 62mph in 4.5 seconds and have a top speed of 187mph. That makes them a good deal faster than the Taurus so they'll soon have Xander in custody.'

'They're mainly used for display purposes at parades and public events. It's the supercar's actual appearance that scares speedsters out of their wits which means it contributes a good deal towards road safety. It also encourages police recruitment,' de Graaf added as he entered the office. 'You have a lead on both suspects?' he asked turning to Peters.

'Vos Xander is just leaving Amsterdam and we plan to ambush him with the Spykers. We've had another report from Amsterdam that a Professor Calder tried to sell six large diamonds to Klaas van Jansen and when he failed to do so he vanished into thin air. They sent us a security picture that confirmed it was him. The car he had stolen was found in a nearby street, which means we can no longer track him; we can only assume he knows it's been compromised.'

'OK, we'll leave that hunt to the Amsterdam police while we do a little ambushing ourselves.' He waved a sheet of paper above his head as though in triumph.

'Is that the warrant, sir?' Peters asked with a growing smile that positively beamed when de Graaf nodded. 'Then I'll assemble the team and we can leave immediately,' he said as he took an automatic from his desk and the warrant from his chief.

Peters made a phone call and signalled to sergeants Mesman and Westhuizen. 'You'll be joining the search once the armed-response team have rendered van Rijn's house safe.'

James looked at Peters expectantly.

'As you are a civilian, and a foreign national at that, you'll have to stay here when we execute the raid,' Cheswell added with an apologetic expression. 'We don't want van Rijn's lawyers using your presence as an excuse for some legal shenanigans.'

'Can't I go in once the place is completely secure,' James pleaded. 'I've been trying to recover this charter from the very beginning and I have to see it through to the end.'

Peters folded the warrant and tucked it into his jacket pocket as he pondered the problem. 'Only if you promise to stay in the car until I signal you to come out.'

Cheswell began objecting but a look from Peters stopped him.

James gave a sigh of relief and joined the officers as they went to the armoury to be equipped with Kevlar vests and automatic weapons. He stood to one side watching the hive of activity until Westhuizen gave him a vest.

'The inspecteur insists that you wear one too, sir,' he said. James took the vest, slipped it on and fixed the side buckles in a way that surprised the senior constable.

'You've worn one before, haven't you sir?' Westhuizen commented.

'Please call me James, and yes, quite a few times, Cobus. I was a policeman myself three years ago.' The two men joined the others and trooped out into the walled compound where a large armoured vehicle was waiting. Peters asked James to ride with Westhuizen and himself in the command car.

Van Rijn lived in Hillegersberg, commonly regarded as the jewel of Rotterdam. A leafy suburb on the north-east of the city, it had escaped wartime devastation. The old village centre from which elegant residential streets radiated attracted the wealthy and expatriate workers. Ironically the master criminal's address was only ten minutes from the central Politiebureau Noord and the command car stopped outside a decorative pair of wrought-iron gates.

They could see a drive winding up to the house between well-tended box hedges. A heavily built man was standing by a small gatehouse and talking on his phone in a distraught manner.

Peters approached the gate with his hand hovering over his holster. 'Open up or face arrest for obstructing the police,' he demanded and the man took one look at his expression, closed his phone and pushed a button that activated the electric gates.

The inspector got back in the car as the guard was handcuffed and hustled into the black truck. The convoy swept up to the house and agents wearing balaclavas poured from the armoured van; some took up their positions at the front door while the rest trotted round to the rear of the house.

The door opened and van Rijn stood with legs apart, arrogantly defying Peters to enter. 'You do realize I know influential people who will not take too kindly to this invasion of my privacy. I suggest you go back the way –'

Peters pushed the warrant into the man's face and thrust past him to enter the spacious hallway where he planted his feet firmly on the marble floor and turned to face the startled criminal as the rest of the team flowed around him and began to search every room. The cries of 'safe' echoed off the marble as Cheswell, James and Westhuizen stepped into the house.

'I'm sorry, sir, but James insisted on coming instead of waiting as you ordered,' Westhuizon said just as a heavily armed Chinese man appeared at the top of the curved staircase and opened fire with an automatic gun. Three of the rounds ricocheted off the marble floor before one of the officers brought him tumbling down the stairs with a short burst from his sub-machine gun.

'Christ, that was close,' James exclaimed as he looked at the chipped marble by his right foot. Luckily I took my medication, he thought.

The Sergeant came out of a room and beckoned to Peters. 'Something you should see here, sir,' he said and gave his superior a gleeful look.

Peters ordered one of the team to handcuff van Rijn and take him into the huge living room adjoining the hall. Peters and Cheswell followed the sergeant into the kitchen at the back of the house. Mesman pointed to a large cupboard beside an open door leading into a pantry stacked with produce; pheasants and other game birds hung from ceiling hooks beside large smoked hams.

He swung the cupboard door open to reveal a flight of steps descending to a basement that was lit by a single bulb. Peters followed his sergeant and found himself between two rows of floor to ceiling wine racks that were fully stocked. Curiosity prompted Cheswell to remove one of the dust-covered bottles and study the label.

'You'll find that's one of three cases, sir,' Mesman said. 'Thirty-six bottles of Henri Jayer Cros Parantoux.'

'Vosne-Romanee Premier Cru,' Peters finished.

'And about six thousand pounds sterling per bottle,' James completed, startling all three men with his sudden appearance behind them and his knowledge of wine.

Mesman walked to the end of the cellar and seemed to disappear. Peters caught up with the sergeant who had gone behind a screen wall and was standing by an open door. The broken bolts and large padlock lying on the brick floor were testimony to Mesman's enthusiasm in forcing the door open.

'Welcome to Aladdin's cave, sir,' he announced with a flourish. A black curtain was draped across the entrance and as they pushed it to one side they were almost blinded by the brilliant light of a dozen spotlights in a veritable museum of fine art. Fine oil and watercolour paintings crowded the walls and more than a score of sculptures stood on floor pedestals.

'Heavens, there's a Picasso,' James exclaimed. 'And a Mondrian, a Damien Hirst and a Klee.' He pointed to each masterpiece he was able to identify.

'Good Lord, is that what I think it is?' the sergeant asked pointing to one painting that stood on an artist's easel. 'Is that a Rembrandt?'

They well all spellbound by the sight confronting them.

Cheswell was the first to speak. 'I know this work,' he murmured in awe as he stepped closer. 'In 1990 it was stolen from the Isabella Stewart Gardner Museum in Massachusetts. It's called *The Storm on the Sea of Galilee* and was painted in 1633. It was never recovered.'

'Until now,' Peters added.

'I read about this when I was at college. It's mentioned in the fourth chapter of the Gospel of St Mark and shows Jesus calming the storm,' Westhuizen said as he crossed himself.

The four wandered round the room in wonderment at the art collection, probably worth millions, that had been illegally accrued by van Rijn. James stopped at the large La-Z-Boy recliner that stood in the centre of the room.

'Van Rijn most probably sat in this to gloat over his collection in complete solitude,' Peters said.

'It is kind of sad, isn't it?'

'For Piet van Rijn, aka Count Berendzen, yes. For the owners of these pieces, no, they'll be overjoyed even if their insurance companies do give them a bit of a headache in sorting out the old claims.'

'It's a rather ironic coincidence that he has the same family name as the man who painted this magnificent work of art; I'm sure Rembrandt must be turning in his grave.'

There was a sudden cry of alarm from Westhuizen who had been circling the walls. He stepped back and withdrew his automatic from its holster.

'Something behind this wall, sir,' he whispered as Mesman and Peters joined him. Cheswell and James slowly edged closer until Peters angrily waved them back.

'Sounds like voices,' Westhuizen whispered. 'Women's voices,' he added as he began searching the wall for any cracks that would indicate a hidden door. Peters focused his attention on a giant painting in an ornate gilt frame hanging on the wall before him.

James crept up behind him. 'That's *The Virgin and St John the Evangelist* by Giovanni Francesco Barbieri that was stolen in 2014 with an estimated value of €5-6 million.'

'I remember that case,' Peters whispered. 'Our department was also involved in the hunt for the thieves.'

'I also think the frame could well be the doorway leading to those voices,' James responded.

Peters signalled silently to his men to test the frame and after a few seconds Westhuizen pressed a small button in one corner of the frame. There was an instant humming sound followed by clicks and metallic whirring. When the mechanism fell silent Westhuizon gripped the edge of the frame with his fingers and swung the painting away from the wall. The painting had been mounted on a thick steel door with a number of bolts aligned with holes in the doorframe.

'It's like a giant safe,' Mesman said and with gun levelled he stepped through the entrance into a large well-furnished bedroom. Cowering in the centre of a super-sized bed were two young Asian girls in sheer nightclothes. They knew they were looking at van Rijn's latest imports and there was no doubting that he was the one who tried them first to make sure the Snakeheads gang was selling him the best merchandise.

'Radio for two policewomen, Sergeant,' Peters murmured and holstered his weapon. The girls, who couldn't have been any older than fifteen, stopped weeping and looked nervously from one man to the next. Cheswell went to the wardrobes along one wall and on the third try found two silk dressing gowns. Without going too close he tossed them onto the bed and gestured that the girls should put them on. His contortions seemed to touch a nerve and they giggled at his mimed efforts.

'Well done, Chief Inspector,' James laughed. 'You'll have to sign up for the Wisbech Christmas pantomime.'

Cheswell pulled a face that caused the girls to giggle even louder. It was only after they had made themselves more presentable that the men noticed they were attached to the metal bed posts by thin chains attached to their ankles.

'My God, he chains them like slaves,' James growled.

'And that's what they are to him, sex slaves,' Peters said. 'We now have enough evidence to put the bastard away for a very long time.' The men heard the sound of high heels and two plainclothes police officers entered the room and absorbed the scene with one glance. Peters asked them to take pictures of the girls who were still in chains for use as evidence. The women reassured the girls that all would be well. One of them was of Chinese origin and she was able to speak a little Cantonese which the girls could understand.

The men went back to the main hallway where a sullen van Rijn stood next to a stranger in a dark suit who introduced himself to Peters as the Count's lawyer.

'You're going to need more than legal defence where you're going you bastard,' Westhuizen snarled. 'A little gossip in the prison exercise yard about child abuse will soon shorten your sentence, permanently.'

'I'd like to do that now,' Mesman muttered.

'Touch me and my lawyer will have your badge,' van Rijn said self-righteously.

This was more than James could take. 'You may think you can sue the Netherlands police for striking a prisoner in custody but you'll need an extradition order to get me into court.' He took two swift steps to get close to van Rijn and before anyone could react James kicked the man in the groin with the point of his shoe. As he doubled up James brought his knee up sharply, breaking the sex trafficker's nose. Blood drops spattered the immaculate marble as Cheswell forestalled James from doing any more damage to Peters' prisoner.

'Somehow I don't think any judge will be signing an extradition order after reading the charges being brought against you by the Public Prosecution Service,' Peters explained in a slow, threatening tone. 'Get him out of here,' he ordered and one of the armed-response team roughly dragged van Rijn out of the house by his shackled wrists.

'You do realize that I can bring a civil suit against this civilian for violently and unlawfully attacking my client without any provocation,' the lawyer stated pompously.

'You must have imagined the incident because nobody else saw it,' Peters said as he suppressed a grin without too much success.

'I can assure you that everyone was provoked by what your client has been doing,' James snapped as the policewomen shepherded the two Asian girls, wrapped in blankets, past the group of men and out of the house. 'These are only two of the unfortunate children who have been brought here on the promise of legitimate employment with respectable families and companies, and found themselves instead forced into sex slavery.'

The lawyer remained impassive, ignoring the passing girls.

'They will be taken to hospital for medical and psychological examinations before being returned to their families.' The lawyer was still unmoved. 'Despite the legality of registered brothels there are still more than two thousand girls who are forced to work in Rotterdam as sex slaves. Your client is a principal supplier and will be charged with trafficking under-aged girls for the purpose of providing sexual services against their will and that's what we call rape of a minor in the Netherlands.'

The lawyer shrugged and strode from the house.

'There's one thing we didn't find in the basement, Inspecteur,' James said morosely.

'The king's charter?' Peters asked.

'I know you have to leave things untouched for the forensic investigators but can I at least take a final look in the other rooms?'

'Sergeant Mesman will accompany you to make it official,' Peters said and he handed James a pair of latex gloves. 'Just make sure you use these.'

Followed by Cheswell James wandered into the large living room as he pulled on the gloves and began searching while Mesman started on the other side. 'What are we looking for exactly?' the chief inspector asked James.

'It's most probably a large art folder, the kind students might carry, or it could even be the same cardboard tube I had the document in; it's beige in colour with black plastic end caps.'

When they were satisfied that they had covered every inch they went across the hall to the dining room and following the same search pattern they worked their way around the room until they all met by the kitchen door.

'If it's rolled up in a tube where would be a good temporary hiding place that's right in front of our noses?' James said suddenly, his eyes bright with excitement. When both officers remained silent he continued, 'You'd put it where there are hundreds of other tube-like objects in a dimly lit place.'

'The wine cellar!' Mesman exclaimed and James clapped the sergeant on the back. They hurried through the kitchen and down the steps to begin their search of the wine racks. Fifteen minutes later Mesman gave a hoot of success when he reached the top of a rack that had been laid down with Vino Nobile de Montepulciano. The cardboard tube was half hidden close to the vaulted brick ceiling and he carefully climbed down the steps holding it like a new-born baby.

'Well done, Sergeant,' James said. 'You've at least given me one thing to take home as a souvenir of my vacation in sunny Rotterdam.' They returned victorious to the hallway just as the forensic team entered, stamping their feet and shaking raindrops from their heads. Contrary to the James' description they had arrived in a minor rainstorm.

'I'm sorry, James, but you can't take that with you,' Peters said as he slipped the tube from under his arm. 'We have to log it in as stolen property along with all the other works of art and sculptures. It will be returned once the trial is over and all the paperwork has been completed.'

'How long will that take?' James asked in a glum voice.

'It'll be quite a few months, I'm afraid. It depends on van Rijn's trial period but don't worry, we'll arrange for it to be given to the British Embassy for dispatch to Chief Inspector Cheswell in Norfolk.'

'Then I'll put it in the safe hands of the British Museum,' Cheswell added with a smug grin.

And get all the glory, James thought ruefully.

24

THE TWO OFFICERS WAITED with growing impatience, their C8 Spyder purring idly. When the call finally came the driver slowly moved down the access road as his partner looked back up the motorway. They had been notified of the suspects' progress and were timing the start of their pursuit to coincide with the car passing them. The suspect flashed past and the sports car snarled into action and the Taurus was neatly sandwiched between two Spyders. The experienced police driver put his foot down and they were soon exceeding 110mph and fast catching up on the Taurus.

Vos Xander had been cruising comfortably at 70mph and planning what he would say to van Rijn when he saw the rapidly approaching sports car in his mirror. He recognized the distinctive blue-and-red livery and knew the police were chasing him. Somehow they discovered that he had the whore's car and had been tracking him by the CCTV cameras on the highway. He pressed down hard but the old car was unable to outrun the Spyder that was still accelerating and closing the gap. Xander knew he didn't stand a chance and he slowed and turned the wheel to take the inside lane where he let the car idle along at a crawl.

The Spyder braked hard with smoking discs and came alongside the Taurus. The officer indicated that Xander should stop but he ignored the signals and producing his automatic he fired into the police car until the magazine was empty. The police car swerved, hit the side of the Taurus and then careered into the fast lane where it was struck by a passing petrol tanker.

Xander accelerated to avoid the spinning car and seeing his chance took the exit road to leave the motorway and take the N445 to Leiden. He knew he had to dispose of the Taurus as soon as possible and on the outskirts of Leiden he abandoned it outside a shopping plaza. Putting on the backpack he strode down a wide avenue until he saw a silver Audi parked in front of a brand-new house. A middle-aged woman was unloading her shopping and when she noticed him he gave a cheery wave and a smile to allay any suspicions until he was standing beside her.

'Don't scream or try anything foolish or I will kill you,' Xander said. He produced an automatic and prodding her in the back instructed her to go inside the house.

'Is that you, Hanna?' A voice called out and a bald-headed man appeared in the hallway. Xander put a finger to his lips and showed him the gun. 'Keep very quiet or I will kill your wife.' He waved the couple into the kitchen and then into a large windowless larder where he gagged and bound them with kitchen twine. 'If I hear you attempting to escape you will both be shot?'

Xander locked the door and checked the rest of the house for any other occupants before strolling to the car. The keys were still in the ignitionand he decided to take the E19 to Rotterdam. He would be relatively safe in the Audi until a neighbour or visitor discovered the imprisoned couple.

When he arrived at van Rijn's house two police cars were parked at the gates and two more plus a large black van in the drive. Xander kept driving and parked a safe distance from the house and settled down to see what transpired.

James and Cheswell left van Rijn's house and turned their collars up against the light drizzle. 'Apart from Xander and the coins you've done a good job, Goodfellow,' Cheswell said and there was genuine praise in his voice.

'We may still recover the coins when that psychopath is apprehended and safely behind bars,' James said with a frown. 'I'm sure he has the coins with him and the British Museum will get their silver bonus.'

Both men laughed and climbed into Peters' car, with Sergeant Mesman behind the wheel.

'What an unbelievable hoard. And how can anyone take pleasure in a precious collection if they can't share it with the world,' Mesman started saying when the radio crackled into life.

He took the message and the three men learnt of the fatalities on the motorway. One officer had died instantly from a bullet in the brain whereas the other, although suffering multiple gunshot wounds, had died in the conflagration as the Spyder spun into the fuel tanker.

Mesman sprang from the car to break the news to Peters who immediately wanted to know if the second Spyder was in pursuit. 'No, Inspecteur, the Taurus never caught up with the police car.'

'He must have sensed that we have been tracking him with the cameras,' Peters deduced. 'He's taken a minor road that doesn't have CCTV and, if I'm not mistaken, he'll want to get back to van Rijn which means he's heading here.'

'That would also mean he plans to bring the silver coins here,' James remarked and instinctively looked back down the drive as though expecting the man to materialize suddenly.

Two armed-response officers stayed in the house with instructions to keep out of sight while the forensic team stayed in the basement gathering evidence; two of the best marksmen remained in the hallway as everyone else climbed into their vehicles and left. The two cars that had been parked in the street followed to complete the convoy returning to central Rotterdam.

Xander saw the vehicles departing and slumped down lower to avoid any recognition as they passed the Audi. As the third police car went by the Audi Xander spotted the familiar figure of James Goodfellow sitting in the back and he instantly felt an overwhelming desire for revenge.

A black limousine went past and he recognized van Rijn's legal representative; his employer was in custody and in big trouble. Xander looked at the backpack filled with silver on the passenger seat and decided to start up his own operation in a new city. His contacts in Antwerp's Snakeheads gangs would help him with any difficulties concerning rival operations. However, there was one thing he still had to do that required lingering in Rotterdam a little longer.

When the last police car had turned the corner Xander pulled out and shadowed the convoy back to the politiebureau. He again settled down out of sight to wait for his prey to emerge and give him the opportunity for a clean shot.

Two hours passed before James and Chief Inspector Cheswell came through the plate-glass doors and went down the steps to where a police car had arrived seconds before to take them to dinner. The two felt they had fasted long enough and as they were scheduled to return to England the following day they decided to take in one of the most famous sights of Rotterdam with Westhuizen as their driver.

Xander pulled out and followed the car for five miles, passing the Museum Boijmans Van Beuningen whose staff would undoubtedly rejoice on the return of the Rembrandt painting. It became obvious where they were going and he wasn't surprised when the car parked at the foot of the Euromast.

The officers got out and strained their necks to stare up at the colossal tower that was catching the last of the sun and reflecting splinters of light in all directions. The tiny figures hanging on ropes slowly grew larger as they abseiled from the 100-yards-high observation terrace above the restaurant.

'Wow, that looks like fun,' James said.

'Why don't you give it a try, James,' Westhuizen asked but James shook his head with a rueful grin.

'We all thought you'd like to go up in the world for that final meal in Rotterdam,' Cheswell said.

'I'm not sure my secretary would approve of this extravagance.'

'Even if it's on the house?' Cheswell's grin seemed to go on forever. 'The Rotterdam politie are so grateful for your help in bringing van Rijn and his cronies to justice and saving those young girls from a dreadful life that they felt you deserved a slap-up meal on them.'

'What about Cobus?' James asked, nodding towards the driver.

'I'm the one with the credit card, sir. I *have* to come with you,' Westhuizen said with a knowing wink as he left the car with them. 'I can recommend the beef carpaccio followed by grilled sea bass and pannacotta,' Westhuizen said with the air of an experienced Euromast diner.

'You come here often, Cobus?' James asked as the officer showed his pass to the attendant.

'Not as much as I would like to, James. A senior constable's pay is a little limiting when it comes to pleasures such as these.'

The three laughed as they stepped into the lift and were whisked up to the brasserie level in seconds. As they were led to their reserved table Xander was paying his entrance fee on the ground floor. The attendant looked at his backpack with some suspicion but as she was at the end of her shift and eager to get home she let him pass.

The lift door opened and he was greeted by the maître d' who asked whether he had a reservation. Xander shook his head and was led to a table close to the centre of the tower where the views of the city were limited. This suited the killer, as he needed to work out how he was going to kill Goodfellow and make a clean escape afterwards. It was very early and the restaurant was only a quarter full. He scanned the diners by the windows and on the far side saw Westhuizen's party toasting each other in red wine. They were also engrossed in the magnificent views and if he strolled across they would hardly notice him. Xander looked the other way and saw ropes hanging past the window.

'Are those for the window cleaners?' he asked the waiter who had brought water and a menu to his table.

The man gave a small laugh. 'No, sir, those are for the abseiling tourists who come for the thrill of dropping a long way on a thin piece of cord,' he said and shuddered in an exaggerated manner. 'You wouldn't catch me doing that. The lift may not be as fast but it's certainly safer as far as I'm concerned.'

Xander ordered a simple salad to get rid of the man and then checked under the table that the magazine in his semi-automatic Sig Sauer 9mm was fully loaded. He stood up, slipped his arms through the straps of the backpack and had walked to within ten metres of his target before Westhuizen saw him and in an instant recognized the scarred face.

'Xander!' he warned and leapt up only to be gunned down by a single shot to the chest. Diners screamed and some fell to the floor while others ran to the lift to escape. Cheswell looked down in horror at the fallen officer as Xander stopped at the table and pointed his weapon at James.

'You've been a troublesome bastard since you arrived in my city,' Xander snarled and the scar became a livid white streak. 'It's time I took care of you.' Movement on his left caused him to spin and he fired the 9mm without aiming. The frightened abseiler dangling outside the window stared at the man seemingly pointing a gun at him and then at the splintered glass before releasing the brake to drop out of sight.

James had instinctively leapt to one side and rolled under the next table and the one beyond that while the chief inspector dived over their table into Xander. The two men fell to the floor and Cheswell punched the thug in the face with one hand while he grasped the weapon in Xander's grip. Cheswell tried to twist the large gun away but the big man was able to bring the barrel round and pull the trigger. Nothing happened; the magazine had jammed and he resorted to striking Cheswell with his free hand and then with the defunct weapon rendering him unconscious.

Xander turned his attention back to his original target but James had disappeared. He dropped the useless gun and walked into the panic-stricken crowd by the lifts. His target was nowhere to be seen and ignoring the terrified people he climbed the stairs to the rooftop where two young men, oblivious to the pandemonium below, were climbing into special harnesses. Xander pulled a large knife from the side of the backpack and ordered them to remove the harnesses and sent them scurrying to safety. Once he had worked out how to manipulate the harnesses he prepared himself for a swift descent – someone was bound to have called the police and he wanted to avoid being greeted by an armed-response team.

Cheswell stirred first and sat upright, a constant searing pain in his head. A waiter rushed from the kitchen carrying wet cloths and seeing the blood running down the side of the officer's head he placed a cooling pad against the wound. Another waiter bent over Westhuizen fearing the worst.

'He still lives but needs an ambulance urgently,' he shouted with relief and the maître d' used his phone.

'How are you, Chief Inspector?' James called out as he ran across the restaurant and knelt beside Cheswell.

'Splitting head but still in the land of the living and so is Cobus,' he said. He groaned intermittently at each stab of pain.

'And Xander, where did he go?' James said as he inspected the wound before using a clean napkin to staunch the trickle of blood.

'The waiter told me he went out to the lifts. I was lucky his gun jammed.' Cheswell picked the weapon up and ejecting the magazine saw that the next bullet had been fed at an angle jamming the whole spring-mechanism. He ejected the errant round to allow the next to move into place, pushed the magazine back into the stock of the Sig Sauer and cocked it. 'It'll work now so let's go and get the sonofabitch,' he suggested. James checked that the maître d' was seeing to Westhuizen and then left the restaurant with Cheswell to find a crowd of diners were blocking their way to the lifts.

James jerked his thumb up. 'If we've got a problem so had Xander, he's gone up onto the roof.'

'Then we've got the bastard trapped,' Cheswell panted as they ran up the stairs and burst out onto the roof where Xander was about to climb over the parapet. 'Stop or I'll fire,' Cheswell shouted but the big man ignored him and disappeared from sight to start his descent while one hundred yards below spectators were looking up and pointing, not knowing of the drama being enacted.

'I can't risk shooting, James, I could hit someone down on the ground.' Cheswell's scream of frustration was whipped away by the growing wind. When he turned round James was harnessed and attaching himself to the spare lines that hung over the vertiginous drop.

'I'll get him, Chief Inspector,' James growled. 'I've had a little experience with these.'

'Good luck, James.'

Taking care not to tangle his lines James climbed over the edge and began lowering himself. He could see that Xander was thirty feet below him and moving cautiously. James had abseiled in the Yorkshire Dales and now expertly released the descender to reduce the friction and move down the line until he was only five feet above Xander. They were now both hanging free from the building and dangling in the void.

As the big man began opening the rappel device to increase his speed he became aware of movement above him and looked up in shock when he saw James abseiling rapidly towards him. Reaching round into the backpack he took out the big knife and applied pressure on the braking bar to stop and wait for James to reach him.

'I'll make doubly sure this time, Goodfellow,' he called out, slicing the air with the blade.

Aware of the danger James started bending and straightening his legs in playground fashion to create a swinging effect until he had achieved a thirty-foot arc. Releasing his descender he dropped on the outward swing and on his return, when he was level with Xander, he used the locking bar. James straightened his legs, leant back so that his full weight would be behind his feet and struck Xander in the head and chest.

The impact was a massive shock and Xander, partially stunned by the blows, almost dropped the knife. He wildly clutched at James with his free hand and James responded by gripping Xander's knife-wielding hand by the wrist. He made doubly sure his braking bar was locked hard to remain hanging beside Xander. As the two men fought for their lives in free space 70 metres above the Euromast's concrete apron their ropes began to twist together.

Xander recovered from the impact and began to punch James in the face and throat while he tried to free the knife-wielding hand. James began to tire and knew he wouldn't be able to keep his grip on the powerful wrist for much longer. He looked at the twisted lines above their heads and it was difficult to tell which was which.

Xander noticed James' upward glance and saw his opportunity. The rope going through his rappel device had yellow stripes while James' had a red thread in the weave. He struggled to move his knife close to the rope and James, realising his intention, put greater pressure to bear on Xander's wrist but his strength was rapidly draining.

Xander brought his knee up suddenly in an attempt to strike his opponent in the groin but James blocked the blow with his thigh and reached across to lock both hands onto Xander's wrist. The extra leverage helped to wrench Xander's knife hand up and over to the taut lines above their heads.

James guided the sharpened blade to slice through one of the lines as though it didn't exist and Xander realized in a split second what had happened. He dropped the knife and tried to grab hold of James who kicked himself free from the man as he fell, his line with the yellow thread no longer attached to anything.

James watched the killer plummeting and shrinking in size to the sound of distant screams from the crowd below until unyielding concrete ended Xander's flying career.

There was a lone cry of victory and James looked up to see a white-faced Cheswell peering over the parapet and punching the air with a clenched fist. He gave a tired smile and released the brake to begin the descent to terra firma.

The ambulance was waiting by the time James had touched down to be surrounded by police officers. Without realizing what was happening to him he was rudely handcuffed and being led to a police car when a voice boomed, 'Bring that man to me.'

Hoofdinspecteur Ernst de Graaf strode across the Euromast apron scattering officers left and right.

'I've had the story by phone from Chief Inspector Cheswell and I want to thank you for bringing that damned animal to justice,' and he gestured over his shoulder to the covered remains of Vos Xander. 'The lifts are jammed with people at the moment but as soon as Cheswell arrives I want you both to be my guests.' He gave a winning smile. 'I promise it will be less eventful than your last attempt at al fresco dining but the food and the wine will be just as exciting.'

'I'm so sorry about Cobus,' James sighed sadly. 'He stepped between Xander and myself to give me protection.'

'He's alive and will soon be in the care of the hospital. I hope you didn't think the ambulance was for that bit of garbage,' and de Graaf said as he pointed with disdain at the shape under the sheet.

James didn't know what to say and instead made a quick apology to call Jennifer and tell her, with fingers crossed, that he would be on his way home in the morning.

25

THE TWO MEN STROLLED on the top deck to watch the sun rising out of a glassy sea. Thanks to a wildcat strike by the air traffic controllers their flight to Stansted had been cancelled and James and Cheswell had no other option but to return by sea, ferrying from the Hook of Holland to Harwich.

They had been given a big send-off the previous night by Inspector Peters and all the other officers at the station and, after being reassured that Cobus Westhuizen was out of danger and had sent them his best wishes, the two men had finally staggered to their beds feeling a little worse for wear. The next morning they climbed wearily into the courtesy police car supplied by de Graaf and were taken to the ferry port.

'When I first met you, James, I thought you were one gigantic pain in the proverbial,' Cheswell said as they sat on one of the top-deck benches and watched the sea-going gulls soaring overhead as though filmed in slow motion. 'Now I know you are one of those rare men who have a sense of honour.'

'That's nice of you to say, Chief Inspector,' James said. 'I believe my wife's boss, Detective Inspector Tilley, could be your twin when it comes to knowing when to turn a blind eye or close both when searching for the truth. Since that first day in Wisbech I have seen you bend the strictest rules but never break them which is the foundation of successful police work as far as I'm concerned.'

Cheswell leant back against the bench slats and gave James a quizzical look but he detected no cynicism. Years of experience in questioning suspects had taught him how to read body language and voice intonation but all he could sense was a genuine compliment from the private investigator.

'You were a policeman yourself, James. Why did you leave the force?' he asked politely.

'When my narcoleptic condition was exposed I was asked to either take a desk job or retire. I chose to retire as I have always wanted to be a detective and the only way I could achieve that was by going private. I opened my own investigation agency in East Steading within the month and since then I've had reasonable success. More importantly, I've found my true vocation and despite the occasional danger which my wife abhors I love it.'

'Occasional danger? Hell's bells, James, you've been in nothing but mortal danger since you first came to Norfolk.' Both men began to laugh and when they lapsed into a comradely silence Cheswell offered to buy them both a warming coffee. Cheswell disappeared inside to use the vending machine and James speed-dialled home to tell Jennifer that he would be a little late as they were no longer flying.

'We're both missing you, James,' Jennifer complained. 'I suppose you've been having a lot of fun in the fleshpots of Rotterdam,' she said and then laughed as she pictured James gawping at the scantily-clad ladies in bay windows.

He didn't tell her about the Euromast incident but gave her a potted history of events ending with the recovery of the king's charter and the silver coins.

'What about Daniel's murderer, has he been apprehended?'

'I believe that could have been Bernard Davies at the Green Fingers Garden Centre. However, we'll never know because he was killed. I thought at first he couldn't possibly be a murderer but on looking back realized he knew of the two treasures and had the greatest opportunity.'

'Shall I tell Agnes and then she can call Margaret to put her mind at ease?'

'Not yet, I'd like to think about it a bit more before we give closure to this case,' James said slowly as he became aware that a man in a long dark coat had come out onto the deck and was standing close to the bench. 'I'll talk to you later about that when I get home, darling,' James said and before they could exchange their usual fond farewells he was tapped on the shoulder.

'Be so kind as to come with me, Mr Goodfellow,' the man in the coat said and he turned to face James with an automatic pistol held before him.

'Calder!' James exclaimed and slipped the phone into his pocket. 'I didn't expect to see you again and especially not on the same ferry as myself.'

'I'm sure you didn't, now walk over to the ship's rail.' Calder strode to the polished oak rail and briefly looked down at the seething water rushing along the hull forty feet below. 'Your interference has ruined me and you and your damned wife have cost me a fortune.'

James slowly walked to the rail and stood before the man whose unblinking hate-filled eyes were fixed on him. 'Now I only have these to show for my life's work,' and he held up the small packet of diamonds. 'Less than a million pounds worth of diamonds if I can find a buyer.'

'Is that all you could get for the charter?'

'I was cheated by an arrogant fool who didn't appreciate the history-changing value of such a document.'

'I can only guess that van Rijn wouldn't pay your price.'

Calder's eyes glinted dangerously. 'He tried to double-cross me.'

'And it looks like he succeeded,' James replied looking at the small package. The automatic angrily prodded his chest before Calder stepped away and shifted his aim to James' head.

'Before you do anything foolish, Professor, just answer one question,' James demanded as he avoided looking down at the lethal weapon. 'Did Davies kill Lightbody?'

'Davies, that incompetent owner of the garden centre?' Calder mocked. 'He couldn't kill aphids on a standard rose.' He spat contemptuously on the deck. 'The moron deserved to get one in the eye and he got it.'

'You shot him?'

'I got rid of an awkward obstacle as well as that bloody farmer and now I will do the same to you,' Calder mocked.

'Daniel Lightbody?'

'Was that his full name? Yes, I had to dispose of the man because he flatly refused to give me the king's charter when I turned up in Ravens' Wood. Having the charter for myself, and knowing it to be genuine, I was duty-bound to take it. I am the only one who knows its true historic worth and I have to be the one to present it to the world.'

'Let's be honest, Calder, you wanted all the glory for yourself.'

Both men steadied themselves against the rail as the ship listed slightly but Calder's aim remained fixed as he continued with his peevish complaint. 'For years I've been stuck in that dusty, archaic college and it's time my expertise and leadership in the field of archaeology was recognized. The king's charter was my crowning moment.'

James looked hard into the man's face and realized he was dealing with an egomaniac and a psychopath. 'But why come all the way from Cambridge in the first place?'

Calder thought for a while. 'There have been rumours and investigations into King John's lost treasure for centuries and in recent times whenever something new cropped up I, as the country's leading authority on the subject, was compelled to go and check the stories for myself. Your stupid farmer didn't anticipate that I would actually travel from Cambridge so soon after receiving his e-mail about his discovery.'

'Why did you go direct to Ravens' Wood and not Daniel's home?'

'I wanted to carry out authentication checks on the spot. I went to see Davies first and he told me where Lightbody had found the chest and how to get there.'

'But you didn't go alone, did you?'

'No. I had a friend living in the area that I thought might be useful and I asked him to come with me.'

'Raul Moran, aka Whitey, the fugitive from Morocco?' James said and Calder gave a bemused look.

'Clever bastard, aren't you, Goodfellow.'

James ignored the jibe and looked beyond Calder but the cold morning breeze coming down from the north had kept the deck deserted and he knew it would be the same behind him. James had to keep the psychopath talking to stand any chance of survival.

'Raul was very useful although rather impatient and before I could stop him he knifed the man to convince him to give me what I wanted and like all the idiots who constantly surround me he didn't kill him.'

'It was you who did the deed?' James murmured as all the pieces dropped into place. 'You used Daniel's own chainsaw as a rather efficient way of killing him and then mutilating his neck. You clearly thought it would be a foolproof way to hide the initial attack with the knife.'

Calder had a smug smile on his face. 'I thought it was a rather neat way to ensure it looked like a very tragic work accident or even a suicide.'

'Unfortunately for you, Calder, the postmortem was very thorough and it revealed the preliminary cut on the neck that had wounded Daniel; out of interest, what kind of weapon did Raul use?'

'It was the farmer's own box-cutter.' Calder laughed as he continued, 'The fool had given one of the silver coins to me to authenticate and I asked to borrow a sharp blade to scrape away some of the tarnishing that had formed on the surface. I handed it to Raul when I'd finished.'

James was running out of questions. 'So after you had gone straight to Ravens' Wood to do the authentication . . .' The ship listed a few degrees and James grabbed at the rail to steady himself, '. . . you found that they were the real thing? They were coins that King John had minted?'

As the ship listed the other way in a particularly strong swell Calder simply leant harder against the rail to steady himself and he grinned at James.

'Yes, I told him they were genuine and said he should give me the coins so that I could do a thorough check at the university but the dullard wanted to wait until the next day so he could accompany me to Cambridge.' Calder sneered, 'It was as though he didn't trust me.'

'He was right to think that, wasn't he?'

'And that was the fool's mistake.'

'Cambridge professor dupes local farmer, that would have been quite a headline so you had to kill him, didn't you?'

'Enough of this chit-chat Goodfellow. I can tell that you're just wasting my time so I think you should join Lightbody where you'll have plenty of time to discuss this matter further.' Calder raised the gun to point at James' left eye, exactly as he had done with Bernard Davies; his finger had started to tighten on the trigger when he saw a movement in the corner of his eye. He turned his head in time to be bludgeoned in the mouth by a large red-and-white lifebuoy that was spinning horizontally like a discus.

The combination of densely compacted polyethylene and polyurethane ringed with tarred rope smashed into his front teeth, ripping them from his gums and throwing him backwards against the polished wood. The gun fired harmlessly into the air as he toppled over the rail and plunged down into the water hissing against the hull.

Cheswell was standing by the open door clutching one spilt cup of coffee while another lay in a crumpled mess at his feet. He discarded the cup and ran across to where James was starting to collapse from shock.

'Where the hell did he come from?' he asked as he put a supporting arm round James. He briefly glanced over the ship's rail at the roiling wake behind the ship in an attempt to catch a glimpse of the professor. There was no sign of him and if the wounded man had survived the fall he would undoubtedly have been drawn into the churning screws.

James mumbled something as he sank down to sit on the deck with Calder holding him. His vision was returning slowly and he saw the blurred image of a white packet lying in the scupper. Calder had dropped the precious object when he was struck and as the tingling sensation faded from James' legs and arms he was able to reach out and pick it up.

'Where the hell did he come from indeed, Chief Inspector?' James echoed as he turned the packet over in his hand. 'Somehow, he managed to get aboard and was planning to return to England to sell these before disappearing forever.' He handed the packet to Cheswell.

The officer helped him rise to his feet and with his arm still clamped around the investigator's waist he walked him to the bench beside the door. 'What's in this?' he asked as they both sat down.

'To use a very old-fashioned expression, they are his ill-gotten gains. It's what van Rijn paid him for the king's charter,' James said, his voice now fully recovered.

Cheswell unfolded the white paper on his lap very carefully and then whistled softly. 'How many are there or should I say how much are they worth?'

'Calder boasted that they would bring him one million pounds sterling but that was just a rough estimate.'

This received another whistle. 'Let's go in. I think we both deserve some fresh, hot coffee and then we can decide on what to do with these.' He slipped the packet into his jacket pocket and helped James to his feet.

When the two men were warmly ensconced on a corner settee, well away from the hubbub of the returning tourists and Dutch day-trippers, they warmed their hands round the cups of coffee and started talking at once.

James apologized. 'After you Chief Inspector.'

'Please James, we've been through a lot and you should be calling me Alan by now.' James smiled and Cheswell continued. 'I had the coffee and was stepping onto the deck when I saw Calder pointing a gun at you. The only thing I could do was drop a coffee, I think it was yours with the sugar, grab a lifebuoy off the hook on the wall and throw it like a frisbee as hard as I could.'

'Lucky for me that you did, Alan,' James said thankfully.

'Calder must have sensed I was there and he was turning his head as I let go of the lifebuoy. The effort threw me off balance but fortunately it struck him and knocked him backward and over the rail. As I said, I had meant to just distract him sufficiently for you to grab his gun hand. I hadn't intended to hit him in the mouth and throw him overboard.'

'Lucky you did because he fired the gun, didn't he?'

'Yes, but it was a reflex action to the lifebuoy hitting him in the face and the bullet went God knows where. Now it's your turn to tell me what went on before I arrived on the scene to save your miserable hide.'

James put his cup down. 'And I'll be thanking you for the rest of my life for that, Alan, and no doubt my wife will have a few words to add to that too.'

'It was nothing, it was just years of training that instinctively came into action.' Cheswell grinned and the mature man suddenly resembled a cheeky boy. 'I admit that lifebuoys weren't included in the weapons training course at Police College but . . .' he hesitated as it sank in what James had said. 'Did you say Calder actually confessed to murder?'

'Yes, and not only did he kill Daniel but he murdered Bernard Davies and his own wife, too. That one I believe you suspected.'

'My God!' Cheswell murmured to himself. 'How can a respectable, educated professor of archaeology change into a serial killer?'

'Greed, Alan. It's as simple as that.'

'Unfortunately, we only have your word that he confessed to all those crimes and my superiors will undoubtedly file this as an unsolved case.'

James was listening with growing disappointment on his face when he suddenly reached into his pocket to retrieve the phone. 'I forgot Jennifer,' he cried out, causing a few curious passengers to look in their direction.

'What has your wife got to do with what has happened here?' James didn't reply but smacked the phone against his ear.

'Are you still there, Jenny?' he asked and a broad grin spread across his face. 'Yes I'm perfectly all right which is more than I can say for Professor Calder.' James listened for a while before handing the phone to Cheswell. 'She's done telling me off and now she needs to talk to you, Alan.'

'Chief Inspector Cheswell speaking,' he announced formally with raised eyebrows and then laughed when Jennifer demanded to speak to Alan. The two spoke for a considerable time during which James began to feel tired and leaning back into the corner drifted into a light sleep.

'She heard everything?' James asked when Cheswell nudged him awake.

'Not only did she hear everything but your clever wife had the presence of mind to switch on the recording device you've got attached to your landline phone,' he replied, his admiration for Jennifer's professionalism evident in his voice. 'However, she must have been terrified by what she was listening to.'

'I knew by the way she was *so* angry with me that she had been frightened but you can always rely on Jenny to use her police training to stay cool.'

'You've got a damned fine girl there, James. By the way, she will be contacting your secretary and Margaret Lightbody to tell them that justice has finally caught up with the murderer and Daniel can now rest in peace.'

'Thanks, Alan.'

'That recording will help me to wrap everything up when I get back to Wisbech and no doubt it will be a relief to the Chief Constable that the case has been concluded satisfactorily.' He paused and then muttered. 'However, I'm not sure what to do when it comes to this,' and Cheswell poked his forefinger at the packet lying between them.

'No doubt the authorities will sell them and use the money to fill a few potholes across the country,' James suggested and gave a hollow laugh.

'It's more probable it will go towards repairing dykes in the Netherlands,' Cheswell added and then a twinkle appeared in his eyes. 'However, we could say that they went overboard with the professor and are now lying on the bottom of the North Sea.'

James was puzzled by Cheswell's words. 'I don't understand, are you saying that we don't turn them in and rather keep them for ourselves?'

'When van Rijn is interrogated he is bound to say that he gave Calder a quantity of diamonds for the king's charter which means the Dutch police will want to know where those stones are. If we surrender them they will be returned to Rotterdam and a furore will ensue as to who should be the rightful owners. I'm positive that van Rijn got them as payment for a large shipment of young girls for the sex market.'

'Then what should we do with them?'

'I'm pretty comfortable on my policeman's salary but you and I both know that Margaret Lightbody no longer has a husband to support her . . .' Cheswell paused leaving a large question mark hanging in the air.

'I could sell them very discreetly, one at a time, to different diamond traders in Hatton Garden and give the money to Margaret,' James finished.

'Not forgetting to return a little to your secretary's petty cash. I believe you've been tapping into her sacred reserves rather generously while working on this case,' Cheswell said knowingly and gave a wink.

'How about a substantial donation to Eaves' Poppy Project first?' James asked and when Cheswell gave an inquiring look he went on to explain. 'It's a non-profit organization that provides support for women who have been trafficked for sex.'

Cheswell nodded with enthusiasm and then said, 'As a last thought I hope you and your family will go on a long relaxing holiday somewhere a little warmer than here.'

Looking out of the window at the gathering storm clouds that had now turned the sea leaden both men laughed.

Epilogue

IT WAS FIVE YEARS LATER and a severe depression in the Bay of Biscay meant that the morning weather forecast was as accurate as the one given by Michael Fish in 1987. The reported mild, pleasantly temperate breezes turned into a violent, extra-tropical cyclone. As barometers plunged to 934 millibars the megastorm made Cornish landfall with a deafening hurricane force of 220 kph.

East Steading was spared severe damage and only a few tiles were dislodged and tossed onto greenhouses and cars, for the main force of the wind was crossing the country and devastating Plymouth, Oxford, Milton Keynes, Cambridge and King's Lynn.

Cars were overturned and thrown into the air, trees were uprooted and tossed about like matchsticks and people stayed in behind locked doors and prayed.

Many of the trees in Ravens' Wood fell like ten pins except for those in the middle of the wood sheltered by their unfortunate beech, birch and maple companions.

However, despite being within the protective ring and having survived the elements for hundreds of years, Oliver Cromwell finally gave up its life as the rotting part of the trunk exploded. Sending slivers of oak whistling through the wood it finally collapsed in on itself. The upper part of the tree fell to the north, downing many of the smaller trees surrounding it, while the lower bole wrenched huge roots from the soil as it was pulled to one side.

Many months later Tom Rogers began the task of clearing Ravens' Wood. Heavy chains were attached to transportable lengths and they were dragged to the waiting articulated lorries. Three weeks after work started he finally came to where Oliver Cromwell once stood in all its regal splendour.

Tom put his chainsaw aside and respectfully gazed at the fallen giant. A large crater had been formed to uncover snapped roots as thick as a man's thigh. For over a millennium they had kept the proud English oak firmly anchored to the land.

He walked to the edge of the huge hole and thought he saw something glinting in the upturned earth. He nudged a clod of soil with his Doc Martens and gasped when the small glint of gold became a dazzling display of precious gems set in a gold crown. King John's most prized possession, thought lost to the forces of the sea, had been returned by the raging power of the wind.

Tom fell to his knees and deferentially raised it up to catch the midday sun filtering through Oliver Cromwell's bared roots. The secret of simple thirteenth-century men-at-arms called Hugh and Geoffrey had at last been revealed.

It was the moment the deceased Professor of archaeology had killed and died for.